A Rage at Sea

A Party Every Night

Lorenz Heller writing as
FREDERICK LORENZ

Introduction by
Nicholas Litchfield

Stark House Press • Eureka California

A RAGE AT SEA / A PARTY EVERY NIGHT

Published by Stark House Press
1315 H Street
Eureka, CA 95501, USA
griffinskye3@sbcglobal.net
www.starkhousepress.com

ISBN: 978-1-944520-99-1

Book design by Mark Shepard, shepgraphics.com
Cover design by Jeff Vorzimmer, ¡caliente!design, Austin, Texas
Proofreading by Bill Kelly
Cover art from *Master Detective*, October 1953

First Stark House Press Edition: May 2020

Heller's Tough, Gusty Tales of Drunkards, Knaves, and Washed-up Hotshots
by Nicholas Litchfield

Lorenz Heller, more commonly referred to as Larry, was a prolific American novelist and screenwriter who used various pseudonyms—principally, Laura Hale, Burt Sims, Larry Heller, Larry Holden, and briefly, his own name, Lorenz Heller. His best-known pen name, however, was Frederick Lorenz.

Details on his life are sketchy, to the extent that nobody seems too sure exactly when and where he passed away. His draft card asserts he was born October 5, 1910 in West Hoboken, New Jersey, and according to a 1956 feature on him in the *Sarasota Herald-Tribune*, he studied journalism at Rutgers University and worked on various New Jersey newspapers, including the *Newark News*, the *Hudson Dispatch*, the *Palisadian*, and the *Carney News*. A 1956 article on him in the *Tampa Bay Times* mentions that prior to becoming a full-time writer he was an ordinary seaman on a freighter running between New Jersey and the West Coast, a fruit picker in Payallup Valey, Washington, a building assistant, a farmhand, an interior decorator, a manager of a movie theatre, and a biller for the National Biscuit Company headquartered in East Hanover, New Jersey.

During WWII, he worked in the New Jersey plant of the American Radio Corp. After the war, he became a dedicated writer, penning dozens of short stories for numerous mystery-detective periodicals. His earliest works, a series of dryly amusing and brisk paced whodunits featuring a tough private eye named Dinny Keogh, were published in the short-lived *Mammoth Mystery* magazine, which folded after only eleven issues. True to its name, *Mammoth Mystery* started as a bulky bi-monthly magazine that, initially, was set to total a whopping 320 pages—the same size as *Mammoth Detective*, its sibling publication. The final page count turned out to be 274, and it eventually shrank to 178 because of post-war paper shortages. Another Ziff-Davis owned publication, the sci-fi pulp *Amazing Stories*, was so popular that the paper was allocated to that magazine, instead, to accommodate its increased circulation. Heller regularly contributed to both *Mammoth Mystery* and *Mammoth Detective* using the pen name Larry Holden. The *Mammoth Mystery* editor offers this apt description of his work: "Holden writes in a hard, fast, crisp style and he has a feel for colorful language and characters that makes the stories sing."

Both magazines contained a distinguished list of luminary writers, among them Robert Bloch, John D. MacDonald, William P. McGivern, and Roy Huggins, as well as prolific pulp fiction maestros like Bruno Fischer, Chester S. Geier, and Arthur Leo Zagat. Despite the mammoth talent on display, these periodicals ceased operations in 1947.

Heller, who was contributing to many other pulps during this period, soon became a full-time writer, and in 1950 he moved from New Jersey to Nokomis, a town along the Gulf Coast of Florida. He churned out commercial fiction with regularity, his tales frequently appearing in *Dime Detective Magazine*, *Detective Tales*, *New Detective Magazine*, and a variety of other long-running magazines, many owned by Popular Publications, the largest publisher of pulp fiction in America. According to newspaper reports, by the mid-1950s, he had authored approximately 500 short stories and published fourteen novels.

Half a dozen of his novels published in the 1950s were paperback originals for Lion Books, a company established by Martin Goodman, an American publisher of pulp magazines, paperback books, men's adventure magazines, and comic books. The paperback line, which lasted a mere nine years, is noted for having published early crime noir works by Jim Thompson, David Karp, and David Goodis, among other influential writers. Heller's contributions include the novels *A Rage At Sea*, *The Night Never Ends*, *The Savage Chase*, *A Party Every Night*, *Ruby*, and *Hot*.

The first of these, *A Rage At Sea*, the leadoff story in this collection, is a tense, unpredictable, high-seas adventure that came out in June 1953. Heller had penned a number of prior novels using the pseudonyms Lorenz Heller and Laura Hale, but for this and the subsequent five works, he used the pen name Frederick Lorenz. As with the later novel, *The Savage Chase*, which he placed with Lion Books the following year, the central character here, boat captain Frank Dixon, is a down-at-heel, devil-may-care type of guy. Having lost his boat in a poker game in Key West, several months earlier, he now spends all his time in gin mills in Miami, brawling, accumulating debt, and drinking himself to death. The only thing he has going for him is the beautiful blonde, Helen, who he has been dating for the past year. However, despite his strong affection for her, his love for the bottle takes precedence, and his reckless, heavy drinking has caused her interest in him to wane. When he turns down a much-needed job offer to skipper a rich man's yacht through the Bahamas to the Virgin Islands, she pretty much calls an end to their affair, no longer willing to see him destroy himself and believing he is too far-gone into alcoholism to save.

Ironically, the job he initially rejects, though later accepts, in part to appease Helen, is a disaster waiting to happen, and it ultimately proves his undoing. He knows it is a bum job from the onset because a crooked gigolo named Theron Addams is involved. Addams, aware of Dixon's drinking problem, recommended him for the job with the aim of getting a twenty-five percent cut of Dixon's wages. As lousy as the deal is, Dixon has to accept the terms, believing that once he completes the four-month cruise, he will be completely rehabilitated and with his reputation as a responsible and sober captain fully reestablished.

Unfortunately, once out on the ocean, alcohol withdrawal symptoms and his reputation as a captain are the least of his worries. The guests, who are often inebriated, are a boisterous lot, and the fat owner, Charles Hunt Allard, is soused from the moment they set sail to the moment they dock. And when he's drunk, he turns into a mean, vicious brute. The touchy youngster Wirt, who is a kind of combination of engineer and deckhand, hates Allard's guts and is spoiling for a fight and needling the owner at every opportunity.

And then there is Addams, the slippery con artist who affects an English accent. Forever toadying to Allard, his cash cow, he has managed to worm his way into the rich man's confidence. Keen to keep Dixon in his place, he starts to make trouble for the captain, messing with equipment and planting liquor in his cabin to give the impression Dixon is back on the bottle.

With tensions high, and conflicts flaring, and the booze flowing freely day and night, it isn't all that surprising that something bad happens. What is surprising is how the author escalates the petty squabbles and bickering to the point of sheer madness, implanting fear and outrage and mistrust and hatred in his four prime characters until they become ruthless, savage beasts, committing sabotage and double-cross and plotting against one another in a desperate bid for survival.

When it came to storytelling, Heller's primary concern was to focus on character over plot, making a deliberate effort to show a contrast between his key protagonists and creating believable conflict between them. Out of this conflict, he maintained, "the plot will evolve." In *A Rage At Sea*, this careful, conflict-centered approach fosters a hauntingly edgy, hot-tempered environment where an imprudent remark might alienate one person, enrage another, or rouse violent behavior in all four of the overwrought men.

The other novel in this collection, *A Party Every Night*, published in January of 1956, has an equally strange, shifting storyline and a miscellany of volatile eccentrics who gravitate around a thriving gin mill called the Pelican Lounge. Front and center is Vance, the sociable, hardworking, highly paid barkeep whose natural charisma helps ensure there is "a party every night." Almost everybody likes Vance, especially Hully, a rough, friendless, slow-witted helper whose sole ambition in life is to please his friend. And then there's Cora, a flirtatious waitress who longs for a husband and wishes it could be Vance. But she can't get a look-in because Vance is besotted with Maddie, the well-to-do wife of Wes, a rich but miserable rummy. The only ones who aren't so taken with Vance are the old skinflint bar owner, Tate, who has "the soul of a mouse being forced to share the last ounce of cheese on earth," and the humorless, manipulative Durkin, an insatiable collector of gossip who's regarded as "the toughest policeman in the county."

Heller takes his time delving into the lives of the abundance of characters, shifting settings and viewpoints, and allowing the story to unfold in a natural, measured way. Although the vivid descriptions and interesting character dynamics make it a compelling drama, for the most part, the narrative seems wholly unremarkable, making one wonder where the story is going. The first hint of a crime then sets in motion a frantic search that is reminiscent of the one in *The Savage Chase*. In that tale, various unpleasant lowlifes engage in a relentless hunt for an affluent, intoxicated, kidnapped gambler. Here, the initial pursuit is to locate a wealthy lumber merchant who is driving his car while drunk. The fear is that he will get into an accident and cause injury to other motorists.

As the drama evolves, violence, death, robbery, infidelity, and foul play ensue. Then unsubstantiated allegations are bandied around when suspicions of murder circulate. Greed, guilt, and anxiety prevent the key characters from behaving rationally, and inadvertently, they start to incriminate the one they care about, setting up a stunning, dire situation that culminates in a wild and chaotic, yet rewarding finale.

Once again, Heller's devotion to constructing well-defined, multi-layered characters helps bring the story to life. Considering the regularity with which he placed his stories with publishers, and the favorable reviews his novels received, his character-driven approach proved highly effective.

Possibly his biggest advocate was famed *New York Times* book critic Anthony Boucher, who regarded him as one of "the real pros of suspense." Heller was one of those writers whose books Boucher wanted to read the moment they reached his desk. The interesting and unusual premise of *The Savage Chase,* together with its "realistic Jersey background and sharply observed, almost Chekhov-Odets dialogue," impressed him greatly and made him keen for more. Heller delivered the goods with his subsequent three novels for Lion Books, all published in 1956. Of these, *Ruby* may have seemed "more conventional" in terms of plot and style, but Boucher still found it "very readable." In his summer of '57 salute to consistently rewarding writers who had spoiled him with good novels, Boucher included the novel *Hot,* remarking: "For powerful story-telling, keep an unflagging eye on the products of Frederick Lorenz."

As for *A Party Every Night,* Boucher described this novel as "a sharply developed story somewhat in the James Cain tradition, with nice observation of believably complex people." The "vigorous and exciting narrative" is, in many ways, comparable to *The Savage Chase.* Although set in Florida rather than Jersey, there's a familiar feel to the dingy bars and the assortment of boozy patrons. Boucher deliberated if the author had once worked as a bartender, remarking: "his understanding of bars and their denizens is phenomenally acute."

Undeniably, there is an authenticity to the author's excellent depictions of the bustling Pelican Lounge and rival community taverns like the grimy Dick's Bar, with its dilapidated jukebox and "dirty floor speckled with flattened cigarette butts." Or the commercial fisherman's hangout C & C Bar, where the owner is so anxious to be liked by everybody that he's "practically neurotic." Or the dreary Ella's Bar, which is run by a shrewd, tough woman who looks "slightly like a half-mad albino horse."

Going by the advice Heller once gave budding writers, we can surmise that the author was in the habit of carrying a notebook with him wherever he went, jotting down "interesting phrases and character descriptions." Even though barman isn't included among his long list of occupations, it isn't a stretch to assume he spent much invaluable investigative time in establishments such as these, absorbing noteworthy conversation and drinking in their palpable charm for the sake of literature.

Information on Heller beyond the early 1960s is scarce indeed. News articles list him as a former North Harbour resident, as well as a former Venice resident, and a feature story on famous names in Florida's writing community, published in 1963 in the *Tampa Bay Times*, indicates he had become a resident of Sarasota. As for his writing, his publication credits show he was still finding success placing his work with publishers like Pyramid Books and the popular, though less reputable, Beacon Books, which mainly churned out paperback sleaze. Curiously, though, by 1963, the author's prolific output seemed to have dwindled to zero.

Exactly what became of him remains a mystery. Thankfully, he was so dedicated to his craft and so uninhibited in his creative endeavors that there are hundreds of tough, gutsy tales to savor. Among them are these two dazzling gems, featuring hot-blooded drunkards, deranged brutes, unscrupulous bullies, and shipwrecked hotshots with too much ambition and too little sense.

—October 2019
Rochester, NY

Nicholas Litchfield is the founding editor of the literary magazine *Lowestoft Chronicle*, author of the suspense novel *Swampjack Virus*, and editor of nine literary anthologies. He has worked in various countries as a tabloid journalist, librarian, and media researcher. Formerly, a book reviewer for the *Lancashire Post* and syndicated to twenty-five newspapers across the UK, he now writes for *Publishers Weekly* and the *Colorado Review*.

A Rage at Sea

FREDERICK LORENZ

Chapter One

The bartender looked at the man and continued to polish the highball glass with his white towel. "Sorry, mister," he said, "but I ain't seen him."

"But they told me he hangs out here all the time."

"Nobody hangs out here all the time but me."

"Are you sure you know the one I mean? The name's Frank Dixon. He's big and he's got black hair ..."

"I know the one you mean, and I ain't seen him. This ain't the only bar in Miami, mister."

"Do you expect him in tonight maybe?"

"I never expect nobody," the bartender said indifferently. He picked up another highball glass and began to polish it. "When they come in I serve them, and when they don't come in I don't worry about them."

"When was he in last?"

"I don't know. A couple days ago. I don't keep count."

"Was he looping?"

"I wouldn't know. If they don't break glasses or start a fight, I let them alone. What was it you wanted him for, mister?"

The man said angrily, "I had a job for him but the hell with it." He turned and walked out.

The bartender held the highball glass to the light and then set it on the shelf behind the bar. He went to the door and looked thoughtfully up the street. The man was a half block away, walking fast. The bartender watched until the man had passed Sonny's Bar & Grill on the corner. He stepped back, closed the front door and plugged in the buzzer so that he could hear if any customers came in. He took a bottle of rye from the bar and walked into the back room.

A big black-haired man was slumped on the edge of the cot, his hands dangling between his spread knees. He looked up dully.

"How are you feeling, Frank?" the bartender asked.

Dixon's hands moved meaninglessly. "Wonderful," he said with self-derision. "Fine and dandy. Is that a bottle?"

The bartender picked up a glass from the window sill beside the cot. He blew a dead fly out of it and poured in two ounces of rye. He handed it to Dixon.

"That's the end, Frank," he said. "I can't carry you no more. It's two hundred bucks now. I can't afford no more."

"Here, take this back if it's that bad."

"Don't be like that. Two hundred bucks is a lot of money."

"You're a liar. Since when was two hundred bucks a lot of money?"

"Since just now. Since right this minute."

"Here. Pour it back in the bottle. I don't want to see you starve to death."

"I won't starve to death but you …" He stopped and looked away.

Dixon scowled. "Go ahead and say it."

"Say what?"

"That I'm drinking myself to death."

The bartender shrugged. "It ain't doing you no good, Frank, the way you go at it, a week at a time. Not that it's any of my business."

"You're goddamn right it's not."

"I said it wasn't. Drink your drink. I wouldn't like to see you go out of here without a pickup."

"The hell with it and the hell with you, too."

The bartender took the glass and set it back on the window sill.

"I wish you wouldn't be like that, Frank," he said. "You can always come in for a shot or two, but a week at a time is too much." He looked unhappy.

"All right! That's the second time you said it, now let's forget it." Dixon sat straighter on the cot and began to button up his shirt. His hands were not very steady. He bent over and fumbled on the floor for his shoes.

"I almost forgot, Frank," the bartender said, trying to be friendly. "A guy was in looking for you. I didn't tell him you were here. I thought he might be a cop on account of that guy you beat up on Tuesday."

"What'd he look like?"

"He was medium and kind of thin. He didn't look like a cop, but cops come all sizes. I didn't want to take no chances. He said he had a job for you. He might have been on the level, but I didn't want him to see you the way you look anyway."

Dixon was bent over, tying the shoelaces, and he grunted. "What kind of job?"

"He didn't say. He got sore and walked out when I wouldn't tell him you was here. He was a medium guy, kind of thin, brown hair. He's got a little bunched up scar in the middle of his left cheek. You know him maybe?"

"No."

He put both hands on the edge of the cot and pushed himself to his feet. He swayed, but he did not put out his hand to steady himself against the wall. He just clamped his teeth until the dizziness passed.

"Suffer, you son of a bitch," he growled to himself, "suffer."

The bartender looked unhappier. It did not take a professional to see that Dixon was in bad shape. He wished Dixon would drink the pickup, but he knew better than to offer it again. Dixon always had been touchy.

Dixon walked to the door without staggering. He stopped and appeared to think something over. He turned and looked at the bartender.

"Forget what I said back there," he said. "You're okay."

"Sure, Frank."

"I mean, you're really okay. I'll pay you back that two hundred when I get it."

"Anything you say, Frank."

Dixon said, "Don't kid yourself," and walked out, still going fairly steadily.

Dixon's room was on S.W. 22nd Avenue, six blocks west. He walked the first half block in the sun and when he began to feel sick, he crossed the street and walked the rest of the way in the shade. On the corner was a drugstore and he went in. The druggist was behind the soda fountain mixing a large lemon-coke for a fat woman who was perspiring almost as much as Dixon. She sat on the stool with her legs apart, her mouth open, gasping, and fanned her face with her hand. Dixon went to the back and leaned against the prescription counter. He was feeling sick again and he was drenched with sweat. It poured out of him. It ran into his eyes and mouth and dripped from his armpits. His blue sport shirt was plastered to him and looked black. This was the worst, sweating like this and not being able to stop it without another drink. Without another three drinks. It always took around three to stop it. He stood there with the sweat running down his face and thinking grimly, Go ahead, suffer, you stupid son of a bitch, go ahead and suffer.

The druggist came back to the prescription counter wearing a gravely interested expression, like a doctor or an undertaker, but it changed to shocked surprise when he saw that it was Dixon.

"My god, Frank," he said, "what happened to you?"

"I want some of those pills they give rummies to sober them up before they kick them out of the psycho ward." It was hard coming right out with it like that, but he was deliberately punishing himself.

The druggist looked grave and regretful. "That takes a prescription,

Frank," he said.

"All right. Write me one."

"I can't do that. Only a doctor can write a prescription. You know that."

"I'll beg if you want me to. I'll get down on my knees. Do you want me to get down on my knees? What do you want me to do? I wouldn't even ask if I didn't need them."

The druggist frowned at the fat woman, who was hunched over her glass noisily sucking up the last drops of the lemon-coke through a pair of straws. He pursed up his lips and without looking at Dixon again, walked behind the frosted glass partition of the prescription room.

The fat woman fished a piece of ice from her glass and put it in her mouth. Her dress bunched up between her massive haunches as she waddled out of the store. When the druggist came back with a small box already wrapped, he looked relieved to see that the woman had gone. He put the box on the counter, still not looking at Dixon.

"The directions are on the box," he said in a prim, disapproving voice. "And please do me the favor of not putting me in this position again." He pressed his lips tightly together, nodded once, sharply, and walked behind the glass partition again, turning his back on Dixon's thanks.

Dixon picked up the little wrapped box. His fingers closed around it and the box crackled drily. He had the jerking impulse to hurl it into the frosted pane of glass, yet at the same time he knew it would be a futile gesture of defiance. He had asked for the pills, and the druggist had given them to him. Not graciously, but he hadn't had to give them at all, graciously or ungraciously. And he hadn't had the right to ask for them in the first place without a prescription. He had shamed himself, but he would shame himself deeper if he hurled the box into the pane of glass.

His room was on the third floor of a guest house, a small slanting room directly under the roof. He put the box of pills on the bed without opening it. He took off his drenched clothes. He put on a terry cloth bathrobe and went down the hall to the bathroom. He returned a half hour later. He had shaved and cut himself in several places, stopping the blood with bits of toilet paper pressed against the cuts. His face looked slightly swollen from all the drinking he had done. He was beginning to sweat again. He had deliberately put off taking one of the pills, punishing himself again. He opened the package, wrapped in green paper. There were three capsules in the box, and on the label he was instructed not to take more than one capsule in any twenty-four hour period. He had no water to wash the capsule down and had to go back to the bathroom. He did all this with tight-lipped deliberation, as if by hurrying he might be coddling himself.

After he finally swallowed the capsule, he took off his terry cloth robe and lay down on the bed. In a short time he was asleep. It was late afternoon when he awakened. The sun was heavily yellow and slanted through the windows from the west. A girl was sitting in the lounge chair by the window with one leg thrown comfortably over the arm of the chair. It was a magnificent leg with a long tanned thigh. Her blonde curly hair was cut short and looked like a beautiful cap that had been made especially for her by Hattie Carnegie. Her high-boned face was sullen in repose, but her skin was smooth and clear.

The mattress springs pinged as Dixon moved on the bed and the girl lowered her magazine and looked at him.

"That must have been a wonderful sleep," she said. "I thought you had St. Vitus dance. Do you always sleep like that?"

Dixon grinned at her and sat up. He was feeling good, refreshed by the sleep and lifted by the drug in the capsule. "You should know," he said.

"I should, but I don't. Not anymore. I used to, but I've got out of practice. You keep going away."

"Ah, Helen."

"No, no, I mean it. You go away and hide behind a bottle and nobody can find you. Is there something wonderful behind that bottle? I'd like to know. I've never been there, but there must be because you keep doing it. It must be really enchanting. What's so enchanting behind the bottle, Frank?"

"I'm not going to fight with you," he grinned. "I feel too good. Come over here and give me a kiss."

"No, I won't give you a kiss until I find out what's behind that bottle where you keep secreting yourself," she said in a bright brittle voice. "I'm really very curious. I'd like to know because if it is something wonderful I'll get a bottle of my own and hide behind it the next time you hide behind yours. I mean, if you've found something really and truly heavenly, it would be very selfish of you to keep it from us poor humdrum people who have to worry along from day to day."

He sat up and covered himself from the waist down with the terry cloth robe.

"You've got a right to be sore, honey," he said.

"Well, thank you. Now that you approve, I can go right on being sore, can't I?"

He saw that she was in earnest and was also very close to tears. Her lips were working and her hands were closed tightly on her magazine. She blinked her eyes and gave her head a sharp shake as if determined not to cry where he could watch her.

"We've been looking for you since yesterday," she said. "I went down to Dominick's a half dozen times, but he said you weren't there."

"I was there. I was in the back room. Who do you mean, 'we'?"

"The man who came to give you a job. His name is Addams. He said you knew him."

Dixon frowned. "I don't know any Addams."

"He said you did. Wait a minute. He had a funny first name. Theron. That's it. He said it meant hunter. Theron Addams."

"Oh the hell, that crud!"

"What do you mean, that crud?" Helen demanded angrily. "He was good enough to come and offer you the job. It's a good job on a yacht. The owner is very rich. You'd be captain, he said."

"He's a crud. I met him down in Key West a year ago. He was on a yacht then, too. Steward. He specializes in yachts. This one was owned by some rich bitch from Michigan. He took her for everything he could get. He took her for about ten thousand bucks, they say."

"*They* say! Who are *they?* I've heard of 'they' before, but 'they' never seem to have a name, and 'they' always seem to know everything about everybody. What do they know about it? And what do you know about it, as far as that goes. Did you see him get ten thousand dollars? Did you see him get anything? Did you see him get even *one* dollar from her?"

"No, I didn't see him get even one dollar from her. You don't *see* things like that, but everybody knew it all the same. She slobbered all over him in the bars, and he had a gold cigarette lighter and a gold cigarette case that she gave him, among other things. He was loving her, and she was paying him for it. Does that satisfy you?"

She gave him a steady, level glance. She opened her hands and the magazine slid to the floor. "What are you driving at, Frank?" she asked.

"Nothing," his voice was angry now, "nothing at all. Why should I be driving at something?"

"Are you going to go and see Addams about this job? He gave me the address where you're to go." She swung her leg down from the arm of the chair, covered her knees with her skirt, and picked up her scarlet plastic bag from the floor. She took out a piece of paper and looked at him. "You don't seem very interested."

"Why should I be interested? What kind of a job could he have to offer me? A crud like that. Or maybe he has a yacht with two women aboard this time. Is that it?"

The girl took a deep breath. She closed her eyes for a moment. She opened them and said quietly, "I saw the yacht. It's named the *Almacor.* It's very pretty. It's white. I met the owner, Mr. Allard, and he's very anxious to have you. He wants to take a cruise through the Bahamas and down to the Virgin Islands. Addams told him you know those waters better than anybody around here, and it's true. You do. You fished them often enough when you had the *Madame*. It's a good job, Frank. I talked with Mr. Allard, and he does want you."

He ignored the pleading in her voice and said stolidly, "If Addams is running around to get me into that job, there's a catch someplace. He never did anybody a favor in his life. Unless there was something in it for him."

"So you're not even going to look into it, are you, Frank?"

"What the hell do you think?" he yelled. "Do you think I'd go to a goddamn gigolo for a job? Think again. I'm not that hard up."

"But it's not Addams, Frank. It's Mr. Allard who ..."

"The hell with Allard. If Addams wants me in, he's got an angle, and the hell with him, too. Anyway, I don't want a yacht job. I've worked on yachts before. You're nothing but a lousy sea-going chauffeur. The hell with it."

The girl, Helen, smoothed her dress down her thighs and let her hands come to rest on her knees. She looked down at them, her blonde curly cap bent. She was silent for a long while. He stepped out of bed and swung into the terry cloth robe. He walked across the room, sat on the arm of the chair and put his arm around her. He put his hand under her chin and tried to raise her face for a kiss. She turned her head away from him, keeping her face down.

"Don't, Frank," she said.

"Oh, come on, Helen. If you knew Addams as well as I do, you'd say the hell with him, too. Forget him. I'll get dressed and we'll go out to dinner. I have a few bucks put away ..."

"No, thanks, Frank."

She stood abruptly and walked across the room. She put her red plastic bag on top of the chest of drawers and took a small bottle of brandy from it. She turned and showed it to him.

"This was for the celebration," she said bitterly. "This was to celebrate your new job. I'm finished, Frank. This is the end. You're not going anywhere from here, and I don't want to go anyplace with you.

I'm done, Frank. I don't want any more of it."

"Just because I won't go to that gigolo for a job?"

"No. I've been sleeping with you for a year now. A whole year, twelve months, fifty-two weeks. When you had your boat, you were wonderful. You were real. I used to walk down the street and get light-headed just thinking about you. Even after you lost your boat in that poker game in Key West, I still thought you were wonderful, though God only knows what's so wonderful about losing a boat like the *Madame* in a poker game. Twenty thousand dollars just like that in a four-day poker game! That's not wonderful. That's stupid. Anyway, I still thought you were wonderful. Maybe because when you told me about it you laughed and didn't seem to mind. Perhaps there was something a little wonderful about it at that. Not everybody could laugh. Yes, at that moment you were wonderful."

"What did you expect me to do, cry?"

"No. I didn't expect you to cry. But I didn't expect you to backfire the way you did. Drink, drink, drink, all you did after that was drink. Did you feel sorry for yourself, or what? Why did you drink like that? I think the *Madame* was the best ninety percent of you, and the ten percent that's left, now that she's gone, is nothing, just nothing."

He did not answer. He turned his head and looked out the window. The cocoanut palm outside lankly waved its long fronds in the slight breeze. The green fruit looked like gigantic grape clusters. He could hear the dry rattle as the fronds scraped against each other. The slanting sun was a puddle of yellow on the floor at the foot of a shaft of flickering gray dust motes.

"Don't you have anything to say?" Helen asked dully.

He shook his head. This was the third time today that he had been told that this was the end, that this was all. One, two, three. Dominick, the druggist, and now Helen. The end, all the way through. If he jumped out the window, he thought with a return of that self-derision, it would make four. But he wasn't going to jump out the window, now or any time.

The girl threw out her hand. "Nothing, nothing at all?" she sounded a little hysterical. "You never explain and you never apologize, do you! Take it or leave it. Well, I'm leaving it, Frank. I'm leaving it right now. Your turning down this job just confirms something that I've been trying not to think about. You've gone away. I don't know where it is you've gone, but I do know that I don't want to be there with you."

She took her scarlet plastic bag from the top of the chest of drawers and stood the small bottle of brandy in its place. She indicated it with a tired toss of her hand.

"It's all yours, Frank," she said. "Drink it down. Hide behind it, and all I have to say is, thank God I don't have to worry about you or it or anything anymore!"

She walked out.

Chapter Two

Long after she had gone, Dixon remembered her sudden tears before she closed the door behind her. There had been two hard, racking sobs and then a softening as the tears came. He remembered the sound of her heels on the hallway outside, and the quick, diminishing whispers of her soles as she ran down the stairs. His mind was empty. He had no thoughts. He felt sodden. There were images, remembrances, but none of it was real, really real.

Helen in the fighting seat of the *Madame*, gripping a U-shaped rod while a marlin beat the water into a white froth a hundred yards from the boat, jumping and jumping, standing on his tail, taking the line from the reel, and her crying, "I've just got to put on the drag, Frank, he's taking it all!" And him saying, "Let him take it, honey, I'll follow him with the boat. Pump your line in when it sags. He'll make a run and then round. He'll take most of the line on the run."

She had boated that one. Not a record, but a big one for a woman.

Helen at Boca Grande, tarpon. The silver king. Another rod U-bent. Helen half risen from her chair, hanging on to the rod.

"I've got him, Frank, I've got him. I'm not letting him go!"

And she hadn't, either. A hundred and two pound tarpon on light tackle. Three hours and twenty minutes by the clock. She had brought it up to the gaff, though, she had brought it up to the gaff.

Helen. Helen in the whispering darkness. "Darling, darling! Oh please, yes, please, yes, yes, darling, darling … oh, yes, yes, yes, darling … oh, darling …"

Helen.

He had meant to marry her. He really had. She was his kind of woman. She liked the same kind of things, she liked to do the same kind of things, she was always *there*.

The sunlight faded as the early night began to seep up into the easterly sky as if the sky were a blotter and the gathering darkness ink. Dixon rose heavily from the arm of the chair and dressed, taking a clean shirt, underwear and socks from the chest of drawers. He put on a tie and took his seersucker suit from the closet. He did all this with a frown of concentration, as if dressing properly were of great importance. Lastly, he went back to the chest of drawers for the money he had put aside. There were almost six dollars in loose change—nickels, dimes, quarters and halves that he had emptied into the drawer from his pockets, an old habit—and about twenty dollars in crumpled bills. He put the half pint bottle of brandy that Helen had brought into the top drawer of the chest and covered it carefully with his handkerchiefs. After glancing from the mirror, adjusting his tie, his eye fell upon the slip of paper that Helen had left on the top of the chest. On it was written Theron Addams, Yacht *Almacor*, Biscayne Yacht Basin, owner Charles Hunt Allard. He put it into his wallet with the twenty dollars in bills. The loose change he poured into his pocket. It was heavy and his pants sagged on that side.

He walked deliberately, almost sedately, down the stairs, a man conscious that for the first time in a long while he was wearing a clean shirt and a proper tie, a suit that was pressed, shoes that were shined.

He was on his way back to Dominick's. As he came from the front door and walked down the steps to the sidewalk, a man's voice cried out exultingly, "That's him!" and three men came boiling out of an old gray Chevrolet parked at the curb. Two of them were tall, lanky men, brothers, and the third was shorter, squat and heavy and had a face that looked much too big for his size. The squat man came first, swinging a huge fist at Dixon's jaw. Dixon turned the blow on his hunched shoulder and hit the man in the body as hard as he could, pivoting on the ball of his left foot. He ducked under the fist of the second and chopped him across the back of the neck with his forearm as the man staggered from the force of the missed blow. He closed with the third and kneed him savagely in the crotch. It was all over in less than thirty seconds from the time the three men spilled out of the old Chevrolet. All three men were sprawled on the sidewalk, the last one doubled over with his knees to his chin, both hands grasping his groin, and going *uh-uh-uh-uh,* his mouth open showing the brown-and-green of teeth rotting at the gums. His pale eyes were spread in agony.

Dixon recognized him as the guy with whom he had had the fight on Tuesday.

A thin woman, obviously wearing only a pink slip, leaned from the second floor window of the house and cried excitedly, "I saw it. I saw it all. I saw those men deliberately attack you. I'll be a witness."

Dixon looked up. "That won't be necessary, thanks," he said heavily.

Dixon caught a cab at the corner of S.W. 8th Street. He sat in the back seat for a long moment, staring at his hands.

"Well, where to, buddy?" the cab driver finally demanded.

Dixon's head jerked up as if aroused from sleep. He made a vague apologetic motion with his right hand. "The Biscayne Yacht Basin," he mumbled. He had lost every desire to go back to Dominick's.

The yacht *Almacor* was tied up about fifty feet from the restaurant in the yacht basin. It was a white boat about seventy-five feet long and broad enough in the beam to be steady in a heavy sea. The sun deck behind the bridge was shielded by a gaily striped awning in dark green, chartreuse, and a bland *café au lait*. A boy of about twenty, with blond crew-cut hair, dressed in white sneakers, white ducks, and a blue and white striped Basque shirt, was sprawled on the lounge with the big-limbed awkward grace of the young.

He rose to his feet as Dixon stepped aboard. He was as big as Dixon but less heavily muscled. His grin was ingenuous. He looked like a college halfback on vacation.

"You wanted to see somebody, mister?" he asked.

"Is Addams aboard?"

"Well, right now he's over in the restaurant having dinner. He'll be right back though. It's his turn for watch tonight. Did you want to see him about something special?"

"Yes. Who are you?"

"Me? I'm Wirt. I'm a kind of combination engineer and deck hand. Hey, are you the new captain Addams been talking about?"

"Is Mr. Allard aboard?"

"He won't be back till late. Him and the others went over the Beach for dinner and stuff. They won't roll in till two, three in the morning. They never do. But say, are you the new captain?"

Dixon ignored the question and looked at the sun deck. It was littered with newspapers, crumpled napkins, magazines and books; the low table had not been cleared of the debris from the cocktail party of that afternoon. Glasses with lime peel swimming in melted ice still stood, olives and pickles in low dishes, *hors d'oeuvres* partly gnawed, a collapsing chicken-in-aspic on a platter in the middle of the low cocktail table. Dixon looked at the boy.

"Who's supposed to clean this up?" he asked.

Wirt flushed.

"Me, I guess," he said.

"Then why isn't it cleaned up?"

"Well, I … I didn't get around to it, I guess."

"Clean it up."

Wirt stared at Dixon, his mouth half open, a magazine dangling from his hand.

Dixon snapped, "I said, clean it up!"

He turned his back and stepped down to the dock. He walked up to the restaurant. He recognized Addams immediately. Addams was sitting at a small table in a corner of the room, eating steak, quickly, neatly and with small, sharp bites. Addams looked much the same as he had at Key West, but more sure of himself. It was nothing Dixon could put his finger on. Possibly the angle of the chin, or possibly the way Addams smiled a quick thanks when the waiter obsequiously poured him a fresh glass of water. Addams looked just a little like the Duke of Windsor, but his manners were just a little more ducal.

Addams raised his eyes as Dixon walked up to the table and sat down.

"Well, well, well," he murmured in that British voice, "Lazarus arisen. Coffee, old boy? Or would you rather have a straight rye?"

"Coffee," said Dixon. "Is that job still open?"

"Well, yes. In a way," Addams smiled neatly and cut himself a thin slice of steak. He put it into his mouth and nibbled like a rabbit, with his front teeth. He looked up at Dixon. "In a way," he repeated, smiling again.

"What's that supposed to mean?"

"Nothing. Nothing, really."

"Well, is it or isn't it open?"

"That, old boy, depends on you."

"I don't get it."

"Perhaps you will, or again perhaps you won't. That's a joke. It's this way," Addams bent over his steak, probing along the bone with his knife for a last tender morsel. "The job pays four hundred a month. The projected cruise is down through the Bahamas and to the Virgins. You know those waters. It would be just nonsense asking if you did. You know them better than I do. However, old boy, being that I'm getting you this job, I expect a sort of commission." He looked Dixon full in the face and said flatly, "A hundred a month. The cruise will last four months. I want four hundred dollars."

"Go to hell."

Addams shrugged. "Think it over."

"The hell with you. I'll go to Allard himself."

"Go ahead. But after you do, I will very regretfully inform his nibs that I've just discovered that you've been spending all of your time in the back rooms of gin mills, drunk and, as they say, disorderly. Go right ahead, apply to Allard, but I'm afraid you'll never take the *Almacor* from the dock. Nobody in his right senses, and His Nibs sometimes does have flashes of sanity, would possibly employ a drunkard, or even an ex-drunkard. Do as you wish, however. I can very easily find someone else for the job."

Dixon gripped the table edge and started to rise from his chair, but that new trick of self-derision blunted the edge of his rising anger. What was he going to do, hit Addams? Get himself arrested? Thirty days in jail for disorderly conduct would be all he'd need right now. Or maybe sixty days for assault and battery. He sank back into his chair.

"Four hundred dollars," he said. "That's kind of lousy."

"Not at all, old boy. In fact, I think I'm letting you off cheaply. You can't get a job anywhere else. Everybody knows how you've been hitting the bottle. I'm really doing you a big favor. When you come back from this cruise, you'll be completely rehabilitated and your reputation will be reestablished. Four hundred is really very little when you think of it that way now, isn't it?"

"It's still lousy."

"I say, let's stop talking about it, shall we? All I'm interested in is the four hundred dollars. You've made up your mind to take the job, so there's nothing further to discuss."

"How do you know I'll pay you?"

"Because," Addams looked amused, "you're an honest man, and honest men pay their debts. Their word is their bond. Anyway, I've already explained to His Nibs that you owe me a sum of money, and he'll pay me off at the rate of two hundred a month. With your permission, of course."

"I should have known you'd cover all the angles."

"Of course. I never take chances with money. I'm too fond of it. I never gamble. I'm not like you. I would never have lost my boat in a poker game. I think gambling is a stupid, futile kind of emotionalism."

"You're right about that," said Dixon grimly.

Chapter Three

Dixon did not wait to see Allard that night.

"There'd really be no sense in it," said Addams. "He won't be back until the bars close in his face, and by that time he'll be so tiddly he won't be able to understand English anyway. You might just as well go to your place and get your clothes and anything else you need for the cruise. Come back tomorrow around noon. I'll have the edge off his hangover by that time. Unofficially, you're hired, you know. But turn up sober, will you?"

Dixon looked at him and said, "I wouldn't keep that up if I were you."

"Don't be so touchy. You've been drunk for a week. I'm just warning you. And there's one more thing. His Nibs is going to seem like an easy touch, especially after a few bottles of scotch. Don't promote him for anything. Is that understood? Not anything. If I catch you putting the bite on him for even a ten dollar bill, you're finished."

"In other words, no poaching, eh?"

"You heard me."

Dixon took a cab back to Miami. He called Helen on the phone.

"I took that job," he said. "That yacht job."

"You did?" She sounded cool. "For how long? Until the first bar ashore in Nassau?"

"I'm over that. But I don't think much of the cruise. The owner sounds like a drunk, and Addams is out to take him for everything he can get. The way he did with that woman in Key West."

"Really? Are you sure you want the job, Frank? Are you sure it measures up to your standards?"

"I had that coming, I guess. How about having dinner with me?"

"No thanks, Frank. Call me up when you get back from the cruise."

"That'll be four months."

"I know. Call me then. Good luck, Frank."

He stared at the mouthpiece as if he did not understand that the click meant she had hung up. He replaced his receiver on the hook and walked slowly out of the store. Four months. She had meant that. She had meant it when she walked out of his room that afternoon. He should have seen that. He should not have called her. It had been thoughtless cruelty, forcing her to go through it again. He would call her in four months.

He took another cab and went to his room. It did not take him long to pack. He uncovered the small bottle of brandy when he took his handkerchiefs from the chest of drawers. He weighed it in his hand for a moment and then slipped it into his bag. When he finished, he stood the bag beside the door and went downstairs. The landlady, a gray tired woman, was sitting on the front porch listening to the radio.

"I'm leaving in the morning, Mrs. Striker," he said. "My rent's paid till the end of the month ..."

"I can't give you a refund," she interrupted quickly.

"That's all right. I was just going to say, you can rent the room tomorrow after I leave if you want to. I don't expect to be back for four months."

"You have a job, Captain?"

"Yes. On a boat. We're going for a four month cruise."

"That's nice. I've always wanted to go for a cruise someplace, but it takes money."

"I'll leave the key in the door when I go. If anyone wants to look at the room before I go, bring them right up. It's all right with me."

"Have a nice trip," she said. "Have a good time."

He went back to his room and sat in the dark for a long time, smoking and thinking of Helen and Addams and the kind of cruise it looked as if it were going to be. It was about two a.m. before he was able to go to sleep.

He awakened at ten-thirty in the morning, covered with that alcoholic sweat again. He took one of the two remaining capsules and in about fifteen minutes he was able to dress without drenching his clothes with perspiration. It was a bad start for the day, and he almost decided not to go to the yacht after all. Almost, but not quite. It would be bad, really bad, if he did not go. He picked up his bag and left the house.

This time he took a bus to the yacht basin. As he walked down the dock, he saw Addams step out on the sun deck of the *Almacor* carrying a tall glass of tomato juice in a tray. He was wearing a white mess jacket, black trousers and white sneakers, obviously his uniform. Dixon wondered if he were expected to wear a uniform. He did not like the idea. Yachting uniforms with brass buttons and gold braided caps was something he'd wear to a Halloween party, but not on a boat. Voluntarily.

Addams spied him and called out in his cheery British voice, "Ah, good morning there, Captain Dixon. Come right up on deck. Mr. Allard would like to see you."

Mr. Allard was a short, fat man, limp in a deck chair, and wearing a dark blue robe with a large white monogram on the breast pocket. His fair hair was thin and looked pink. His eyes were bloodshot and he squinted painfully in the bright sun reflected from the dock. He clutched a twelve ounce glass of tomato juice in his hand and drank it thirstily, nodding at Dixon as he drank. Addams stood behind Allard's chair and winked at Dixon. Allard was in the grip of a very bad hangover. Dixon set down his bag and gave both of them a short nod.

"I'm glad you finally got here, Dickman," Allard grumbled peevishly. "Maybe now we can get going. You all set?"

"It's Captain Dixon, Mr. Allard," said Addams. "D-i-x-o-n. Captain Dixon. The Captain assured me last night that he could sail at any time."

"Let's go then. Let's get out of here. This town's worse than Atlantic City."

"About the money," said Dixon.

Addams shot him a sharp glance.

Dixon went on, "I understand I'm to get four hundred a month."

Allard looked up at Addams. "That what I said?"

"That was the amount we agreed upon, sir."

"All right then, all right. You want an advance, Dixon, is that the idea?" he squinted up at Addams again. "Give it to him. Don't bother me with it. You're the purser. When can we get out of here, Dixon?"

"The clearance paper will not be ready until late this afternoon, sir," said Addams taking the empty glass from Allard's hand. "We can sail in the morning with the tide. Is that right, Captain?"

"Whenever you say," said Dixon stolidly. Then to Allard, "I'd like to have one thing understood before we sail. I don't want any sightseers up on the bridge with me while we're at sea. That's a rule I always make."

Allard flushed and Addams cut in smoothly before the man could open his mouth. "That's customary, sir. Bahamian navigation is very tricky, and furthermore, there have been instances of guests burning holes in valuable charts with their cigars and cigarettes. You can't replace a chart at sea, sir, and in rough weather you have to have charts. Captain Dixon's rule is an excellent one, if you don't mind my saying so, sir."

Allard bunched up his lips and said petulantly, "Well, if it's a rule, it's a rule, but do you mean to say I got to stay off my own bridge?"

"Of course, no one can forbid you the bridge on your own boat, sir, but with the treacherous navigational problems ahead, I'm certain you won't insist on that privilege. It would actually be against your own interests." Addams winked again at Dixon over Allard's head. "After all, sir," he said reproachfully, "the captain *is* responsible for the safety of the yacht. Let me put it this way. The captain of a yacht is comparable to the comptroller of a large corporation. Before you sold your factory, Mr. Allard, would you have permitted indiscriminate and, if you'll pardon my saying so, ignorant visitors in your accounting department? I'm sure you wouldn't. It would soon have demoralized the system."

Allard kept nodding. His hangover was leaving him and he was feeling better. "Right," he said, "right. In business I made it a rule never to interfere with department heads. Same thing goes here. Check. It's your responsibility, Captain, but don't forget, if you fall down on the job, you're the one that gets hell, and no alibis. If there's anything else you want to know, ask Addams here."

Addams picked up Dixon's bag. "I'll show you your cabin, Captain," he murmured.

Dixon's cabin was in the forecastle, separated from the main cabin by the galley. The galley was a gleaming model with large double Monel-metal sink drains, a huge white refrigeration unit, a bottle-gas stove fed from two upright cylinders, both of which were topped by pressure gauges, plenty of mahogany lockers and dish-cabinets, and superfluously, a dishwashing and garbage-disposing unit.

Addams tapped a hatch cover in the deck with the toe of his neat foot and said, "We've enough canned goods to take us around the world, Captain. Canned guinea hen, canned partridge, rabbit, truffles, caviar, venison, Westphalia ham, and everything else you can possibly think of. That's for us, of course. Mr. Allard's gastronomic peak is a rare sirloin steak with peas, mashed potatoes and apple pie. This is your cabin. I bunk after with Wirt in the fantail."

He opened the mahogany door and Dixon saw the usual two bunks, one over the other, with lockers beneath. There was a closet behind the galley door, and forward was the door to the head. There was a short, narrow alley down the center, and the side opposite the bunks was filled with cases of liquor lashed securely. Dixon looked at the cases.

"A party every night, eh?" he said.

Addams smiled that small, demure smile with which Dixon was going to become so familiar. "Mr. Allard has commissioned me to purchase a thousand dollars worth of spirits in Nassau," he said. "I'm afraid we're going to be a little crowded in the fantail after it is all aboard. You actually have the best cabin, Captain. If you want more head room, I can have the carpenters take out the upper bunk this afternoon. Mr. Allard won't mind."

"Who's in charge, you or Allard? You seem to have everything under control, Allard included."

"We-ell, you know how it is. Allard is a little lost sheep on a boat, and I've had the experience. He leaves most things to me."

"You're doing all right."

"I manage."

"What's this purser business? I never heard of a purser on a yacht. I thought the captain did the buying if the owner didn't want to be bothered."

"Oh, come, come, Captain, you really don't think I'd let you have a plum like that, do you? Don't be silly. You can't handle Allard, and I can. You bark at him. You get his bristles up," Addams looked complacent. "I can smooth him out every time. You leave Allard to me, old boy, and I'll leave the navigation to you. Right?"

"Turn your English accent off with me, you bastard. I know where you came from, and it wasn't dear old London. If it was London anything, it was London, Ohio."

Addams chuckled. He put Dixon's bag on the bed, opened it and began hanging the clothes in the closet. "I can't hide a thing from you, can I, Captain? Too true. It's positively shaming. I wasn't born in London at all, but many of the best people weren't, you know. Oh my, my, my, what is this?" he held up the duck-billed cap Dixon always wore while at the wheel. "This won't do, you know. We'll have to get you one of those gold-braided objects with which yacht captains always adorn their noble brows. You'd really look intrepid."

He looked up brightly and flourished his slim hand across his forehead.

"Captains Courageous," he said. "Dear old Kipling. Now, listen," his voice turned sharp, "and I mean this. You take care of your department, and I'll take care of mine. Allard is my department. The boat is yours. Don't interfere with me, and I won't interfere with you. Let's have that understood immediately. You're the Captain. Allard is the owner. I'm only the purser, cook and steward. If you want me to shine your shoes, I will. But, and this is a definite warning, if you step over the line into my department, I'll get rid of you like that!" he snapped his fingers. "Allard is my pigeon. Mine!" He tapped his chest and smiled complacently. "Don't poach, old boy, don't poach. To use your own words. Don't poach."

Dixon said harshly. "Now I'm beginning to see how you did it to that old dame down in Key West."

Addams laughed angrily. "I don't give a damn what you see."

"You took her."

"Sure I took her. If I didn't, somebody else would have."

"And you're going to take Allard."

Addams smiled.

Chapter Four

Dixon took the *Almacor* out on the four-thirty tide the next morning. Addams cast off the stern lines while Wirt stood on the dock and held the bow snubbed to the dock as Dixon eased the stern out into the stream. There was a bare five feet clearance from the yacht tied up astern and just about the same from the one on the bow. They really stacked them in here, bow to stern all the way down, like buzz-boats in a Coney Island concession. Dixon kept the rudder over, watching the stern as the *Almacor* swung its arc, the slim nose a pivot against the dock, held by Wirt's line.

That Wirt, he was all right, a sailor even if he was a college boy with that crewcut and grin. He held the nose with a half hitch against the piling. Addams was very crisp and efficient, too, but different. Efficient like an attendant in a parking lot. That Wirt was all right. Dixon's eye touched him briefly, mechanically to make sure, though he had been sure from the moment the boy took the line and snubbed it in a half hitch that could be tossed off when Dixon gave the diesels full astern. In this close birth, the tide was a joker trying to slam the *Almacor* back into the liverwurst aft—Lord, who had designed that one?—the minute Wirt cast off. It had to be just right. If Wirt let go wrong there'd be a mess of smashed rails and fantail and Lord only knew what else with this tide. This was the lousiest berth in the world right here. Close, too close and too fast. But Wirt was all right. You can always tell when they're all right, just by the way they handle a line. Clean. It was a little thing, but not such a little thing at that. The line was the umbilical when you were coming out from the dock in a close berth. Women again, but it was always that. Up on the bridge, he could handle the rudders and the motor, but the umbilical was the line on the deck, and if Wirt didn't cut it just right, what an abortion this would be with this lousy goddamn tide.

Damn, thought Dixon in a post-alcoholic sweat, streaming, blotting it on his forehead with his handkerchief, *what is this, the DT's?*

He was afraid. To smash up now, to let the tide ram him back into that sausage of a boat astern, and the yells and the police and the delay, he'd forgotten how lousy the tide could be here and the wind straight from the south. What a lousy break. Something in him was screaming for the steadying muscle of a drink, just one, just one double rye, but it was too late now. He had the yacht half way out with the tide and the wind trying to drive her back.

He saw Wirt holding the line, looking up to the bridge, waiting for him to get her out so they could cast off. Dixon wanted to slam the diesels over and get her out of there, but if he hit them too hard she'd rip the cleat clear out of the screws, maybe even pull the piling or the line—how old was the line? He had to ease it.

She was quivering. She was a beautiful boat. Slim in the flank and maybe too ready to roll in a heavy sea, but quick and eager. Alive. She was alive, all right. Too much alive. Quivering and trying to draw away from him, sensitive, pulling back like a young girl.

Dixon blotted the alcoholic sweat from his forehead and rigidly watched as the stern swung out into the stream. The back room of Dominick's, that was the place. Safe. Secure. Mother, mother. Lord, let me put this goddamn thing out of here, I'll be all right the minute I pull it out of here, but Lord let me get it out of here, that goddamn tide and that stinking wind, that goddamn stinking wind, I could shuck her out like an oyster without that goddamn stinking wind …

She was swinging back and, panicky, he gave it too much gun. The piling groaned and Wirt leaned back, holding the line, his face sharply up-angled as he shot a startled glance to the bridge.

Addams, staggering and reaching for the rail at the end of the bridge, snarled at him with a nasal Boston flatness and barely managed to keep the carafe of hot coffee erect on his tray. Behind him was Allard, clutching the handrail. Addams was first on the bridge, setting down the tray with the carafe of hot coffee beside the compass rocking in its gimbals.

He hissed at Dixon like a spitting cat. Dixon scarcely heard the words, but he knew that Addams was issuing commands. He lashed out with the back of his hand and hit Addams across the side of the face. Addams tumbled into the cushions, making mewling sounds, crouched, his arms crossed before his face.

Allard bleated, "What's the trouble here now, what's the trouble?"

Dixon snarled, "I said keep off my bridge and goddamnit, I mean it! Get out of here!"

He took the *Almacor* out, yelled, "Cast *off!*" to Wirt, and took her out into the stream. Wirt flipped off the line and nimbly leaped on the bow as the yacht backed into the stream. Dixon took her around and pointed her out toward the Atlantic. The buoy light was on the bow and she was running easy. He reached for the carafe of hot black coffee.

"I told you sons of bitches to keep off my bridge," he said woodenly.

"If you want to play shuffleboard up here, I'll take you back and you can have it. But keep the goddamn hell off my bridge when I'm taking her out."

He turned his back on them and sipped at the cup of steaming coffee. He heard Allard say sharply, "You've got a temper, man!" but he paid no attention. It hadn't been temper. It had been near-hysteria, but it was all right now. They were running free and clean. The Atlantic met the bow with only a slight swell which the yacht took so easily that there was the feeling of riding a bubble. Dixon relaxed on the high stool of the wheel, beginning to feel the deep and quiet exhilaration of having the broad sea ahead of him. It was a familiar thing, a sanity and a reassurance. When dawn seeped into the sky and shadows and half-seen bulks became solids, he had the curious feeling that the boat was a slim hand holding him protectively in its palm.

It was about nine o'clock when Allard came back to the bridge. He had the slightly muddled satisfaction of one who had recently conquered a hangover with three or four fast ones. He sat down on the bench and lit a cigar. He sat for ten minutes without saying anything, and then he cleared his throat, as if announcing his presence.

"So we're on our way, eh, Captain," he said heartily.

"That's right."

"Nothing like it, is there? I mean, all this."

"No," Dixon smiled a little, "there's nothing like it."

"You seem to have had a little trouble getting away from the dock. There's nothing the matter with the boat, is there, Captain?"

"Not a thing. We had a strong south wind and a close berth."

"That's all right then. I don't know anything about boats, and I thought they might have sold me a lemon. Where we headed for now, the Bahamas?"

Dixon chuckled. There were about three thousand islands in the Bahaman group, stretching across eight hundred miles of sea like the jagged-toothed jawbone of a shark.

"Addams mentioned Bimini as the first port," he said.

Allard had no recollection of this. "Bimini? What's at Bimini?"

"Fishing, chiefly. Marlin, barracuda, amberjack, bone-fish."

"Just fishing?"

"That's about all."

"Isn't there anything else there?"

"There's an aquarium and a few small hotels, but people go there mainly for the fishing."

"What do they do after they fish? I mean, nights. Or do they fish at night, too?"

"Sometimes. Mostly they sit around nights and tell each other how good the fishing was last year."

"No night clubs, no shows?"

"You can hire some of the native boys to come up to the boat and sing calypso."

"And that's all?"

"After a good day's fishing you don't feel like doing very much except sleep."

"You're not taking me there," Allard said emphatically. "I never had the patience for fishing. I always had to be up and doing. Fishing's all right for kids or old men, but not for me. Where else can we go?"

"Well, there's Nassau," he said mildly.

"What's at Nassau?"

"Night clubs, floor shows."

"That sounds more like it. We'll head for there."

Addams appeared at the end of the bridge with a tall glass of orange juice so amber in color that Dixon could see that it had been well laced with bourbon. Allard said, "Ah!" and took a long swallow.

"Why didn't you tell me about Bimini, steward?" he asked accusingly.

"Sir?"

"The Captain just told me there's nothing but fishing there."

"That's right, sir. It's one of the most famous fishing spots in the world. Everyone goes there."

"I don't care who goes there. We're going to Nassau."

Addams shot Dixon a venomous glance, and started smoothly, "But, sir, I've already engaged a charter boat for several days …"

Allard shouted, "Cancel it, damn it!" his face congested like that of a baby in a tantrum. "I don't like fishing and that's all there's to it."

He stepped down from the bridge and stalked aft toward the sun deck where the guests had already started their day's drinking. Dixon heard him say loudly, "In case you hadn't heard, girls and boys, we're on our way to Nassau."

Addams looked at Dixon and said in a low furious voice, "I thought I told you to keep your nose out of things."

Dixon shrugged. "He asked me, and I told him."

"I'm warning you for the last time, keep your nose where it belongs. The next time you step out of line, you're going to find yourself on the beach."

Dixon said lazily, "Ah, go to hell."

Addams turned on his heel and ducked down into the main cabin. Wirt looked up from the opposite end of the bridge, grinning.

"You stepped on his tail, Captain," he said. "You stepped on him where it hurt."

"Get out of here and do your work."

"Yes, sir. I am doing my work. I'm listening to the diesels turn over down there. I'm the engineer, the chief engineer."

"You're also going to get a boot in the tail."

"Yes, sir. I was only setting you straight, that's all, sir. I'll bet you don't even know why Addams was so sore, do you?"

Dixon laughed. "I suppose I'm going to get told whether I want to be or not. Go ahead, tell me."

"It's that boat he chartered in Bimini. He chartered it for a whole week in Mr. Allard's name, forty bucks a day whether they used it or not. I heard him on the radio telephone."

"So?"

Wirt winked. "It's like this. Once in a great while when he thinks nobody's looking, Addams likes to tie one on. Well, it seems that last night he really tied one on. I don't know who he thought I was, but he didn't know I was me. He kept calling me Charley, and did he give me the lowdown on this Bimini deal, and laughing like the dickens all the time. He was going to keep Allard and party so drunk in Bimini that they'd never use the charter boat at all, and the guy who owns her would be free to take out anybody he wanted. Addams' cut was to be a hundred bucks. And that, Captain, is why he flipped his lid when you put the match to that one."

Wirt grinned and looked back toward the sun deck. "And right now," he said, "he's back there serving drinks like crazy, trying to get Mr. Allard soused enough to change the course back to Bimini. I guess I'll get down to the engine room. It's nice and clean down there compared to some other parts of this boat."

After a while Dixon began to see how really funny it all was. No matter how hard Addams ran, there were more dollars in the world that he would ever be able to overtake, running, running with arms outstretched. Dixon laughed softly and lifted his eyes from the compass to the quiet sea rolling ahead.

Chapter Five

The sailing route was to Gun Cay, over the Great Bahama Bank to the Northwest Channel Light, and from there southeast to Nassau. The *Almacor* was running light and fast on a calm sea, and Dixon figured that they would dock at the Nassau Yacht Club no later than seven that evening.

They were a few miles east of Gun Cay when Addams came to the bridge again, bringing Dixon a turkey sandwich and a glass of tomato juice. His neat, careful face was very bland.

"They've drunk two bottles since breakfast," he said confidingly to Dixon. "They're so blind they don't know if they're here or on the Staten Island ferry."

"That's terrible," said Dixon, just as blandly. "When I drank like that, I used to wake up in the damnedest places."

"In Lauderdale they were drunk for a week, and all the while they thought they were in St. Petersburg. His Nibs kept wanting everybody to go out and sit on a green bench with him. They don't care where they are when they're drunk."

"I know. That's the way I was. I spent a night under the grandstand at Hialeah." Dixon kept a straight face. Addams had no sense of humor; he wouldn't know he was being kidded.

Addams went on thoughtfully, "You know, Dix, I was really counting on getting to Bimini this trip. It means a lot to me. A lot."

"Gosh, that's too bad."

"Charley Hatch is thinking of selling the *Fly Boy*, and he's chartering out of Bimini. I wanted to look it over. I've got some money laid away, and I'd like to put it to work. The *Fly Boy's* a nice boat, and I hear the price is right."

"Sounds good."

"Yes, it'll be a nice deal. I wanted to talk to you about this before. I want to get somebody to work it for me. Now I know you're broke, but if I can close the deal with Charley, I'll take your note for half interest in the boat. I think we could make some money, and you'd be doing what you like to do. Frankly, I'm tired of working for people like His Nibs back there. I want to work for myself for a change. How does is sound to you?"

Oh, you cute son of a bitch, thought Dixon delightedly, you cute, conniving son of a bitch. Aloud, he said, "Sounds great. What are you going to do, wire him an offer from Nassau? Or why don't you go down and talk to him on the radio telephone? He's got a ship-to-shore on his boat."

"You don't do business like that, old boy. I'll have to go over the boat first. And I'd want you to go over it with me."

"How can we manage that? We're not putting in at Bimini."

"That's what I wanted to talk to you about. Why can't we put in at Bimini?"

"Mr. Allard …"

"Forget Mr. Allard. I'll take care of Mr. Allard. He'll be drunk from the time we put in until the time we pull out. And even if he does come out of it, I'll tell him he changed his mind, but he won't, so don't worry."

"Oh no. I couldn't do that. I have definite orders to go to Nassau. I can't change the orders. You know that."

"Don't be a damn fool! I just told you …" Addams smoothed his voice, "Put the blame on me, if it comes to that. Tell him I came to you with a message to change course."

"No, no, I just couldn't do that. It wouldn't be right."

Addams said angrily, "For God's sake, use your head!" He turned away and as he left the bridge he flung back over his shoulder, "I'm not keeping that offer open forever. We're only an hour away from Bimini, so there's still time to turn back."

With Addams gone, the joke curdled and Dixon suddenly felt very tired. What had been the point of it, the laugh?

Sooner or later Addams would wake up to the fact that he'd I been kidded. Addams would maybe understand being doublecrossed, but he'd never forgive being kidded. But what the hell, Addams had been kidding him, too and not for laughs. Using that business about Charley Hatch's boat to get them back to Bimini. Charley Hatch wasn't selling any boats, especially the *Fly Boy*. But that wasn't the lousy part of it. The lousy part was the way Addams had used the bait, knowing how he felt about losing the *Madame*, knowing that he would rise to bait like that. He hadn't. That was something. He wasn't that far gone. And that's why the tiredness had come. Helen had said, *I think the Madame was the best ninety percent of you.* She was wrong about that. She didn't cut deeply enough, but how could she know everything there was to know? The time he had the *Madame* up in Brielle, New Jersey, for the tuna fishing and the four sporting types from the Newark Athletic Club chartered her. They were sportsmen, all right, with muscles from handball and sun-lamp tans, out to do the fish a favor with expensive tackle. That was the day the tuna weren't running, and all they got was albacore. Nobody got anything that day. There wasn't a single tuna flag up in the whole fleet. But from the way the four of them went on, you'd have thought that even the kids were catching them from the jetties with bamboo poles, and Dixon couldn't have got one if it had been stuffed and mounted and nailed to the deck. They let him know, all right, and not for laughs. He didn't say a word all the way in, but when they got up on the dock he took on the whole four of them, and when they were all stretched out, he took the money they had paid him and stuck it in the open mouth of the last one he had clipped. It wasn't the fight, and it wasn't the satisfaction of giving them back their money and it wasn't even that he had showed them that he didn't have to take their abuse. It had been clean out there, and they had dirtied it. There had been that.

And there had been the time out of Bimini when they lost that big black marlin. It was a monster and when it felt the hook it beat the sea to a froth until you'd have thought it was a whole school of porpoise killing a shark. Then something let go and it went bucking out and away like a suddenly freed wild horse and they stood there watching it until it was out of sight. If the guy who'd lost it had been sore, it would have been understandable, but all he said was, "God!" in a kind of awe. There had been that, too.

And there had been other things, the whisper of the boat through the water coming in at the end of day, talking loudly, not boasting, but because they were happy and they had a two hundred pound tarpon lashed to the stern. That was Boca Grande in the Gulf of Mexico. And little things like the rain and a high sea and the boat stubbornly taking it all and bringing them in, or the quiet days when the engines hummed and the props gurgled under the stern.

All of it, all of it.

He had turned the boat over to the automatic pilot, for the water was as serene as a sleeping young girl, and only once in a great while did he have to lean forward to check the compass. It was at the Northwest Channel Light that he had to change the course for Nassau. This involved more care, and he did it resentfully, for it interrupted the sensuous and almost tactile gathering in of the past. The course laid, he switched over to automatic again and relaxed on his stool, closing his eyes.

When the engines changed their heavy beat and faltered, he started up, his head jerking from side to side, as if he had been aroused from deep sleep by a cannon shot, but in the next instant he jerked the twin control levers back to Neutral. The engines sped up but hawked irregularly. Then they stopped. Dixon swore.

He leaned over the end of the bridge and roared, "What the hell's going on down there?"

A few moments later Wirt looked up at him from the main cabin door. "Fuel pump on the port engine," he said shortly.

"How long will that take?"

"I won't know till I take it down. Two hours maybe."

"How's the starboard engine?"

"Okay."

"Turn her on. We'll limp along on one."

Wirt said, "Limp is right. Wait till I disconnect the port engine." He disappeared back into the cabin.

Dixon walked over to the chart, spread flat under glass to the right of the controls. The nearest anchorage was at the west end of Chub Cays, a little cove well protected from easterly winds. He had known that before, but he didn't trust his memory. He heard Wirt's muffled shout, and he pressed the starter button. With only one engine running, the sound was thinner now, like the shallow breathing of a sick man. He switched off the automatic and, taking the wheel, turned the slim nose of the yacht due east. He had to keep compensating for there was a strong pull to starboard with only one prop turning. It was a good two hours before he dropped the bow anchor in the cove just north of Chub Point.

When he squeezed down into the cramped engine room, Wirt was squatting on the narrow runway between the engine, arms, face, hands and chest smeared with heavy grease, cleaning the fuel pump in a bucket of kerosene. He was swearing, and from the monotonous beat of it, it sounded as if he had been saying the same words over and over for so long that they lost meaning.

"What's the trouble?" asked Dixon.

Wirt looked up furiously. "The trouble!" And then his lips quirked. "Well," he said, "it could be a brassiere got caught in here, they're all over the place, or it could be one of those tosspots poured in a quart of redeye, or on the other hand it could be just a plain ordinary everyday act of God."

Dixon said drily, "Very funny."

"It gets funnier," said Wirt earnestly, waving a sopping piece of rag. "Do you want to hear the funniest part of it?"

"If I don't have to buy a ticket for the performance."

"You know what I'm cleaning out of this thing? Mud, sludge,

garbage, scum, sewage, and I'll have to clean it out of both engines and suck out the fuel lines as well. They must have dug that fuel oil out of the Okeefenokee Swamp. The only thing it hasn't got in it is dandruff. And when I get finished cleaning this end, I'm going to have to try and figure out some kind of filter to put in the fuel tanks so maybe we can go a mile or two without getting stuck again. If you ask me, somebody gave us roofing tar instead of diesel oil by mistake." And then he added woodenly, "Only it wasn't a mistake."

"What the hell's that supposed to mean?"

"Who does all the buying of everything for this floating establishment of joy?"

Dixon said, "Oh."

"And who gets a rake-off on each and every item? And who'd buy fourth grade oil and charge for first grade oil? But leave us mention no names. That is, leave us not take the name in vain …"

Dixon said angrily, "Cut it out, for God's sake! There's nothing funny about it. Suppose we'd got stuck out there and a blow came up, that'd be sweet, wouldn't it? Give me some of that sludge in a can."

Wirt pursed his lips and looked down into the bucket of dirty kerosene. He stirred it with his finger. "I made a mistake," he said finally. "The tanks must have been dirty before the oil was put in. I should have cleaned them. If you took a can of that muck to Mr. Allard, you'd be getting me in trouble." He held up his finger. It was covered with black scum. "Addams has a bill that says first grade oil, and that's what he'll tell Mr. Allard he bought. If Mr. Allard checks back with the oil company, they'll say they delivered first grade oil. What else can they say? If you make a stink, Addams'll throw it in my lap and I'll get canned. I don't want to be canned for negligence. That'd make it rough for me to get another job." He kept his head down and said thinly, "So if anybody asks me, I'm going to tell them we had a defective bleeder line between the fuel pump and cylinder head and weren't getting any injection."

Dixon leaned over him. "*Did* you clean those tanks?" he demanded.

"What do you think?"

"Okay. Okay. How long is this going to take you?"

"I'll be finished in four hours."

Dixon nodded and straightened up. He climbed the narrow metal ladder to the main cabin. The yacht was as silent as a Sunday afternoon on a long country road. Allard and his friends were sleeping it off in their cabins. The life cycle of the mosquito—drink, coition, sleep. But then, the mosquito didn't know any better.

Dixon walked back to the fantail. Addams was on one of the day beds, reading a magazine. On the cover was a picture of one of the models clad solely in roller skates.

"If she ever fell down on the rink," said Dixon, "she'd get a tail full of splinters."

Addams thrust the magazine down between the bed and the bulkhead. "What's the matter with the engines?" he asked coldly.

Dixon sat on the edge of Wirt's bed and lit a cigarette. "Wirt told me it was a defective bleeder line," he said. "We were lucky it was only the port engine. If it had been both engines and any kind of wind came up, we'd have broken loose from the anchor. In a heavy sea, we'd have broached to and turned over like a canoe. It could easily have been both engines."

Addams snapped, "We didn't, so what?"

"Oh, nothing, nothing," said Dixon pleasantly. "I just mentioned it. And by the way, I happened to check the fuel tanks. We've got the wrong kind of oil. Come on down. I'll show you."

"Why should I look at it? I don't know anything about oil." And then realizing he had spoken too quickly, Addams said warily, "What do you mean, the wrong kind of oil. It's diesel oil, isn't it?"

"It's diesel oil, all right, but it's non-detergent. It gums up."

"You're crazy. There's nothing the matter with the oil. The tanks must have been dirty."

This was exactly what Wirt had predicted. Smart boy, that Wirt.

"It's not dirty at all," said Dixon blandly. "The oil's as clean as a whistle, but it's non-detergent. If you know anything about oil, you can feel it between your fingers. Detergent oil feels lighter but actually has more viscosity than non-detergent." This was pure fiction, but Addams wouldn't know the difference. "We'll have to empty the tanks when we get to Nassau," he went on. "This stuff we got is for a different type of engine. Who sold it to you, by the way? They should have known better. Mr. Allard should write them a good stiff letter, and I'll tell him so. He should demand a refund."

Contentedly, he watched Addams squirm, trying to think of a way out.

Addams muttered, "Thanks for telling me. I'll take it up with him."

"Great, great. But be sure to take care of it. It could have been serious. If both engines had gummed up, well, you can imagine what would have happened to us. So when we get to Nassau," he added casually, "do you mind if I look over the oil before we fill the tanks again? Purely as a safety measure, of course."

Addams lay very still, and then he relaxed. There was no movement, but the tension had gone out of him. He had been like a cat on a low fence, watching a dog approach, and pass.

"Of course," he murmured. "The thing to do. Thanks for offering." He looked at Dixon from behind that neat, closed-in little smile. "The thing to do," he repeated. But his eyes were as hard and cold and opaque as glacial ice.

Dixon rose from the bed. "Mind giving me a hand with the dinghy?" he asked. "I'd like to take a look around outside."

"Not at all." Addams bounced up from the bed, willing and friendly, except for the eyes.

The dinghy hung on davits off the fantail. There was a small inboard motor mounted in the center of it. Dixon checked the gasoline tank before they lowered it. He tied a line to a cleat and tossed it over the stern. He slid down into the little boat. As he chugged away from the yacht, he looked back. Addams waved, still smiling. Dixon waved back, thinking—*you're not as cute as you thought, you little son of a bitch.*

He took the dinghy up around the north arm of the anchorage. Behind there, the cove forked into many small bayous, walled in by the mangrove that stood on their trestling roots above the surface of the water. The roots were thick with clusters of coon oysters. He went in until he could no longer see the yacht, and then turned off the motor. He tied up to a mangrove root and looked over the side into the water. He had been here before, and he knew what to expect. Before long, little fish began to cluster curiously around the boat, a few at first and then by the thousands until the water was alive with them, swimming in and out the shadow of the dinghy, or just lying back, perfectly still except for a faint flutter of their tails, looking at it.

They were striped and spotted in every color of the spectrum. Dixon leaned slowly over the side until his face was within an inch of the water. The fish scattered. When he did not move, they returned slowly until they were all there again, peering up at him and swimming in and out of his shadow as if playing. It was a showcase of living light and after a while, in a kind of transposition, he felt that he was the core of it and was weightless as if his body had fallen away from him.

Later, he sat up and looked at the sky, letting his eyes drop slowly to the mangrove around him. The leaf clusters, turned toward him, toward the sun and light, looked like green lotus blossoms. A single white ibis, black on the wing-tips, sailed over the bayou, its long legs trailing, and planed down into the mangrove. Somewhere in another bayou there was a violent thrashing in the water as a feeding fish, possibly a jack, struck into a school of smaller fish. It lasted but for a split second, and it was quiet again. It was not the lonesome quiet of a deserted city street, but a tranquil, breathing quiet.

Dixon looked at the mangrove and thought, if I could clear a few hundred feet of that, I'd build here. And he could have a boat, a small Bahama smack, so that when he wanted to come out all he would have to do would be to raise the sail. You could go almost anywhere in a Bahama smack. The thought of Helen crossed his mind and resentfully he brushed it away.

She wouldn't like it here. She liked nightclubs and shows and things like that. She liked to be up and doing. He had an uneasy feeling that somebody had said those exact words to him very recently. Up and doing. He did not try to remember who had said it. His thoughts had no course, but now the pleasant drifting had been interrupted. He lit a cigarette and sat hunched on the stern seat, staring down at the bottom of the dinghy. He thought, it needs a good varnishing. The sun down here in the sub-tropics played all hell with varnish. The *Madame* had had a varnished deck and cockpit, and when he wasn't washing it down with fresh water—expensive stuff in Bimini—he was giving it another coat of varnish. The next boat he got would be white with yacht-blue trim. The *Almacor* had teakwood decks. And there was Allard, an unvarnished crud if there ever was one. No varnish on him. Plastered was the word for Allard. And what was the word for Addams? Addams had the knife out for him now. He had seen it in his eyes. Addams liked to be sure of himself, and he had been caught unsure. You didn't like that, did you, Mr. Addams? You've got to be sure every minute of the time and sixty seconds of every minute. The hell with you, Mr. Addams. If that's what Addams had to go through to make a buck, he could have it.

Dixon flipped his cigarette over the side and looked up the bayou into the maze of mangrove. Probably lousy with snakes in there, and the little fish were all right to look at, but you couldn't eat them. Moodily, he reached for the starting rope of the motor at his feet. It was getting dark.

Chapter Six

Lights were burning on the yacht when Dixon swung the dinghy under the stern and reached for the line from the davits, gathering both of them in his hand. He hooked into the ringbolts, bow and stern. He went up the manila line to the fantail, hand over hand. He was about four feet up when the line came loose and he fell back into the dinghy, uselessly holding himself to the rope. His right foot struck the motor housing, turned under him, and he sprawled against the stern seat, skinning both forearms as he flung out his hands to save himself. The boat careened wildly, shipped water, but did not overturn.

He lay there for a moment in total astonishment, and then heavily he pushed himself up, wincing as he moved his head. His neck had taken a sharp blow against the edge of the seat. He looked up at the yacht. The rope lay in a tangle over the motor. He picked it up. It hadn't broken and it hadn't been cut. The end was still wound tightly with fishline to prevent fraying. But it couldn't have pulled loose for he had thrown four half hitches over it before pulling it tight to that cleat on the deck, and the line would break before you could pull out four half hitches. Unless some damn fool had been playing around with … His hands tightened on the line. You lousy conniving son of a bitch, he thought grimly. Addams. Nobody else would fool around with a line tied to a cleat in the deck. Nobody but Addams had a reason to. He looked up at the stern again. The yacht was high-sided with about a nine foot freeboard. If he had fallen the whole nine feet, or even seven or eight, he could have broken a leg or an arm. Easily. Maybe his back. An accident. Who could say it wasn't. The rope wasn't cut. Then tomorrow the *Almacor* would pick up a new captain in Nassau, and Addams wouldn't have anybody around making remarks about the crappy diesel oil and perhaps get Allard thinking about things. Neat. Just as neat and sweet as Addams' own little smile.

Dixon stood, flinching again as he put his weight on his right foot. He had turned his ankle when he hit the motor housing.

He climbed the line to the davit and swung over to the deck. He hoisted the dinghy and covered it carefully with the canvas. He looked at the line he had first tried to climb and then quickly stooped and threw one half hitch over the cleat from which it had pulled loose. That was the way Addams had probably done it. One half hitch. Two half hitches might hold, but one would slip. He looked at the cleat and thought, now let's see you figure *that* one out.

He walked forward. Addams was making dinner in the galley. His eyes sprang wide for an instant when he saw Dixon, but he had so honed himself that it was no more than a flicker.

"Well, well now," he said cheerfully. "Have a nice jaunt, old boy?"

"Old boy had a dandy jaunt," said Dixon, showing his skinned forearms. "Is there a medicine chest aboard?"

"Good heavens, what happened?"

"I didn't know enough to keep out of the mangrove. Those roots are slippery. Now if you don't mind my asking again, is there a medicine chest aboard? I want to clean this off. That slime can be pretty poisonous down here."

"Sorry, old boy. You looked so bloody, I was taken aback. Forgive me. We have a very complete medical and surgical cabinet. I stocked it myself."

He opened the door of what Dixon had taken for the broom closet beside the refrigerator. It was stocked from ceiling to floor with everything from aluminum splints and Benzedrine to a rack of gleaming hypodermic needles and aspirin. Addams had made more than a few dollars on that inventory.

"What, no operating table?" said Dixon. "Give me some iodine."

He took the small bottle and went into his cabin. Stripped to the waist, he was washing at the handbasin in the head when Wirt came in and leaned against the stack of liquor cases, dribbling smoke from a cigarette that hung from the corner of his mouth.

"You have a run-in with Addams?" he asked.

Dixon reached for the towel. "Why?" he asked carefully.

"I heard him talking to somebody in Nassau on the ship-to-shore. He was asking if there were any captains around who could take a yacht down to the Virgins." Then, anxiously, "You didn't sound off about that fuel oil, did you? If you did, then I'm on my way out, too."

"Don't worry about it, kid. This is just something between Addams and me. I think he was counting on something that didn't happen."

Wirt was silent, and there was such an odd expression on his face that Dixon said, "Is there more?"

"I don't know if it means anything but he said, 'This time Mr. Allard wants a captain who doesn't drink.' After he switched off, he came in your cabin here and stayed about ten minutes. I thought you ought to know about it."

Dixon looked quickly around the cabin. "He came in to make up the bunk." But he knew this was not true. Addams was systematic and did such housework in the morning immediately after breakfast. He looked around the cabin again.

"He threw something overboard," Wirt offered. "I heard two splashes, but I didn't see what it was."

"He was cleaning up."

"He cleaned your cabin this morning."

"But what the hell would he throw overboard?"

He looked in the closet, but nothing had been disturbed. That was silly, anyway. Addams wouldn't throw his clothes overboard, even in a fit of pique. Addams was subtler than that. He knelt and opened the locker beneath the bunk. Everything was there, even the half pint of brandy Helen had left in his room back in Miami. He glanced around the cabin for the third time, and this time he saw that the case of bourbon on top of the stack beside the galley door had been opened. All the others were glued shut, but one of the flaps on this one stood open about an inch. He pulled it back, peered into the case and grunted. Two bottles were missing. He lifted out a third. There were about three fingers of bourbon left in it. He looked at Wirt. "Two splashes, eh?" he said.

"Two," Wirt craned his neck and looked into the case. He glanced at Dixon but said nothing further.

"The idea is," said Dixon, "that I'm supposed to have drunk those two bottles and most of this one."

"Oh?"

"I didn't. Addams threw two full bottles through the porthole and probably poured this one down the sink." He glanced toward the door to the galley.

"He's setting the table up on the sun deck," said Wirt. "You mean Addams is going to tell Mr. Allard you drank all that?"

"Even Allard would be impressed by that kind of drinking. That's why Addams asked Nassau for a captain who didn't drink." Dixon's voice was flat, as if he were reading from a newspaper.

"Why does he want to get you canned?"

"He probably," said Dixon drily, "considers me a threat to his earning capacity."

Wirt put his fingers to his lips and glanced warningly at the door to the galley. Dixon heard the clink of dishes out there and then the clatter of silverware being put on a tray. Addams was whistling the *Londonderry Air*. He rarely whistled, only when he was exceptionally self-satisfied, and it was always the *Londonderry Air*. It was part of his pretense at being English, like the accent he used.

Dixon waited until he heard Addams walk out of the galley with the tray of dishes and silverware, and then he said, "Where's the current liquor supply kept?"

"In the main cabin in the big sideboard. Wait," Wirt put his hand on Dixon's arm. "Let me get it. If you're caught with your hands in the sideboard, Addams won't even need this." He tilted his chin at the liquor case.

Dixon said, "Thanks. But don't you get caught, either."

"Me?" Wirt laughed. "I've got a fishing license. Addams told me to help myself any time I wanted. That was in the beginning when he was trying to schmooze me."

"He's a great little schmoozer," said Dixon, thinking of how Addams had told him of all the tins of guinea hen, partridge, and other delicacies in the galley hatch.

"I'll get those bottles for you now, Captain."

"Any time before Nassau. Don't take any chances."

Wirt grinned and went out. Dixon sat down on the edge of the bunk. He was very tired. He didn't want to think about Addams, he didn't want to think about anything, but he knew he was going to have to do something about the man. Or get himself canned, and he didn't want that. Not now, not the way things were with Helen. If he lost the job, no explanation would impress her after the way he had acted when she told him Addams was looking for him.

And there was another thing. If Addams didn't succeed in getting him fired, he'd get rid of him another way. Addams would not be afraid to use violence if he thought he could get away with it, if he could make it look like an accident, like the fall into the dinghy. With surprise, Dixon realized that Addams was actually dangerous. He had thought that trick with the line over the stern a sneaking, cowardly kind of thing, but it was more than that. Addams was playing for big money. He had taken ten thousand from that silly woman in Key West, and God only knew how many thousands he'd milk from Allard before the cruise was over. Whatever it was, it wouldn't be peanuts, and if Addams got the idea he was muscling in, anything could happen.

Dixon knew he was going to have to do something about Addams, but his mind balked. He couldn't beat Addams up. That would be a sure way to get fired. Addams was high man with Allard. Anyway, Addams was so much smaller that such a thing was out of the question. But what could he do? He was going to have to do something.

Something, something, something. That was as far as he could get. Well, he'd think of something. Tomorrow. They wouldn't be in Nassau until almost noon tomorrow. There was plenty of time.

The door opened and Wirt came in with three bottles wrapped in a sweat shirt. He was grinning very widely.

He held up one of the bottles for Dixon to see. "Exactly the same brand," he said. He took out the partially filled bottle and put the others in the case. "You want this?" he asked, offering the bottle he had taken out.

Dixon's hands lifted from his knees, dropped back. He wanted a drink so badly he could taste it on his tongue, feel the warmth of it in his stomach and spreading through his chest.

"Throw it out the porthole," he said.

"Si, si, compadre," Wirt reached over the stack of cases and dropped the bottle through the open port. "Boy, I'd like to see Addams' face when he finds that case full."

Dixon said wearily, "Yeah." Addams would think of something else. He was thorough, if nothing else. First that doctored line over the stern, and then the liquor. Addams was really having a run of bad luck, though. Two duds. Poor Addams.

"Anything else, Captain?" asked Wirt, still very happy.

"No. And thanks again."

Wirt went out jauntily. Dixon sat on the edge of the bunk for a while, and then slowly undressed. He stretched out on the bunk. He was bone tired. He closed his eyes, but he could not sleep for thinking of Addams. He deliberately made himself think of Helen. He'd have to send Helen a postcard from Nassau. Having wonderful time. Or maybe he'd better not write that. She might think he was drinking again. Skip it, he told himself.

Later, Addams looked into the cabin and said softly, "Are you sleeping, Captain?" He sounded very solicitous.

Dixon said, "Close that damn door." The light bothered him.

"Aren't you going to have dinner?"

"No."

Addams' voice dropped to a whisper. "It's guinea hen tonight, Captain. Just for us."

"Beat it. I want to sleep."

Addams backed out and closed the door very quietly. Dixon lay staring up into the darkness. It was a long time before he went to sleep.

Chapter Seven

When he came awake with a leap that took him out of the bunk, the girl was screaming continuously, shrill and terror-stricken, in the galley just outside his door. He bounded out. She was standing at the steps to the main cabin, her head thrown back, her mouth wide open, the shrieks coming out of her with a terrible rhythm. Her arms were rigid at her sides and her fingers were cataleptic claws.

Dixon thrust her aside and she fell to the deck and lay there still screaming senselessly. He stopped short in the doorway. He was hardly able to believe what he saw. Wirt's big body was sprawled face down, one arm crooked under him and the other outflung. One of the male guests, the one called Dave, was stumbling around the cabin holding both hands to his face and making small, empty noises like the sound of pigeons. There was blood on his hands. Someone was breathing hoarsely and Dixon turned his head. Allard was gagging against the screen door on the starboard side of the cabin, a liquor bottle half raised in his right hand. He was drooling, breathing through his open mouth, and his eyes were distended. He was very drunk. Then Dixon saw the blood on the label of the bottle. He started across the cabin.

"Give me that bottle," he said.

Allard bleated, slid across the screen door, the side of the cabin and backed into the corner, raising the bottle higher. Addams came running down the companionway from the fantail, wearing only a pair of nylon drawers.

He yelled at Dixon, "Let him alone." He took a step toward Allard and held out his hand. "May I have the bottle, sir?" he asked politely. "It's empty. I'll fetch you another if you wish a drink."

Allard lowered the bottle and looked at it dazedly. Addams took another step and cupped his hand under Allard's elbow. "I'll take you to your cabin, sir."

Allard went docilely, mumbling to himself. Addams steered him down the companionway without a glance at either Wirt or Dave, who was now leaning against the other side of the cabin, whimpering.

"Mind the steps, sir," said Addams as Allard staggered.

Dixon went down on one knee and gently turned Wirt on his back. There was a large lump on the boy's left temple and it was already beginning to discolor, but he was not hurt badly for his breathing was quiet and steady. Dixon left him and went to Dave. The blood ran down his face from a diagonal gash in his forehead. It was deep and long.

"Sit down," said Dixon, guiding him to a chair. He took out a handkerchief and put it to the wound. "Hold it there. I'll be right back."

He went to the medicine cabinet in the galley. He found a surgical needle and thread. He also took back a bottle of iodine, some absorbent cotton, bandage and a basin of water. He was stitching the cut when Addams came back into the cabin.

Dixon paid no attention to him until the gash was bandaged. Dave's head was limp against the back of the chair. He had passed out, either from liquor or the stitching. Dixon went back to Wirt, saying over his shoulder to Addams, "Allard ran amuck with a bottle."

"Why?"

"He was soused."

"But there had to be a reason, even if he was drunk."

"Ask your friend over there, I'm busy," Dixon flipped his hand at the unconscious Dave.

He went to the galley again. The girl was still on the floor, sleeping. Her dress had ridden up around her hips when she lay on the floor threshing her legs and screaming. Her legs were beautiful but there were four dark bruises on the inside of her left thigh and one on the outside. Dixon thought sourly, you sure earn your money, honey. He took three ice cubes from the refrigerator and wrapped them in a towel which he pounded on the Monel-metal sink until the ice was pulverized. When he returned to the cabin, both Addams and Dave were gone and Wirt was dizzily trying to sit up.

Dixon said, "Okay, kid," and helped him to the chair. He went to the sideboard and took out a bottle of bourbon. He did not even think about taking a drink as he poured some in a glass for Wirt. The boy gagged over the first swallow. He was able to grasp the glass. Dixon held the wad of crushed ice against the lump on the boy's temple.

Wirt said thickly, "Give me another one of these," and held out the glass.

Dixon gave him another stiff one and the boy drank it straight down and shuddered. Dixon watched the young face harden, the eyes thin.

"What was the shenanigan, kid?" asked Dixon. "Did you get in the way when those two comedians started swinging at each other?"

Wirt said harshly, "Like hell!"

Wirt looked leaner, older, and mean. His big hand was clenched tightly around the glass. Dixon could see the knuckles whiten. All the soft, awkward youngness had gone out of him. There was the sound of a foot kicking against a wooden step and the girl came lurching out of the galley. She was very drunk. Her mouth was loose and ugly. She staggered across the cabin without a word and stumbled down the companionway and fell to her hands and knees. Wirt watched her hate-filled eyes and made no move to get up and help her. She pushed herself up, steadied against the wall and staggered on. Dixon watched the boy narrowly. Something *had* happened.

Dixon said, "You don't have to tell me if you don't want to."

Wirt looked around at the sound of his voice but still said nothing. Dixon shrugged.

"Okay," he said. "See you in the morning. Keep the ice pack on that bump."

Wirt let him get all the way to the door to the galley before he blurted. "I'll tell you. I'll be glad to tell you. I'll be glad to tell everybody."

Dixon turned. "As bad as that?"

"They were having their usual party up on the sun deck," he said. "Addams came back to the fantail at twelve. He gets off at twelve. He went to bed, but they were making so much noise up on the sun deck that I couldn't sleep, so I went to the galley to have a cup of coffee or something." He stopped and looked at the galley as if it had become a loathsome place.

"I was making a cup of hot chocolate on the gas stove when the girl came in," Wirt continued heavily. "She came over. She stood close to me, looking up into my face. She didn't say anything right away. She just stood there. And then she said, kiss me. I could see she'd been drinking. I didn't want to kiss her. I mean, she was drunk. I said, 'You're in the wrong cabin, honeybun,' and took her by the arm and started her out of the galley. She threw her other arm around my neck and kissed me, and then I started kissing her back. I didn't mean to, but hell, I'm not made of wood. Know what I mean?"

"I know."

"Well then she started working on me a little, running her hands through my hair, pulling my head down tighter against her mouth, moving against me and, well, you know, all that. And then I heard somebody and I looked up and there they were, both of them, standing in the doorway, watching and giggling. I knew right away they'd put her up to it. I saw red. I mean, I really saw it. All I wanted to do was get at them. They squawked and jumped back into the cabin. I went right in after them. I didn't give a damn. I just wanted to get at them. Allard hit me with the bottle. I didn't go right down but I could feel myself slipping. Somebody said, Don't hit him again! Somebody bumped into me and I went down and passed out."

He reached for the bottle and poured another drink, spilling some on the polished surface of the sideboard. Dixon watched him.

"Sounds pretty lousy," he said, trying to make it sound like a mild sort of lousiness, like someone deliberately jostling you to get into a revolving door ahead of you. Wirt was worked up enough. He didn't need any encouragement.

Wirt threw down his drink. He was getting a little tight now.

"I'm going to beat the hell out of him," he said. "The dirty, filthy ..."

"He's got it coming," said Dixon carefully. "I meant to ask you something before, but I forgot. How are the engines?"

Wirt looked at him blankly.

"The engines," said Dixon, "they're all cleaned up?"

Wirt squeezed his brows together, thinking it over. "Right," he said finally.

"Will we have any trouble getting to Nassau?"

"No trouble, no trouble. Don't push'm. Filters not so hot." He was beginning to sway.

"Suppose we turn in. I'm getting sleepy. You can have the upper bunk in my cabin for the rest of the night. We'll have to be getting up together in the morning to shove out of here. And anyway, it's a long walk back to the fantail. Okay?"

Wirt grinned. He threw a loose arm across Dixon's shoulders. "Okay," he said.

Chapter Eight

Dixon woke at seven the next morning. He felt dull and heavy. Wirt was still sleeping in the upper bunk. His knees were drawn up and his arms crossed over his chest, but he was not relaxed, even in sleep. He was mumbling. Dixon bent closer but the words were not understandable. He scowled and went into the head to take a shower. He felt better afterward, though not much. Addams was making an omelette at the gas range when he went out into the galley. The sliding door to the main cabin was closed to keep the cooking odors from the rest of the boat.

Addams turned his head as Dixon came in. "How's Wirt?" he asked.

"He'll wake up with a headache. He's got a nasty bump. How's Dave?"

Addams shrugged. "Did Wirt tell you what happened last night?"

"No." He knew why Addams was worried, and he was going to let him go on worrying. Addams was afraid Allard had really stepped out of line this time. The incident had happened in British waters and they were headed for a British port where Allard's money would not impress the authorities if Wirt signed a complaint. This could mean the end of the cruise and the end of Addams' easy graft. Addams had reason to worry.

"Didn't you see any part of it?" Addams asked.

Dixon rubbed it in. "Sure. I got in at the end when Allard was waving that bloody bottle around and Wirt was on the floor with a bump the size of a walnut on his head and Dave was bleeding all over himself. What does Allard have to say about it? Or isn't he awake yet?"

"He's awake. He doesn't remember a thing."

"He was blotto, all right. Your omelette's burning."

Addams jerked the pan off the flame. Dixon went to the refrigerator and poured himself a glass of milk and took a fresh pear from the hydrator. He heard the sliding door open and close and Dave came down the steps.

He looked terrible. He was a flabby man and his face hung slack, and above the bruised-looking pouches his eyes were painful slits.

"Give me a Benzedrine," he said sluggishly to Addams. He looked at Dixon. "How's the boy this morning?"

"Sleeping."

"It was a dirty trick and I'm sorry I had any part in it. Tell him that."

"You tell him."

"I will."

Addams was at the medicine closet and his ears were cocked sharply. Dave touched the bandage across his forehead.

"How many stitches, Captain?" he asked.

"Five. You'd better see a doctor when we get to Nassau."

"Yes. Thanks for taking care of it last night. Where's that Benzedrine, Steward?"

"Right here, sir. Here you are."

Dave took the tablet and drank the water that Addams gave him. He plodded back to the door. He turned.

"When you get the chance, Steward, I want my things packed. I'm getting off at Nassau. Miss Lamont will be getting off also. Pack her things too." He nodded once shortly and went out, sliding the door closed behind him.

Addams gave Dixon a flickering glance and walked back to the gas range. He pretended to study the pressure gauges on the two tall gas bottles. His face was screwed tighter than before. Dixon smiled and walked out through the main cabin and stood at the rail looking across the water at the green tangle of mangrove on the Cay.

It was a fine morning. The sky was slightly hazy at the horizon as it usually was and overhead it was clear and blue and there were no clouds. A light breeze moved over the water from the north-east scarcely ruffling the surface. The boat rose and fell gently as if breathing. Dixon went up to the deck at the bow and stretched out, looking up at the sky.

It was around nine o'clock when he heard the rushing hiss of water in the shower beneath him. He rose, stretched, and went down to his cabin. Wirt was drying himself angrily with a white Turkish towel on which the name *Almacor* had been embroidered. His expression was tight and compressed.

"How's the head, kid?" Dixon asked.

Wirt said shortly, "Okay."

"Let's take a look at that bump."

"It's all right." He was hard, uncompromising and smoldering and had withdrawn to the bitter core of himself, excluding even Dixon.

"After you have breakfast, I'd like to get going," Dixon said.

"I'm not hungry. We can get going right now. But what do you need me for? The engines are all right."

"I want you to keep an eye on them for a while."

"All right."

Dixon went up to the bridge, making up his mind to keep the boy occupied until they reached Nassau. Occupied and out of Allard's way. He didn't want the kid to get in trouble. He let Wirt stay down in the engine room for an hour and a half and then called him up and told him to take the bow and watch for shoals. The boy nodded and went without a word.

No one was on the sundeck, which remained empty even through lunch. Addams brought Dixon a tray of sandwiches. Ten minutes later Dixon saw him walk up to the bow with another tray for Wirt. He did not leave. He squatted down on his heels and lit a cigarette.

When Dixon glanced at them again, Addams had edged closer to Wirt and was talking fast and earnestly. Wirt was sitting stiff and staring straight ahead, as if he had to listen only because he could not leave. Dixon watched them. Addams was being smooth, very smooth, and his hands moved in ingratiating gestures. He tried to put something into Wirt's hand and the boy slapped his arm away.

Addams talked some more, leaning closer. This went on for several minutes before Wirt responded.

"All right, all right!" his voice rose harshly, carrying to Dixon up on the bridge. "But tell him to keep away from me, that's all, just tell him to keep away from me."

Addams stood, slipped something into Wirt's shirt pocket, said something and patted the boy on the shoulder. He was wearing his neat, demure little smile when he came back.

It was about fifteen minutes after this that Addams appeared on the bridge, ostensibly to take away the tray.

"A very touchy youngster," he said, shaking his head. "Did he tell you what happened last night?"

"He did."

"Dave told me. It was very silly and inconsequential actually, you know."

"Including the five stitches and the lump on Wirt's head?"

"I can't tell you how badly Mr. Allard feels about that. If he'd been himself, it never would have happened. You know that as well as I do, old boy."

"Do I?"

"Oh, come, come, old boy. Everybody had been drinking ..."

"Wirt hadn't."

"I know, I know, but let's not exaggerate the importance of this. After all, it's not as if it were deliberate, you know, and Mr. Allard is deeply grieved."

"I'd be deeply grieved too if I beat two people over the head with a bottle and stood a good chance of being picked up by the police for it."

"Now look, Dix, let's be sensible about this. You've been around and you know how such things happen. His Nibs is really quite cut up about this and wants to make it up to everybody for what happened. Why don't you forget the whole thing?"

Dixon said drily, "Sure. Just like that."

"Think it over," Addams said. "And when we're in port, let's keep it to ourselves. Talk to the youngster. He likes you. He'll listen. There's no sense in starting a lot of silly gossip in Nassau."

"When I work for a man," Dixon said with slow emphasis, "I don't talk behind his back. Not as long as I work for him."

"Naturally," Addams murmured, "naturally."

He picked up the tray and left by the starboard end of the bridge. A few minutes later when he consulted the chart, Dixon saw the bill sticking out from under the frame. He picked it up. It was a crisp new fifty dollar bill. Dixon put it in his pocket and bent over the chart again.

They tied up to the Yacht Club Dock in Nassau around three-thirty that afternoon. Dave and one of the girls—not the one who had approached Wirt in the galley the night before—came out of the main cabin carrying their bags. The other male guest was with them, talking in a low urgent voice. As they went down the gangplank, he made a grab for Dave's bag, saying;

"Come on, Dave, come on, don't be like that ..."

Dave pulled the bag away from him and took the girl's arm as they walked toward the Yacht Club building. "I'm going and that's all there's to it, Harry," he said flatly. "Don't bother me. I've got a headache."

"Listen, Dave, just listen for a minute ..."

Dixon watched them go. Harry was still arguing when they disappeared around the corner of the Yacht Club and Dave was still not having any. The girl didn't look as if she cared one way or the other.

Dixon had Wirt supervise the pumping out of the fuel tanks and check the new diesel oil before they took it on.

Addams stopped on the deck to talk to Dixon. "Mr. Allard would like to sail first thing in the morning," he said.

"I thought he wanted to see Nassau," said Dixon innocently. "The night spots, floor shows and all that. I thought he'd spend about a week here, from the way he talked."

"He changed his mind. Really, you know, Nassau *is* rather stuffy. He wants to go to Haiti, Puerto Rico, and then to the Virgins."

"It's three days to Haiti. He'd better get in a little night life while he can."

"Oh, Mr. Allard's not going ashore tonight. He's not feeling very well. There won't be any need for a watch, so tell Wirt he can have the night to himself." And then with a sharp upward glance into Dixon's face, "Everything all right?"

Dixon knew he was referring to the fifty dollars left under the chart frame.

"Fine," he said blandly. "Great. Everything all right with you?"

Addams looked at him with open dislike and walked away without answering. He saw nothing funny in serious things, and things were still a little on the serious side. Until they got out of Nassau.

Dixon felt good until he saw the boat that looked like the *Madame*. It had an open cockpit, two tall slim outriggers, a yacht-blue cabin top, white sides and a varnished deck. He looked away quickly. There was a stone in his stomach. To have a boat of his own again! But he had nothing to mortgage but his soul, and that wasn't mortgageable, he thought wryly.

At five-thirty a truck came with a load of liquor for the *Almacor*, and Dixon remembered that Addams had told him in Miami that he had been commissioned to buy a thousand dollars' worth. They needed more liquor like they needed a hole in the hull. There was already enough liquor aboard to keep the party going twenty-four hours a day. Allard had been talked into that one, all right. It was loaded into the fantail, case after case. It didn't leave much room with the two day beds, the chest and the two reserve bottles of cooking gas. Dixon counted the cases as they came aboard. He was pretty well acquainted with liquor prices in Nassau and after the last of it was in the fantail, he figured that Addams had short-weighted Allard by around a hundred and fifty dollars. The bill, of course, would read a thousand. Dixon looked at the truck to see from whom it had been bought, but there was no name on the truck. It had been hired for the delivery. Addams had bought the liquor from one of his pals. He had pals all over the place.

You had to hand it to Addams, all right. He was a busy little man. Yes sir. None busier. Dixon chuckled. He happened to glance down the dock again and there was the boat that looked like the *Madame*. A boy was hosing off the varnished deck with fresh water. Dixon looked hungrily at it and then went aboard the *Almacor* and down into his cabin, but it was so utterly lonely there that he left it quickly and walked back to the fantail. Wirt was standing there, a thin twist on his lips, looking at the pile of liquor cases.

"Let's have a party," he said. "Let's invite everybody. Let's have a regular brawl for a change." He kicked at the cases and tore a hole in the side of one of them. "Have a drink. It's on the house. In fact, it's all over the house. A couple more cases and there wouldn't be any place to sleep."

"I came in to see if you'd like to have dinner with me," Dixon said.

"I don't feel like going out."

"It's my birthday," Dixon lied. "Don't make me have dinner all by myself." The last thing he wanted was to leave Wirt alone on the boat with Allard. Not until that bright anger had embered a little anyway. "A man likes to have company on his birthday to keep him from bursting into tears."

"I can just see you bursting into tears," Wirt grinned a little. "How old were you the last time you bawled? Four? Five?"

"I cry once a year on Jefferson Davis' birthday."

"You're a southerner?"

"No, but I'm very fond of Virginia baked ham." He watched the boy snapping out of it. "And I'm nuts about grits and gravy and candied yams and Southern belles and I had a wonderful time in Biloxi once. The fine was something like fifty dollars as I remember. I loved Biloxi."

"I think I'll cry on Marilyn Monroe's birthday," said Wirt. "Not for Marilyn Monroe herself, but for the same kind of reasons you used for Jefferson Davis."

"How about having dinner with me instead?"

"I will, thanks. I feel better now."

"Good. Let's get dressed up and go to a fancy place," Dixon was feeling better too. "Let's go to the Royal Victoria."

As they left the boat a half hour later, Wirt said, "I suppose Addams bought all that new liquor for Fatguts."

"I'd be surprised if he didn't."

Wirt nodded with satisfaction. "I hope he steals the son of a bitch blind."

Wirt got very drunk that night.

Chapter Nine

Dixon waited until daylight the next morning before he took the *Almacor* out of Nassau Harbor because the flashing red gas buoys, that marked the channel, were hard to distinguish in the dark with the other lights ashore. The wind had freshened from the north-east and outside the bar there was a fairly heavy sea to buck. The *Almacor* dug her slim nose into it and the spray flew as if she were a lean dog shaking herself after a wetting, but it wasn't too bad for they were quartering south-south-east and the wind was on the port stern.

When Addams brought the breakfast tray to the bridge, he told Dixon that everybody was seasick except the crew.

"Mr. Allard would like to know if you can make it less bumpy," he said.

"Tell him we got a flat and that's what makes it bumpy," Dixon grinned. "Tell him it'll be fine after we change the tire."

"I gave them Mothersill's so they're probably asleep by now."

"Have a big night?" Dixon asked. "Wine, women, and song?"

"I met an old friend, a ship's chandler. We talked."

So that was the source of the liquor deal. Dixon wondered what they talked about, these birds of a feather. Did they talk like other people? Did they talk about women, or politics, or reminiscences? Or did they just sit and talk about the fast buck they were making or had made or were going to make? The pursuit of the fast buck was such a full time occupation that there couldn't be much time for outside interests. Dixon would like to have heard the two of them together. For say five minutes. After five minutes they'd probably be as deadly as a couple old potbellies about their golf scores.

What was really interesting was that Addams had been hitting the bottle again. Addams had never been much of a bottle man, but here he had got plastered two nights ago in Miami, and again in Nassau. The pursuit of the fast buck must be a pretty rugged marathon.

Addams stared dully through the windscreen at the rows of creaming waves ahead. They were very regular and looked plowed.

"How long will it be like this?" he asked, "I've never been farther south than Nassau."

"A week, a day, an hour. Feeling rocky?"

"I didn't get much sleep."

Dixon took pity on him. "Lie down, take a nap."

"I'll be in one of the vacant cabins amidships. There's too much motion in the fantail."

Later Wirt came up to the bridge. There was not much deck work he could do with the sea so rough. He had a bad hangover and looked it.

"Take a Benzedrine pill," Dixon told him. "They're in the medicine closet."

"I never take pills."

"They *say* suffering's good for the soul."

"That's why I don't take pills. My soul's in bad shape. It needs exercise." The *Almacor* took a heavy wave and heeled to starboard. Wirt clutched Dixon's arm and steadied himself. "I'm beginning to feel like a broken piston."

"It'll be a little calmer when we get opposite the Exumas. The cays'll break the wind. Why don't you lie down for awhile?"

"I tried that. The fantail's terrible and your cabin's like the inside of a bass drum."

"Lie down there." Dixon pointed over his shoulder with his chin at the wide cushioned bench behind him.

Wirt smiled feebly. "That's what I was leading up to," he said. "But thanks for bringing it up first."

"I'm the Great White Father," said Dixon. "I just sent Addams to bed, too."

Wirt stretched out on the bench, curled one arm under his head and was asleep in ten minutes. Dixon looked back at him from time to time to make sure he wasn't too close to the edge. Wirt was a good kid. He liked him. He hoped there wouldn't be any more trouble with Allard, but there probably wouldn't. Allard had had a good scare, which was another thing that was good for the soul. He wondered, chuckling at the thought, if a little suffering and a few good scares might not make a new man of even Addams, but he doubted it. If Addams suffered, he'd want to be paid for it.

The sea did become calmer when they paralleled the Exumas and within an hour after that the wind died away almost entirely and Dixon was able to give the engines full throttle. The *Almacor* could really run when it had the chance. It was like that cat, slim and long and smooth, the cheetah, the fast one.

Dixon had his anchorage for that night already selected. Crab Cay. A little speck of nothing in the middle of nowhere. There was a small but adequate cove on the western side. It would save running miles eastward to the Exumas for a harbor. He had never been to Crab Cay, for it was well off any of the routes, and it was too small to have any sightseeing interest, but it looked good on the chart.

Wirt awoke at two o'clock and took the wheel. The nap did not seem to have done him any good. He was silent and moody. Dixon gave Wirt the course and lay down on the bench. He closed his eyes but did not fall asleep immediately. He kept thinking of that boat back there at the Yacht Club Dock, the one that had reminded him so sharply of the *Madame*.

There was the time he had taken Helen over the Cross State Canal to Fort Myers and then up to Boca Grande for the tarpon fishing. They took three the first day on crabs, and that night they anchored out in Charlotte Harbor because the mosquitoes were so bad inshore. They had also taken a number of black grouper and Helen pan fried one on the tiny gasoline stove and they had asparagus tips and artichokes with it. Afterward they lay on the cabin roof looking up into the night and Helen said the stars weren't stars at all but holes in the fabric of the sky where it had worn and what they were seeing was Heaven shining through and someday the sky would wear out entirely and they would be able to see the whole of Heaven instead of just little specks.

"But that would be the end of the world," he said.

"Of course. There'd be no point in staying here then, would there? That's what I used to think when I was a little girl. I'm glad I'm a big girl now and there aren't any holes in the sky."

"I'm glad you're a big girl, too," he said, kissing her lightly.

"Sometimes the holes frightened me. The idea of Heaven frightened me too. Not because I didn't think I'd go there. I was sure I would but I was equally sure that no one else I knew would and I'd be dreadfully lonely. Oh I was a lovely self-righteous little brat, but then little girls usually are. I used to ask God as a special favor to let my family come with me. I was certain God would be only too glad to do me the favor because I was so sanctified. Weren't the tarpon wonderful this afternoon. I'm glad we let them go after we got them to the boat."

"You always let them go, unless they're a record."

Helen had fought one for an hour and twenty minutes and it had been very spectacular for it had been in the air half the time, lithe and silver, fighting her in her own element. When he gaffed it over the stern and brought it part way up out of the water so that its big overlapping scales shone in the sunlight, he was sure she'd object when he freed the hook and told her he was going to let it go, but she didn't.

"Oh, please let it go, darling," she said, still panting. "Please. It wasn't really a fair fight."

"That's a fact," he said solemnly. "And on top of that, you outweighed it. It was a mismatch. I hope the Fish and Game Commission doesn't hear of this. You'll be suspended."

He let it go and they watched over the stern as it sank without movement. Her hand tightened on his arm. "Oh I hope it isn't dead!"

"It isn't. Just bewildered, and probably resentful of your patronizing attitude. I wouldn't be surprised if it became neurotic. I'd suggest that the next time you jump over the side and catch one with your bare hands."

"That wouldn't be fair either. To me."

"What's fair, then?"

"Nothing, really. Wait. Yes, trees are fair, and flowers and vegetables. They don't hurt anybody."

He had then turned and kissed her and held the kiss for a long time but very gently and without passion or violence.

Later she said, "If you look very intently at the moon it gets bigger and bigger and closer and closer."

There was a full white moon and he stared up at it. "It doesn't do anything," he said. "It just looks chilly."

"You didn't look at it long enough. I'm looking again … it's moving toward me, I can see it." And then suddenly he felt her shiver.

"Let's go to bed, darling," she said.

There had been other trips and they had all been wonderful, but all through, the *Madame* had been the catalyst. He *had* to have another boat! That wasn't over-simplifying. It was important. It was his whole way of life. And Helen was important.

He did not know whether he thought all that or dreamed of it, for when he came awake it was still very fresh and clear in his mind and though he kept his eyes closed, trying to keep it that way, it began to recede as the sounds of the boat took definite form, the steady mumble of the engines, the swishing of the cutwater, the bubbling astern from the props. He sat up.

Wirt was sitting on the high stool at the wheel, one leg dangling.

"What time is it?" Dixon asked.

Wirt turned his head. "Five. You had a nice sleep."

"Everybody still below decks?"

"One of the body beautifuls came up and plopped herself in the sun for a half hour, but nobody brought her a drink, so she went down again."

Wirt was feeling good again. Things were going to be all right, Dixon thought. Wirt was still very much of a kid. He liked to prance around and laugh. He'd be very formal and distant with Allard, but there wouldn't be any trouble.

At six o'clock Dixon took the glasses from the leather case beside the wheel and scanned the horizon off the port bow. They'd be raising Crab Cay pretty soon now. It was right where it was supposed to be. He patted the hydrographic chart and said, "I love you." But when they came to the Cay he found that he had to anchor a half mile offshore. It was low tide and there was less than a fathom of water on the bar. The chart had given him deep water right into the cove. He looked at the chart and said, "Go to hell." There was nothing he could do about it now except hope the wind didn't freshen during the night. He looked up at the sky. At least it wasn't the hurricane season.

He took the glasses from the case again. He raised them to his eyes and examined the Cay. It was about a mile in length. The northern end was low and thick with mangrove. The center portion looked as if it had been cultivated at one time, although now the trees were almost hidden by ground weeds and climbing vines with intense scarlet flowers. A citrus grove, Dixon guessed, orange, lime, lemon or grapefruit. The small cove was midway on the shore line and was partially enclosed with two mangrove-covered pincers that did not quite meet, leaving an entrance about a hundred feet wide. There had once been a dock on the inside, a narrow platform of gray boards that now lay drunkenly on its side in the shallows. Dixon ranged the glasses along the path that ran from the dock to the high southern end of the Cay. Something moved swiftly among the trees and he swung the glasses sharply. It was a goat. Then he saw more, and in the end he counted twenty-three and saw two pigs rooting in the ground at the base of a guava tree.

"That's a gloomy looking place. A dead end." It was Allard. His bare feet had made no sound on the deck. He was wearing dark blue nylon pajamas with a big white A on the breast pocket. "Is anybody living on it?"

"Natives, I think. I saw goats and pigs. I think there's a house up there. I can just about see it through the trees. Oh-oh."

"What's the matter?"

"There *was* a house. There's a wall wedged among cocoanut trees, and there's part of the roof."

"What do you think happened?"

"Hurricane." He held the glasses on the cocoanut tree The wind was coming in strongly from the northeast. The Cay broke the wind and they didn't feel it down here in the anchorage. It was scarcely more than a gentle breeze down here.

"Will we be getting into Haiti tomorrow, Captain?" Allard asked.

"The day after, with luck."

Allard stared at him. His face flushed angrily. "For God's sake," he blared, "why didn't you tell me that before we left Nassau? Who the hell wants to go floating around for three days? It's so goddamn monotonous, all we do is sit. This is supposed to be a pleasure cruise, not an endurance contest. Why didn't you plan some decent stops on the way down instead of this!" He glowered at the Cay through the windscreen.

Dixon's hands tightened around the glasses. "We can put in to Great Exuma tomorrow," he said evenly. "You'll find some night life in Georgetown."

"That sounds a little better. But hereafter, use some sense. *Think*. We don't want to be sea-going hermits, man. Don't make me tell you your job. Use your head."

As Allard turned to stalk off, Wirt came up over the end of the bridge and they were face to face less than five feet apart. They both stopped. Wirt's whole stiff body was a frozen snarl. He was half crouched, but with his big shoulders blocking the end of the bridge, he must have looked enormous to Allard. Dixon heard Allard suck in his breath with a small cry. Wirt did not move. He stared at Allard with widening eyes. Dixon knew that he was the one who'd have to break it up.

"You wanted to see me, kid?" he asked casually.

Wirt's head jerked. He looked at Dixon. He looked back at Allard and the muscles clenched at the hinges of his jaws. He turned on his heel and walked heavily toward the fantail. Allard's hands were shaking badly and Dixon could see a sheen of perspiration on his face. He was breathing shallowly.

Dixon stood looking at the end of the bridge long after Allard had disappeared around the end of it. Dixon was abruptly sick of the boat. He went down to the galley. Addams was making dinner at the gas range. He looked pleased. He had heard the bawling out Dixon had got.

Dixon said, "No dinner for me," and went to the refrigerator. He took out three bananas.

"Aren't you feeling well, Captain?"

Dixon caught the gloating note in his voice. "Go to hell," he said and walked out, hearing Addams chuckle as he closed the galley door.

Wirt had rolled up the canvas that curtained the fantail and he was sitting on his bed, reading a book. He had taken off his shirt. His torso was creamy brown and squarely muscled. His shoulders were tremendous. He was a powerful boy. He looked up when Dixon came along the rail and said, "Hi."

"I'm going to take a look around the Cay," Dixon said. "Like to come along?"

Wirt lifted his book. "Got to study."

"Study what?"

"Engineering. I'm going to finish school as soon as I get the money together. One more year. Carnegie Tech."

His tone was so offhand that Dixon knew he was shy about it and didn't want to do much talking. Somebody had probably kidded him, maybe Addams. Addams could be very mocking.

"Good for you," Dixon said. "Could you give me a hand with the dinghy?"

"It's going to be dark in a half hour."

"I know."

"You'd better take this." He took a long flashlight from under his bed and handed it to Dixon.

They let the dinghy down into the water and Dixon slid down the line into it.

Wirt leaned over the rail. "If she's got a sister," he said, "give me three blinks on the flashlight and I'll swim ashore."

"Go and build yourself a bridge. I'll take care of the sister myself."

The tide was running out and Dixon felt the prop churn sand as he crossed the bar. At low tide the bar would be entirely out of water, but it was a sand bar and not coral and he was pretty sure now why it had not appeared on the chart. The prevailing northeast winds were washing away the north end of the island and the sand had been swept southwest, forming the bar. The cove shelved gently and the dinghy nuzzled into sand about six feet from shore. Dixon took off his shoes and socks, rolled up his pants and stepped over the side into the tepid water. He pulled the dinghy up on the beach and tied it to a clump of sea grapes. He put on his shoes again. Beyond the beach, the Cay was very rocky.

The path to the southern crest was overgrown with flame vine and other creepers but it was very easy to follow. All the taller trees, he noted, leaned toward the southwest. The trade winds had done that. He could hear the goats and pigs in the underbrush to his left, but they were very wary and wild and he could not get a glimpse of them. The sun was setting when he reached the top of the path.

He poked around the remains of the house that had been blown down in the hurricane. The wooden flooring still remained although almost completely rotted and the wall that was wedged in the grove of cocoanut palms was spongy and he could push his finger through it. It had been there a long time. Not as long ago as the big hurricane of '35, but probably the one of September, '47, which had been a brute, too. It was a silly place to have built a house, here on the very peak of the Cay, exposed on all sides. It must have been a man and wife, for up here the view had the effect of infinity with nothing but water from horizon to horizon and a woman would think of that first. A man left to himself would have built lower and against the rocky slope for protection.

So they built their house up here and the hurricane came and they opened a window but the flimsy walls could not take the battering force of the terrific wind. The aluminum roof was lying among the trees. It looked like a piece of paper that had been crumpled in a fist. Dixon wondered if they had got out alive. It bothered him and he went back down the path nosing ahead of him with the beam of the flashlight for it was quite dark now.

The southern end of the Cay, as he had seen through the glasses from the yacht, was covered with mangrove and was quite swampy, but there wouldn't be any mosquitos. There never were on these lonely Cays. The everlasting wind carried them off. He could hear the wind in the mangrove. It sounded like the rush of water in a shower as heard from another room.

There was a citrus grove in the center of the island and the trees were laden with oranges. There were oranges fully grown, half grown and some the size of peas, hard and glossy green, and there were fragrant blossoms that would make more oranges. He plucked one, bit a chunk of skin from the stem end and squeezed the juice into his mouth. He spat it out and grimaced. It was very sour, bitter. But of course. He should have guessed that. Sweet oranges had to be shipped and that would be a problem here. Bitter oranges could be made into marmalade and they—who had *they* been? what had *they* looked like? had *they* been young? … It was futile to think about them, but it was sad all the same.

He went back to the beach, sat down on the powdery sand and lit a cigarette. He did not look at the yacht. He lay back and looked up into the star-pierced darkness, remembering when he'd had the *Madame*. His mind fumbled back into the past with a kind of hungry hope …

It wasn't an explosion, it didn't sound like an explosion, it sounded like an exaggerated grunt, and he sat up. An arm of fire hung over the forepart of the *Almacor* and fell back. A moment later there was another grunt and the fire shot up at the fantail, and in an instant the yacht was bathed in flame from bow to stern. Dixon stared at it incredulously. The yacht had lifted on the second grunt or had seemed to lift. The flames thrust fiercely into the darkness.

He bounded across the beach and tore the line loose from the clump of sea grape. He thrust the dinghy into the water and leaped in, pushing hard with his leg to give it momentum. Five times he spun the motor with the starting rope before remembering that the choke had to be adjusted, for the night was cooler. The motor bellowed when he spun it again. The dinghy moved sedately up the yellow path of brilliance toward the yacht. It was a safe, tubby boat, but there was no speed in it. Dixon rocked back and forth on the seat in an agonized rhythm. He knew he had to get out there as fast as he could. He groaned when the dinghy slithered up on the bar and the motor stalled. The bar, about twelve feet wide, was now completely out of water. He jumped over the side and dragged the boat. He fought it over the bar, slipping, falling, ankle deep in the sodden sand, no purchase for his feet. The prop dug into it and it became a lunatic tug of war between him and the dinghy and he strained, fighting savagely to claw it forward another foot, another inch. He wrenched it, screamed at it as if it were alive and he could impose his will upon it. It was only when he was almost ready to drop, his head spinning and the nausea filling his throat, that a kind of sense told him what to do, and he dragged it stern-first, lifting so that the prop would not cut into the sand. It floated free and he fell into it, retching. He tried to raise himself and tumbled dizzily on his side. He tried again and fell into the motor, tearing his cheek on the edge of the housing.

Now he could hear the fire. It was the great carnivore, snarling over a bloody carcass. He thrust himself up and back onto the seat, swayed, and clumsily wound the starting rope around the magneto flange. His hands were shaking badly from the violence of that insane contest with the dinghy. The motor started on the first weak pull of the rope.

All this time, he had not looked up at the yacht, and when he raised his head he had the feeling that the whole night had gone crazy, for the *Almacor* was farther away now than it had been, the flames jabbing and slashing the darkness the entire length of her. She was moving away. She was moving on the tide, driven by the wind. The anchor line had burned through, and she was adrift. Dixon pursued it, pounding the canvas side of the dinghy with his fist as if he were a jockey on an exhausted horse. He was actually overtaking it when the motor sputtered, coughed twice, and stopped dead. He lunged at it with the starting rope, wound and jerked, wound and jerked, bending, straightening, staggering to keep his balance with the frenzied angular movements of a man dancing on hot coals. He was beginning the same senseless fight again, this time with the motor, but he stopped and said thickly, "Wait a minute, now, wait a minute, we'll look." He fumbled for the wire to the spark plug. It was still in place, and he unscrewed the cap of the gas tank and felt inside with his finger. It was a long, flat tank and he touched the bottom. It was dry. There was no gasoline and there was no emergency can of it in the dinghy.

This final calamity was too great to be borne and he reached up his arms and clawed at the sky, shrieking at it. Calm settled over him almost immediately. There were no oars. The seat just ahead of the motor was held in place by a brace at either end, and he splintered them with a heavy thrust of his heel. The seat was still screwed down, but without the braces, it could be wrenched free.

There was no point in pursuing the *Almacor.* There never had been a point. There was no one alive aboard. The flames were devouring everything. His pursuit had been a madness. He turned the flashlight beam on the Cay to take a bearing, and then knelt in the bottom of the boat and paddled clumsily toward the spot where the *Almacor* had originally been anchored. The water was quite rough and he had to paddle furiously to keep the dinghy moving without broaching to, but the frenzy had gone out of him. The creaming chop made it almost impossible to see any floating objects. He called and listened, but there were no answering shouts. He paddled in a wide arc, combing the water with the flashlight beam and calling. He tried to keep his voice high and out of his throat so that he would not go hoarse so quickly. And then he caught the glitter of a splash off to his right. He crouched and tried to hold it in the beam. It was definitely someone splashing out there, for the chop had a rhythm and this was counter to it. He paddled, digging harder with the clumsy seat, stopping frequently to find the splashing again with his flashlight. Twice he lost it and had to stand precariously in the bobbing boat before he found it again among the whitecaps.

It was fifteen minutes before he was close enough to see that it was Wirt. He switched on his flashlight and the boy flailed weakly toward the dinghy. There was a long gash across his forehead. The salt water had stopped the bleeding and the edges of the wound were puffed and waxy. Dixon had to help him over the side and into the boat. Wirt looked at him with wide, empty eyes. Dixon let him lie in the stern, and carefully raised himself to his feet. He made a slow full circle of the area with his flashlight but he could see nothing now but the pattern of the heaving water. The burning yacht was far to the southwest.

He paddled around until the muscles of his legs and arms and stomach and back coiled and knotted and the seat with which he was paddling began to slip from his fingers at every stroke. He looked back over his shoulder. Wirt was still lying in the same position, his eyes still distended. Dixon turned the dinghy toward the Cay and forced himself to take it foot by foot through the chop.

They were a hundred feet off the bar when he heard the cry. It came in a harsh and regular beat, like the keening of an idiot. Dixon picked up the flashlight with bent, shaking hands and fumbled the switch forward. He had to brace it on the gunwale. It was some minutes before he found the two heads among the leaping peaks of the water. It was Addams and Allard. Allard was on his back, his head clear of the water by a life preserver, and Addams was towing him. Addams was also wearing a life preserver.

Addams was swimming with one arm and at each stroke the breath came out of him in that harsh rattle. His strength was going for they were being slowly swept southwest, out to sea. Addams did not even turn his head when the beam of the flashlight moved over to him.

Dixon croaked, "Hold it, boy!" and turned the dinghy. It was easier going with the wind.

He reached for Addams when they were alongside and something happened in his stomach when his hand slipped from the naked, hairless skull. Addams had no hair. Dixon hooked his fingers in the life belt before the dinghy swept past. Addams cried out and heaved convulsively to pull himself free, clawing at Dixon's wrist.

"Take it easy, boy," Dixon panted. "We'll take you in."

Addams turned his head and tried to bite the hand that was holding him, protectively thrusting himself between Dixon and Allard. He did not have much strength, but he fought with all of it. He got his teeth in the ball of Dixon's thumb, and when Dixon jerked back, he tried to swim off with Allard, thrashing desperately. When Dixon caught him the second time he feebly tried to fight free, but he had nothing left. Yet, he still managed to keep Allard behind him. Dixon pulled them both to the side of the dinghy. He closed Addams' hand over the gunwale.

"Hang on," he said. "Dammit, hang on! I'll take care of Allard."

Addams' fingers closed around the gunwale, but he would not let go of Allard, even after Dixon tied the man securely to the bit with the starting rope of the motor. Dixon used his own belt and Wirt's to lash Addams to Wirt's ankle.

They had drifted several hundred feet south of the bar. It was an inch by inch struggle to paddle back. It would have been easier to angle in toward the Cay, but the Cay curved sharply to the southeast, and if he missed it and was carried past the end, he would be exposed to the full strength of the wind and would never get in. He paddled. He was a pinpoint of pain in the measureless dark. His arms rose and fell, and even after the dinghy nosed into the sand, they continued to rise and fall, digging at the water with the flat of the seat. The dinghy yawed. He struck the bar with the paddle and finally understood where he was. Doggedly, he leaned over the gunwale and let himself fall into the shallow water, hanging on to the dinghy with one hand. He crawled up the bar, pulling it after him. He stopped only when the dinghy grounded firmly and he could not move it. He turned and sat, resting his head on his arm.

He stared numbly at Addams and Allard. The water was much calmer here, and they rolled slightly on the swell against the side of the boat. Wirt was sprawled and motionless against the stern seat. Dixon lifted his eyes. It was an effort. The *Almacor* was still flaming but it looked no larger now than the length of a hand.

Then, abruptly, the burning yacht vanished. It flared brightly for an instant, like a nova, and was gone.

He frowned. "She went down," he muttered. He nodded several times. The empty darkness confirmed it. He felt sad, as if an acquaintance had gone. Not a friend, just an acquaintance who might have become a friend.

He looked at the flimsy dinghy, at the three unconscious men, turned his head and looked at the dark bulk of the island. The first thing was to get them ashore. They couldn't stay here on the bar. There would be three feet of water when the tide came in. The little anchor would never hold the dinghy.

He pushed the little boat until it floated free and then he plodded down the bar, pulling it after him. He walked half bent. The end of the bar was about two hundred yards south of the mouth of the cove. He brought the dinghy around and pulled it through the water up the landward side. When he was opposite the entrance to the cove, he stepped into the dinghy, knelt painfully, and picked up his awkward paddle again. The water was very calm in here, but his muscles had stiffened, and paddling was worse than drudgery. They moved so slowly that there was hardly any ripple from the canted nose of the dinghy.

He'd make it to the shore, he knew. He'd get there. His thinking was all right again. He paddled soddenly, but steadily. Row, row, row your boat, he thought, *gently down the stream, merrily, merrily …* Keep it up, Dixon, you're doing fine, there's another six inches behind that you don't have to worry about. Shall we try for twelve? Fine, we'll try for twelve. Who tied the anvil to this damn paddle? Who threw the overalls in Mrs. Murphy's chowder? Who stole your heart away, who? It's the suspense that counts. He looked over his shoulder. Addams and Allard were still alongside, their heads still above water, Wirt was there. He turned back and sat slumped, resting. He straightened up wearily.

"Let's go," he said.

He let himself over the side when they were still in four feet of water. It was easier to walk with the dinghy than to paddle it. He drew it up on the shore as far as his strength would allow him and tied the line to the clump of sea grape again. He splashed out to the boat. He unbuckled the strap from Addams' arm, but Addams was clinging so tightly to Allard's life preserver that Dixon had to use all his strength to pry the clenched fingers loose. Addams mumbled and actually tried to fight him again but he was too enfeebled to do more than push at Dixon's hand. Dixon laid him high on the sandy beach and went back for Allard. Wirt was the hardest. He had to be lifted over the side of the dinghy, and he was heavy and completely limp. His eyes were closed now. Dixon made the last trip for the flashlight.

As he trudged up the sand, he was vaguely aware that something was different, and when he looked up at the trees, he saw that the sky was becoming light behind them. It was a gray light, seeping up from the east. That would make it around six in the morning. He stared at his wristwatch. It had stopped at ten minutes to twelve last night. That must have been when he was first wrestling the dinghy over the bar. He'd been out there six hours. He looked down at his legs. The thigh muscles were twitching.

"No wonder," he said. He snickered and shook his head. "You never know when you've had enough, do you?"

He shuffled up the slope to where he had laid out the three men side by side. He bent over Wirt and looked at the gash in the boy's forehead by the light of the flash. It was deep, and looked pulpy from the salt water. Dixon took off his shirt and tore it into strips. He had to keep blinking to keep his eyes open. The forehead had to be bandaged so Wirt wouldn't get sand in the wound if he rolled over. Next he went over Allard, but aside from the skinned cheekbone he could find nothing. Addams had a large bump behind his right ear, his arm was scraped from shoulder to elbow, and there was a dark bruise as big as a fist on his ribs. His hair was gone, but his scalp did not look badly burned. Dixon took off Allard's shirt and bound Addams' head in it.

Addams' eyes opened vacantly, and then spread with alarm.

"Where's Allard?" he whispered, trying to sit up. Dixon pushed him back.

"He's right here. You did a good job, boy. You held him up till I got there."

"Where is he, where is he?"

"Right next to you."

Addams struggled up on one elbow and peered uncertainly into Allard's face. "He's all right?"

"He's just dandy. He's going to have his usual hangover when he wakes up, is all."

"Yes. He was dead drunk. I had to get him off. The chairs were burning. But he's all right?"

"He's fine," said Dixon gently.

Addams lay back on the sand and closed his eyes. "Everything was burning," he mumbled. "I had to get him off …" He was saying more, but his voice was an unintelligible drone.

Dixon crawled beyond him and stretched out on the soft sand. He'd never have thought it of Addams. The man had deliberately gone into the fire to get Allard out. That was guts, and not just the guts as when you were fighting for your own life. Nobody made him go after Allard. He would never have believed it before, and it showed you could never figure those things …

He turned on his side, rested his head in the bend of his arm and was asleep.

Chapter Ten

About twenty inches above his face, the broad sea grape leaves made saucer-shaped patterns against the blue sky, and the blue of the sky was very restful but very far away. The leaves were much closer and restful too. They were dark green and they made you think of sleep and peace and invulnerable places. He was vaguely pleased to have awakened here in the shade under the sea grape, and then he remembered last night.

"Just wake up, compadre?" said Wirt.

Dixon moved and grimaced. His muscles felt wired to his bones. "What time is it?" he asked.

Wirt crawled under the overhanging branches and squatted at Dixon's feet. He had an orange in his hand and he sucked at it.

"It's afternoon," he said. "It makes a difference?"

"Anybody else get ashore?"

"Addams and Fatguts."

"I know. Anybody else?"

Wirt shook his head.

"What happened out there last night?" Dixon asked. "What set it off?"

Wirt said, "God!" and looked away, out through the leaves toward the water. He shivered.

"Do you *know* what happened?"

"It's … well …" Wirt's hands moved unhappily.

"Was it very bad?"

"No. It's just what you think afterward. I mean, you picture all kinds of things. Maybe none of them actually happened, but you can't help thinking."

"Talk about it and get it straight and it won't be so bad. How'd it start?"

"Well, they were up on the sundeck. They had a phonograph and records and they kept making Addams bring all different kinds of drinks, stingers, sidecars, manhattans, martinis, and a lot of crazy ones too. They were trying to have a hell of a time, but you could tell it wasn't working. I guess they'd had a hell of a time too many times, maybe, and they couldn't think of anything new. Know what I mean?"

Dixon said, "Yes."

"Once one of the girls yelled, 'You cut that out!' She sounded sore. And Fatguts said. 'What's the matter with you all of a sudden?' He was sore too, drunk-sore. The other guy cut in fast and sang out like a master of ceremonies, 'Hey, sweetheart, do like they do in burlesque for us. Come on, everybody, give this little girl a big hand.' I guess he wanted her to do a strip tease, because she said, 'It's too damn cold.' And then this other guy said, 'Say there's an idea, let's have some hot buttered rum.' That was about the only drink they hadn't had, so he went down to the galley to make it. Fatguts and his girl friend had another scrap and she said she was getting off this damn boat the first chance she got and she'd let everybody know what kind of a son of a bitch he was, but the other girl finally patched it up, and they started smooching. I mean, that's what it sounded like and the second girl said, 'It looks like three's company,' and I heard her go away, calling to the other guy. I wasn't trying to listen to all this. I didn't even want to, but I was right there in the fantail."

Dixon didn't say anything when Wirt paused and glanced at him. He nodded and Wirt went on.

"Anyway, they were quiet for about fifteen minutes, and then this other guy came back from the galley with a pitcher of hot buttered rum. 'Just a wee drap and dorris,' he said, and then they all started talking in a Scotch accent. This went on until it kind of died away. And then the first girl said, 'Oh God, he's passed out.' And then they tried a lot of stuff to bring him around, slapped him and pulled his ears and things like that. I got the idea they were getting back at him, because the other guy said, 'You don't have to pull so hard,' and the girl gave a funny laugh and said, 'That ear won't come off, lover-boy, see?' The other girl said, 'Oh stop it, now you got his nose bleeding, let him alone. Anyway, he can't be a pain in the ass when he's sleeping. Don't you know when you're well off? Let's make another pitcher of this stuff. It warms you up. Who said it was hot in the tropics?' The first girl said, 'Hey, I'm coming with you. You don't think I'm going to sit here with the body, do you?' And the three of them went. The next thing I knew was the explosion. The boat shook. I jumped out of bed. Something pushed me hard and I couldn't breathe. That's the last I remember."

"You said you had it figured out," Dixon said.

"Oh. Yes. They didn't turn the gas range all the way off in the galley when they made the first batch of hot rum and the galley was full of gas when they walked in. You can't smell that bottle gas very much. Not like natural gas. They lit a match. They might have smelled something if they'd been sober, but they were all pretty high. The second explosion, the one that knocked me, was the emergency gas tanks in the fantail. They were connected by copper tubing so when the ones in the galley were empty all they had to do was turn on the ones in the fantail. That's the only way I can figure it."

Dixon looked up at the sky through the sea grape leaves. It was a light and very impersonal blue and it was very far away. It always looked farther away when you were lying on your back. He knew what was bothering Wirt. Those three who had been in the galley when the gas exploded.

"Where was Addams all this time?" Dixon asked.

"He was in one of the guest cabins. He moved all his stuff there yesterday afternoon. It was pretty crowded in the fan-tail with all those cases of liquor."

Dixon pulled in his legs and sat up. "Let's take a look around," he said.

Wirt said, "Wait a minute. You ought to know what you're going to run into out there first."

"What do you mean?"

"Fatguts. It's all your fault. It would never have happened if you hadn't brought them here in the first place, and you should have been aboard, and he's going to see that you get what's coming to you when we get back to the States."

Dixon shrugged. "Let him try."

"Both of them," said Wirt. "Him and Addams. Addams eggs him on. Addams keeps saying, 'I can't understand Dixon at all. He used to be a good man.' He's got Fatguts thinking you were drunk and came ashore to sleep it off where nobody'd notice. He believes everything

Addams says. He thinks Addams is the only friend he's got in the world."

"Maybe he is. Addams pulled him out of the fire."

"I know, and so does Allard. Addams told him often enough, told him how he had to crawl through the flames up to the sun deck and how he kept him from drowning and all that. And Fatguts keeps patting him on the knee and telling him he'll never forget. He slobbers."

Dixon felt something like a laugh in his throat but not really because the joke was on him. He had fallen asleep last night thinking that Addams had done a brave thing, and Addams had done a brave thing if you considered it all by itself. Only it wasn't heroism or bravery or anything like that. Dixon understood it very clearly. He should have understood it before, but it needed Wirt telling him how Addams kept reminding Allard that he had been the rescuer.

Addams had never been out of character for a minute. Allard was money in the bank, alive. Dead, he wasn't worth a nickel. Addams would risk a burn or two if there was something in it for him. Burns heal, but it isn't everyday you get a chance to cash in on them. Yet, Dixon didn't feel very good, thinking like that, because there was always the chance that it had been a spontaneous and selfless act. He made up his mind to find out if Addams had made any attempt to get to the three who had been trapped in the galley. That would be the answer.

Wirt said, "I'll go to bat for you when the time comes."

"Thanks, kid. How's the head?"

Wirt rolled his eyes to show the extent of his headache. "You're going to have a scar," said Dixon. "It should have been stitched."

Wirt grinned. "You gave me the shirt off your back. What more could I want? Is it your fault I forgot to bring my knitting needles? Anyway, when I get back I'll tell everybody I got it fighting head hunters. That scar's going to make me a celebrity."

"Don't count on it," said Dixon. "If it's worth money, Addams'll lift it some night while you're sleeping."

"Tell him to get his own scar. Tell him I'll be glad to do everything I can to help."

The boy was all right. He had the right kind of reactions. It had been bad for a while, but he was all right now. He was really a very healthy kid. He had good recovery.

"Let's take a walk in the sun," Dixon said.

He had to squint his eyes against the piercing white glare of the beach. The sand was like snow and in the moonlight it would look as cold as an Alpine Christmas card. There was a slight haze and the horizons were very pale, almost white. And there was wind, of course. There was always wind from the northeast. It sounded like a wide, running brook in the trees. The tide was quite high and there was no sign of the bar at the mouth of the cove. The dinghy tugged restlessly at its line.

As they passed the little boat, Wirt looked at it and said significantly, "You were the one who brought us all in, weren't you?"

"I thought I might need company."

"Addams and Allard didn't get in by themselves."

"When we found them, they were trying to make Cuba. They won't thank us for picking them up. There isn't a bottle of liquor on the cay. In Cuba they could have had all the rum they wanted."

Wirt said, "We?'"

"You were with me every minute," Dixon lied easily. "I couldn't have made it alone. We were out there six hours."

Wirt touched the bandage on his forehead. "That must have been some wallop," he said. "I don't remember any of that." He sounded a little awed.

"You were there all right."

"Isn't that something? I just can't remember it. That's the first time I ever blacked out. I'm glad I wasn't dead freight, anyway. I suppose it'll come back to me someday." He was happier, now that he thought he hadn't been dead freight.

Allard and Addams were in the shade of a cluster of young cocoanut palms high on the beach at the other side of the path to the top of the Cay. Allard was sitting on the ground, his sweaty torso very white. He was eating a banana. His legs were sprawled out ahead of him, thick and soft and without grace, like two stuffed flour sacks. With all that heavy fat on him, there was the curious impression that he was melting into the ground. Addams was standing. Allard's shirt was still wound around his head. There were burns on his face and he had no eyelashes or eyebrows. From the way he stood there, legs apart, hands behind him, he had the appearance of standing guard. Allard pulled another banana from the stem and ate it in two bites.

"Why did it have to be him," said Wirt bitterly. "There were four of them, and it had to be him."

"I would have preferred the blonde myself," Dixon said.

"I don't mean that."

Dixon said, "Relax, kid. It's a small island."

"Any island would be too small, even for ten minutes. Just look at the fat hanging all over him. Doesn't he make you want to puke?"

"Not especially, kid. I wasn't thinking of eating him."

"Eat him! I couldn't get that hungry. Jesus!"

Allard paid no attention to them until they were right there, and then he looked up at Dixon, his lips bunched.

"Well, here we are, Captain," he said coldly, "thanks to you."

Dixon lifted his eyebrows. "How do you figure that?" he asked.

"Nobody but an imbecile would have brought us here. Don't you have any brains, or don't you know how to use them? Why didn't you take us to a safe port instead of anchoring us a half mile out in the ocean here? There is a safe port at Exuma. You admitted it yourself yesterday. Why didn't you go there?"

"This is the straightest route to Haiti, and you wanted to go straight to Haiti."

"Straight to Hades, you mean!" He was shouting. "You're a moron! You're a halfwit! Even I'd know enough not to anchor a boat a half mile out in the ocean. You were drunk. You were drunk all the way down, and you were drunk in Miami before that. Deny it, go ahead, deny it!"

Dixon glanced at Addams. Addams' face was impassive. Dixon looked down at Allard.

"Consider it denied," he said.

"He wasn't drunk," said Wirt heavily.

Allard ignored him, but you could see he was conscious of Wirt, and wary. He kept his eyes on Dixon.

A moment ago he had been working himself up. That was over. Wirt had made the difference. Dixon was startled to see that Wirt made that much difference. Allard was afraid of Wirt, or more truly, afraid of the hatred in Wirt's eyes. It was the bigness of it that frightened him.

"You were incompetent, Captain," now Allard was being very severe and very judicial, almost impersonal. "You were negligent and stupid. Criminally negligent. The boat was in your care, and you went off on a pleasure jaunt without a word. Three people are dead, Captain, and when I get back to Miami, I'm going to see if something can be done about *that*."

Dixon's face went white. He was suddenly very angry. Allard had gone too far. He took a step toward Allard and said harshly. "Now you're going to listen to me ..."

Addams said sharply, "Get back!"

Wirt yelled, "Watch him, Captain!"

Dixon turned. Addams had a gun half way out of the waterproof bag at his waist. He did not bring it all the way out. For the space of several breaths, no one made a sound or moved. The gun seemed to fill the whole beach where they stood. Addams' mouth looked pinched. Dixon thought, he'll shoot, he's just waiting for me to give him the excuse. Wirt made a noise in his throat. Dixon put out his arm and closed his hand around the boy's waist.

"Relax, kid," he said.

Allard slumped a little against the tree and let out the breath that had caught in his chest.

Addams said, "All right, Mr. Allard."

Allard sat up straighter. He lifted his jaw. "I think I'd better take charge of the gun, steward," he said curtly. He held out his hand.

Dixon looked quickly at Addams. Oh God, he thought, he's going to do it!

Addams hesitated for only an instant. "Of course, sir," he said and gave Allard the gun, but he didn't like it very much.

Allard held the gun with his finger on the trigger, but he did not point it at anybody. He rested his hand on his thigh. Now he was a man with a gun. It was a responsibility. He looked stern.

"I'm taking over, Captain," he said in a clipped voice. "You should be the one, but I'm afraid that is out of the question. In view of past performances."

"Good. Now I won't have to worry about getting us off here."

"We'll be picked up by the next ship that passes."

"Yes. When it passes."

"What do you mean by that?"

"They don't pass here."

"Of course they pass here. This is the route to Haiti, isn't it?"

"The shipping lane is about a hundred miles south. We had to anchor here for the night. The big ships go right through."

"If we stopped, somebody else will stop."

"It's possible, but I wouldn't want to wait that long. It might be next year. Nobody cruising through the Bahamas would come near here, and not many yachts make the jump from Nassau to Haiti."

Allard said angrily, "I don't bluff easy, Dixon."

"That's fine. As long as you're in charge, there are a few other things you ought to know," Dixon's teeth gleamed. This is childish, he thought, really childish. He squatted down on his heels and made a dot in the sand with his finger. "Here we are," he said, "Crab Cay. Here are the Exumas," he made a diagonal line, "seventy-five miles. Here are the Jumentos," a curved line, "seventy-five miles. Cuba's way down here, and up here is Andros, a good hundred miles. See all that space around us? Water, empty, nothing. Trading steamers stay close to the Cays. There's nothing for them out here. You'll never see one. Most freighters and passenger liners go from the States to Havana and then along the southern coast of Cuba. There's not much shipping along the north coast, and what little there is doesn't come within a hundred miles of us. So much for the big boats. Not much hope there." He could hear Allard breathing shallowly. Addams was very intent, and Wirt was hunkered down with a funny little smile tucked in the corner of his mouth.

Dixon went on, deliberately drawing it out. "Now, about the small boats. The natives go all over the banks in them. Sometimes they go out and don't come back, so you can see they're not out picnicking. They're businessmen," he said for Allard's benefit. "They're in the fishing business, and they don't take chances with their boats. Anyway, the fish feed among the reefs closer inshore, and they go where the fish are. Is that clear so far?"

He looked blandly at Allard. Allard was staring at the crude map in the sand. Addams' lips were compressed and he, too, was staring at the map. Wirt was rocking back and forth on his buttocks, his arms clasped around his knees, looking up at the trees and whistling gravely. Dixon smothered a grin. Wirt knew what he was doing and was very happy about it. It was all true, nonetheless.

"These fishing boats," Dixon continued, "do run into storms, and our chance is that one of them might be blown in here. They'll never come here on purpose. So let's not count on somebody picking us up by accident. We can light a signal fire if it'll make you feel better, but it won't mean much. The natives won't investigate, and other boats will think it's some fisherman camping out for the night. When do your friends expect you down in the Virgins, Mr. Allard?"

Allard ran his tongue over his lips. He opened his mouth and had to swallow before he spoke. "They don't. I mean, I don't know anybody down there."

Addams sucked in his breath. Dixon whistled. The *Almacor* was not expected. There would be no search when she did not arrive. That was a chilly thought. It was a very sobering thought. Dixon tilted his head and regarded the map he had drawn. He reached out and carefully drew a circle around the dot he had made for Crab Cay.

"What about the dinghy?" Addams demanded abruptly.

Dixon nodded. "There's the dinghy," he agreed. He turned and looked over his shoulder at it sitting dumpily on the ruffled water.

Compared to the outside, the cove was calm, yet the dinghy was rocking and bobbing as skittishly as a fat and frightened old cow. You could never take it against the wind to the Exumas. You'd have to go east-south-east to the Jumentos and it would be a miracle if you ever reached them. The wind would be at you every minute, turning you toward Cuba, and in any kind of blow at all, you'd be safer with waterwings.

"It'd be a long row," he said to Addams, "especially without oars. Would you like to try it?"

"There's a motor in it."

"No gas."

Allard clenched his hands. "He's lying!" he shouted at Addams. "It's a bluff. He's been bluffing all along."

"Tell him," said Dixon. "You saw the chart. You know where we are. Tell him."

Addams hated him then, completely. He would never tell Allard an unpalatable truth while Allard wanted to hear a comfortable lie, and Dixon was forcing.

"It's not as bad as he says," he said flatly.

Allard said triumphantly, "I thought so."

Dixon said, "Oh hell." He was tired of it, disgusted with Allard, disgusted with Addams' eternal buttering-up. He stood and slapped the sand from his hands.

"There's only one thing we can do with the dinghy," he said. "We have to take the motor out and put in a centerboard, otherwise you won't be able to control it. Then we have to step a mast and see if we can find something for a sail. After we do that, it's barely possible that one of us might be able to reach the Jumentos in it."

"Not you!" Allard said nastily. "You'd let us rot here. Can you handle it, Mr. Addams?"

Addams pointed his chin at Wirt. "He can," he said.

Wirt said violently, "You can both go ..."

Dixon said, "Hold it, kid. Let's be sensible. Can you sail?"

Wirt's face looked swollen as he glared at Addams and Allard, and then he said reluctantly, "Yes."

"It won't be like sailing on a lake. It can get rough out there. You'll have to know what you're doing. I'll take it myself if you have any doubts."

"You will like hell," said Allard loudly. He lifted the gun. "The hell you will."

"I can handle it," said Wirt. "But if you'd rather do it yourself, I'll take that gun away from him. Just say the word."

"No. Let's see if we can do this without anybody getting hurt."

"The two of us could go in the dinghy. The hell with them."

"One."

"It's big enough."

"I know, but it'd be safer with one."

"We'll see."

"You'll see nothing," said Allard in an ugly voice. "You'll do as you're told."

"He's the boss," said Dixon ironically.

"You're damn right I'm the boss. And we're getting things organized around here too. Do as you're told, and there won't be any trouble. You two get to work on the boat. That's your job. Addams, you take care of the food end of it."

"And what are you going to do?" Wirt snapped. "Just sit on your fat ass?"

Dixon took his arm and turned him. "Let's go, kid," he said. He did not relax his grasp until they were down the beach. Allard might have popped off with that gun out of sheer fright.

"Boss, for God's sake!" Wirt muttered.

"Don't let him bother you, kid. We're the ones who are going to have to figure this out."

"All right, but if he starts on me again, I'm going to let him have it right in the teeth."

"Fine. I'll help you when the time comes, but let's get the job done first."

The dinghy was bobbing about six feet out. Dixon pulled it ashore. He laughed softly and tapped it with the side of his foot. "No tools, no mast, no sail," he said. "And we're fighting about who's going to sail it. How ridiculous can you get, eh, kid?"

Wirt was open-mouthed for a moment and then he began to laugh.

"Let's see what we've got here," Dixon said.

They bent over the dinghy. The motor was fastened to the mount by four heavy bolts, and then there was the stuffing box through which the propeller shaft ran. The big question was, would she sail.

"She'll be clumsy as hell," Wirt said.

"If it's too bad, we won't take it out."

"Are we in as much of a mess as you told them?"

"Just about. Sooner or later, I suppose, somebody'll start wondering what happened to the *Almacor*, and they'll come looking for us, but things could get pretty bad in the meantime. And I mean that, kid."

"You mean Allard," said Wirt.

"I mean all of us. If things keep going the way they were back there, it *will* be bad. If you start on Allard, you won't stop with just a punch on the jaw."

"No. I guess not. I'd kill the son of a bitch."

"All right. But if you knock him off, you're going to have to knock Addams off too, or you'll be up for murder. Not in the States. Here in the Bahamas, and the English are very tough. So you'd have to take care of Addams."

Wirt did not answer. He was thinking about it, turning it over in his mind.

"Maybe," he said in a low voice.

"No. You'd have to. Or hang. That would leave you and me, and after awhile …"

Wirt blurted, "No!" shocked.

"Yes. If we're stuck here for awhile, I'd start getting on your nerves, or you'd start getting on mine. You might not think so now, but you can take my word for it. It's happened. Maybe I'd be the one who'd start wondering if I'd be next, and I'd catch you looking at me in a certain way, and in the end I'd let you have it before you got me."

"I don't believe it."

"What I'm driving at is, let's not try to find out. It's up to you and me. Leave Allard alone. It won't stop at one killing. There'd have to be at least two. If we keep calm, there won't have to be any. There won't have to be anything."

"All right."

"Maybe you think I'm talking through my hat with all this killing. Maybe you think it's far-fetched."

"No. I'd have killed him that night on the boat if I'd got my hands on him."

"Then let's watch ourselves, kid."

Wirt nodded. He was feeling very bad.

Dixon said, "There used to be a house on top of the island. Let's take a look around up there. I'd like to get off this place if we can manage it."

He turned and strode across the beach toward the path that wound up the rocky hill to the summit of the Cay. Wirt followed, keeping pace. Addams and Allard were talking earnestly under the palm trees. They did not look up when Dixon and Wirt passed within twenty feet of them. Addams was making marks in the sand with a slender twig of mangrove. Dixon glanced back at Wirt. The boy was walking with his head bent; he had not even noticed the other two.

The wind was stronger on the summit and the tall palms, tossing their fronds, looked anguished and made a dry withered sound. The water, now visible on all sides, looked emptier.

Wirt and Dixon went silently to work, picking through the ruins of the house. It was Wirt who found the remains of the tool shed behind the house. He picked up a long-handled spade, crusty with rust, and when he tapped the blade against a tree, it crumbled like dried mud.

"We're about five years too late," he said. "Look at this." He kicked at a hoe lying on the ground and it disintegrated. "We can't work with any of this stuff."

They found many other gardening implements in the weeds among the trees, pruning shears, trowels, rakes, snips, an ax, all corroded and useless. The ax head, when cleaned of rust, became a blunt stub the size of a child's hand, and the handle broke suddenly, rotted through. Wirt dropped it and wiped his hands down the sides of his thighs.

"Let's keep looking," Dixon said. "We might turn up something."

Wirt muttered, "Yeah, *might*," and turned back to the weeds, flattening and probing them with a dead citrus branch. He was depressed and Dixon thought, *I was too rough on him down there*. He had been rough, but it was the only way. He himself did not believe much of what he had said I about the killing, but he'd had to make Wirt listen. Wirt hadn't yet grown out of that black-and-white kind of thinking you do when you're very young, and you had to give him a black-and-white picture or he wouldn't be able to see it. *I was right about the trouble though*, Dixon thought defensively. He didn't want trouble, or even bickering. It could be avoided. You could walk away from it.

He found a garden fork hanging in a lime tree. It had a springy ring when he flicked it with his finger. He showed it to Wirt.

"See, everything isn't rusted out," he said.

"But what good is it? You can't fix the dinghy with a pitchfork."

"I can make a gig out of it. We can spear fish off the rocks."

Wirt was not interested. They had enough food. The dinghy was the only important thing.

Later they found two pots and a frying pan, all aluminum, and Dixon put them at the head of the path with the fork. Wirt found a large tarpaulin that could have been made into a sail, but it came apart in his hands when he picked it up.

Dixon said, "Keep looking, kid."

Gradually they separated again. Dixon found a tree of ripe guavas.

He plucked one. It was coarse and had a strong odor, and he remembered what everybody said about guava that if you let a cat smell a guava, the cat would immediately bury it, the cat being a very clean and sanitary animal. Dixon ate five while he stood looking down at the crumbling aluminum roof of the ruined house, wondering if they could use it for something. There was a lot of it. An idea was forming in his mind when Wirt yelled to him from the cocoanut palms. Dixon bounded through the weeds. Wirt was standing beside a wooden chest. The clotting depression had gone out of his face and his hands were shaking with excitement.

"A tool chest," he cried. "It's a tool chest."

The chest was about three feet long and twenty inches wide and deep. It was made of Cypress. Cypress did not rot. The cover was held down by a hasp fastened with a peg of wood.

"I didn't want to open it till you got here." Wirt was literally dancing, and Dixon grinned.

"Open it up," he said.

Wirt dropped to both knees and jerked at the peg that held the hasp. It was swollen tight and he could not move it. His eyes darted over the ground and he snatched up a rock and pounded at the peg. He kept missing and gouged splinters from the side of the chest. His blows became furious and he began to swear and blood dripped from skinned knuckles. He attacked the hasp, but it was made of heavy brass and all he did was wedge the peg more tightly. He threw the rock into the trees and searched the ground for a heavier one. He was panting and his hands were trembling badly. He found a rock the size of a watermelon, stood and raised it over his head to smash the chest. Dixon stopped him.

"Hold it, kid," he said. "We might need that chest, let me take a shot at it."

He straightened the hasp with a smaller rock and gently tapped the peg loose. Wirt grinned sheepishly.

"Oh, go to hell," he said. "Open it. What're you waiting for?"

The hinges squealed as Dixon lifted back the heavy lid. Wirt bent over his shoulder, breathing heavily. It was a tool chest, all right, and it was full.

Wirt whispered, "Babybabybabybaby …" and Dixon suddenly knew why Wirt had not opened the chest when he first found it. He had been afraid it wasn't really a tool chest.

The tools were in very bad shape. The chest was not watertight or moisture proof, and it had been here a long time. They were in better condition, however, than the garden implements. It was a full set of carpentering tools. There were saws—rip, crosscut and a backsaw—squares, three hammers, two planes, adjustable open-end wrenches, a monkey wrench and a Stillson wrench, clamps, a set of twelve bits in a mahogany case in graduating sizes, a brace, screwdrivers, several punches and nailsets, a spirit level, a wood rasp, a hacksaw, tin snips, and a variety of copper nails and brass screws.

Wirt whooped. "We could *build* a boat!" he crowed.

Dixon took out the crosscut saw and felt the teeth. It left an orange rust mark across his finger. The teeth were rounded and blunt. He looked into the chest. There were no files. Wirt reached for the backsaw. The tiny teeth were entirely useless. The rip saw was a little better, but, not much.

"I'll sharpen them with something," he said confidently. "I've always been able to do anything with tools. Hell, I cut my first tooth with a chisel. Hey!" He bent over the chest. "No chisels. And he called himself a carpenter. Shame on him."

He was in a high state of elation and undismayed by the condition of the tools. He whipped the saw and the steel made a singing sound. He laughed happily.

"The hell with the dinghy." He slapped Dixon on the shoulder. "We'll build a schooner and sail around the world, just you and me and the hell with the Gold Dust Twins down there."

"Let's build a bar," said Dixon, "and have a drink." He wanted a drink and wanted it badly. Now he was beginning to feel depressed. Maybe it was the reaction. He looked away from Wirt's jubilant face.

The sun was setting, flat and orange in the cloudless sky. Sunsets were usually not very spectacular in the tropics: you had to have clouds.

"We'd better be getting downstairs, kid," he said. "It'll be dark in about fifteen minutes."

They put the saws back into the chest. There was a brass handle on either end, which made it easy to carry. They went slowly down the path, taking the pots, frying pan and garden fork with them. A flock of ducks whirred over the eastern side of the Cay, circled and settled slowly behind the citrus trees.

"Duck dinner for Sunday," grinned Wirt. He was interested in food again. He paused. "Say …"

"What?"

"You and Fatguts. Do you think he's really going to make trouble for you when we get back to the States?"

"I can only think of one thing at a time," said Dixon stolidly, "and right now I'm thinking about the dinghy."

Chapter Eleven

The camp had changed. Allard was sitting under a frame of bamboo roofed with broad banana leaves. He was wearing a shirt again, and Addams had covered his burned head with his own shirt. There was a heap of pink and white conch shells and a pile of the white, rubbery meat on a flat stone. Some of it had already been pounded flat to tenderize it. Addams was squatting by a fire, roasting pieces of the meat on a long sliver of bamboo. There were piles of bananas, cocoanuts, oranges, grapefruit and papaya neatly arranged at the back of the new lean-to.

Addams handed the roasted piece of conch to Allard on a clam shell. Allard sniffed at it with an expression of petulant dislike. He glowered at Wirt and Dixon.

"I thought you were supposed to work on the boat," he barked.

"Go to hell," said Wirt casually. They had left the tool chest at the foot of the path, closer to the dinghy.

Allard said nastily, "Off on another one of your little jaunts, Captain?"

"We couldn't work on the boat without tools," Dixon said.

"So we went and got our teeth sharpened," said Wirt. Allard did not bother him tonight.

Addams was cutting up another piece of conch with a clasp knife. He did not look up as he skewered the meat on a sliver of bamboo and held it over the fire.

"We found tools," Dixon told Allard, keeping his voice mild. "We can start on the dinghy tomorrow morning."

"Tomorrow morning! What's the matter with tonight?"

"Nothing's the matter with tonight," said Wirt promptly. "It's a beautiful night. Don't go blaming it on the night. It's the union. The union won't let us work at night. And don't look at the Captain. He hasn't got a thing to say about it. And on top of that, stupid, we want to see what we're doing when we start cutting holes in the boat. I'll explain it to you after dinner."

Allard kept his head toward Dixon. Wirt had not spoken. Wirt had never spoken. Wirt was not there.

"How long are you going to take on this job, Captain?" Allard asked curtly. "Can you be ready to sail in three days?"

Wirt hooted with laughter. He flung himself on the sand, kicking his legs, slapping his hands together like seal flippers, guffawing every time he looked at Allard. His merriment was so completely derisive that Allard furiously half rose and reached for a conch shell.

Addams said quickly, "There's quite a bit of work converting to a sailing dinghy, sir."

Allard sat back. His face was fiery. "How long?" he snapped at Dixon.

"I can tell you better tomorrow. After we get an idea what we're up against. I'm not going to rush the job. We've only got one dinghy."

Allard grunted and put the piece of conch into his mouth. He chewed for a few seconds and then turned his head and spat it out. He glared at Addams. Dixon ran his hand down the slender length of bamboo that held up the outer edge of the lean-to.

"Where'd you find this?" he asked.

Addams pointed toward the northeastern portion of the island. "The other side of the orange grove."

"Is there any thick enough for a mast?"

"Some."

"I'll take a look tomorrow." He sat down by the fire. He was tired. He'd been stiff when he'd got up and he'd been on his feet for hours. Addams silently handed him a clam shell on which was a curled and browned piece of the conch. It tasted a little like a very tough deep sea scallop but the flavor was mainly woodsmoke.

"We got two pots and a frying pan for you," Dixon told Addams. "Also, there are goats and pigs on the hill. You might try getting a shot at one tomorrow."

Addams nodded. He was cutting up a pair of papaya melons with the clasp knife. Dixon wondered what else Addams had brought in that little waterproof bag that hung at his belt. He had an idea that Addams had always kept that bag packed and ready for just such an emergency as this. Addams gave Allard the first piece of melon and a shell to use as a spoon.

"They call these the pepsin melons, sir," he said. "Excellent for the digestion. Would you care for a pig hunt in the morning, sir? It might be sport."

"They're wild?"

"Yes, but I don't imagine ..."

"You go."

"They're man-eaters," said Wirt. "They're as big as horses. They run in packs, like wolves. Very dangerous." He looked sidelong at Allard and laughed.

Addams snapped at Wirt, "I think we've had about enough of that now, haven't we?"

"Yes, sir. We certainly have, sir. I apologize, sir. I won't speak again unless spoken to. I'll be seen but not heard, like a good little stooge."

Addams carefully wiped his knife on a palm frond and dropped it back into his bag. His eyes were hard and speculative. Then he went over to the fire and roasted himself a piece of conch which he ate with small, neat bites, nibbling fastidiously with his front teeth. Dixon kept changing position as he ate his melon. His legs were sore and he could not get them comfortable. He wondered vaguely where he was going to sleep and decided that the spot under the sea grape was as good as any. He'd take Wirt with him. It would be better to separate the party. He finished his papaya and ate some bananas that Addams passed around on the stalk. Addams took one of the pots and walked down the south beach with it. When he came back, he had water. It trickled out of the rocks, he told Dixon. There was a small pool. There were gulls nesting in the rocks, too. Tomorrow he was going to climb up and see if there were any eggs. Dixon nodded drowsily.

"Want me to look at those burns on your head before I turn in?" he asked.

"I put vaseline on them," Addams said.

Dixon felt a surge of anger. "Why didn't you say you had medication?" he demanded. "We could have put something on the boy's cut forehead."

"I've got iodine."

"What were you saving it for? Let's take a look at your head, kid."

Wirt unwound his bandage. It stuck on the wound and he eased it off gingerly.

Dixon tilted Wirt's head toward the fire. The gash had a thick, healthy scab and there was no inflammation. "It's doing all right by itself. We'd better leave it alone." He threw the soiled bandage into the fire and held out his hand to Addams. "Give me some gauze and adhesive tape."

Addams took them from his bag and gave them to Dixon together with a pair of small scissors. Dixon said drily, "You really thought of everything—except that somebody needed it." He knew that Addams was saving it in case anything happened to Allard.

"Don't worry about me," said Wirt. "I could grow a new head if I had to."

Dixon said, "Sit still, dammit," and finished the dressing. He stood. "I'm turning in. See you in the morning. Let's go, kid."

Allard took a heavy breath. "Who's taking care of the signal fire?" he asked in an ugly voice.

"Not me," said Wirt. "I'm on the day shift."

Dixon said incredulously, "You mean, sit up with it all night?"

"I'll take care of the fire, sir," said Addams.

"No. You stay here. Let them do it." He did not want to be left alone.

"Okay," said Dixon. "We'll sit up with the fire, and you work on the boat tomorrow while we sleep."

"I can enlarge this fire, sir," Addams said.

"It's no good here."

Dixon turned and walked up the beach toward the cluster of sea grape. Let Addams figure it out. Addams always boasted he could handle Allard; now let him do it. Wirt trotted at Dixon's side.

"I just got an idea for the sail," he said loudly so that his voice would carry back to the fire. "Fat boy Allard's pants. We can get a mainsail and a jib out of them and have enough left for a half dozen napkins."

Dixon said savagely, "Now I'm getting sore at you myself. I told you to lay off Allard. You needled him all evening. Cut it out from here on in, you hear me?"

Wirt gasped, and Dixon strode away from him. He crawled under the sea grape, made a hollow in the sand for his hip, and lay down on his side. A few minutes later, he heard Wirt worm under the other side of the bush, dig out a bed for himself and settle into it.

"Say, compadre," Wirt whispered.

"What?"

"I'm sorry. I'll lay off him."

"Good."

"I don't want to mess things up for you. I was just horsing around. I'll cut it out."

My God, thought Dixon, does he think I'm sucking around Allard? He wasn't sucking around anybody. All he wanted was a little peace for a change.

Dixon did not reply and at length he heard Wirt let out a long easy breath as he turned over to go to sleep, but he himself did not close his eyes for a long time. The night was very dark without the moon and down the beach the fire was only a handful of yellow light. The dark had never made him uneasy, even in strange places, but tonight he wanted to reach out and push it away from him with his hands. He wanted a drink, a good stiff one in a water glass, a whole bottle so that he could lie there and drink it all night until the light came in the morning. He tried to think of Helen but he could not form her image in his mind. It blurred and dissolved and went away from him. Sleep came very slowly. When he awakened in the morning, Wirt had the dinghy out of water and was sitting cross-legged beside the open tool chest. Dixon walked down to him. He had a headache and felt drearily tired. Wirt had five wrenches spread out on a flat piece of driftwood and was methodically tapping the sixth with the hammer.

"Frozen tight?" said Dixon, squatting down on his heels. He picked up the Stillson.

"Every damn one of them," said Wirt in disgust. "And not a drop of oil to soak them in. I've been hammering on this bastard for an hour. No dice."

"There's oil in the motor."

"Too thick. It wouldn't touch this stuff. You need penetrating oil."

Dixon took one of the open-end wrenches and began rapping it with the Stillson. About an hour later, Addams came down the beach and told them breakfast was ready.

"Bring it down here," growled Wirt. "We're busy."

Addams walked away. Dixon thought he'd let them go hungry, but he was back in fifteen minutes with a pot and two huge clamshells, which he filled from the pot. It was crabmeat stewed in cocoanut milk and it was delicious and they ate a potful between them.

"Where'd you see those pigs?" Addams asked Dixon.

"Just walk up the hill. You'll hear them. They're pretty shy."

"How's the fat boy this morning?" asked Wirt, poking in the pot for the last piece of crabmeat. "Will he live?"

Addams looked contemptuously at him for a moment and turned to Dixon. "You can eat where you want," he said, "but he'll have to eat down here. Mr. Allard doesn't want him around."

"I'll eat with Wirt."

"At least I can eat," said Wirt, grinning. "I was afraid I'd be sent to bed without dinner."

Addams ignored him and said to Dixon, "You're making a mistake. Mr. Allard said you were welcome to eat with us."

"I'll eat down here."

Addams frowned. "Suit yourself," he said coldly. He picked up the empty pot and the two clamshells and went back down the beach. Allard was sitting under his canopy, hunched and heavy with fat. Even from that distance, he looked like a discontented eunuch.

Wirt said seriously, "I don't mind if you don't eat with me."

"You don't think I'd let you eat by yourself, do you?"

"No, but it's like the man said, you're making a mistake."

"Then I'll make it."

"Just listen to me for a minute. He can make it rough for you when he gets back to the States …"

"Dammit, I'm not going to suck around him, so let's forget it."

"That's not sucking around. Addams is sucking around. You don't have to kiss his foot the way Addams does, but you're not using your head when you as good as tell him to go to hell."

Dixon shook his head. He wanted to smile, but it wouldn't come. "It's all settled," he said. "Let's get back to work."

Wirt picked up his hammer and regarded it thoughtfully. "Well," he said finally, "I don't blame you for wanting to eat with me."

Dixon tried not to think about it, but it kept coming back to him all morning. Allard was vindictive, and Dixon for the first time squarely faced the fact that he was going to be in a mess when they got back to the States. Allard was going to make a royal stink; he had to have a goat. He was small-minded. That was the whole thing. When he had a goat to kick around, he felt big and he could justify himself and perhaps even get a lot of sympathy. The hell with him, Dixon thought stubbornly, I'm not going to suck around.

They worked on the wrenches until noon and suddenly Wirt swore and threw down his hammer. "Look at that!" he said. He shoved the wrench at Dixon and pointed out a hairline crack across the upper jaw. "Cast-iron crap." He jumped to his feet and hurled the wrench into the cove. "Yours loosening up any?"

Dixon tried it. "No."

"The hell with it. We'll try something else."

He rummaged in the tool chest and found three punches.

He climbed into the dinghy and crouched over the motor. He held the punch on the flat of the nut that held the propeller shaft and hit it smartly with the hammer. Within an hour he had the shaft disconnected and out of the boat. He looked at the heavy bolts that held the motor, muttered, "Brother!" and went to work.

Addams brought them some hard-boiled gulls' eggs, four avocados and clam broth for lunch and went away without saying anything to either of them. Wirt ate very rapidly and jumped back into the dinghy.

They changed about every half hour, which was long enough to work in that crouched position, and while one squatted in the boat, the other walked up and down the beach, easing his cramped muscles. The bolt turned reluctantly, but it turned.

They heard a shot in the middle of the afternoon, and later Addams came down the hill path, dragging a pig. It was quite a large pig, but it was skinny and long-legged. They watched him display it to Allard and saw Allard wave him away with repugnance. Wirt grinned and leaned on his hammer.

"Fat boy don't like blood," he said. "Fat boy throw up."

Allard pointed peremptorily and Addams dragged the pig among the trees to butcher it out of sight. The next time Dixon looked up, Addams was running across the beach with something in his hands that gleamed redly when he heaved it into the water. Almost instantly the water was lashed to a boiling froth and it continued for several minutes. Wirt stared.

"What the hell was that?" he said.

"Barracuda," said Dixon. "Big ones."

"Barracuda hell. That was shark."

"Barracuda will run to a hundred pounds down here."

"And I was going to take a swim!"

"They won't bother you. All you have to do is tickle their bellies and they go to sleep."

"Not me. I'm not fooling around with a fish that's got a mouth like a keg of nails."

He crouched and pounded at the bolt, swearing at it. They did not get it loose until sundown. Wirt pulled it out, screwed the nut back on and threw it into the tool chest. He stood and stretched.

Dixon glanced down the beach. Addams had the cook fire going and Allard was still sitting grumpily under his canopy. He had not moved all day.

"Man," said Wirt, "I'm tired. And all we got out was one lousy bolt. Think we'll get home for New Year's?"

"Personally," Dixon said, "I'm taking a swim."

He stripped and ran down the beach and hit the water in a fast shallow dive. He swam up and down while Wirt stood on the shore and told him that barracuda ran to a thousand pounds down here. He tried to get Wirt to come in, but the boy said, "No, sir. When I give up a leg, I want a Purple Heart in exchange." And when Dixon came out, Wirt said, "No wonder they didn't bite you. You're so goddamn hairy, you'd get in their teeth." Dixon ran to the mangrove and back several times to dry himself and Wirt said, "You looked pretty good on the half-mile, but how are you on the running broad jump?" Somehow or other, it was a very happy moment, and Dixon was never to forget it.

The dinner was very good that night. It was pot-roasted pork, bananas stewed in gravy, heart of palm salad, orange juice, and papaya which Addams in one of his British moods called pawpaw. Dixon was feeling very good and he was not bothered when Addams told him severely that Mr. Allard was displeased, very displeased. They turned in early and Dixon slept very well, awakening refreshed in the morning.

He and Wirt walked down the beach to the dinghy, despite the monotonous drudgery ahead. With the meager means they had, it would take about two days to loosen the three remaining bolts. By late morning they had devised a faster method. Dixon, lying prone, tapped the nut at the bottom of the bolt while Wirt simultaneously tapped the head. At the end of the day, they had the motor out of the boat, and despite the fact that it would probably never be used again, Wirt nailed together a wooden box for it and put it aside for later.

When Addams brought the evening meal it was baked barracuda steaks moistened with fresh limes.

Wirt said incredulously, "Barracuda! My God. What did you do, shoot it?"

"Really," said Addams, "it's much simpler than that, you know. One uses one's head." He was very superior and British as he always was when he was at his snottiest.

He had taken thin sharp strips of bamboo, wound them tightly and put them into pockets he had made in chunks of raw pork. When the barracuda digested the pork, the bamboo sprang open and the sharp points literally stabbed the fish to death from the inside.

And then, still very superior, he washed his hands of Dixon. "You know," he said, "I've lost all regard for your intelligence. In the past two days you've managed very thoroughly to cut your own throat. Mr. Allard was quite willing to let bygones be bygones. He made a very friendly gesture, inviting you to eat with him, which you very stupidly ignored. Now he's quite certain that you're skulking down here from a sense of guilt and that you're ashamed to face him."

"You mean if I go up and eat with him he'll forget all that business about turning me in when we get back to Miami?"

"Aren't you over-simplifying just a bit, old boy?"

"Then there *is* more to it. I'll have to scratch his back and wipe his nose and things like that, too, is that the idea?"

"Nothing of the sort."

"Then I don't get it. Why is he so anxious all of a sudden to have me eat with him? What's he after?"

"A friendly understanding, a willingness to listen to your side of the story."

"Hell."

Addams drawled, "There really are expensive luxuries even here, aren't there?" He picked up the flat piece of driftwood he used as a tray and walked away humming the *Londonderry Air*.

Afterward, Wirt said, "I think the fat boy can't stand not being liked. I think he's beginning to get scared. What do you think?"

"I think you're right."

Wirt ate a piece of the barracuda. "Watch out for bamboo slivers," he said. He frowned and stopped chewing and looked up the beach to where Addams was bending over the fire. "You know," he said, "that guy gives me the creeps."

Dixon looked up in surprise. "Addams?"

"Yes. It came to me when he said how he caught the barracuda."

"Hell, that's an old trick. He didn't invent it. Natives have been using it for centuries."

"I know. I've read about it. I didn't mean just that. It's lots of things. He gives me a funny feeling," he was very serious. "He's got everything figured out, he's always way ahead, and you can't stop him. For instance, say God or somebody came up and said, 'Only one of you guys is going to get off this island alive.' You know who that guy'd be? Addams. One way or another, he'd be the guy. Maybe he'd feed all three of us bamboo splinters, or maybe we'd have accidents, like falling in the water when the barracuda are feeding, or maybe we'd just plain disappear like Houdini's rabbit. I don't know how he'd manage that, but he would. He'd *learn* how. But no matter what, one day he'd turn up in Miami with a pocketful of folding money, a hundred-dollar blonde and a Cadillac."

Dixon smiled. "He's not that good, kid. His survival drive is wound up a little tighter than most people's, that's all."

"Sure. It's wound up tighter and it's got points at both ends like those slivers of bamboo he feeds the barracuda."

"Well anyway, you don't have a thing to worry about, kid. You're not a barracuda."

"Oh, go to hell."

Later, as they were falling asleep, Wirt murmured drowsily, "You know, you're really a hard-boiled son of a bitch. Maybe you'll be the one to wind up in Miami with the hundred-dollar blonde."

"If it's anybody," said Dixon, "it'll be Allard. The guy with the most money always wins the crap game. Now go to sleep."

The next day before they could start work on the dinghy they had to find the wood for the centerboard and they went up to the summit of the hill. They didn't think of that ruined house as debris anymore; it was their stockpile. Even Addams used it and had found three aluminum cups, silver forks and spoons, a Mason jar of salt, a plastic comb, and a briar pipe. It was a treasure chest. Wirt called it Macy's.

All the wood they found, however, was unsuitable for the centerboard. Either it was too badly warped or cracked or it was rotted completely. This was serious. Without a centerboard, the dinghy would roll like a ball in the water. But Wirt solved it with the crumpled aluminum roof.

"We could make a wooden frame and nail an aluminum sheet to each side; then we could fill the bottom of it with all the old iron we can find and give it some weight like on a keel."

It took time. The tin snips were frozen, just as the wrenches were, and had to be loosened. This time the motor oil helped. It took about six hours to make the centerboard. Now a slot had to be cut through the bottom of the dinghy, and there were no tools. Rust and corrosion had eaten the sharp life from everything. The wood of the dinghy was very hard and tough, and there were three thicknesses of it, the batten board that ran down the center, the ribs, and the sheathing.

Wirt threw the case of useless bits back into the chest. "This damn job's been jinxed from the beginning," he said bitterly.

"I wouldn't call it jinxed," Dixon said. "We didn't have any tools."

"We got tools."

"Ha."

"And where the hell are the chisels? There should be chisels. If I had a chisel, I could sharpen it on a stone and we could cut the slot with that." This was the third day of nagging frustrations. "We'll never get this damn thing fixed," Wirt said.

He was very depressed and Dixon knew that the best thing would be to get him away from the dinghy for awhile. A drink would fix him up, Dixon thought automatically. Then he thought, sure it would, it would fix him up like it fixed me up.

Then he said aloud, "Should there really have been chisels, kid?"

"Everybody in the world who buys a set of tools buys chisels," Wirt waved a limp hand, "except this guy."

"Maybe he did have a set. Maybe he had them in the house when the hurricane hit. Why not go up and take a look around?"

"Now why the hell couldn't I have thought of that? I don't have brains. Where did I ever get the idea I had brains?"

"Oh hell. Get your tail out of here, will you? We've got work to do."

Wirt's chin jerked up angrily, and then he managed a sick grin. "My hard-boiled compadre," he said.

"Beat it."

Wirt short-cutted up the hill through the citrus grove. Dixon squatted in the dinghy and with the points of a copper nail marked out the cut they were going to have to make. The wood was very hard and the nail barely scratched the paint. You'd better find those chisels, kid, he thought.

A voice said, "The work seems to be going right along, Captain."

It was Allard's voice, but it couldn't be. Allard hadn't left his end of the island for three days. Dixon sat up incredulously. It was Allard, all right. He was standing about eight feet to the side of the boat. He looked pretty awful. He was wearing a kind of conical hat made from broad banana leaves, and under it his pendulous face was covered with white stubble. His shirt and pants, once white, were dirty, greasy down the front and thighs, torn and wrinkled.

Dixon said expressionlessly, "The work's coming along all right."

Allard tried to look into the dinghy but he did not come any closer. "If there's anything you want Addams to do," he said, "just let me know."

"Sure."

"Do you … have everything you need?"

"We'll manage."

"Oh, I'm sure you will, I'm sure you will."

Dixon watched him. Now what the hell are you up to this time, he wondered. He hadn't come down to ask about the boat. Dixon was sure that Addams gave him a full report three times a day.

At length Allard mumbled, "I've been wanting to talk to you, Captain. I may have misjudged you. I … didn't know all the facts."

Here comes the pitch, Dixon thought. "Which facts do you have in mind?" he asked.

"Your, well, your boat, your losing it. I mean your own boat, your charter boat. A thing like that, anybody would take it hard."

"I lost it in a crap game," said Dixon without compromise. "Or didn't Addams tell you?"

"He did, he did. Very understandable. A man can lose his head. I play poker myself."

"All right."

"And the drinking part of it. Very natural, under the circumstances. I'm quite convinced that it's over and done with. I spoke hastily the other day, and I regret it. Deeply." He looked up at Dixon, looked quickly away. "Deeply," he repeated.

"All right," Dixon said again.

"I think these things should be brought out into the open and aired. I'm a great believer in frankness."

"Me too."

"It gets things settled. It gets them back on an even keel again."

"Sometimes."

"You're still sore?"

Oh Lord, thought Dixon, am I still sore! You come around with a mouth full of mush, and I'm supposed to jump with joy? Forget all about everything, particularly the criminal negligence part of it? Sure, sure. I don't mind being kicked in the ass as long as you apologize later. That's what apologies are for, so you can get that big feeling both ways. But the hell with it. "No," he said, "I'm not sore."

"I wouldn't blame you a bit. You had every reason. Of course, I was upset. It was a very shocking thing. Losing three friends. You can understand."

"Sure."

"Then everything's all right again?"

"Everything's fine."

"I'm very glad." A patently insincere smile swam to the surface of Allard's thick, moist lips. "I have every confidence in you, Captain."

"That's good."

"But ..." Allard glanced quickly over his shoulder, "I can't say as much for that boy, what's his name, Wirt."

"He's a damn good kid," said Dixon flatly.

"But irresponsible, Captain, irresponsible. I've been thinking and I've come to the conclusion that it would be a mistake to trust him with the boat."

"No. He'll be very good with the boat. He'll get it through."

Allard's face shifted, revealing the terror and trembling venom behind it. "Captain," he cried, "that boy hates me. He'll never send anybody back to pick us up if we let him take out the boat. He'll let us all rot here, just to get back at me!" His voice fell away into a whine, "I played a very harmless joke on him one night. Anybody else would have laughed, but he's got a bad streak in him. He's vindictive. You've noticed, too. I know you did. And I know you're the only one who's holding him back. If we let him take the boat, we'll never hear from him again."

Dixon said, "Oh, Lord." He was disgusted. He stepped out of the dinghy. He turned his back on Allard and went over to the tool chest.

Allard followed him, trying to grasp his arm.

"You don't know," he babbled. "He doesn't look at you the way he looks at me …"

Dixon pulled his arm free and knelt down beside the chest. "For God's sake stop blubbering," he said. "He won't touch you."

"You don't think so? I *know*. He's just waiting his chance. Listen," he pawed Dixon's shoulder. "I'm going to make you a proposition. A business proposition. You're interested in a business proposition. You take the boat when it's ready and take me along. You can't leave me alone on the island with that young cut-throat. I won't stay here. I want to live. I'm going in the boat. I'll make it worth your while. I'll pay you. I don't expect you to do this for nothing. It'll be a business proposition. A thousand dollars. I'll give you more. I'll give you two thousand."

"You won't give me anything. Now beat it before I get sore."

"Five. I'll pay you five," he bent over and tried to look into Dixon's face. "Five thousand dollars. That's a lot of money. You can use five thousand dollars. You don't have to do anything, just take me with you. You wouldn't leave me here to be murdered, would you? You can do a lot with five thousand dollars."

Dixon said furiously, "Stop spitting in my face!"

"Yes. Of course. I'm sorry. I didn't realize," he backed away a step, his mouth twitching and formless. He tried to smile ingratiatingly and it was horrible. "I'm not asking you to make up your mind now. I want you to think it over. It's just a straightforward business proposition. Consider it from all angles."

I'm going to hit him, Dixon thought wildly, I'm going to shove his teeth down his throat. But he did not move. He clenched the edge of the tool chest and his own hands were shaking. This was all outside reality. Allard wasn't real. He wasn't contemptible or disgusting or pitiable or any of those things. He was fantastic.

Dixon said meagerly, "You're not going to be a hell of a lot safer in the States if Wirt's really after you. Did you think of that?"

Allard mumbled, "We don't have to think about that now."

Dixon watched him and saw the eyes shift uneasily in their pockets of fat. "You son of a bitch," he said. "You don't intend to send anybody back to pick him up. But what about Addams? If he hadn't got you off the boat, you'd have burned. He saved your miserable life. What about him?"

"How could I stop you from sending back a rescue party?"

"By making it part of the business proposition. That's what you had in mind, wasn't it?"

"And have you blackmail me for the rest of my life?"

Allard was almost calm. His hands were still snaking, but he was not hysterical any longer. Dixon scowled.

"There's something," he said. "You've got it figured."

"No. You can tell the authorities the minute we land. Think it over," he sounded surer of himself and surer of Dixon. "Sleep on it and we'll talk about it again when you're ready. Try to see it my way."

He walked away holding his arms a little out from his body the way fat men and penguins do. A drop of sweat fell on Dixon's wrist. He pulled his hand across his face and stared at his wet fingers. He felt a little sick.

A few minutes later, Wirt came across the sand from the citrus grove. He stared after Allard.

"What did Fatguts want?" he demanded.

Dixon hesitated. "Hell, he just wanted to make sure we weren't cutting up the dinghy to make a checker set." It came out strained and not funny at all.

"Did he give you the business again?" Wirt asked.

"No. He was all right. He's anxious to get out of here."

"Good. Why doesn't he go? Why doesn't he start right now?"

"You really hate his guts, don't you?"

"I don't want to talk about it," he bent over the tool chest. "I didn't find the chisels. I'm going to see if I can sharpen a screwdriver. It might work."

He sat down on the sand with a flat rock between his knees and began morosely to rub the tip of the screwdriver up and down on the hard surface.

Dixon watched him. He wanted to get up from there and go away, but he did not move. It was a sick fatigue and a growing congestion as if he were literally choking on his lie. It became intolerable and he knew he'd have to go or blurt it out.

He said abruptly, "Allard offered me five thousand dollars to take him off the island when the boat's ready."

Wirt gaped, and then his mouth thinned with contempt. "What's he afraid of, that we'll leave him marooned here?"

"Something like that."

"I hope you grabbed it."

Dixon shook his head.

Wirt made a guttural sound of exasperation. "Why the hell not?"

"I had a feeling."

"I have feelings all the time, but I'd never let any of them cost me five thousand bucks. What do you mean, a feeling?"

"I got an idea he's figuring something scummy."

"Like not paying you afterwards?"

"No. He'd be all right that way."

"Then how scummy can he get?"

"I don't know. There's something. I could see it." He did not want to tell Wirt his real suspicions. "When he thought I was nibbling, he started to get shifty."

"Outside of not paying off. I don't see a damn thing he can do. You can pile five thousand bucks pretty high."

"I'm going to think about it first."

"There's nothing to think about. The dinghy'll carry two. I've always said so. You'll be a damn fool if you don't take him up on it."

"We'll see."

"See, hell. It's all settled. Now let's get this boat operating so you can collect."

The screwdriver took an edge very quickly. It was a cheap one and the metal was quite soft and when they began the actual cutting of the slot for the centerboard, they found that it had to be resharpened every few minutes.

"This is going to be a shooting pain in the tail," Wirt said.

Chapter Twelve

That night it was very bad. There was no sleep or peace in it and Dixon lay under the sea grape trying to think and at the same time trying not to think. Considering Allard's business proposition at all was practically accepting it, and there was a dirtiness because Allard was a dirty man, and because the offer had been made in terror and malice and in secret. And because of the money.

It always came back to the money. Five thousand dollars would be the down payment on the kind of boat he wanted. Without the money, it would be the simple act of helping a terrified man. If the man had not been Allard. The only clean and honest thing, when everything was sifted, was Wirt. But there was the money, and as long as the money was there, everything could not be sifted.

And in the end, coming to no decision, Dixon realized dully that no matter what he did after this night, whether he accepted or repudiated, there would always be the dirtiness. The morning came very slowly.

Going back to the dinghy with Wirt was an extension of the bad night, but worse because in the light he could see the boat and Allard and Wirt, and the open sea beyond the curved, guarding claws of the cove. Dixon went doggedly. There was little or no conversation. They chipped away at the reluctant wood, sharpened the screwdriver, chipped and sharpened, chipped and sharpened, and very little progress was made. Addams came down an hour later wanting to talk privately to Dixon.

Wirt muttered, "Be smart, compadre. Take it."

Addams led Dixon down the beach toward the mangrove. They could hear the surf growling as it gnawed at the northeastern edge of the Cay.

Addams took two cigarettes from his waterproof bag, gave one to Dixon, and lit them with his gold cigarette lighter. Dixon glimpsed two flat tins of fifty cigarettes each before Addams closed the bag and his temper flared. It had been smoldering anyway. He cursed and threw his fist at Addams' face. Addams flung up his arm, but the force of the blow sprawled him on the sand. He rolled and spun to his feet, crouching. He was very quick and fluid. A knifelike blade glinted coldly in his right hand and with his left he scooped up a handful of sand to fling into Dixon's eyes.

Dixon snarled. "You had cigarettes all the time, and we're doing the work!"

"I didn't think."

"You're a goddamn liar. You saved them for Allard."

Addams circled backward for firmer footing on the packed sand closer to the water as Dixon came heavily toward him.

"That's right," he said. "I saved them for him. I didn't even smoke any myself. And what have you got to say about it anyway? You didn't bring them. I did. If I want to give them to Allard, I will. And if I want to throw them in the ocean, I can do that too. I can do anything I want with them." He saw that he had slowed Dixon and he kept talking. "Did I ask you what you have in your pockets? Did I come around asking for my share? For all I know, you might have a couple bottles of liquor buried up there, but that's your business, not mine."

"If you thought I had anything, you'd knife me to get it for Allard so you could suck around him." He stopped. There wasn't any point to this anymore. His fury was gone and it hadn't even been honest anger in the first place. Disgust drenched him. He walked back to the cigarette he had dropped and picked it up. A minute ago he would have ground it under his foot. Addams followed him warily.

"I'll give you a box," he said. "Here. It's a full fifty."

"Shove it."

"Now come, come, old boy," he knew that there was no longer any hazard and he tried to thrust the box into Dixon's hand. "Take them. They'll taste just as good as if I hadn't had my filthy hands on them, you know."

Dixon opened his hand and let the cigarettes fall to the sand. Addams let them lie, but he said, "Your young protégé might enjoy a smoke, too, you know." Then, casually, "The boss said he had a little talk with you yesterday."

Dixon felt a dull stir of surprise that Allard had actually told Addams. "What did he tell you?"

"Oh, about taking him off in the boat and all that."

"And leaving you and the kid here?"

"He said that seemed to bother you and it really does, doesn't it? It doesn't bother me a bit. It would be for such a short time, and the lodgings are good, the cuisine excellent, and actually it's very restful after a life misspent in toil. I shall quite enjoy it."

"Sure."

"He was serious about the money."

"He was hysterical."

"Oh, quite. Still is. He fairly gibbers. He has nightmares and all sorts of odd notions. He's taken it into his head that some fine night Wirt is going to creep up and cut his precious old throat from ear to ear. I have to do sentry-go every night. It's not real hysterics with him; it's driveling idiocy. Wirt is a bloodthirsty savage. Utter nonsense, but you can't talk him out of it. Why else would he offer you such an incredible amount of money to take him away from here?"

Dixon said slowly, "If he's so damn scared, he's going to want more than just getting away."

Addams looked up sharply. "I don't follow you."

"He sounds scared enough, for instance, to pay you to take care of Wirt while you two are alone here."

It seemed to Dixon that Addams' laugh completely masked his face. When a man laughs, it fills his face and nothing else can be seen, and anything can be hidden behind it. Addams' laugh ended in a wide smile.

"You'll really have to make up your mind," he protested. "I'm either a slimy bootlicker, as you have so broadly hinted, or I'm a cold-blooded killer. I can't be both, you know. It's a temperamental impossibility. But you honestly don't believe that, do you?"

"It's a thought."

"Let's be practical for a moment, shall we? I'm tired of people flying off into tizzies and having tantrums. Seriously, Dix, he'll definitely pay you five thousand dollars. He was never more earnest in his life."

"That's quite a pitch. What're you getting out of this?"

"My share," said Addams cheerfully. "You know, the poor old thing is really quite capable of a sort of gratitude, which is very nice when it takes the form of good hard cash. And speaking of hard cash," he took a manila envelope from his bag and opened it to show a sheaf of bills. "Your retainer. A little over nine hundred dollars. Call it nine hundred. Don't look so surprised. You don't think I'd take a few odds and ends and leave my cash aboard, do you? You know me better than that. Go ahead. Take it. It's your down payment."

Dixon took a last drag from the stub of his cigarette and snapped it into the water. "I haven't made up my mind," he said.

"Oh, good Lord! It's the …" Addams paused and looked thoughtfully at Dixon. "I wouldn't try to raise the price, if I were you. You'll make out better if you don't."

Dixon shouted, "I told him yesterday I'd let him know and that's all there's to it! I'll make up my mind when I'm damn good and ready, so tell him to stop bothering me or he can go to hell!"

Addams backed away. He watched Dixon with pale, clinical eyes.

"You know, Dix," he said. "You're not looking well. Your eyes are bloodshot and you've got rings under them. I've got some quinine. Do you want it?"

"Oh, for God's sake," Dixon said, "take your damn grab bag and get out of here."

Addams walked away, pursing his lips. He looked a little uneasy and once he paused to glance back over his shoulder. Dixon sat down on a palm log, his hands dangling inertly between his knees. He stared out over the water. It was quite rough beyond the bar and the caps on the chop were as white as teeth.

The hell with it, Dixon thought, I'm not going to take him, I'm not going to have anything to do with him, we'll do it the way it was in the beginning, Wirt takes the boat, and I'll tell the fat crud the next time I see him.

On his way back to the dinghy, he bent over and picked up the flat box of cigarettes.

Chapter Thirteen

Wirt was sharpening the screwdriver on the flat stone beside the dinghy and he sat up when Dixon came across the beach. He wiped the sweat off his forehead with the back of his hand.

"How'd it go?" he asked.

"It didn't." Dixon looked down at the screwdriver. It was becoming stubbier from repeated sharpenings.

"You turned him down?"

"I'm calling the whole goddamn thing off. You're taking the dinghy just the way we had it set."

"Did something come up?"

"No."

"I mean, were there any strings attached?"

"No!"

"You just plain turned it down for no reason?"

"Yes."

"I don't get you," Wirt blurted. "If Fatguts wants to hand you five thousand bucks, take it. If you don't have to kiss his foot for it, take everything you can get. Make him pay through the nose, the son of a bitch. I don't get you at all. Honest to God I don't!"

"Goddamn it!" Dixon yelled. "Shut up!"

Wirt leaped to his feet. His face was white and for a moment he looked as if he would hit Dixon, but he turned on his heel and went striding across the beach and disappeared among the citrus trees. Dixon stared at the grove in astonishment, not realizing how savage he had sounded when he yelled at the boy. Nerves, he thought, this place is getting on everybody's nerves. He looked at the box of cigarettes in his hand and threw them into the boat.

Wirt came back about two hours later. Dixon was hunkered down in the dinghy, chiseling away slivers of wood a half inch at a time. He had to hammer heavily for the screwdriver would not hold an edge.

Wirt said coldly, "I'll take it for a while."

Dixon straightened up. His hand was cramped from holding the screwdriver and his leg and arm muscles ached and he had a headache from the sun.

"Are you sore just because I yelled?" he asked sourly.

"I'm sore because you're burned up about something and you're trying to take it out on me."

"Oh, hell. Will it make you happy if I apologize?"

"Not interested."

"What do you want me to do, send you a Mother's Day card?"

"I don't care what you do. You're not going to kick me around just because your monkey's up, that's all. Get out of the boat and let me go to work."

Dixon stepped out of the dinghy. He knew he could fix everything up with a really friendly gesture, but now he was sore. If Wirt wanted to sulk, let him. The hell with him. I kick five thousand bucks out the window on account of him, Dixon thought resentfully, he'd know that much if he had any sense, and look at the snoot on him, a yard long, you'd think I broke his yo-yo, *he's* mistreated!

He dropped the tools in the boat and said, "Help yourself." As he walked away he said back over his shoulder, "There's a box of cigarettes."

The boy did not answer and as Dixon started up the hill he heard him hammering in the dinghy. He saw Allard peer anxiously at him from under his banana-leaf canopy and he strode on without a word or a glance, knowing that Allard still watched. Let him wonder, Dixon thought, changing his mind about telling him right away that he wouldn't be leaving in the boat. He gave me the business, now let him squirm.

At the top of the hill, he thought about the signal fire again. To satisfy himself, he gathered together a heap of dry palm leaves and cleared the area around it so nothing else could catch fire. His cigarette lighter needed fluid, but the tinder caught hungrily at the flame. Dixon threw on more palm leaves and then some of the rotted wood from the house to make smoke. He stood back and watched it critically. There was always a wind up here. It swept strongly over the dome of the hill and the fire roared hoarsely. There was a lot of yellow flame at first and after awhile the rotted wood began to burn and white smoke billowed out in a continuous roll like dirty cotton. There was a lot of it and the wind blew it southeast into the trees and laid it almost parallel to the ground and within very few feet it was nothing but a slight haze. He laughed shortly and without humor. The invisible signal fire.

He poked aimlessly in the debris while waiting for the fire to die and after awhile he found a rusty machete lying in the cross-hatch of a cabbage palm where it had been placed after trimming the tree.

He sat on the ground with his back to the tree and began indifferently to clean off the rust with a piece of coquina stone. He had no use for a machete, it was just something to do. The wind was cool and refreshing but it made a lot of noise in the trees and eventually he found himself irritably trying not to listen to it. He went over to the fire, kicked off the smoldering wood and stamped out the embers. He hung the machete at his hip from his belt with a loop made from a piece of copper wire he had also found. It had a sharp, jagged edge. Coquina stone was a very coarse abrasive. He went down the eastern face of the hill. There was no path. At the edge of the hill was a sheer drop of fifty feet to a very rocky beach and, peering over the lip, Dixon could see the fish swimming among the rocks in the water. Farther down the hill he found the pond to which the ducks went every evening. There were no ducks on it now. Addams was picking papayas at the northern end of it and he stopped when he saw Dixon coming toward him. He noted the broad-bladed knife swinging from Dixon's hip, and unconsciously he drew himself together in a tighter, defensive stance. He could see that Dixon was in a peculiar mood. His eyes darted to the trees.

"Give me your lighter fluid," Dixon said.

Addams silently took the can from his bag and gave it to him. Dixon filled his lighter, whistling dissonantly. He handed the fluid back.

"You ought to open a department store," he said.

"If you need a flint, I've got some."

"I wouldn't be surprised. Tell your boss I'm still thinking."

"All right."

"How's he holding up?"

"He's waiting."

"Tell him I said, that's the spirit. Tell him that from me."

"I'll tell him."

"No, you won't. You'll make up a nice little fairy tale with a happy ending for him. You're his dear old pal. You wouldn't dream of saying anything that would upset him."

Addams took a deep breath. Dixon looked at him, smiling.

"Now, where's that bamboo?" he asked. "We've got to get the boat ready for the big voyage. We have to make it comfortable for the passengers. We can't waste time gossiping."

"It's about three hundred yards straight ahead, just before you get to the mangrove."

Dixon walked on, looking for the bamboo. There was not much spring in his step. That bit of cruelty with Addams had made him feel worse. Everything was getting dirtier all the time. You did things you didn't want to do and you knew how it was going to be while you were doing it but you couldn't stop. It was all getting loused up for fair. Everything, everybody. The hell with them, he thought angrily.

He found the bamboo without any trouble. It was growing in clumps and there was a lot of it. The feathery tips whipped in the wind twenty-five and thirty feet above his head. Many of the dark shiny green canes were six inches in diameter, and there were scores of slimmer ones. There would be no problem about a mast for the dinghy. The only thing now was the sail, and suddenly he thought of that great sheet of aluminum roof up there on the hill. It could be flattened and cut. It wouldn't give much speed but it would work. He became a little excited and hurried across the island to tell Wirt.

As he came out of the citrus grove, he saw Wirt leave the boat and walk up the beach and away from him, his back stiff. It was a moment before he realized that Wirt had seen him coming and had deliberately walked away. He clenched his big hands. The box of cigarettes was still there, unopened.

That night Wirt slept farther up the beach among the cabbage palms.

It was the same the next day. They worked in two-hour shifts. Twice Dixon tried to reach the boy and after the second time he didn't try again. I'm not going to crawl, he thought grimly.

It was on the third day of working on the slot for the centerboard that the accident happened. Dixon was in the boat and Wirt was nursing his morose and complicated grudge somewhere on the Cay. It was late afternoon and the westering sun hammered down relentlessly. There was never much breeze on this beach. Dixon was sodden with sweat. Perhaps he brought down the hammer too hard, or perhaps the screwdriver slipped in his sweaty hand. It could have been either. The tip of the screwdriver shot off the rib he was cutting and tore a narrow, fifteen-inch-long strip from a sheathing board, broke it off completely. He carefully pulled the screwdriver from the hole in the bottom of the boat and leaned over to look. He could see the sand beneath the boat through the long hole and he felt his stomach fall away from him. He stepped out to the beach and turned the boat over. There was a long triangular tear in the canvas, longer than the hole and about a foot across at the base. This was the true catastrophe, for the canvas was what made the dinghy watertight. The sheathing was not caulked. He picked up the strip of wood that had broken off and saw that the long edge of it was gray. It had been cracked for a long time. He turned the boat back and found many other cracks in the sheathing. He examined the canvas bottom again.

There were bubbles all over it where the canvas had become unglued from the sheathing. He lifted the torn flap. It was brittle. That was why it had torn so easily. The life had gone out of the canvas. It had lain too long in the sun and salt air without paint at some time or other. My God, he thought, it wouldn't fill up faster if you held it under a faucet!

Something churned in his chest and suddenly he was roaring with laughter. Great gusts of it came out of him. He gasped and the tears poured from his eyes and he staggered into the ankle-deep water, guffawing and beating his hands together. There really was a vast and infinite humor in it, a humor beyond tragedy, a humor that so revealed everything that it was truth. He saw it all very clearly, and he himself was not exempt from the revelation. He was right there under the microscope, a frantic little nit suspended in a speck of water.

Sure. Why had he been so lousy to young Wirt? Because deep in his mind he resented the kid for standing between him and the five thousand dollars. That was the whole thing. And on top of that he'd wanted to be congratulated for being noble and turning down the money, wanted the kid to be grateful.

But had he really made up his mind to turn down the money? Had he? Why hadn't he told Allard flatly? Why hadn't he come right out and put it in words? Because he *hadn't* made up his mind, and Wirt knew it, and that was the reason he threw *his* wingding. Despite all his urging to the contrary, the kid didn't want him to take that offer, and now the kid felt that he had been deserted.

And what had all the agony been about and what was left after the wars? A rotten, worthless dinghy that couldn't sail across the cove.

And who was the clown, Dixon thought, me; the joke's on me. It was all very clear and very funny and rather horrible.

He turned. Wirt was standing by the dinghy fingering the torn flap of canvas.

"What happened?" he asked. He looked stunned.

"The screwdriver slipped when I hit it."

"Can it be fixed?"

"If we had tacks, we could tack the hunk of wood back in place and caulk it, if we had caulking. Then we'd need waterproof glue for the canvas. We don't have any of those things."

"Then we can't use it?"

"Not unless we want to commit suicide."

"We can't do *anything?*"

"I just told you."

"There's got to be something."

"Not here. In a boatyard. The whole dinghy's in bad shape. We don't have a prayer unless we can get that canvas glued down with something that won't come loose."

"There's *got* to be something," Wirt cried, his voice rising.

"Maybe we can figure something out," Dixon said pityingly.

"Goddamn it, stop saying maybe all the time!"

"All right."

"Why didn't you watch what you were doing, why didn't you watch it?" he was strident and losing control.

Dixon did not answer and Wirt yelled, "You were too goddamn anxious to collect your five thousand bucks. You couldn't wait to get your hands on it!"

Dixon said wearily, "And maybe I even did it on purpose. Maybe I did it so I wouldn't have to make up my mind."

Wirt hit him. He saw the fist coming and he did not duck. It caught him on the side of the jaw and he spun around and fell down on the sand. He pushed himself up and Wirt hit him again. He dropped to his knees and fell forward on his face. He did not move. Wirt seized the dinghy, dragged it violently across the sand and overturned it on Dixon's back.

"You wanted it," he yelled. "Now you've got it!" He ran into the citrus grove as if fleeing.

It was some minutes before Dixon stirred. He pushed the dinghy off and sat up. He felt his chin and opened and closed his mouth. His jaws were very sore and there was a pain across the small of his back where the gunwale of the dinghy had caught him when Wirt overturned it. He rose to his feet, lurched into the water and knelt down. He splashed water into his face but it did not help him much because it was warm. He wobbled back to the shore and sat down dizzily on the boat. It passed off slowly. He picked up the box of cigarettes and tore off the cellophane wrapper. Neither he nor Wirt had smoked any. He lit one and drew the smoke deep into his lungs. When he finished the cigarette, he dropped it between his feet and ground it into the sand with his toe.

"Let's break the news," he muttered.

He shoved himself off the dinghy and plodded up the beach. Addams saw him coming and, shooting a glance at the napping Allard, went to meet him. Dixon stopped and waited for him. His back hurt and walking was an effort. Addams approached warily. He could see in Dixon's face that something was wrong.

"What's the matter?" he asked.

"We can't use the dinghy," said Dixon without much expression.

"*What?*"

"The tool slipped and I punched a hole in the bottom of it."

"Can't you plug it?"

"It's no use."

"For God's sake, man ..."

"It didn't come with the yacht. Where'd you pick it up?"

"In Lauderdale." Then sharply, "Why? There's nothing the matter with it. It didn't leak."

"I had an idea you made a buck on it someway or other. It's no good. It's old. The canvas is falling apart. It won't float," Dixon smiled drearily. "You made your fast buck once too often."

Addams drew his lips back from his teeth like a ferret. "It was all right when I bought it!" he snarled.

"It was old when you bought it. It had been sitting in somebody's backyard for years. The sun sucked it dry. But you can forget it now," he sounded drowsy and listless.

Addams whispered, "God!" and bit his lip. He glanced back over his shoulder. "Now what am I going to tell the boss!"

"Don't worry about it. You'll get out from under. You'll tell him I knocked a hole in it and ruined it."

"You did, didn't you?"

"Yes. I did."

"*Now* what are we going to do?"

"I don't know. We'll sit. Does it make any difference? We'll be picked up. Sometime."

Addams made a harsh sound and swung around and walked away from him. Dixon started up the path to the crest of the hill. He was not very far up when he heard Allard screech shrilly and a second later there was the sound of a shot and the bullet went slap-slap-slapping through the leaves of the orange tree high over Dixon's head. He looked back. Addams was struggling with Allard, holding his right arm with both hands and Allard was flailing at him with his left. Dixon shrugged and continued up the path. On the summit he propped a piece of wall from the house against two trees to make a windbreak and lay down behind it. He turned on his side and pillowed his face on his curled arm. He was worn out. What he needed was some sleep.

Chapter Fourteen

The following days passed without anything to mark them, empty, lethargic days, swimming slowly by like something barely realized in cloudy water. Dixon did not leave the hill, and no one came up. Once or twice he saw Addams in the water below at low tide, catching spiny lobsters. The second time, Addams saw him peering down and he picked up his lobsters by their long antennae and hurried away.

Wirt, Dixon knew, was living alone at the other end of the Cay, north of the duck pond. He had glimpsed him several times moving among the trees, but Wirt did not look up and Dixon did not go down to meet him.

Most of the time Dixon did nothing at all. In the nights he tried thinking of Helen but she always evaded him. He could never see her when he closed his eyes. It was the same with other things. When he tried to recall a certain incident that had happened in Sarasota or St. Augustine they became mixed up with other things that had happened in other places.

Then one morning he woke up and knew that this day was different from the others. He was clear headed and there was an eagerness all through his body. He leaped to his feet and walked through the cocoanut palms and when he stood on the brim of the hill, looking out over the restless water, he knew what it was. It came to him so complete and perfect in all details that he knew it must have been simmering deep in his mind for days.

He knew how he could get off the island. He could make a raft of bamboo. There were scores of canes six inches in diameter and he could lash them together with the tough vines that grew all over the island. Three bars across the bottom would keep it rigid. He would use the same plan for the sail as he had been going to use for the dinghy— a sheet of the aluminum roofing. He could make a sweep for steering from a length of bamboo and one of the thwarts from the dinghy. It would be slow in the water, but it would move and it would be unsinkable.

He quickly ate a half dozen bananas, impatient now to start working. He went down the eastern side of the hill, taking along a chunk of coquina stone to sharpen his machete when it became dulled. As he passed the duck pond, he heard something moving heavily through the brush to his left. It was too heavy for a goat or a pig, and he knew it had to be Wirt. Just before he reached the stand of bamboo he came upon Wirt's camp. Wirt had made himself a tented frame of slim bamboo and covered it with the broad banana leaves, as Addams had covered Allard's canopy. There were clam shells in a neat pile to one side and a stalk of bananas hung from a cabbage palm. The banana trees were at the southern end of the island. Dixon felt a surge of pity, affection and guilt and determined to make his peace with the boy at the first opportunity. He called several times, but there was no answer. He walked on to the bamboo clumps.

He felled fourteen of the heaviest canes and dragged them out into the open where he cut them into fifteen foot lengths. That would make his raft about seven feet wide and fifteen feet long. He took a length in each hand and started across the island, dragging them. The raft would have to be built on the shore of the cove, for that was the only spot from which it could be launched. The thick weeds made it heavy work and he perspired freely. When he had all fourteen piled on the beach, he sat down and smoked a cigarette.

Next he had to cut the three crosspieces and a long cane, for the mast.

He was planning a rail around the raft so that he would not roll off in a heavy sea when three shots shattered the quiet. There were two more shots before he could spring to his feet. He looked up the beach and saw the sprawled body on the sand about ten feet from Allard's canopy. Dixon sprinted toward it. It was Wirt. Dixon knelt down beside him and when he gently turned him over he saw all the blood. Wirt had been hit twice in the stomach and once through the head. He was dead. Dixon heard a whimper and turned his head sharply. Allard was crouched at the very back of the canopy against the trunk of the tree. The gun dangled in his hand. Dixon leaped at him and snatched the gun. Allard cried out inarticulately and huddled with his arms crossed in front of his face and his knees drawn up as if to protect his stomach. He was speechless with terror. Addams came running along the shore from the southern end of the island. He stopped and stiffened at the sight of Wirt's body. Now there was blood in the sand around the body.

He looked quickly at Allard, at Dixon, and finally at the gun in Dixon's hand. Dixon was holding the gun by the barrel.

Dixon said, "Here's a mess. Your boss just killed the kid." Addams kept looking at the gun.

"How did it happen?" he asked.

"I don't know. I heard the shots and when I turned it was all over."

"Wirt must have done something. Mr. Allard wouldn't shoot for no reason. I've heard Wirt make threats on other occasions. Why did Wirt come down here in the first place? This isn't his camp. He came down to make trouble, and if Mr. Allard shot him, it was only in self-defense."

Dixon's mouth curled. "What are you trying to do, give him a story to tell? You're wasting your breath. Fat boy isn't hearing a word you're saying."

They both looked at Allard. He still crouched and his eyelids were desperately squeezed together. He was curled up like a fetus.

Addams gave Dixon a hard speculative glance. "How do I know you didn't shoot Wirt yourself?" he said abruptly. "I've only got your word for it. You could have done it. When I came up, you had the gun in *your* hand."

Dixon remained impassive. "Is that the way it's going to go?"

"I didn't say that. As far as I'm concerned, either of you could have done it."

"That's right."

"And if you start accusing each other, it's just your word against his."

"Right."

"The police would give both of you a hard time. They might even assume that both of you had a hand in it. The police are very tough about things like this. And we're still in the Bahamas, you know. This is English soil, and the English are very harsh about killings."

"Very. Do you have any suggestions?"

Addams shrugged. "If Mr. Allard shot him, it was self-defense. If you did it, you had your reasons. We're living under unnatural conditions. Things can be excused here that can't be excused elsewhere."

"In other words, let's forget the whole thing. Right?"

"Frankly, yes. It would be best. No one knows Wirt was here with us. He could have gone down with the yacht. To say anything else would be asking for trouble."

Dixon did not answer. He was looking at Wirt's body. He walked back and picked up a small basket crudely made of green palm leaves that lay on the sand beside the body. In the basket was a handful of dry cocoanut fiber and three heavier pieces of wood. He examined it very carefully, rubbing the cocoanut fiber between his fingers, puzzled. Addams watched him narrowly.

"What's that?" he demanded.

"There wasn't any self-defense," said Dixon bluntly. "Wirt didn't come down here to make trouble. All he wanted was some of your fire so he could do his own cooking. He was going to carry it back in this basket. Here's the tinder and wood enough to keep it burning till he got back to his own camp. Allard wasn't defending anything. He saw the kid walking up and got hysterical, so don't give me self-defense."

"It's *still* only your word against his!"

"Yeah? Look at this," he thrust the gun toward Addams. It was silver plated and had a smooth pearl handle. "His fingerprints are all over it."

Addams looked thoughtfully at the gun and Dixon said ironically, "I'm going to take good care of this gun. I'm not going to let anything happen to it."

Addams moved his hands, giving up. "Well," he said at length, "he can certainly plead temporary insanity."

"I'll go along with that. He's been temporarily insane for a week, but they'll probably hang him anyway." There was a sudden hot choking in his throat. The shock had frozen him emotionally, but now it flooded out of his chest. He turned away. "I'm going to bury him now," he said in a muffled voice.

"I'll give you a hand," Addams said.

They carried the body up the beach to the citrus grove. Dixon had covered Wirt's face with his handkerchief. The grave was very shallow because of the rocky substratum. They pushed the earth over Wirt with their hands and piled heavy stones on top of that so the pigs would not root it up.

Addams made a cross of two orange branches, which he trimmed neatly with his clasp knife. He pushed it into the earth at the head of the grave. It made Dixon feel a little differently toward him. He had not thought Addams capable of such sentiment.

As they walked somberly away from the grove, Addams asked disinterestedly about the bamboo Dixon had brought to the edge of the cove. "Going to build yourself a shack?"

"A raft," Dixon told him, equally disinterested.

"A raft! To get off this place?"

Dixon told him about the raft. It was something to talk about. When he was talking he wasn't thinking about Wirt. He explained the raft in detail. Addams listened intently and kept glancing at the pile of bamboo, visualizing everything Dixon was saying, and in the end he knew exactly how it was going to be made.

Suddenly he said, "You've made up your mind to turn Allard in?"

"You're goddamn right!"

Addams took a step ahead, turned, and made a vicious upward slash at Dixon's belly with his knife. The blade struck the wide belt buckle and slithered across Dixon's ribs, tearing a long, shallow gutter. He swore, recovered his balance and made a backhand cut at Dixon's throat but missed. Dixon roared and clubbed him across the side of the head with his fist. Addams staggered, tripped in the heavy sand, but before Dixon could get at him, he scrambled to his feet and fled toward the citrus grove. Dixon bounded after him, wrenching at the machete at his hip. Addams was fifteen yards ahead when he plunged into the high weeds among the trees.

Addams was much the fleeter, and Dixon lost him before he had gone three hundred yards. He stopped, panting, and listened, but Addams had also stopped and the only sounds were the ordinary sounds of the Cay, the birds, the wind and the growling sea. Dixon searched for another half hour and then gave it up. There were too many places where Addams could hide and the sun was setting. Before going back, Dixon went to the bamboo. He found a cane that was about seven inches in diameter and chopped it down with the machete. He cut off one segment. The gun slipped into it very easily. All he had to do now was make a plug for the open end and he had a waterproof container. He went back to the beach at the cove, taking two papaya melons with him.

Allard was still where they had left him. Dixon paid no attention to him. He ate his melons and started figuring where he was going to spend the night. Addams would be watching, he knew, waiting for him to drop off to sleep. Trying to stay awake would be a damn fool thing to do. Sooner or later he'd have to have sleep. The mangrove, he thought, I can bed down in the mangrove. And then he thought grimly, he's in the same boat; he'll have to sleep too, but he won't sleep tonight. He heard a sound and looked up sharply, reaching for the machete.

Allard was standing about twenty feet away from him. The tears were running down his face. When Dixon moved, he scrambled back three paces. He made a trembling, conciliatory gesture with his hands.

"I didn't mean it," he whimpered. "I didn't mean to shoot him. I was just trying to scare him."

"Get back where you belong."

"I didn't mean it. Why didn't he say what he wanted? Why did he just keep coming like that? He had a look on his face. How was I to know?"

"All he wanted was some of your fire."

"I didn't believe him, the way he looked and …"

"So he did say what he wanted!" Dixon rose slowly to his feet. "He *did* say, didn't he?"

Allard babbled. "You wouldn't have believed him either. That look he had and the way he kept coming. I was all alone. I told him to go away. I told him. He didn't listen. I didn't mean to shoot him. I only wanted to scare him."

"Thanks," said Dixon with satisfaction. "I wasn't sure before, but that ties it up."

"What are you going to do?"

"Me? Not a thing. That's up to the police."

"But I *didn't* mean *it!*"

"Tell that to them when they come to pick you up."

"Please, please, *please!*" Allard dropped to his knees and crawled toward Dixon, holding out his hands beseechingly.

"Please!"

Dixon looked at him with disgust. Allard kept crawling toward him, babbling, begging, weeping, and Dixon became disgusted with himself for allowing it to continue.

He yelled furiously, "Shove it!" and strode up the beach.

Allard shrieked after him, "I'll do anything, anything you want, anything at all, just tell me and I'll do it."

The crashing of the dry weeds underfoot drowned out the sound of Allard's screeching voice. He drove on without caution and then, suddenly remembering Addams, stopped and listened and this time he heard a stealthy rustling to his right. He sprinted straight ahead for a hundred yards and then as quietly as he could circled through the trees toward the mangrove. In the mangrove he made no sound at all, stepping carefully from one arch of roots to another. He found a small clearing. It was dry. Silently, he sawed off several branches with the machete and when he lay down he covered himself with them. He was completely hidden. He lay with the machete beside him and listened for Addams and then he began to think of Wirt and how the boy called him compadre and made jokes, but mostly he remembered how the kid had looked up to him in the beginning and depended on him. Later, he wept.

Chapter Fifteen

The next morning he took a roundabout way out of the mangrove so he would not show Addams where he had slept. He finally emerged at the eastern side of the Cay near the bamboo. On the way across the island, he cut long lengths of tough vine and dragged them with him. Now he wanted to get the raft made as quickly as possible. He worked facing inland, the cove protecting his back. Addams was somewhere in the weeds or among the trees, watching. He wouldn't be finicky about where he planted his knife.

Lashing the long lengths of bamboo to the first crosspiece went very quickly because the pieces could be manipulated when he threaded the vine over and under to bind them tightly. Tying the second cross strip was much harder and he worked more slowly, steeling himself against haste.

Allard came slowly down the beach toward him. Dixon sat up. Allard was very pale, veal white, and he was drenched with nervous sweat.

"I want to put something up to you," he said.

"Not interested."

"Wait. You want a new boat. I'll buy you one. I'll buy you any boat you want. I'll equip it complete, everything you want on it, rods, reels, radio-telephone, refrigerator, everything. You can have your own boat again. That's what you want, isn't it, your own boat? You can have it. You can have the best."

"That sounds as if you've been talking to Addams," Dixon said heavily. "That sounds like his kind of proposition."

Allard said hurriedly, "What difference does it make? I'm the one who's making the offer."

"And I'm the one who's turning it down."

Allard tried to keep control of his face. "Wait. A boat of your own, all equipped ..."

"And I'm telling you for the last time," Dixon interrupted fiercely, "stay away from me!"

Allard fled, showing a terrified face over his shoulder. Dixon looked down at his hands. They were shaking. That goddamn Addams! He snatched up the machete and walked grimly up the path to the top of the hill. He looked down over the Cay. The tops of the citrus trees were a green blanket across the middle of the island. Beyond it was the mangrove belt and to the east were the feathery tops of the bamboo. He watched. If Addams moved down there, he would see him. Later he went to the opposite side of the hill and watched from there. He saw goats and pigs and birds but there was no sign of Addams. He went down the hill and around the rocky shore where he had seen Addams catching lobster. There were so many hiding places. It was the rush of gravel that warned him and he leaped back as a huge rock came tumbling and struck the shore with a splintering crash. He looked up and saw Addams climbing rapidly up the face of the bluff. He ran around to the side of the hill but Addams was gone by the time he reached the summit. That was the last he saw of Addams though he searched relentlessly for the rest of the day. At nightfall he was tired out. He had no appetite but he ate some bananas before going into the mangrove for the night. He lay sleepless for an hour. Suddenly Addams' voice called:

"Dixon, Dixon …"

He clenched a mangrove root beside, his head to keep himself from leaping to his feet. He listened tensely.

Addams called again. His voice was muffled by the foliage. He was not very close. Dixon cocked his head. His fingers curled around the handle of the machete.

Addams spoke, "I know you're in there. I'm not trying to find you. I just feel like having a bit of a chat."

Keep talking, Dixon thought, just keep talking. He turned his head. It was hard to hear from where the voice was coming.

Addams said, "Can you hear me, old boy?"

Dixon thought for a moment and then craftily turned his mouth close to the ground and rumbled, "I can hear you." Let Addams try to get a direction out of that!

Addams went on in an easy, conversational tone. "You know, chappie, you're really off on a tangent. You haven't thought this out properly. I've got the notion you're lashing out in all directions because you feel a bit of guilt yourself. It's sheer nonsense to lay all the blame on Mr. Allard. He was no more responsible for his actions than an idiot child. If you want to blame anybody, blame me. I'm more at fault than he. At least I had my sanity. I should have taken that bloody gun away from him. He wasn't to be trusted with a gun. Good Lord, he almost popped *me* one night. It was obvious that sooner or later he was going to pot somebody. I didn't take his gun because he'd have gone completely off his chump, but I could have taken the bullets out. So blame me. It's my fault too."

Don't worry about that, friend, Dixon thought. Carefully he removed the camouflaging mangrove branches that covered him. It was impossible to get a bearing on that voice while lying on the ground.

"Are you there?" Addams called.

Dixon grunted, "I'm here." He propped the branches to make a screen and sat up.

"And you're to blame too, old boy," Addams reproached. "You could have taken the gun away from him. He'd have squawked and flopped like a trout, but you wouldn't have had any trouble. Good Heavens, man, up in the States you wouldn't have let a dangerous lunatic run around a crowded railway station with a loaded gun if you had the chance of taking it away from him, would you? Why didn't you take it away from him? Because it wasn't your particular hide that was in danger? Because it was only the boy and you couldn't be bothered about anybody but yourself?"

Dixon stiffened. There! He had Addams placed. The voice was definitely coming from the southeast, closer to the bamboo. *Got you!* he exulted. Stealthily he rose to his feet and started through the mangrove, circling to come up behind Addams. He moved very slowly, testing each step before he came down with his weight. The mangrove roots were springy and slippery.

Addams continued. He sounded very sad, but a little too lugubriously, like a hired mourner. "And what about young Wirt? I know he's dead and it's a foul thing to talk about him like this, but he wasn't lily white. Wirt deliberately goaded Allard every chance he got. Aside from being a rather cruel thing to do, it wasn't very sensible. There were only four of us here on the island and good Lord anyone with any intelligence at all would have realized that under these extraordinary circumstances even the smallest tiffs would be bound to be exaggerated. Dammit all, the young fool put all of us in danger. *I* almost got shot, and *you* actually *were* shot at. That day of the accident to the dinghy. If I hadn't grabbed his arm that day, you'd be dead and buried instead of Wirt. Now really, when you consider it, the boy recklessly provoked the whole unfortunate incident. From start to finish. Be fair now, old boy. That's all quite true, isn't it?"

Dixon carefully propped himself. He turned away from the voice and muffled his own voice against his chest with his cupped hands. "You're doing the talking," he said gruffly.

"Right you are," said Addams cheerfully. "And I'm talking sense too, you know. Coming right down to the point, Allard was actually the least culpable of all of us, you and I included. He fired the shots but consider how he'd been bullied and goaded and harried and just generally kicked around by everybody. He's a selfish, blubbery swine, and I know you dislike him, but you don't hang a dog because you don't like the set of his ears. We're all guilty and we should all suffer, or none of us should suffer. If you make Allard the scapegoat, you won't be satisfying your conscience. It'll gnaw at you for the rest of your life. You'll always remember you had the chance to prevent tragedy and you didn't. You turned your back. You let Allard keep his gun. You *permitted* the boy to be killed. It will nag at you, Dixon. It's nagging at you right now. Isn't it, Dixon, *isn't* it?"

Dixon groaned, shut up, you son of a bitch, *shut up!* He took a long step and his foot shot off the slippery root. He grabbed wildly for an overhanging branch and dropped the machete. He was in the swampy part of the mangrove and it struck the water with a noisy splash.

Addams cried out shrilly, "You bastard!" And then viciously, "You won't get off this place alive, Dixon. I'll take care of you, don't worry!"

Dixon heard him running through the weeds. He swore futilely. He fished in the water for his machete and, after he found it, went slowly back to his hiding place. He lay down and covered himself with the branches again. With open-eyed horror, he realized that Addams was right. It *was* gnawing at him. And more than Addams knew. He had completely repudiated the boy. He had driven him away.

He could almost hear Addams jeering—the boy's dead. You're partly to blame, but what can you do about it? You can get Allard hanged, but that won't help *you*, old boy. Hang Allard, and someday you'll end up by hanging yourself from a rafter in the attic.

Helen, Helen, he groaned!

When he came suddenly awake the next morning, the sky was overcast and lean gray clouds raced over the Cay. The wind moaned in the trees. The surf was a thudding roar. There was a storm coming. Northeaster, Dixon thought dully. He plodded out of the mangrove. He hesitated at the papaya tree, but he was not hungry. When he reached the cove, he saw what Addams had done to his raft during the night. All the lashings had been cut, all his work undone. The now separate lengths of bamboo were neatly stacked. It was the kind of taunting gesture Addams would make. Build it up again, old boy, and I'll cut it to bits while you sleep. He shrugged and listlessly carried the bamboo to higher ground so that it would not be washed away when the storm came. He hammered pegs into the ground and lashed the pile down.

He had no desire to work today and the coming storm was a good excuse. It was coming all right. It was going to be a big one. Not a hurricane. You didn't get hurricanes this early. But there would be a lot of wind. He looked up the hill and saw the way it was tearing through the trees. The cocoanut palms were leaning away from it. It was rising steadily. He remembered the crumpled aluminum roof up there and decided to lash that down too. He could not afford to have that blow away. Before he went, he worked a half hour on Wirt's grave, adding stones and arranging them more neatly. He marked the head of the grave with a tremendous rock that left him shaky and dizzy after he lifted it into place, and he had to sit down. There was more work to do on the cairn. The name has to be carved in the stone, he thought. Wirt had to have a fitting memorial. The cairn should be bordered too. It had to be right.

When he started up the hill, he saw Allard standing outside his canopy, watching him. Allard looked worse than ever. Dixon stopped. Allard watched him haggardly. Dixon half raised his hands in a gesture of defeat. He'd had no clear idea of doing this before he stopped, but now that it was done, he knew that it had been inevitable since the night before. Allard stared in disbelief and suddenly sat down on the sand and began to cry. Dixon watched him without feeling anything one way or the other. Allard was not very pitiable. If anything, he looked rather repulsive, like a dissolute baby. He cried very badly. But it didn't make any difference. Allard's reactions were unimportant.

Dixon said, "As soon as the storm is over, I'll finish the raft and we can go."

Allard wept, "ThankGodthankGodthankGod …"

"It'll take a few days. If Addams doesn't break it down every time I get it together. I'll have to stop that. Will he be coming to talk to you when I go away?"

"Yes. He comes when you're not around."

"Keep him talking this time."

"I'll do that. I'll keep him talking. Yes," he looked up craftily. "What are we going to do?" he whispered.

Dixon understood the look and the whisper. "You're a murderous bastard, aren't you," he said indifferently.

"He'll kill you. He promised. You can't take chances. He's very sly."

"Why are you tying up with me instead of him?"

"You can get me away from this place. He can't."

"You *are* a swine."

Allard said sullenly, "I'll go crazy if I have to stay here." Then anxiously, "You're going to take me, aren't you? You're not going to leave me here. I'm going to buy you a boat, you know. You remember that, don't you? I meant every word of it. I haven't forgotten."

"Neither have I," said Dixon shortly. Wirt had said—*Make him pay through the nose, the son of a bitch!* Wirt would appreciate this. He'd agree and say it again and take great satisfaction in it. "You're going to get me a boat all right," Dixon said woodenly. "Now keep Addams talking when he comes."

He went up to the top of the hill. He concealed himself at the clump of cabbage palms and presently he saw Addams moving stealthily in the citrus grove. It was only the glimpse of a lean brown back between two of the smaller trees, but it was enough to show that Addams was working his way toward Allard. Dixon ran toward the eastern slope, crouching to keep himself concealed. He bounded down the hill. It took him about twenty minutes to make his way around the rocky southern end of the island to come up at the opposite side of Allard's camp. He could hear Addams and Allard talking.

Addams was saying, "You've got me to thank. I talked to him last night. I got him to change his mind. What did he say? What were his exact words?"

Allard mumbled, "He said we'd go when he finished the raft."

"But how did he sound? Did he mean it?"

"He meant it."

"Are you sure? You can't afford to be mistaken. It'll be too late afterward. Did he really sound all right?"

Dixon was at the last of the concealing rocks and he was still fifty feet from where Addams and Allard were sitting, and Addams would see him the moment he exposed himself. But it was Allard who saw him first and he got up and walked nervously up and down at the other side of Addams so Addams had to turn his back on Dixon.

"What's the matter?" Addams asked.

Dixon thought, the fool is going to give it away, but Allard whined, "It's my indigestion. I can't eat this food anymore. I get gas pains and I have to walk them off."

"You should eat more papaya. It's good for the stomach."

Allard said petulantly, "I can't stand it anymore. It makes me sick. It tastes like soap."

Dixon moved very slowly. He was still too far away to make a rush. He remembered how quick and agile Addams was. He could see that the suspense was becoming unbearable for Allard. Allard kept glancing at him and becoming more agitated. In a moment, he *would* give it away, but suddenly he went out of control and flung himself on Addams. He wound his arms desperately around him, pinning Addams' arms to his side.

He screamed, "I can't hold him, I can't hold him!"

But Addams was so stupefied that he did not move until Dixon was almost upon him, and even then he nearly escaped. He kneed Allard, rolled frantically, but slipped in the sand when he tried to scramble to his feet and Dixon clubbed him across the side of the neck. He tumbled in a heap, unconscious. Allard writhed on the sand five feet from him, holding his crotch. Dixon quickly stripped a climbing vine from the palm and bound Addams' hands behind him. Allard sat up, groaning. He bared his teeth at Addams.

"Kill him," he panted, "kill him, *kill him!*"

He tried to crawl to Addams and Dixon kicked him in the belly. He curled up, retching. Dixon did not give him another glance, but picked Addams up, threw him over his shoulder and trotted down the beach with him. He took Addams deep into the citrus grove. He cut long lengths of vine, sat Addams against a tree and tied him securely.

He squatted down on his heels and lit a cigarette. Addams' eyelids flickered. He was conscious.

He said harshly, "What are you waiting for?"

Dixon said drearily, "I don't know."

"Get it over!"

"Oh. You mean that. I'm not going to do anything to you."

Addams stared incredulously. He was not going to be killed? Dixon was going to let him live? Relief came drenchingly and he almost vomited.

"Give me a cigarette," he ordered contemptuously. "I've got some in my bag if you've finished yours."

Dixon took the cigarettes from Addams' bag, lit one and put it between Addams' lips.

Addams jeered, "You'll have to manage it for me. I've got a sore hand." He felt perfectly safe now. He inhaled, nodded his head, and Dixon took the cigarette from his mouth. He nodded his head again and Dixon gave him another puff at the cigarette.

Dixon said expressionlessly, "I'll tell you what kind of guy you've been working for. He wants me to knock you off."

Addams sneered. "He's smart."

"What?"

"Sure. He knows the score. You're just kidding yourself."

"Oh, brother. You are a pair of swine, aren't you."

"No. We don't kid ourselves, that's all."

The rain came in a melodramatic slash of lightning and a bellow of thunder. Both men were drenched almost instantaneously. Dixon leaped to his feet, remembering the aluminum roofing he had meant to lash down.

Addams said sharply, "You're not going to leave me here alone, are you?"

"You won't starve. I'll feed you."

"It's raining."

"It won't hurt you."

"Good Lord, man, this is a storm!"

As if to emphasize Addams' words, there was another wild cut of lightning followed immediately by thunder. It was very close. Dixon gave Addams the bare bones of a grin. Addams struggled frantically against the vines that bound him to the tree.

He screamed, "You can't leave me here! You can't do it you can't do it you can't *do it …*"

Dixon ran.

At the top of the hill, he lashed the roofing to the two trees between which it was crumpled. The rain was blinding and the wind howled through the palms. The surf bit and tore and snarled at the rocky eastern side of the Cay.

It was a big storm. The small craft warnings would be up on this one, he thought. But someone would get caught, someone would go down before the day was over. A heavy branch hurtled from a cocoanut palm and crashed to the ground twenty feet from him. He ran for the path. The hill was too exposed and it was becoming dangerous. It was quieter on the beach below but it was raining very hard and he crawled under the overturned dinghy.

The storm continued all day. He fed bananas to Addams at noon and again in the evening. The man was drenched but he was safe enough there, protected by the citrus grove. His eyes followed Dixon with silent hatred, and when he did speak it was only to fling bitter obscenities at Dixon's back. Allard had not come out from under his inadequate canopy, where he huddled in sopping misery. It was dusk when the rain stopped but the wind blew harder than ever. Dixon dropped into uneasy sleep listening to the monotonous pound of the surf on the opposite side of the island. Later, he thought he heard the sound of a yell. He listened, only half awake, not moving. There was another yell and then a third and fourth. It was Addams. Dixon rolled the dinghy off him and sprinted across the beach toward the citrus grove. The moon shone fitfully through the scudding clouds. Addams was yelling continuously and his voice shrilled on a rising note of terror.

When Dixon burst through the trees, he saw Allard prancing jerkily in front of Addams, jabbing at Addams with a long stick. Each time he jabbed, Addams yelled and dodged and tried to fend off the stick with his shoulder. Addams was bleeding from the cheek and neck. Allard panted and lunged at him again, tearing a long, jagged gash in the shoulder. Horrified, Dixon flung himself at Allard, grasped him by the arm, swung him around and hit him three times in the face. Allard fell into Dixon and Dixon stepped back and let him drop to the ground. Addams was slumped against his tree, breathing heavily. Blood ran down his cheek and neck. They were superficial scratches and the blood was already beginning to coagulate.

Dixon picked up the stick with which Allard had been poking at Addams. It was a slender length of bamboo that Allard had sharpened by rubbing against a stone. It had a point like a dagger.

"He was trying to stick me in the eye," Addams said.

"He won't pull that trick again."

"He'll pull it the next chance he gets, you fool."

"He won't get another chance."

"Don't leave me tied up here! You saw what he tried to do. He'll do it again. For God's sake, give me a chance, will you!"

Dixon said shortly, "You'll be all right."

Addams swore at him.

Dixon dragged Allard down the beach and tied him to the cabbage palm under the canopy. Allard grunted as Dixon pulled the vines tight across his chest just under the armpits. He made no other sound even when Dixon lashed his wrists under his knees.

Dixon said curtly, "And don't get ideas if you know what's good for you."

Allard pressed his lips together and did not answer and Dixon said in final warning, "Leave Addams alone or I'm not taking you with me when I go."

Allard looked away and appeared to lose himself in reverie. Dixon ate a half papaya melon and later made a bed of dry banana leaves and went to sleep.

The morning came quietly. The winds had died away in the night. The sky was a pale, spotless blue and the sun swung over the eastern rim of the island. It was several minutes before Dixon discovered the boat on the bar just outside the entrance of the cove. The tide was low and the bar was completely out of water and the boat lay on its side. It was a Bahamian fishing smack with a tall mast and a patched sail. Dixon stared at it and then with a wild yell ran crazily into the water, dived shallowly and swam out to the bar. The boat was empty and there was no sign of the fisherman who had sailed it here. Dixon knew what had happened. The boat had got caught in the storm and the fisherman had let his boat run ahead of the wind. He had tried to run into the cove and had run aground on the bar and the impact had thrown him into the sea. Dixon scanned the shorelines though there was not even a remote chance that the fisherman had survived.

He examined the boat. It looked battered and cranky but most Bahamian smacks did and Dixon knew that despite their disreputable appearance they were very seaworthy and you could sail anywhere in them. The mast was not sprung and the sail, though patched beyond recognition, was still serviceable. He felt no elation. The future wasn't anything to be elated about.

He righted the boat and bailed out the water. Four hours later it floated free on the incoming tide and he sailed it into the cove. He loaded it with enough oranges, bananas and papaya to last several days. Only when he was ready to sail did he cut Allard loose. Allard showed no curiosity about the boat.

"It doesn't look very safe," he said sullenly.

"It's safe enough. Get in."

"What about Addams?"

"I'll take care of him." And when he saw Allard's eyes narrow, he added sharply, "I don't mean that way."

Allard stepped into the boat. He scowled. He did not like it. "Where are we going?" he asked.

"Cuba."

"There are closer ports than that!"

"They're all English, and the English will ask too many questions. Do you want to answer a lot of questions? Sit down. I'll be right back."

He went into the citrus grove and untied Addams' hands. "You can manage the rest yourself," he said.

Addams stammered, "You're leaving?" He was very pale and there was sweat on his face.

"Yes, and if you hadn't tried to be smarter than everybody else you'd have been going with us."

Addams said savagely, "Oh, shut up, and get the hell out of here, will you!"

Dixon got the bamboo length in which he had put the gun. He had put a cypress plug in the open end and waterproofed it with pork fat. He left the machete on the beach for Addams. He pushed the boat into the deeper water and climbed in over the stern. The sail caught the wind and they moved across the cove.

Two days later he and Allard landed on the beach south of Santiago in Cuba.

Chapter Sixteen

Dixon stood at the window of his hotel room and looked down at the traffic on Biscayne Boulevard while he buttoned his shirt. Rat race, he thought morosely. It hadn't looked like a rat race three weeks ago when he flew in from Havana with Allard. It had looked pretty damn good then. Everything had looked pretty damn good. Even Havana had looked pretty damn good after Santiago, and Havana had always been something for the birds as far as he was concerned. A town as phony as those frozen daiquiris they served.

But it hadn't taken very long to find out that it was the same old rat race. Nothing had changed. It was a little worse, if anything, a little drearier. He had money in his pocket, a brand new wardrobe, and Allard's Caddy convertible to drive around in, but for all the difference it made he might just as well have been in Philadelphia on a rainy Sunday afternoon. He stood before the mirror and knotted the batik silk tie into the V of his collar. Now he was wearing five buck ties. And twenty dollar shirts, fifty dollar shoes and two hundred dollar suits. Even the high class pimps over on the Beach didn't dress any better than that. He needed only monogrammed underwear to come up to the standards of the racket men and gamblers. But he had got all that in the very beginning when Allard had the sweats and couldn't do enough for him. Things had slowed down since. Now Allard was giving him the old run-around. He knew that Allard was getting shifty, but he didn't care very much. He hadn't seen the boat he wanted. He hadn't really looked yet. It hadn't seemed very important. He'd get to it. He'd been in a very; funny mood and it had been much easier to let things slide for a while. Anyway, Allard had some naval architect looking around for a boat. That much was on the level. He'd given the guy all the specifications, the snotty son of a bitch.

"That sounds like quite a boat, Captain," very sarcastic. "You won't object if we have it custom made, will you?"

You could see he thought Dixon was taking advantage of Allard's generosity. Allard's generosity was very touching. It had been in all the papers. Grateful millionaire to buy boat for impoverished rescuer. It had made quite a story. Real Horatio Alger stuff. Dixon wondered how lovely everybody would have thought it if they knew the facts.

Dixon poured himself a cognac. Allard had sent him a case. He drank two fast ones and it picked him up a little.

Maybe, he thought, Allard wasn't giving him a run-around at all. Allard was in pretty bad shape. He had thrown a prime wingding. He had started getting drunk in Santiago, but that was only the beginning. He was gory-eyed in Havana and when they carried him off the plane in Miami, they took him straight to the rest home. He had the screaming meemies and had missed alcohol poisoning only because he could no longer get a glass to his mouth without spilling it all over everything. Even at a hundred and a quarter a day, the rest home had not been too happy about taking him in. His blood pressure was so high they thought he'd explode and his heart sounded like a machine shop under full production.

"It's amazing," the doctor told Dixon later, "what the human system can stand."

"Isn't it," Dixon said.

That got him an odd look and the doctor said, "You know, Captain, you don't look in such good shape yourself. There's a look of strain. Quite natural, of course, after what you've been through. Perhaps I ought to look you over while I've got you here."

"The last thing I want is to be looked over."

"Well … you should rest, you know."

"I am resting." And then he gave a short barking laugh and added, "On my laurels."

The doctor really thought him nuts after that.

They all thought him nuts, the nurses, the bellhops at the hotel, the elevator operator, the desk clerk, everybody. He was supposed to be a hero. He was supposed to be sitting on top of the world. They envied him. Everybody has a dream of rescuing a grateful millionaire. Rescue a millionaire and your worries are over. Dixon had taken to giving that short, barking laugh when they congratulated him.

"Don't ever rescue a millionaire," he told them. "They're never as grateful as the stories in the *Saturday Evening Post* say they are."

And then he thought, thank God we didn't get tangled up with the English. Even the thought of it gave him the sweats. The English would have taken them to the cleaners for sure. The English were a hard-boiled, hard-fisted lot. They'd never have let Allard get away with that drunken wingding. They'd have sobered him up and sweated the truth out of him. The English could spot a phony a mile off. But the Cubans had been fine. They didn't really care what happened to a pack of Americans. So long as they couldn't be blamed for it, so long as it didn't cost them anything. The Cubans were realists. It was a very unfortunate incident, yes, but Senor Allard was rich, he could buy another yacht, and after all it is much easier to forget painful moments when you can spend a lot of money and buy happier ones, no?

The Cubans were really fine. Very civilized. Thank God for the Cubans. The English were too grim. They were always fining somebody, or putting them in prison, or hanging them, or something.

Thank God, thought Dixon, that we didn't get messed up with the English!

He had another drink. He put on his jacket, counted the money in his wallet, sixty-three dollars, and left the room without any clear idea of where he was going. Just getting out of the room was enough. He walked down the stairs to the lobby instead of taking the elevator. He did not want to have to reply to the operator that yes it was another fine day.

Downstairs, he stepped into a phone booth and called Helen. "Hello, honey," he said.

"Oh, God," she said.

"What's the matter?"

"I didn't think you'd be alive after last night."

"We didn't have more than a half dozen drinks all night."

"Where was this? In the Copa? We only got there a half hour before they closed. What about the four martinis before dinner, two kinds of wine during, and all that Strega after? Or don't you start counting *until* you get drunk. I suppose you're right. They are the important ones. They're the ones you feel the next day."

"Did you just get up?"

"I'm not up and I'm not going to get up."

"Put on some clothes and we'll go for a drive."

"You mean you'll drive me over to the Beach and we'll have some cocktails and the next thing you know, there we are again and tomorrow will be just a little more hideous. No thank you."

"I didn't mean that. We could drive down to Key Largo and have some broiled lobster. I don't want to start drinking anymore than you do."

"That's just the trouble, Frank," she said, "I do want to start drinking. I want to get up and have a couple of whiskey sours, but I'm not going to. We've been out every night for two weeks. I think it's time to put on the brakes."

He thought of the empty afternoon ahead and said, "We can go for a drive, can't we?"

"I'm in no condition to go for a drive. I'd hate it."

"How about dinner tonight?" He could feel her refusal coming and he added hurriedly, "We'll go to a quiet place and later we can take in a movie."

"Well, all right," she was not enthusiastic. And then she said slowly, "I want to go someplace where we can talk."

"Sure."

"I mean that, Frank, so don't start planning another big night and don't try to talk me into it."

"All right, honey. I'll pick you up at five."

"You'll pick me up at six. If we leave at five, it'll mean an hour of cocktails. I'll see you at six. Now please hang up because I'm feeling rather awful."

He went into the hotel bar and had a whiskey sour and then he walked across the park to the bay where the charter boats were docked. Seven of the boats were tied up without charters and the captains were standing around hoping to get a party for the next day. The tourists were walking up and down the dock, stopping to look curiously into the cockpits of the boats, and one or two paused to talk to the captains, but Dixon could tell that the captains wouldn't have any luck with them. These were out-and-out tourists. When he had tied up to that dock with the *Madame* and saw that kind wandering down the dock, he would say, "Here comes another happy moron," and be right every time. They had a different look when they were shopping for a charter; they didn't look quite so much like cows that had meandered through a break in the fence.

He did not go out on the dock. He knew all the captains there and he did not want to have to get into conversation with them. He did not want to be kidded. Or if they didn't kid him, there'd be nothing to talk about except boats and fishing, and he did not want to talk about that either.

He walked away thinking about going out to Hialeah. Then he thought about the traffic jam there'd be after the races were over, and anyway you have to follow the horses every day or it was just a lot of nags running around a track and where was the point? In the end, he got the Caddy from the hotel garage and drove out to the rest home to see Allard. It was very strange, but in this whole rat race he felt closest to Allard. He didn't like him any more than he ever had, but he kept going back to see him two and three times a week.

The rest home was one of those hot-looking Spanish-Mediterranean things that had been built during the twenties, wrought iron balconies, hollow-tiled roof, tall narrow windows. It had a tremendous tailored lawn, like a golf course. Allard was sitting in the shade of a royal poinciana reading the *Wall Street Journal*. His skin had no more vitality in it than suet. He was obviously not well. He barely nodded at Dixon and, nodding back, Dixon took the other chair under the tree.

"I suppose you're broke again," Allard said sourly.

"I was never broke when I had the *Madame*. I was always chartered a week or more in advance. I never had to stand around on the dock with my hand out," Dixon spoke without heat. "When I get my boat you can kiss me goodby. What's the hitch?"

"Widlund's still looking. You know that."

Widlund was the snotty naval architect, or whatever he was.

"What's he looking *with*, a jeweler's glass?"

"You're a little hard to please, Captain," Allard sneered. "We'd be afraid to offer you just any old boat."

"You haven't offered me anything yet."

"How can we? The boat you want doesn't exist. They don't make them with solid gold anchors these days or diamond studded toilet seats. We're doing our best under the circumstances."

"Show me a real boat. That's all you have to do."

"You mean you'll actually be satisfied with something less than the *Queen Mary?*"

Dixon looked at him. Allard was more vinegarish today than he had ever been, more sarcastic and yet at the same time, more uneasy. He kept fiddling with his newspaper and looking away. There was something on his mind.

"Thinking of calling it off?" Dixon asked.

Allard mumbled, "How can I? We're trying to find you a boat. Do you need any money?"

"No."

"I'll call Widlund later. I'll tell him to find you something within the week." Then, heavily, "I suppose you've still got that ... gun."

"I've still got it. I'll give it to you when I get the boat."

Allard wet his lips. "I don't believe you," he said.

"That's up to you."

"You hate me."

"No. I did but I don't now."

"When you get your boat, you'll turn me over to the police anyway."

"Oh hell."

"You'll do it because you think you're so damned honest."

"I won't even answer that, it's so damned silly. Call Widlund and tell him to have something to show me by the end of the week."

He got up and walked toward the Caddy parked beside the building. He didn't hate Allard. That was all over. If there was any hate, it was all on Allard's side. It had been particularly bad today. It was getting worse. Well, it would soon be over. Let Widlund come up with anything fairly decent and it would be all over there and then.

He killed a few hours in a bar on the Dixie Highway, chewed some chlorophyll gum, and went to pick Helen up. She must have been watching for him for she walked out to the curb from the entrance of her apartment when he drew up. She looked very blonde and very lovely, but when she got into the car and he leaned across the seat to kiss her, he saw the discolorations under her eyes and the tired lines at the ends of her mouth.

"You're worn out, you poor kid," he said contritely. "Where would you like to eat?"

"Anywhere. I'm not hungry."

"How about Lagois'? It's very quiet."

"All right."

It was a silent drive. He was still thinking about Allard and he couldn't tell Helen about that. At the restaurant, when they had their table, she said suddenly, "I will have a drink. A double scotch."

"Fine. We'll both have one."

"You've already had a few, haven't you?"

Dixon told the waiter to bring two double scotches and then said good-naturedly, "Now let's not start the evening that way, honey."

"But you have been drinking, haven't you?"

"Just a couple, and you can't call that drinking."

"I want to ask you something, Frank."

"Go ahead."

"How long are you going to go on sponging off that man?"

"As soon as I get my boat, honey ..."

"But in the meantime, you'll go right on sponging."

"It's not sponging."

"What is it then? We've gone out every night for two weeks. You've spent hundreds of dollars. I don't like it, Frank. I don't like the way you seem content to let him go on giving you money. What's happened to you? You never took charity from anybody."

"It's not charity," said Dixon angrily.

"Do you think he *owes* it to you? Do you think you have a right to it?"

"He owed me four hundred dollars. A month's salary."

"You've spent double that. You've spent more than double that."

"It's only a kind of loan …"

"Please, Frank, don't *lie!* It isn't any kind of loan. A loan is something you have to pay back and you don't spend a loan the way you've been spending money."

The waiter came with their drinks and she stopped talking until he went away.

Dixon said quickly, "I'm getting my boat by the end of the week."

"And I was just coming to the boat, too. Why should you accept a boat from him? You didn't do anything that any decent person wouldn't have done."

"I've been thinking about that myself. I'm going to give him a note for the value of the boat."

"You're lying again."

"All right goddamn it, come with me when I do it, see it with your own eyes. Will that satisfy you?"

She stood. "I don't know. I'll have to think about it. I don't even recognize you any more, Frank. You're somebody else and I don't think I like you very much."

"Good Lord," he shouted, "I just said I'd give him a note, didn't I? What more do you want me to do?"

The other diners turned to look at him and a waiter came hurrying toward the table. Helen said dully, "I'll think about it, Frank," and walked out.

The waiter hovered anxiously. "Is everything all right, sir?"

Dixon gulped the rest of his drink and pushed out his empty glass. "Bring me another one of these." He thought angrily, the hell with her.

He drank several more scotches and left without having dinner. He went back to his room in the hotel and started drinking cognac. He took just one drink and in sudden revulsion, went into the bathroom and emptied the bottle down the toilet. It wasn't the hell with Helen at all. She was what he wanted. What else was there? The boat? She was right.

I'm drunk, he thought, don't try to think when you're drunk.

He called room service and ordered a pot of black coffee. He took a cold shower. He drank the coffee when it came and afterward went downstairs and had something to eat. He was fairly sober when he went to bed.

The next morning there was a telegram for him from Allard. It said tersely, "We have a boat for you."

Dixon laughed. He was feeling very good. Allard was going to fall over. He washed and shaved and drove out to the rest home. Allard was sitting alone under the same poinciana tree.

Dixon said, "I'm going to give you a note for whatever you spend on the boat."

"Very interesting."

"I mean it. All I want from you is a loan. I'm going to pay you back. I don't want anything for nothing."

Allard looked up with sour suspicion. Dixon laughed.

"You'll see," he said.

Allard grunted in disbelief. "This boat," he said, "may not be everything you demanded, but it's a very good one."

"Since I'm going to pay for it myself, I may not be able to afford it. Where is it?"

"The boat belongs to a man named Jorgenson. Here's his address. He'll wait for you until noon if you're interested."

Dixon took the slip of paper. Jorgenson lived in Sanibar about thirty miles south of Miami. "I hope he doesn't want too much for it," he said.

Allard said angrily, "I'm not interested in your jokes."

"It's not a joke."

Allard opened his newspaper and held it up in front of his face. Dixon went back to the Caddy. He was grinning. You'll see, he thought, you'll see.

He wanted to call Helen but he thought it best to wait until everything was almost settled. She'd see, too. It took him a little over a half hour to drive to Sanibar. He stopped at a gas station and the attendant told him the Jorgenson place was a half mile down the beach.

"You can't miss it," he said. "It's the only house down there. But I don't think Mr. Jorgenson's back from South America yet. I haven't seen his car."

"He's expecting me so he must be back."

"Must be," the attendant said doubtfully.

Dixon found the house quite easily but when he stopped at the end of the driveway he saw that the windows were boarded up. He must just have got back, he thought. He ran up on the porch and pressed the doorbell. The door opened.

"Come right in," said Addams, pointing his gun at Dixon's chest.

He walked backward and Dixon followed him into the house as if mesmerized. Addams looked unnaturally intent.

"You're surprised to see me," he said.

Dixon said nothing. Somehow or other, he was not surprised.

Addams said, "Another boat came to the island the day after you left. Natives. They were looking for the boat you used. I told them I hadn't seen it. I told them I had been on my way north from Puerto Rico when my schooner went down. I had the dinghy hidden by that time and they had no way of knowing I was off the *Almacor*."

"You know," Dixon said, "Wirt used to say that when it was all over, you'd end up in Miami with money in your pocket and a hundred dollar blonde on your arm. How right he was."

"He was smart. You weren't."

Until that very moment, Dixon had actually thought that Addams was merely after the gun that had killed Wirt, and then he was incredulous that he could have been so naive. Neither Allard nor Addams could ever have been satisfied with so little.

Addams and Allard. How they complemented each other. Addams, the perfect blackmailer. Allard would never get rid of Addams. Addams would feed on him like a cancer. But someday Allard would figure out how to get rid of him too. How they *deserved* each other.

Something like a laugh was beginning in Dixon's throat when Addams pushed the gun into his face and fired.

THE END

A Party Every Night

FREDERICK LORENZ

Chapter One

The girl came from the shower, her skin red and blotchy from the rough toweling she had given it in her anger. She glanced at the bed. The lean, sandy-haired man was still asleep. He was lying on his side with his right arm curled under the pillow as if to give his head more support, for his shoulders were very wide. His lips moved and she bent over him, scowling when his muttering made no sense to her. Then she remembered that someone had told her that a sleep-talker will answer if you put the question right, and she leaned closer, almost touching his face.

"What was that, Van?" she whispered. "I didn't hear you."

He mumbled again and turned his face deeper into the pillow. She straightened up, looking at him with smoldering resentment.

"Oh, go to hell," she said.

She turned angrily and walked across the room to the chair into which her clothes had been so recklessly thrown the night before. She dressed very quickly, as if afraid that nudity somehow diminished her.

There was a mirror over the chest of drawers at the side of the room, and she stood before it and sullenly combed her thick, tawny hair and made up her face. She used a lot of make-up, especially lipstick, the color of which was much too dark for her medium blondeness. Intent on only herself for the moment, her face became a little less glowering as she stepped back to appraise the result. She used the tip of her finger to spread the lipstick more evenly. She was about to put the lipstick back into her red plastic handbag when the man moved on the bed and the mattress squeaked under his weight. She looked at him and the resentment seeped back into her face. Re-opening her lipstick, she turned back to the mirror and printed on it with sharp, angry strokes:

YOU CAN
KEEP YOUR
GODDAM LINA!

She snatched up her red handbag and walked out of the room, slamming the door behind her. Van stirred on the bed again but did not awaken.

In fact, it was not until three in the afternoon that he opened his eyes and immediately closed them again, grimacing at the stab of light. He had a hangover. He kept his eyes closed, but it didn't do any good. There was a heavy pounding in his head, particularly behind his left eye, and finally he rolled out of bed and stumbled into the bathroom. He turned on the shower and stood under it with his head bent forward so that the hard fingers of hot water could massage the back of his neck. He stood like that until the water began to cool, and then he turned it to full *cold* and forced himself to take that for another few minutes. When he stepped out of the shower, he had begun to throw off the hangover. He dried himself briskly and hung the sodden towel over the edge of the sink. He looked into the mirror and rubbed his hand across his chin, deciding against a shave until after at least a cup of coffee. He brushed his teeth, making a face at the sweetish, minty flavor of the toothpaste. Then he stretched and worked his arms back and forth to loosen the neck and shoulder muscles. He felt much better when he walked back into the other room.

He started to dress, then changed his mind and went to the chest of drawers for his swimming trunks. He stopped when he saw the lipsticked message on the mirror, and that was the first he remembered the girl, and he muttered, "Oh, God!" Up until that time, he had not thought of the night before at all. *Oh, brother*, he thought. *Cora*. Now he remembered closing the Pelican Lounge, switching off the lights, locking the doors, after first putting the night's receipts in the safe under the bar, of course. Then he walked around to the parking lot behind the Lounge, and there she was, standing beside her old '38 Ford, swearing. Some drunken comedian had let the air out of all four tires, and at two in the morning there weren't any service stations open.

"Forget it, Cora," he told her. "I'll take you home."

She was the waitress in the Lounge.

She got in the car. "I'll bet it was that lousy Carl Stover," she said furiously. "He tried to date me and I brushed him off. I'll fix that son-of-a-bitch."

"It could have been almost anybody, Cora," he said, trying to pacify her. "Drunks have a funny sense of humor. I don't think Carl'd do a thing like that."

"I'll find out, and if he did, I'll let him have it right in the teeth."

"How's about a drink? I think we should buy ourselves one for a change. Okay?"

"You're not kidding."

So, he had driven her over to Dick's Bar, an all-night joint in the palmetto east of the Tamiami Trail, about a mile up the old Hammermill

Road. Dick's was nominally a beer-and-wine bar, but you could get a glass of good 'shine if Dick knew you and liked you. 'Shine was thirty-five cents a shot, served in a wine glass. It had a slightly oily flavor, but after the first drink you didn't mind. After the first drink, you didn't mind anything. There were a pine bar and some rickety booths at the side of the room, and behind the bar there were a lot of signs, like, *We Got An Agreement With the Bank; They Don't Serve Beer, And We Don't Cash Checks*; and, *Don't Ask For Credit, You No Pay, I Get Mad, I No Give, You Get Mad, Damsite Better You Get Mad.* And so forth.

They had taken a stool at the bar and had a drink of 'shine. He felt a warm glow as it took hold.

"That does the job," he said.

"You're not kidding."

"A refill?"

"Twist my arm."

The second drink went down much easier than the first, and Cora leaned her elbow on the bar and looked at him.

"You know something," she said, "you're okay."

"Well, thanks."

"And you know something else? When I first seen you behind the bar, I said to myself, woo-woo, what a hunk a man!"

"Woo-woo."

"But I changed my mind."

"Why?"

"You was snotty."

"Me?"

"You're not kidding. I come up to the bar, I give you the drink order, and what do you give me? The brush-off."

"What do you mean, the brush-off? I never gave you the brush-off."

"The hell you didn't. I don't mean there was something you did, but you kind of looked at me like you was thinking—Drop dead, slob. Like that. Know what I mean?"

"You're wrong, Cora."

"Sure, sure. I admit it. I changed my mind back again. You're okay. It was just your way, I guess. You never gave me a rumble. Maybe that was it, huh?"

"I'm sorry you feel that way, honey. It was just that I was busy."

"I know, I know. I said you was okay, didn't I? You're okay. I mean it. You're okay, and I take it all back. And you know what? I used to think you was a wolf."

"A wolf!"

"You're not kidding. It was like this. A guy gets plotzed and drives off and leaves his wife, and nine times out a ten you take her home in your jalopy, and every time I seen you do it, I think to myself—oh-oh, Van's getting his tonight."

He laughed. "You couldn't be wronger," he said.

"You mean you took them home and didn't get nothing out of it?"

"Right."

"Brother," she said, "you must be slow on the uptake or something. Some a them babes, you could hear them sizzle. And you mean to tell me you took them home and that's all?"

"Just a Southern gentleman at heart," he grinned.

"You're not kidding," and then she looked beyond him and her expression changed. "Be right back," she said.

He thought she was going to the john, but she crossed the room and stopped at one of the booths, leaned in and swung her arm. There was a laugh and a big, dark-haired man surged up, holding her wrist. Carl Stover. She tried to pull away, but he held her, still laughing.

"Don't be like that, baby," he said. "I came back for you, but you went."

"You bastard!" she said.

She brought up her knee, but he blocked it with his thigh, pulled her close and kissed her. She must have bitten him, because he swore, shoved her back against the side of the booth and clapped his hand to his mouth. Vance could see the blood on his chin. Stover swore again, and brought his arm around in a back-hander that sprawled her into the adjoining booth. Vance leaped from his stool. Stover saw him coming and swung a mauling fist at his head. Vance slipped inside the punch and hit him once, hard, on the point of the chin. The big man staggered, fell heavily and did not move again. A little late, Dick came running over with a two-foot length of garden hose that had been loaded with sand and plugged at both ends.

There was another man in the booth, but he sat absolutely motionless as if afraid the slightest movement would bring him the same that Stover had gotten.

Dick looked at him and said, "Take that jerk outa here and don't neither a you come back." He patted Vance's shoulder. "You can stay, pal. He ast for it."

Vance went back to the bar with Cora. She didn't seem hurt.

"Man-o-man," she said admiringly, "you sure creamed that son-of-a-bitch. What a smack!"

Dick came down the bar and poured each of them another drink of 'shine.

"That was some clout, pal," he said to Vance. "You musta been in the ring or something."

Vance shook his head and said quickly, "I just caught him right, that's all."

"Don't give me that, pal. I go to the fights every Friday, and I seen how you slipped inside that hook and let him have it. I bet you didn't swing more'n eight inches. You been in the ring, all right."

"Not me."

"Then you should be. You're a natural."

"He really cooled him, didn't he, Dick!" Cora said, laughing and looking excited. "He sure poured it in there."

"He sure did. That poor jerk won't be able to eat steak for a month. Don't tell me you wasn't in the ring, pal. You done that just a little too slick for an accident."

Dick stood there for about ten minutes, trying to argue Vance into admitting that he had been in the ring, and during that time he poured them another drink on the house. Cora was excited and kept feeling his arm muscles and saying, "What a smack!"

By the time Vance had five drinks of 'shine, he was feeling it. He had been off the liquor for over a month, and 'shine was pretty strong stuff. Things started getting a little hazy.

He remembered being out in the car with Cora and her being very exciting and desirable and soft-thighed. This was pretty hazy, but he remembered snatches of it, particularly coaxing her to come to his apartment with him. He winced at that part of it. He remembered lying on the bed and her standing in the middle of the room, throwing her clothes into the lounge chair at the window and becoming dimmer and dimmer, as if the light were fading. That was all. He must have blacked out, because he could not remember a single thing after that.

And now he stood in front of the mirror, reading the message she had printed on the glass with her lipstick. YOU CAN KEEP YOUR GODDAM LINA. He scowled. What the hell was that supposed to mean? Unless Cora noticed ... but no, he'd kept hands strictly off, and besides, he'd never mentioned her by name.

But whatever had happened, Cora had walked out sore, and he felt a definite sense of relief. Not that he had anything against her—she was all right—but he just didn't want to get mixed up with her, that was all.

But what a night!

Well, you had to let yourself go once in a while.

He walked downstairs and got his car from the parking lot behind the apartment and drove to the beach, about a mile below the municipal bathing area where all the tourists went. The sun was still hot and the Gulf of Mexico spread smoothly to the horizon, a deeper blue than the sky. Dumpy cabbage palms hunched along the rim of the beach, and over them a long line of pelicans drifted southward, scarcely moving their wings. Vance sat for a few minutes and watched, letting the peace of it seep into him. Then he sprinted across the beach and hit the water in a shallow dive. He swam out into the Gulf for about a half-mile, and then he turned on his back and floated, closing his eyes against the glare of the sun. The heat soaked into him, and after a while he swam slowly back to shore. He trotted about a thousand yards down the beach to dry off, turned at the clump of sea grape and ran back, sprinting the last hundred yards. He was breathing a little heavily, but not panting, when he reached the car. He was still in pretty good shape. He looked at the clock in the dashboard. It was five, and he had to be on duty behind the bar at six. He brushed the sand from his feet, slid into the seat and stepped on the starter.

Chapter Two

Hully paused at the window and bent over the pail of steaming, soapy water to wring out the mop in his huge hands, but his real purpose was to glance around the bar to make sure no one was watching him. There were no customers this early in the morning, and a clatter from the kitchen told him that Tate was out there, making a pot of coffee. He dropped the mop into the pail and straightened up, quickly snatching a round can of snuff from his shirt pocket. In the window stood a long narrow glass tank, in which swam about twenty goldfish and a large number of guppies. Hully twisted the top from the can and sprinkled a thick pinch of snuff into the tank. He leaned forward intently as the fish darted toward the drifting gray specks, then pursed up his mouth with disappointment when they refused to take it.

"Aaah, go to hell," he said.

It had been going on for quite a while, this thing between him and the fish, and he had experimented with different ways of annoying them—soap, dirt from the floor, spittle, shredded cigarette butts, and once he had poured a glass of beer into the tank. The fish had acted a little funny for a while, but in a very short time they were swimming around as serene and indifferent as usual. Every morning he stopped at the tank to wring out his mop and glance warily around the bar, and every day he tried something on the fish, but so far he had not managed to bother them at all, except possibly for the beer and he was not at all sure they hadn't actually enjoyed that. So, it had come to the point where it was the fish that irritated and baffled *him*.

He really had nothing against the fish, except that they had it so easy. They really had the life, those goddam fish, and what good were they? They didn't even catch flies. But once a day they got fed and they had a nice big tank of lukewarm water to swim around in and down at the bottom was a little cement castle with doors and windows they could swim in and out of, and not a worry in the world. On the other hand, when he was finished cleaning up, Hully could sit entranced and watch them for hours, they were such pretty colors in the sunlight and they moved so slow and graceful, prettier even than birds. There had been a black one with long, lacy fins, and he had been unable to resist scooping it from the water and holding it in his cupped hand, but he had held it too long and it had died. He hadn't squeezed it or anything, but when he put it back into the tank, it just floated on its side. Tate found it later and swore, because the fish had cost five dollars. Hully laughed silently to himself. Imagine paying five dollars for a fish. Hell, for four-ninety-five you could get a wristwatch at the drugstore in Sanibar. Anyway, it was a lot of malarkey. Tate was always saying he paid twice as much for something, and all the time crabbing about it, but he didn't fool Hully for a minute. Tate owned the place and he was making the money hand over fist. That was why Hully had laughed over the dead fish. He hoped it *had* cost Tate five dollars.

He watched the disregarded snuff slowly settle through the water and with another glance toward the kitchen, he spat into the tank. When Tate came out with his cup of coffee, Hully was mopping under the tables ten feet from the fish and on his face was his usual expression of good-natured stupidity, though he knew that any minute Tate would start his "come on, come on, get a move on," the way he did every morning. That lousy Tate, he sure liked to keep you hopping. Tate snapped the expected command and Hully worked a little faster for a few minutes, mumbling, "Yessir, Mr. Tate, yessir, yessir, yessiree."

"You damn crackers don't move an inch faster than you have to, do you?"

"I'm moving now, Mr. Tate."

"When I keep after you, sure."

"I'll have it mopped up in no time."

"See that you do or I'll get somebody else."

Hully had heard this threat many times before, but always he was terrified that Tate might mean it. He did not want to get fired. He did not want to work any other place than here in Tate's Pelican Lounge. There were lots of jobs around, but here there was the juke box and dancing and laughing and Vance cutting up behind the bar, sometimes playing the uke and singing, and everybody cracking jokes and having a good time. It was a party every night, practically. Nothing could be worse than getting fired.

Hully worked still faster, making more noise than progress, watching Tate from the ends of his eyes, but Tate had lost interest in him and was tying on a white apron, preparatory to washing glasses. Hully did not realize that there was very little chance of his being fired. No one else would have worked sixteen hours a day for the pay he was getting. He didn't have to work that long, but he came in at night and carried in ice and bottled beer when Vance got too busy behind the bar, and helped with anything else that came up, because there was always something doing at night, always that big noisy party, and every once in a while Vance would slip him a drink when Tate wasn't looking. Why, you couldn't hardly call it a job at all.

He took the pail into the kitchen to refill it, and when he set it under the faucet, Tate yelled in at him, "Take it easy with the hot water, dammit. Hot water costs money. You don't need it boiling to mop floors."

"Yessir, Mr. Tate," Hully said cheerfully. "I'm taking it easy."

While the pail was filling, he looked up at the calendar over the sink. It was from a plumbing company and it showed a naked babe sitting on a cushion, painting her toenails. Hully had looked at it every day for months and he was familiar with every line and curve, but whenever he went into the kitchen, that was the first place he looked. Man-o-man, he thought. But there was nothing he could do—it was only a picture—and when he went back into the other room with his pail, he shot a venomous glance at the goldfish and thought about slipping a little ammonia into their water. Tomorrow, when Tate wasn't around.

There was a customer standing at the bar, a big heavy man, almost as big as Hully himself. He was one of the regulars, in and out during the day, and two or three times at night during the week with his wife. The wife, though, there was a babe. A redhead like the babe on the calendar. Nossir, a man wouldn't have no complaints about her, no complaints at all.

"Morning, Mr. Elwood," Hully greeted him. "How's the wife?"

Elwood said, "Fine, fine," and as he raised his glass, the large diamond on his right hand blazed in the shaft of sunlight.

It was for just an instant, like a lightning flash, but it seemed to Hully that every color in the world had filled the room with brilliance. He had never seen anything like it. He had seen the ring before, but it had never caught the light in just that way. It was a pretty ring with the big diamond in the middle and two red stones on each side, but he had never even dreamed that such fire and color lived in it, had never imagined such magic. He wanted to ask Elwood to repeat the gesture so he could see that flame again, but Tate was giving him such a sour look that he took his pail up the room and resumed his mopping. At first he couldn't get it out of his mind, but then gradually he forgot it and listened to the conversation between the two men.

"... expenses," Tate was griping. "Listen, I pay my bartender alone a hundred and a quarter a week. Since when is a bartender worth a hundred and a quarter? Tell me that."

"I don't know, Vance is a damn good barkeep."

"But is he worth a hundred and a quarter a week?"

"People go to a place where they like the barkeep."

"That's just it. Blackmail. If I let him go, maybe he takes some of my trade with him to another place, so I got to keep paying him a hundred and a quarter a week, even though I can get a good bartender, the best, for eighty a week. Is that right? Is that fair?"

"That's your problem, I guess."

"And on top of that," Tate said indignantly, "he won't take care of the tables, so I got to hire a waitress at forty-five a week. Where do I come off, with expenses like that? Where's my profit?"

His voice became more hectoring, and Hully stopped listening. He was bored. He had heard all this too many times before, and anyway, Mr. Tate would never fire Vance. Vance had too many friends. Everybody liked Vance. Thinking about that, Hully felt very warm and happy because Vance was *his* particular friend. But suppose Mr. Tate *did* fire Vance! Hully's eyes became fierce. He'd fix Mr. Tate if that ever happened. He'd fix him good. He thought of all the things he could do. He remembered how mad Mr. Tate had been the time the beer compressor broke down. Ha. That'd be the first thing. He'd whop that old beer compressor so hard they'd never put it together again. But that'd only be the first thing. There were lots of other things and, thinking about them, he began to feel good again. He went outside to wash the windows. Later, he would stretch out in the storeroom and take a nap, but what he was really waiting for was nightfall and the party and the noise and the fun ...

Chapter Three

There was seldom much doing in the bar between six and seven, and this gave Vance a chance to get things shaped up for the night—fill the cooler with bottled beer, lay in the ice cubes, make simple syrup from club soda and sugar, squeeze up the fruit juice, and slice the lemons, limes, and oranges for the fancy drinks. Tate never left him more than just barely enough to get by on during that first slow hour. Actually, Tate should have left things stocked up and ready to go, but he never did, and Vance had to work his head off to get set.

It was deliberate, of course. Tate had all the time in the world during the afternoon to do the chores, and it wasn't that he was lazy or preferred to beat his gums with the customers. No, this was his way of making Vance earn that hundred and a quarter he paid him every week.

And he makes tips on top of that, yet! Tate had told Elwood indignantly.

Vance knew all about it. He knew the whole song and dance. The bar was really a Wailing Wall during the day when Tate was behind it. He was a real schmo. He had the soul of a mouse being forced to share the last ounce of cheese on earth. Vance grinned when he thought of Tate's weekly agony when he had to hand over that hundred and a quarter. It was blood, every penny of it.

And to tell the truth, Vance was glad to have something to do during that creeping first hour. He hated a bar where you had to stand around and watch the front door, hoping somebody would walk in. But he'd never breathe a word of that or he'd walk in tomorrow and the place would be stocked for a week.

There was one customer at the bar, hunched on his stool and staring morosely at a bottle of Bud.

"Hi, Jimmy," said Vance, putting on his white mess jacket. "Who died?"

Jimmy pulled at his ear. "It's bleeding."

Vance laughed. He knew what Jimmy meant. Tate had talked his ear off. Tate talked everybody's ear off. He was a real sharp barkeep, all right. Vance took a deck of cards from under the bar.

"Shuffle them, Jimmy, and I'll show you how to get rid of your mother-in-law."

Jimmy shuffled the cards and placed the deck on the bar. Vance put a napkin over the deck, reached under it and snapped his finger and the queen of spades flew into Jimmy's lap. He did a couple more tricks with a running patter, and when he finished, Jimmy was laughing and had bought another bottle of beer. Tate watched from the kitchen door and never cracked a smile, and in fact seemed on the verge of asking waspishly if that was all Vance had to do with his time. Poor old schmo, Vance thought. He'd never learn that it wasn't liquor that brought people into a bar, it was the kind of time they had while drinking it.

Vance said, "You may now resume your nap, Jimmy," and walked back to the storeroom.

Hully was sitting on a case of Seagram's, eating a Hershey bar. He was wearing a pink and green sport shirt, and his hair had been watered and raked back with his fingers. Hully always dressed up for the evening.

"Well, well," said Vance, "if it isn't Hully, the well-dressed man."

Hully grinned happily and held up the Hershey bar. "Have a bite, Vance?"

"Just save me the nuts. How's about giving me a hand with some beer and ice."

"Sure, Vance, sure. Anytime. You know me."

He would have been unhappy if Vance had not asked him. He carried in six cases of beer and several buckets of ice cubes while Vance sliced fruit, made juice, and all the rest of it, working very rapidly. Hully stacked the beer in the cooler the way Vance had shown him, keeping the brands separate—Schlitz, Bud, High Life, Pabst, and then two Florida beers, Tropical and Regal. He did this with care because it was for Vance and not Tate. When he finished, Vance slipped him a bottle of Tropical, his favorite.

"I don't know what I'd do without you, Hully."

"Anytime, Vance. Just ask. You know me. And say ..." he put his open hand at right angles to the side of his mouth, the confidential gesture, and whispered, "anybody starts anything with you out here tonight, just call me. I'll bust'm."

Vance grinned and felt Hully's granite arm muscle and whistled. This was routine and he did it because it pleased Hully. "You really could, couldn't you."

"You bet. I can bust anybody."

Hully walked back to the storeroom, holding the bottle of beer under his sport shirt so Tate wouldn't spot it and get Vance in trouble. Five minutes later, he was back, asking Vance if there was anything else he could do, and it wasn't just the beer that made him so affectionate. He liked Vance. Vance made him feel good. He wanted to do things for Vance. But Vance was getting close to the seven o'clock deadline, when the bar would start to fill up, and he still had more juice to squeeze and the simple syrup to make, nothing for Hully's powerful but inexperienced hands.

Hully stood there glumly for a minute and then wandered into the kitchen and asked Tate if he could feed the goldfish. Tate was busily making hamburger patties for the evening trade. He tended bar during the day and did all the cooking at night. As a matter of fact, he really enjoyed the cooking, fussing over the stove, garnishing the hamburgers and sandwiches with vegetables and relishes of his own invention, and consequently the Pelican Lounge had a reputation for the best hamburger north of Miami on the west coast. He had a hamburger mold into which he pressed the chopped beef with a spatula, slicing it off evenly from the top, for every ounce of beef he bought had to pay its way. Peevishly, he told Hully not to bother him, but Hully was used to this.

"Them goldfish oughta be fed, Mr. Tate. You just can't let them goldfish go hungry."

"I'll feed them myself!"

"But you're so busy, I thought maybe I could feed them for you tonight."

Tate swore thinly, but reached up to the shelf over the refrigerator and gave Hully a small can of goldfish food.

"Now don't give them the whole thing, you dumb ox. Just what you can take between two fingers."

"Oh, sure. I know how to feed the goldfish, Mr. Tate."

"All right, all right, all right. Just what you can take between two fingers. That stuff costs money."

"That's right, Mr. Tate. It costs money. I'll watch myself."

Cupping the small, round can in his hands, he walked outside to the goldfish bowl in the window. He knew Tate was watching him, so he put only one pinch of food into the tank and elaborately replaced the lid on the can and put the can into his pocket. That, he knew, would satisfy Tate. Then he bent over the tank as if watching the fish eat their evening meal and dropped one gob of spittle after another into the water, screening the operation from the kitchen with the width of his tremendous shoulders.

Cora came in at seven. Tate had tried to get her to come in at six, but she had told him what to do with the job. He had looked at her and had seen not only an experienced waitress, but also a full-bodied girl who knew that there was more to milking a tip than mere service, even if it took a pat on the cheek and a hint and a promise. So, he let her come in at seven. There was no trade before that, anyway. She came in the front door, pointedly ignored Vance, and went into the back room beyond the johns, where she changed into her uniform. There were several customers at the bar when she came out, and Vance was talking and laughing with two of them, a man and woman, and he was doing a card trick and traveling salesman story in which the red queens always kept turning up with the black kings. She did not look directly at them, but watched vindictively from the ends of her eyes. She made a contemptuous noise in her throat and turned away. Show-off, that's all he was, a show-off. Hully was bent over the goldfish tank, and she pretended a great interest in him, and for the first time she really saw the shoulders on him and she thought, my God, the muscles! Vance grinned at her and waved, and she turned her back with a twitch of her hips. *Creep!*

A party of four came in and took a booth. She went up to them, all smiles, holding her pad and pencil—but at the same time, quickly appraising the two men. One was fat and bald and had a pot—a jerk; the other was youngish and had false teeth and a sidelong eye. She directed her smile at him. He'd be a good tipper. They wanted hamburgers and—after a short argument pro and con about coffee—beer. She walked away from the table, rolling her hips, knowing that the young one with false teeth was watching.

"Four burgers *with*," she called at Tate in the kitchen, and then went down to the service part of the bar, enclosed by two high curving chromium bars, and set down her tray. "Four Schlitz."

Vance brought her the four bottles, capped with six ounce glasses. There was nobody around, because people didn't sit near the service bar till things got crowded. Vance grinned at her.

"What was the telegram you wrote on my mirror with lipstick?" he asked.

"Go to hell."

"I don't get it."

"You're not kidding."

"What's that supposed to mean?"

"The way you sounded, you wasn't getting it. That's what I mean."

"Come again?"

She looked contemptuously at him. "Lina wasn't giving."

"But who's Lina?"

"You should know. You was talking about her in your sleep all last night."

He grinned, turning on the charm. He didn't want any friction. "Wait a minute. I'm beginning to remember. When I was a kid, I had a dog. It was sort of guitar color with white spots and ..."

"Go to hell."

She took her tray and walked back to the booth with it. She gave the first beer to the youngish one with the false teeth, leaning into him just a little but not too much when she reached across to set the second bottle in front of the skinny bag, obviously his wife the way she yapped. He was the kind that tipped the best if you gave him the treatment. She felt him drop his right arm, not to feel her but to let her leaning cover a more tactile area, and suddenly there was in her a poignant sense of loneliness. She didn't want any more of this. She didn't want any more of this at all. She was tired of it, tired, tired, tired! She wouldn't even care if she was a skinny old bag like that one, just so long as she was married to a guy and he was taking care of her and she didn't have to wait on tables, or make an effort. She stepped back from the table.

"Anything else, folks?"

The youngish one tried to be a comedian, the way they all did, but his wife cut him short, and Cora walked away, feeling bleak.

The customers were coming in steadily now, and by ten o'clock the Pelican Lounge was humming like a machine shop under full production, the rhythm established and constant. There were the voices, masculine and feminine, blending in ordinary talk and argument and laughter, the foundation for the other noises that rose above it from time to time. Occasionally a piercing individual laugh could be identified, just as the sudden and shattering screech of a metal saw could be identified above the pound and thud of the heavier machines, but all in all the beat had been made and the pace set, and it would go on like that until closing.

It was nearly midnight when Wes Elwood came in with his wife, a slim red-headed girl whom everybody called Maddie. Wes was one of the regulars, and he came in almost every night, sometimes with Maddie, but most of the time without her. He was a big, fleshy man, usually a little drunk. The minute they walked in, Vance saw that they were in the midst of one of their periodic spats. Maddie's face was cold and set, and Wes looked petulant. They sat at the bar without speaking, Maddie staring straight ahead and Wes stolidly polishing his big diamond ring with his handkerchief. Vance pretended not to notice and greeted them cheerfully. Wes ordered a double bourbon.

"Why not make it a triple?" said Maddie bitterly. "Why not a quadruple or a quintuple? Why bother with a glass at all? Think of all the time you can save drinking right out of the bottle."

"A double for me and a mickey for the lady," said Wes.

Vance winked at Maddie. "How would you like your mickey," he asked, "with an olive, an onion, or lemon peel?"

That was one way of doing it—turn it inside out and let them laugh at it. He never interfered in family fights, but he usually tried to kid them out of it obliquely before they started throwing pretzel bowls at each other. Not the Elwoods. They never threw things or raised their voices, but somehow or other their fights made Vance feel worse than the noisy ones did. He did not care about Wes so much, but there was a melancholy in the way Maddie's smooth, high-boned face froze up when she was angry.

"On the other hand," he said, "our special mickey comes with Scotch on the side, but you have to watch them. They sneak up on you."

Maddie looked at him, her face still tight, and then unexpectedly she laughed. "With Scotch," she said. "I'll have my mickey with Scotch. I'd love to have something sneak up on me tonight instead of falling on my shoulder and snoring in my ear, the way it does other nights."

"Very funny," said Wes heavily, not looking at her. "Van's in stitches."

"I've been in stitches for years," Vance pulled up the sleeve of his white jacket and showed them a short criss-crossed scar on his forearm. "I had the mumps once and couldn't laugh, so I had this done so I could show the people how much I enjoyed their jokes. I'm always in stitches."

Maddie said, "Oh, no, Van!" in mock protest. "You can do better than that."

"Did we order a drink or didn't we?" Wes demanded. He was beginning to turn nasty, the way most rummies did when the drinks didn't come fast enough. "Come on, get it up."

Vance said, "Aye, aye, sir," and went up the bar, knowing that Wes was really going to tie one on tonight. He had that sullen, dogged look. Nobody was going to stop him, and especially not Maddie.

After his second double bourbon, Wes went to the piano, an old Baldwin that Tate had gotten cheaply, painted apple-green and set up on a small platform with a baby spot in the ceiling over it. It was a bright spot in the neon-lighted cave that the Lounge became after dark. Wes was really very drunk, but his hands had a sober life of their own, and his big diamond flashed and sparkled as his thick fingers raced up and down the keyboard.

Someone said humorously, "Well, he might not be the best pianist in the world, but he certainly is the fastest."

By this time, the usual number of singing drunks were hanging on the edges of the piano like old overcoats, begging Wes to play the old favorites like *That Old Gang of Mine* and *Let Me Call You Sweetheart*, which he did, but with a velocity that defied the human voice. The drunker he got, the faster he played.

The Pelican Lounge was L-shaped, the bar taking up the short shank, and the booths and tables the longer stem. In that part was the juke box and the dance floor. There were booths in the bar too, and Cora's post was at the angle of the two. She could not keep her eyes off Vance, and she seethed as she watched him laugh and joke with the customers.

It made her boil that he could do that after the way he had treated her last night, like she was nothing, and talking in his sleep about that other dame. But what she remembered most acutely was how he *had* turned to her during the night, and had caressed her, his fingers fleeing down her body, and then brutally had thrust her away, hurting her. And what had he said? "No, no, *no!*" Like she was dirt compared to this other dame. She wanted to hurt him. She wanted to dig her fingernails into the top of his face and drag them slowly down to his chin. She wanted to make him bleed and cry out, to match the low cry that was within herself, the terrible loneliness of pain, the bleakness of the unhealed and the bare bones of the unwanted and the death concealed in despair.

She noted jealously the attention he paid Maddie Elwood every time he had a break and how his face became electric and the wisecracks seemed to crackle out of him. She tensed. Maddie ... Maddie ... Her fingers curled tightly into her palms. Maddie, Madelina, *Lina!* The Lina he had been mumbling about in his sleep. She felt a sickness as if she had just been told of her own impending death and had been shown the X-rays of exactly how it would come about. In a moment of terrible truth, she realized that she could never compete with Maddie Elwood. Maddie had class, and she herself, she confessed dully, was nothing but a good-natured slob. That's me, she thought, a good-natured slob, and who wants it? She looked back over her shoulder. The youngish one with the false teeth and the skinny bag of a wife at the table of four was giving her the up-and-down from the side of his eyes, and the next time she served them, he'd probably pat her on the hip and pass it off with:

"That's real service, sweetheart. We appreciate service, don't we, Joe?"

And Joe, not being interested, would just grunt or say yeah—sure, and the jerk would get the mean-eyes from his wife and a bawling out in bed, and when they left, there'd be an exact ten percent tip because the jerk would be trying to cushion what he knew was coming.

And that was it, she thought from out of the years of awakening in the gray morning, that was just about it.

There was tired venom in her eyes when she looked at Vance and Maddie Elwood again.

This was about quarter of one, and Vance had a small break, all glasses filled. He was leaning on the bar in front of Maddie, and she was smiling and crinkling her eyes at him. The juke box was playing Tommy Dorsey's *I'm Getting Sentimental Over You*, and Wes Elwood was no longer at the piano. He was probably in the john, the amount of liquor he had drunk—four double bourbons plus what he'd had before he came into the Lounge. In the john and sick as a ruptured goat. People were dancing all over the place now, and especially in the darker corners where they could pretend that all they were doing was dancing, though at this hour nobody cared what anybody else was doing. Whenever Vance got a break, he spent it with Maddie. He was crazy about her.

"I'll tell you, Maddie," he was saying.

"*Please* don't call me Maddie. I hate it."

"Madelina."

"Everybody calls me Maddie and it's so ugly, like Lizzie or Maggie or Tillie."

"Madelina."

"I hate that too." Vance shrugged. He wished to hell she weren't married. It was just not in his book to make passes at another guy's wife, no matter how you felt about her. How many times had he talked about this very same thing over the bar to the local wolves.

"Maybe I'm simple-minded, but I believe in giving a guy every chance. Then if his wife still wants to play, let her divorce him. I sleep in my own bed and the woman with me has to be there a hundred percent and not on a fifty-fifty basis."

Someone rang a coin against a glass. "See you later, Maddie," he said quickly, and walked down the bar to make the drink.

He saw Hully sitting patiently in the doorway of the storeroom at the end of the bar and guiltily he remembered that the poor guy had been due for a drink over a half hour ago. He waved and told Hully to get another case of Schlitz for the cooler. Hully, he knew, liked to feel that he was being rewarded for doing a chore.

The bottled beer was in the big walk-in cooler outside, behind the storeroom. The moon was bright and full and Hully stood looking up at it. The big dappled disc made him uneasy. The stars he liked, they sparkled, but the moon when it was full gave him the feeling that something was hanging over his head and he didn't like to turn his back to it.

He walked toward the cooler and as he did, he heard somebody being sick in the patio beyond. That made him mad. He had to sweep the patio every morning and when somebody got sick in it, he had to scrub it with soap and water and get down on his knees with a brush. He strode angrily around the cooler, muttering to himself. Wes Elwood was leaning against the round cement table in the middle of the patio, heaving and groaning, hardly able to stand upright. Hully took him by the arm.

He started, "Aw right, Mr. Elwood, I'll take you—" and then that big diamond on Elwood's hand sparkled in the moonlight.

Elwood mumbled, "Wassamatta, wassamatta...."

Hully took his hand and started to work the ring from the finger. Drunk as he was, Elwood realized that he was being robbed and punched feebly at Hully's face. Annoyed, Hully hit him. He staggered and fell, striking the edge of the concrete table with the back of his head. He crumpled to the flagged floor of the patio. Hully bent over him and got the ring. He stood up and held it to the moon to make it sparkle. He smiled and turned it in his fingers, letting each facet catch the cold light and turn it into flaming brilliance. Then suddenly he realized that somebody might be watching, and he glanced furtively over his shoulder, shoving the ring into the pocket of his jeans. He walked hurriedly to the cooler and got out a case of Schlitz and took it into the bar. Vance gave him a slap on the shoulder and grinned, "My pal." That made Hully feel good, and he knelt on the floor and carefully stacked the bottles in their proper place. Vance slipped him a Tropical and Hully went into the storeroom to drink it, concealing it under his shirt so Tate wouldn't spot it and get Vance in trouble. That Vance, he was a swell guy, he was the tops, a fella you liked to do things for. Hully snapped the cap from the beer bottle with his teeth. He was proud of this trick, and he did it even when he was alone.

Some day he'd show it to Vance when Tate wasn't looking.

Vance was busy again. That was the way it went. It came in waves. Sometimes every glass on the bar was up, but the next minute they were all empty and he had to run his legs off, filling them. A good bartender never left anybody with an empty glass. It was three-quarters of an hour before he was able to stop in front of Maddie Elwood again. He had made up his mind to stay away from her but she raised her hand and beckoned to him.

"I think the Wonder Boy has passed out in the john," she said dryly. "That's his favorite spot at home. Would you mind taking a look, Van, just to make sure he isn't tangled up in the plumbing?"

"Sure thing, Maddie."

He went to the kitchen door and told Tate that he was taking a cigarette break. Tate grumbled but came out, taking off his grease-spattered apron. Vance went into the john. There were two men coming out, talking about the fishing in the Gulf, and a third in the booth was just a pair of socks and a pair of shoes showing beneath the door. Vance looked in and the man said peevishly, "For crissake!" and Vance said, "Sorry, friend," and went back to the bar.

"He's not there," he told Maddie. "I'll take a look out in the patio."

"Be sure to look up in the trees too," she said. "He likes to swing by his tail and eat coconuts."

"Ah, give the guy a break," he said, his automatic response to ruffled wives, and walked toward the storeroom.

Hully was sitting on the case of Seagram's, turning the diamond in the light of the baby spot over the piano, and when Vance walked in he hastily closed his fist around the ring. He jumped eagerly to his feet.

"Something I can do, Vance?"

"Wes Elwood come through here, Hully?"

Hully's hand tightened on the ring. "I—I ain't seen him, Vance," he stammered.

"Maybe he's out on the patio."

"Wait." Clumsily, Hully tried to get between Vance and the door. "I'll look. I'll take care of it for you, Vance."

"Thanks, kid, but I need a breath of air anyway."

Hully tried to swallow. Now he was frightened. His impulse was to hit Vance to prevent him from going out on the patio, but he couldn't do that. Vance was his friend. He couldn't hit Vance. Not Vance. The conflicting emotions made him feel dizzy, and he lurched when Vance pushed by him and went out to the patio. Hully stood there trembling, listening to Vance's footsteps on the flagstones. He wanted to run. He knew it was wrong, taking Mr. Elwood's ring, and now he was going to be punished for it. The ring was still in his hand. He looked around frantically and then reached up and put it on the shelf behind a gallon jar of pickled pigs' feet. He was breathing heavily, but now that he was rid of the ring, he felt better. They couldn't blame it on him now. He didn't have it. No matter what they said, he didn't have it.

They could turn his pockets inside out, and if they didn't find it, they couldn't say he took it. He looked fearfully through the open door. The patio was empty. There was nobody there, neither Mr. Elwood nor Vance. Nobody. Shakily putting one foot in front of the other, he walked outside, fully expecting to see Vance holding up Mr. Elwood around the corner of the walk-in cooler, but there was nobody there either. Mr. Elwood was gone. He hadn't told Vance that he, Hully, had taken the ring. Hully's courage flooded back. What the hell. That dumb Elwood, he was too soused to know what was going on anyway. He never knew the difference. What could he tell? He was orey-eyed drunk and couldn't see his nose in front of his face, so what could he tell? Nothing.

Still, Hully's knees felt very weak when Vance came walking back from the parking lot.

"Find'm?" Hully croaked, cleared his throat and asked again, "Find'm, Vance?"

Vance shook his head. "The jerk. He took his car and lit out, and that's all we need, another drunken driver on the road."

"Was he drunk, Vance?" Hully asked slyly.

"Drunk? He was looping!"

"Well, watta you know. He was playing the piano so nice. I never knew he was drunk. He sure had me fooled, Vance. Did you know he was drunk, Vance?"

"I should know. I fed it to him."

"Ah, now, Vance, you ain't got no call blaming yourself for something like that. If he didn't get it here, he'd of got it somewheres else."

"Well, maybe you're right," said Vance tiredly.

"Sure I'm right. And say, Vance ..."

"What?"

"Anytime you want something done, just ask me, okay?"

"What brought that on?"

"Well—you and me, we're friends, ain't we?"

"Sure."

"Well then?"

Vance slapped him on the shoulder. Hully might be a dummy, but he was all right. "My pal," he said.

Vance walked back into the bar and Hully ambled behind him as far as the storeroom. Now he could breathe again. Everything was all right. Hully waited impatiently until he was absolutely sure that Vance was not coming back, and then he reached behind the jar of pickled pigs' feet and retrieved the ring. He sat down on the case of Seagram's again and, concealing the ring in his cupped hands, turned the diamond to the light. Each time the facets caught the white beam of the baby spot, they flamed like a living and personal spectrum. Hully glanced at the goldfish, languid in their tank at the window, but they could not compare to the rainbow that lived in the diamond. He sat enraptured over the ring. There was no greater happiness than this.

"You took long enough," said Tate crustily as Van resumed his station at the bar.

"So what?"

Tate did not answer and walked into the kitchen, putting all his choler into the stiff set of his narrow shoulders. Vance went up to Maddie.

"I know," she said, before he could tell her. "He took the car and went home."

"He was gone before I could get to him."

"Don't worry about it. He's probably fast asleep on the bathroom floor. I don't suppose I can get a cab at this hour of night, can I?"

"I—" he hesitated. "I can run you home, Maddie."

She regarded him from under a speculative eyebrow, and he flushed as if he had made a deliberate pass at her and had been caught at it. She nodded.

"I'll take you up on that," she said, and then she smiled and crinkled her eyes at him again. "I had a feeling something was going to sneak up on me tonight. Wes leaving me stranded, I mean."

Mechanically he said, "Ah, give the guy a break," and turned quickly away when he heard Cora's tray rattle in the service part of the bar.

"Two Collins, two rye and soda," she told him formally; and then, falteringly, "I wasn't really mad at you, Vance. About last night, I mean."

"I didn't blame you a bit, honey. I was pretty drunk."

"You're not kidding. You was looping when we come out of Dick's. You have a hangover?"

"This big."

"Me too," she laughed nervously. "Say listen, how's about us going out for a little pickup after closing? I could use one."

"Not tonight, honey. Some other time maybe."

"Tomorrow?"

"Sometime."

"I ain't doing nothing tomorrow."

"We'll get together one of these times, maybe."

"Oh sure, maybe!" she flared, furious at having offered herself so obviously. "Maybe never, you mean! Well, forget it, brother, that's all, forget it!"

She snatched up the tray of drinks, spilling a little from each glass, and walked stiffly away from him. Vance felt shamed, knowing that he had given her the brush-off because Maddie was sitting so close. He could have done it better, without hurting her feelings. Someone called an order from the end of the bar and he busied himself with ice, glasses and bottles.

It was two-fifteen before he got away from the Lounge. Maddie was sitting in his car waiting, and when he got in, she moved a little closer and touched his arm.

"You're an awfully nice guy, Vance," she said softly. "Did anybody ever tell you?"

Her face, turned up to his, was a delicate, luminous oval. It was very close, closer than it had ever been, and he had an idea that if he kissed her, she would not mind.

Emotion surged up in him, but instead of moving toward her, he leaned back in his seat and shoved the car keys into the ignition lock. It was not a matter of resisting temptation that he did not kiss her. It was more than that. He told himself that once you started that kind of stuff with one guy's wife, you do it with another and then another, and the first thing you know, you're beating the mattress in half the beds in town, and you wake up in the morning feeling like a heel. Worse than a heel, because you were taking something from a guy who couldn't defend himself. Maybe there was a special word for guys who robbed blind men or stole the gold inlays from the teeth of dead men. The same word would apply.

This wasn't the first time he had taken some drunk's wife home, and it wouldn't be the first time he was taking Maddie home. Wes passed out regularly, drinking the way he did, starting before breakfast and drinking steadily all day, before, during and after meals. And then there were the times he had gotten sore and had walked out, leaving Maddie to get home by cab or as best she could.

Wes was a brooder. That was the trouble. He never yelled or had a real scrap, the kind that cleared the air and got the poison out. He brooded, and he drank, and half the time, Vance was willing to bet, Wes didn't know if he was brooding about something real or something fancied. That was the way with a drinking brooder. Sooner or later they came to the point where their imaginations took over and they tormented themselves with situations that never took place or never would take place, inventing whole conversations to inflame an already fevered ego.

Vance had taken Maddie home five or six times, and he had never made a pass at her. Usually she was embittered, the way walked-out-on wives are, or just plain silent, and mainly it had been just a kind of cab-trip to get her home from the gin mill. Tonight was the first time—

He put that out of his mind. Maybe she wanted to, and maybe she didn't. The thing was that once you took the first step off the diving board, you were in deep water and it was too God-damned easy to float around out there rather than swim back to shore and get the hell out of it, especially when you had company.

The only trouble was that it was a wrench not to kiss her when her luminous face was turned up like that and they were alone and nobody around to see or say no or even care if they did fall into a clinch. Only with Maddie, it would be more than a clinch, and it'd go on from there; and that'd be even worse than a one-night stand. If he kissed her, he'd mean it.

He turned the ignition key and stepped on the starter. Maddie sat abruptly back in her seat, and from the way she froze, he *knew* that she had expected him to kiss her.

Of course, there was a reason for that, too. She was sore at Wes. That was the way wives worked sometimes. Also, if you were just a little nice to them, like taking them home, they felt as if they had to do something for you out of gratitude, like kissing you good night and maybe letting you go just a little further but not all the way, though some of them had made it pretty obvious that nothing stood in the way.

But not with Maddie.

She was silent as they drove out of the parking lot and turned into the road toward the causeway to the Key where Wes had built a rather spectacular house which had been photographed for both *House & Garden* and *The Architectural Forum*. Wes was supposed to have quite a sockful, but the word was that most of it was tied up in the lumberyard and in several of the subdivisions in the Sanibar area, mostly expensive stuff on the bays or the Gulf. Wes had the reputation of being able to make one buck do the work of five. Many a cracker had said admiringly over the bar, "Why that joker could take a sandspur and set it in a ring and sell it for pure diamonds!" It was something that Vance could never figure. Wes had made all his money himself. He hadn't inherited a cent of it. In fact, old man Elwood, the father, had been a pleasant, industrious, hard-working old guy, but had never been able to make more than just enough to keep the family in grits-and-gravy. So where had Wes gotten this terrific drive to make money? God knows he had made it. Drunk or sober, he had made money.

Almost automatically, though he was just making conversation, he said to Maddie, "How long have you and Wes been married, honey?"

Her chin settled a little closer to her chest and she said bitterly, "Almost ten years."

"That was just about the time he went into the lumberyard."

"Just before. I lent him the money. Three thousand dollars."

"He sure piled it up since."

This was just talk. He was trying to make Maddie feel better, and he wanted to pass the time impersonally. He had to.

"Oh, he piled it up, all right," she said in that same bitter voice. "But he's got it so scattered that you'd need a native guide to get at it. But he piled it up. He's a great piler-upper anyway you look at him. But he was like a squirrel burying nuts. Every time you turned around, he was burying another nut. Do you know what we live on? We started out on grits and fatback and we're still living on grits and fatback. And liquor. He won that damn diamond ring of his in a crap game down in Key West when he was speculating in shrimp."

Embarrassed at these revelations, Vance said, "But he made it, that's the main thing. I've never had one dime to rub against another."

She stirred and looked at him, turning up on one hip on the seat. "But you've made it. I can tell. I know you've made it."

He wagged his head in a noncommittal gesture. "On and off. But I spend it. Christ knows on what. It just seems to piddle away and in the end I'm still without the two dimes to rub together. That's the way it goes. Some guys make it and multiply it, like Wes, and other guys, like me, make it and slop it up a rope."

"You could do the same as Wes, or better. You're smarter!" There was an intensity in her voice that startled him. "Wes isn't anything but a dumb cracker."

"Well, maybe," he said uneasily, "but I still think he's got something I haven't got."

"What, for instance?"

"He can make it and keep it."

"Anybody can do that. If he's pushed."

"Pushed?"

"Who do you think made it for him? Who do you think kept at him all the time?"

Vance didn't like the way this was turning out. He had started it only to pass the time between the bar and her home, and he certainly didn't want to go into a lot of whoop-de-do about what he was able or not able to do. It wasn't the kind of conversation for two-thirty in the morning. In the first place it didn't get you anywhere, and in the second place it was like all conversations you had at two-thirty in the morning. They had a tendency to turn into hangovers when you woke up the next day.

He drove a little faster. It was actually only seven miles to her place on the Key, but they still had a few miles to go. The roads were pretty winding and lined with cabbage palms, palmetto, Spanish dagger, and sand. The cabbage palm was a dumpy, flimsy tree, but not when you hit it head-on doing forty or better.

For some reason or other, probably to flatter him, she kept insisting that he could make money if he put his mind to it.

"Maybe you haven't had any reason to go after it, Van," she said earnestly. "You have to have a reason. You haven't had a reason yet. You've just been drifting."

"Maybe so," he agreed. Just so there wouldn't be any arguments. "But I'm not going to worry about that right now."

"All the same, you could make it if you wanted to. And keep it, if you had the incentive. I know you. I've watched you in that bar. God knows," that bitter tone again, "I've had little else to do. But," her voice picked up, "I've watched you and I know what you can do. I'm a good judge of character. You're not just a bartender. Anything but that. You've taken the job for some reason or other. I don't know what it is, and I don't care. But there's a strength in you. You're not a clown and you're not a servant. There's something else, but I haven't been able to find out what it is. Something that made you come down here to Florida and take that job. It's just an interim job. I know that. You can't fool me. I'm a good judge of character."

He realized now that she had been drinking and that was why she was talking the way she was. She wasn't drunk or anything like that, but she was at the stage at which there was nothing more exhilarating than an earnest conversation about something, anything at all, the subject didn't matter just as long as it was earnest.

It made him feel a lot better to realize that. Better and worse, to be truthful. Better because it meant that it would be easier not to kiss her and go on from there; worse because, at this stage, she would have been the same with anyone.

"I'll probably be moving on after the tourist season closes," he said. "Tate wouldn't be able to afford to pay me anyway, and I've got a job kind of lined up in Atlantic City for the summer."

"Bartending?"

"There's good money in it."

"You'll change your mind," she said with assurance. "I know you. You won't be satisfied with just tending bar. You're not satisfied now. I can tell."

"Well," he shrugged, trying to pass it off lightly just to end the talk, "round and round it goes, where it stops, nobody knows."

"Well, I know," she said with satisfaction, settling back into her seat. "I just know."

Within five minutes, Vance turned into the driveway of the big, spectacular house on the Key. The broad sheets of plate glass glinted vividly in the sweep of his headlights. Maddie sat stiffly forward in her seat as they rounded the banyan tree before the garage. Wes's car was not there.

"Could he have parked around the other side maybe?" Vance asked.

"In his state, he could have parked in the living room," Maddie said in an angry voice.

"I'll take a look."

He walked completely around the long house, peering into all the shrubbery and even into the palmetto field across the road. Wes had not come home. Vance went back to the car.

"He isn't here yet, honey," he said, leaning in the open window.

Her eyes dilated and, in the brilliant swath of moonlight that made the beach look like spilled white paint, he could see that she was furious.

"My God!" she said, "if he hits anybody tonight in that damn car, they'll sue us for everything we've got. And collect, too!"

"He might just have passed out—"

"He can go on for days. You don't know him. Oh, God!" She beat her pointed fists on her knees. "He can get himself into a crap game in Key West with five thousand dollars on the table just because he's drunk, but all the insurance we carry on the car is ten thousand liability! Ten thousand! If he gets into an accident tonight, a jury would strip us clean."

"Ah wait a minute, honey. You're getting yourself all upset about something that hasn't happened."

"But it *can* happen! It can happen very easily. He's drunk. You know he's drunk as well as I do. He's blind drunk. He's not responsible. You know what'll happen if he gets in an accident and hurts or kills somebody. He won't buy insurance, but he'll get in a crap game for five thousand dollars—"

"Forget that part of it. He won."

"A ring. A diamond ring, which he won't even take off when he goes to bed. His lucky piece, he calls it. Oh, my God! What kind of sense do you call that? A five thousand dollar lucky piece, and what we need is insurance. He could buy a rabbit's foot for a quarter. *Oh, God!*"

She was very close to hysteria, and Vance said, "We could go look for him."

"Where?" she asked hopelessly. "Where does a drunk go? Where could we look?"

"There are only a few gin mills open at this time of night. Dick's—Ella's—the C & C Bar. The all-night joints. I'll make the rounds if you want me to."

"Let me go with you!"

He wouldn't have wanted anything else, yet it was the last thing he wanted.

"Sure," he said, sliding into the car. "Naturally."

Chapter Four

The first stop was Dick's Bar, about a mile east of the Tamiami Trail, out in the palmetto and rattlesnake country, up the old Hammermill Road. Dick, with his dyed, lank hair combed carefully across his bald spot so that it looked like raked coal dust on a white, shiny floor, was behind the bar. His eyes gave Maddie a quick on-and-off, and he barely nodded to Vance, pretending to be busy with the beer taps.

Vance knew what was the matter. Dick liked Cora. Cora was his style. Maddie wasn't. Vance knew that if he had come in with Cora, he would have gotten the big-hand from Dick, but with Maddie it was different. Maddie didn't belong in Dick's Bar, and Dick knew it. People like Maddie were slumming when they turned up in the Bar, and

Dick knew that too and resented it. He resented people like Maddie in the first place. People like Maddie didn't lean their elbows on the bar and give. Dick liked people who could lean their elbows on the bar and give. He was that kind of guy. He didn't know, Vance reflected, that people like Maddie were just as capable of leaning their elbows on the bar and giving. More so, in fact. Dick had just had bad experiences.

As a bartender, Vance knew how people were. Dick should have, but he didn't. People have to be in familiar, comfortable, friendly places before they relaxed. Dick would never let Maddie relax in his bar. He'd be very polite to her, he'd give her a lot of professional attention, but he'd never make her feel at home. It was Dick's fault.

Maddie stopped in the doorway and looked around the room, at the varnished pine bar, at the dirty floor speckled with flattened cigarette butts, at the dilapidated juke box, at the back-bar mirror on which was still soaped *Merry Xmas & A Happy New Year*, at the beer drinkers in their faded blue jeans and threadbare shirts.

Her face tightened and she said with flat distaste, "I don't want a drink here. Just ask him if he's seen Wes or if he knows where he went."

Vance said, "Sure," and went over to the bar, leaving her standing close to the doorway. He knew that Dick wasn't going to be very co-operative about this unless he did something about it, so he tried to make it sound as if Dick were doing them an important personal favor.

"Have you seen Wes Elwood tonight, Dick?" he asked. "That's his wife over there. Wes is out on a toot. He's really looping. I saw him, and she's scared sick."

Dick remained noncommittal. "So that's the wife. I wondered what she looked like. Not bad. No, I ain't seen him."

Vance laid his hand on the bar, palm up. "Look, pal, we're not just checking up on the guy. He's roaring drunk, know what I mean? And he's out tearing around the country in his car and he shouldn't even be near a car, the way he is. He's going to get himself in a mess and there'll be hell to pay. Insurance doesn't cover you if you have an accident when you're drunk, and he's really plotzed."

"He didn't get it here."

"And he didn't get it at Tate's. He was looping when he came in. You know how he gets."

"You should of taken care of him then."

"We were jammed," said Vance with as much patience as he could command, for he knew he wouldn't get anywhere if he lost his temper. "Look. I like Wes. I've known him a long time, and I don't want to see anything happen to him. He's a nice guy, and you know that as well as I do."

"Yeah. Wes is okay."

"And you know me, Dick. As far as I'm concerned, if a wife can't take care of her husband, I'm not going to do it for her. But this is different. He might even kill somebody if he gets out on the highway. He's in no condition to drive."

"I know, I know, but I ain't seen him, Vance, and that's the honest truth."

Vance realized that Dick was breaking a fixed rule in telling him this. Dick never gave out any information about any of his customers to anybody, no matter how innocuous, if it was the matter of a check-up. He wouldn't have a phone in the place for that reason. "Hell," he'd say, "I don't care what you do in here just so long's you don't break the glasses, but the minute your wife starts coming around looking for you, you'll be doing me a favor if you take your business somewheres else. Don't bring your troubles here."

Vance said, "Thanks, Dick. I appreciate that."

"Aaaah, drop dead. But tell the little lady not to worry. If Wes comes in here drunk, I'll take his car keys away from him. I'd do that much for anybody. You can tell her that. Here," he set up two glasses and quickly filled them from a bottle of 'shine before Vance could protest, "on the house. And you can tell the little lady I aged this bottle myself personally for six months. It's not the sewer juice I serve the rest of you cruts. I drink this myself."

Vance went over to Maddie. "He poured a couple drinks on the house," he said in a low voice. "I couldn't turn him down. He said he'll take Wes's car keys from him if he comes in drunk, and that's a big favor, coming from Dick."

"I told you I didn't want a drink here, didn't I?"

"I know, honey, but we're asking him to do something he doesn't usually do for anybody. I think we should take the drink if only to keep him cooperative."

"The glasses are probably filthy!"

"Dick keeps them spotless. I can guarantee that." Maddie made an exasperated noise in her throat. "Oh, very well, but I don't think much of it."

She walked stiffly back to the bar with him and Vance said quickly to Dick, "Mrs. Elwood's very worried about this whole thing and she appreciates what you're doing for her. You know what it is with a drunk on the loose."

"Hell," said Dick, "I'd do the same for a dog. You don't have to be afraid of that drink, lady. I know the guy that makes it and he's okay."

Maddie looked at the oily, light amber liquid in the glass and turned to Vance. "What is it?" she asked, barely concealing her distaste.

"It's 'shine, lady," said Dick. "The best there is."

And Vance said, "It's corn liquor, Maddie. Practically the same mash they make bourbon from. Some people don't like it. Right, Dick?"

"Yeah, it makes some guys puke, but it don't hurt them none. I've seen them puke and come right back for another one."

Vance crossed his fingers as Maddie, wrinkling her nose, lifted her glass for the first sip. He knew how she felt in a joint like this, but he liked Dick and didn't want anything to happen that would hurt his feelings. Maddie took one sip and then another and Vance let out a breath of relief when she smiled at Dick.

"It's very good," she said. "I like it. I like it very much."

Dick beamed. "Well, it won't turn the fillings black in your teeth, lady. I drink it myself."

Maddie finished her glass and set it out on the bar. "May I have another one, please?"

"It's kind of strong, Maddie," Vance tried to warn her, "It sneaks up on you."

"Like a baseball bat," said Dick. "Just like a baseball bat. Wham!"

"But I still want another one. I like it. And I can hold my liquor."

"I guess you can, at that," Dick grinned. "It stayed down, didn't it."

"It packs an awful wallop," Vance said.

"Wallop!" Dick tilted the bottle over Maddie's glass and winked at her. "Listen to who's talking. He's the one that packs the wallop. You should of seen what he don't do to a guy here last night. One smack and the crut was out colder'n an iced mullet. And he's been spittin' out teeth ever since. Lost six in front, I heard. What a smack!"

"A fight?" asked Maddie with interest, looking at Vance, who flushed.

"It wasn't no fight, lady," Dick said. "Blam! and it was all over. If you ast me, Van here used to be in the ring or something, but he says no."

"Were you in the ring, Vance?" Maddie asked. "I used to go to the fights all the time when I lived in New York, especially the Golden Gloves. I loved the Golden Gloves better than the professional matches."

"Yeah," said Dick, "them kids really tear into each other, don't they? But you should of seen Van here last night. What a smack. Blam! I thought he tore the guy's head off."

"*Did* you fight professionally, Vance?" Maddie asked. "Now tell the truth. I used to love the fights when I lived in New York."

Vance said shortly, "No. And I don't like fighting anyway."

"But you will if you have to."

"Anyone will."

"That's not the truth. I've seen Wes back down from fights on several occasions," she said contemptuously, "talk his way out of it."

"I do the same."

"Oh, no, you don't. You proved it last night."

Vance stood up. "I think we'd better get along, Maddie. We've got a few more stops to make if we're going to find Wes."

"I admire a man who'll put up his fists when he has to," Maddie said. "I loved the Golden Gloves up in New York. That was before I was married. The fights down here in Florida are terrible unless you go to Miami."

"That's a fact," said Dick. "Stumble bums is all we have here."

"Are you ready, Maddie?" Vance asked, shaking his head as Dick reached for the bottle to pour Maddie another drink.

She looked a little vaguely at her glass, but nodded and stood up. A bitter look tightened her face. "There's nothing like married life, is there?" She turned abruptly and walked toward the door.

Dick winked at Vance. "I'll bet she was really something when she was a little younger," he said.

"You mean when she was six?"

Dick gave him an odd glance. "No, just a little younger. She ain't no minor, buster."

"In that case I'd better get her home before her grandchildren start wondering what happened to her."

Dick watched him stride to the door and then shook his head. "Figure that one out," he said to himself. "Who's he think she is, Marlin Monroe?"

Vance and Maddie walked silently to the car, and when she got into the front seat she leaned her head against the back of it and closed her eyes.

"I shouldn't have had that second drink," she said. "In fact, I shouldn't have had the first."

"Do you want me to take you home?"

"No. And I'm not drunk," she said with a slight edge to her voice. "I'm just a little sleepy. Oh, *damn* Wes anyway! Where are we going now?"

"Ella's Bar. It's about three miles south of here. And after that, the

C & C over on the bay."

"Are they anything like Dick's?"

"Well—"

"I know, worse. Ugh! Wes is really quite a pig, when you come right down to it. Going into places like that night after night. He's disgusting. Well, let's go and get it over."

"Sure, Maddie."

"Before we start I want to tell you one thing, however. I'm not having any more drinks in either of those places. In fact, I'm going to stay in the car while you go inside. Is that understood now?"

Her voice was sharp but he could see from the way her head lolled on the back of the seat that the strain and the liquor had gotten to her, and he said gently, "Sure, Maddie. You just relax and I'll take care of the rest of it."

"All right, but just remember it. *Oh, God!*" She turned her head away from him and he saw her slim hands clench in her lap and knew what she was going through.

She was asleep before they reached Ella's Bar on the Palmetto Road south of the city. It was one of the original buildings in the area and had once been the office of a turpentine company. It was made of jagged travertine rock, and in the back were still the remnants of the stockade in which the prison labor had been locked up overnight. The old timers still remembered some pretty grim stories about the old turpentine camp—lashings and killings—and the place still had a pretty bad reputation. There had been a knife fight only a week or so ago, Vance remembered, that the police had never been told about, though both men had been badly cut. There would not have been any witnesses, anyway. Nobody would have seen a thing. The crackers who inhabited Ella's Bar still regarded the police as enemies and nothing would ever change them.

Vance looked at Maddie in the bleak light of the single naked hundred-watt electric bulb that thrust out of the wall over the front door of the bar like a toadstool. Her red hair glowed, but her face was strained even in sleep. He kissed her lightly on the cheek and got out of the car.

It was quiet in Ella's. It was always quiet inside. What fights there were usually took place in the cleared space behind the building. Four men were playing a languid game of shuffleboard and about a dozen others lounged at the cypress-plank bar. Ella was a tall, raw-boned woman in a shapeless sack of a stained cotton dress that had once been patterned with red hibiscus on a light green background, but frequent washings had faded it to an almost uniform gray. There was something faintly sinister in her pale hair, pale eyes and angular, high-boned face. She looked slightly like a half-mad albino horse, but she was very shrewd, very tough and ran the bar like a martinet. You had the feeling when looking at her that if there had ever been anything feminine about her, the man who had known it was now dead. The men looked briefly at him and discarded him with their eyes. This was strictly a cracker bar and he was a damyankee in a section where anyone not actually born on the premises was an outsider. Their hostility was passive and contemptuous.

Vance ordered a beer. He had to order or he would get nothing from Ella, though he knew the chances were slim anyway. When she brought his mug of beer, he asked her if she had seen Wes Elwood that night.

She regarded him with an opaque stare that was like wet ashes.

"He owe you money or something?" she asked.

"He's drunk and I don't want him to get in trouble with his car."

"I didn't know you was such a friend of his. What's this sudden interest?"

"I just—"

"Nuts, brother," she said in a bored voice. "Wes comes in here almost every night and there ain't nothin' I don't know about him. He's told me often enough, God knows. And you never figured in any of it. So now all of a sudden you're running around looking for him just because he's soused. He's been soused for years and you never looked for him before. So, what's the interest all of a sudden?"

She had spoken in her usual loud ripsaw voice, and Vance knew that every cracker in the place was listening. He remembered, too, that Wes was a cracker and that these men were, in a way, his friends, or at least one of them.

"He got drunk at Tate's," he said patiently. "I meant to take his car keys away from him, but I got busy and the next time I looked around, he was gone, and he was in no condition to drive. I like Wes, and I shouldn't have let him get out of that place with his car keys."

Ella's expression did not change. "Bull," she said. "In the first place, you got that wife of Wes's out in the car with you. I seen you drive up. Maybe you got a good reason for lookin' for him and maybe you ain't. I don't care either way. But just don't ask me to come in on it with you, that's all."

"I'm only asking—"

"You ain't asking me *nothing*."

"Okay," said Vance angrily, "so I don't give a damn myself, but I'm not asking for myself—"

"You're damn right you're not, brother. I wouldn't tell *you* what way was up."

"Just take his car keys away from him if he's too drunk to drive, will you? Or is that too much to ask? For him, not me. For him, to keep him out of trouble with the police."

"If he comes in drunk, I'll take care of him my own way." She turned her head and looked at the front window of the bleak room, and for a moment she looked as if she had seen all the evil in the world and did not care one way or the other about it, except as a matter of disinterested comment. She looked back at Vance and there was the bloodless glimmer of what might have been a smile on her thin lips.

"Yeah," she said, "I thought it might be something like that. The wife must have done quite a job on you to get you to run around the country half the night looking for a poor drunk that's pickling his brains because of her. That's it, all right. I heard she was quite a piece."

Vance pushed his mug of beer away from him so violently that it spilled on the bar. He stood up. "In your own words," he said, "bull!"

As he turned and walked out, someone snickered and there was a leer in it. He was glad that Maddie was still asleep when he slid into the front seat of the car. He knew that the clench of fury was in his face and that she would have seen it and asked questions, and right now he did not want to answer any questions about what had taken place in Ella's. He drove away as quietly and smoothly as possible so as not to awaken her. She was still sleeping when he stopped at the side of the C & C Bar to the west of Sanibar on the bay. This was a commercial fisherman's hangout, and there was much less of that inbred bitterness here. These men did not sit in shacks in the back country and feed on their own rancor. Most of them worked on the big commercial boats when the mullet runs thinned out, and though they talked about damyankees, it was not in a festering way. They had been around—Key West, Central America, Mexico and most of the Gulf states—and their prejudice had become diluted.

The place was run by a fat, sloppy man called Mush, who stated frequently and loudly that he'd sell a drink to even a Republican if he got paid in advance for it. In a one-party Democratic neighborhood, this was considered quite a joke. He had a large, falsely hearty manner. At frequent intervals during the evening he would shout, Is *e-e-e-everybody* happy?" and slap the bar noisily with his pudgy hand.

"Nobody's drinking beer tonight," he shouted when Vance ordered a mug. "It's rum, cap, and it's only a quarter a shot. I got a couple kags of it today from a friend off a ship, but don't ask me where he got it. Know what I mean?" he winked broadly. "Ask me no questions and I'll tell you no lies. And don't give me that don't-want-none stuff. You been drunk half your life, you son-of-a-bitch, and once more won't hurt you. Your guts are all shot to hell anyways like the rest these bums that come in here."

He guffawed and half the score of men at the bar laughed with him. Mush had the reputation of being a clown, a comedian and a wit. He gave Vance half a beer glass of rum so dark that it was almost black.

"A hunnert and twenny proof right down the line, cap," he said. "One drink of that and you can pop your tonsils like peanuts and you won't have to pay a doctor for taking them out, and all for two bits. Cheap at half the price."

It was strong, raw rum and it tasted heavily of molasses, but it was easy to drink after the first harsh swallow. Most of the men at the bar were already drunk on it, and two were asleep under the shuffleboard at the side of the room.

Vance tried to ask Mush about Wes Elwood, but it was several minutes before he could get Mush to stand still long enough to ask the question. Mush was in one of his generous moods and he kept walking up and down the bar with the half gallon bottle of rum, filling all glasses as he went, scooping change from in front of the drinkers whether they had ordered a refill or not.

"Drink it up, you drunken cruts," he bellowed. "I got two kags of it."

This happened periodically in the C & C when someone smuggled Mush liquor from one of the Latin countries. Sometimes it was rum, sometimes tequila, banana liquor, or even pale, potent moonshine from Mississippi. For some reason or other that no one had ever been able to fathom, Mush was so anxious to be liked by everybody that he was practically neurotic, and even when he was the most generous he gave the impression that it was false and that sooner or later the mean reason for it would be disclosed. Yet, most of the men liked him and felt sorry for him, and laughed at his jokes because he had the same kind of raw humor that they did.

And when Vance was finally able to get a private word with him, Mush's face closed as if he had stepped behind a door.

"Wes Elwood?" he said with a spurious air of interest. "Noooo, I ain't seen him, Vance. And you can see for yourself that he ain't here. Nobody here but us chickens." It was the same thing again, but Vance said, "I know. I didn't see his car outside. But will you do me a favor—"

"Hell, yes. Anything at all, cap. All you got to do is ask. That's what they call professional courtesy among us bartenders." He winked.

"If Wes comes in drunk will you take his car keys away from him, as a special favor to me? He got drunk in the Pelican and I should have done it myself, so I feel a little responsible."

"Sure, sure, Van, and glad to do it. A friend of yours is a friend of mine. Sa-a-a-ay, I hear you busted Carl Stover's jaw last night over in Dick's place. Hear he's in the hospital with his face all wired up like a piano. Over a blonde, wasn't it?"

"I didn't break his jaw," said Vance, knowing that the man would repeat this story every chance he got. "He lost a couple teeth, that's all. It was a lucky punch."

"Made a pass at your dame, huh?"

"It wasn't like that. She slapped him and he smacked her and I smacked him. She slapped him first because he let the air out of her tires, just as a joke. She slapped him first, but you just don't let a guy get away with smacking a woman around, Mush. You know that as well as I do. Especially down here in the South. A guy who does that is asking to have his teeth knocked down his throat."

Mush nodded. These were sentiments with which he could agree. It was something everybody said and believed, and a few of the men who said it had actually never struck a woman.

"Yeah," said Mush, "you can't let a guy get away with a thing like that. I heard it was one hell of a smack, though. They was an hour bringing him to, I heard."

"He wasn't out for even five minutes."

"Well I'll be damned. That just goes to show how things get repeated. You know, Van, if I paid any attention to the lunks in this joint, Carl Stover'd of been dead and buried. All the same, the next time I beat up a woman, I'll do it when you ain't around."

"Let's forget the whole thing. Okay?"

"Sure, sure, cap. But that must be a terrific wallop you got. I ain't never heard of nobody knocking Carl Stover out before. It's usually the other way around."

"Lucky punch, that's all. But if Wes comes in, get those car keys away from him, will you?"

"Surest thing you know, Van. Consider it done."

Vance stood up a little dizzily. It had been very strong rum and he had drunk about four ounces of it too fast. He was not drunk but he could feel the fiery liquor burning inside him.

He said, "Thanks, Mush. I appreciate that," and was surprised to find that he could walk fairly steadily to the door.

He looked at the sleeping Maddie as he got into the front seat, and then eased the car out of the parking lot and to the shore road to the Key where she lived. He heavily discounted Mush's promise to look after Wes. Mush would promise anything to anybody, out of his desire to please, but Vance was very well aware that if Wes did not want to give up his keys, Mush would do nothing about it, even if Wes were so drunk that he couldn't remember his own name. Mush would want to please Wes, too.

Maddie moaned a little in her sleep, moved closer and rested her head against the side of Vance's arm, and he had to suppress a desire to put his arm around her and hold her very close as they drove. He passed Dick's on the way home and went slowly by but did not see Wes's car there. He also watched the sides of the road, but there was no sign of Wes anywhere. Nor was Wes's car in the garage or on the grounds when Vance finally stopped again at the house on the Key. Vance felt angry now at the useless stupidity of what Wes had done. He sat at the wheel and stared at the dark, breathing rise and fall of the great placid Gulf.

"The jerk," he thought, "the God-damn jerk."

Chapter Five

He touched Maddie on the shoulder. Her eyes half opened and she looked vaguely around. She became fully awake when she saw the bulk of the house against the sky. Her fingers tightened on her thigh and he heard her draw in a heavy breath.

"We didn't find him," she said.

"No, but every place I went, the bartender promised to take his car keys away from him."

"Something's happened. I know it has," her voice began to rise. "He should have been at one of those places. He—"

Vance cut in sharply, "This isn't the first time he's gone out on the town like this, so stop it!"

His voice had the effect of a slap, and though her hands still clenched, the rising hysteria went out of her.

"Of course, you're perfectly right, I know you're perfectly right and it isn't the first time, I know that, but I get like this every time. I can't help it, sitting there wondering if this is the night he's going to run into somebody with that car of his—he drives like a madman when he's drunk—and I know that some night he's going to run into somebody and kill a half dozen people in some dreadful wreck on the highway. You read about such things every day in the newspapers. And in one second like that he can lose every cent he's worked years to get. You don't know what it's like to sit night after night thinking about those things, Vance, you just don't know what it's like!"

"I have a pretty fair idea," he said, to soothe her.

"Yes, I think you do. You're a very sympathetic person. I think you know what it's like or you wouldn't have done what you did for me tonight and—but would you do just one more thing for me? Just one more thing?"

"Sure."

"Call the hospital and the police for me. I'd do it myself but— I just couldn't do it tonight."

"Of course."

"You're so good. You're so understanding." She tried to smile but her face was so stiff from strain that her mouth quivered as the ends of it raised, and he could feel the tremor in her when he held her elbow as they walked up the path to the dark house. Inside, she went immediately into all the rooms, looking for Wes.

"I thought someone might have brought him home," she said to Vance. "The phone is over here in the living room. You don't mind, do you?"

"Of course not."

He called the hospital first, but no accidents had been reported, nor had Wes been brought in. While he was calling the highway patrol, Maddie sat down on the sofa beside him and put a tall glass in his hand. It was dark with bourbon despite the ice cubes. He sipped it almost absently.

"Okay at the hospital," he told her. "Right now I'm calling the state highway patrol."

She whispered, "I don't know how I can ever thank you, Vance. I don't think I could have gotten through this night without you. I just got myself in a state, I guess."

"Everybody gets that way once in awhile and—hello ..."

He talked to the highway patrol headquarters for a few minutes and grinned reassuringly at Maddie. "Nothing on the highway," he told her. He then called the sheriff's office, with the same result, and finally police headquarters in Sanibar. The desk sergeant there knew all about Wes.

"Ah, hell," he said, "is that dumb bastard got himself another snootful again? What's the matter with him anyways? Jesus Christ. The boys is always taking him home or something and we even got him out of a couple of scrapes we shouldn't of. I swear to God the next time we find him plotzed, we're going to throw him in jail and keep him there till he grows some brains. You're calling for his wife, you say?"

"That's right. You haven't heard anything about him, have you?"

"Not yet, and the boys report in over the radio all the time. Ah, hell, tell Miz Elwood not to worry. If the boys pick him up, I'll tell them to bring him home. It's the last time though, understand? You don't have to tell her that."

"Thanks, sergeant, she'll appreciate that."

"Well, I don't. I'm getting sick and tired of Wes Elwood. If there's anything I hate, it's a rummy. They make more work for us than all the crooks in the county. If it was up to me, I'd drownd the whole mucking lot of them in a vat of alcohol. Except they wouldn't drownd. They'd drink it. Tell her—wait a minute ..."

Vance could hear the two-way radio squawk in the headquarters room, but he could not understand the words and he crossed his fingers while he was waiting for the sergeant to return to the telephone.

When the sergeant came back he said disgustedly, "Nope nope nope nope. It wasn't about Wes. This dame, she's got men on the brains. They keep looking in her window, only we ain't ever found no sign of none of them yet. But about Wes, here's what I think. He pulled off the side of the road somewheres and he's sleeping it off, and it won't be the first time. The boys're always finding him parked in somebody's front yard or someplace. You tell Miz Elwood not to worry. We'll take care of it when we find him."

"Thanks again—"

"Don't mention it. Jesus Christ, Wes used to be a good steady boy. I can't figure out what's got into him."

Vance hung up and told her what the sergeant had said. She smiled mistily and touched his cheek with her fingertips.

"You're so good," she murmured, "so understanding. And do you know something? I'll tell you something. I'm not worried anymore. Isn't that wonderful? I'm not a bit worried. I was worried sick, but I'm not worried now and I think it's wonderful. That's what you've done for me."

She kissed him quickly, partially on the cheek and partially on the side of the mouth, then jumped up from the sofa and snatched the empty glass from his hand.

"I'll fix you one more drink before you go," she said brightly. "We'll have a nightcap. I think you've earned it. You've really earned it if anybody has."

The liquor he had drunk was washing through him in pleasant, languorous waves and he did not notice how she staggered a little as she crossed the room to the built-in glass and chrome bar on the west wall. It was straight bourbon and ice cubes that she brought back in the tall glasses. She sat very close to him on the sofa and put her head on his shoulder.

"Oh, I don't know what I would have done without you tonight, darling," she said in a dreamy, far-off voice that seemed to come out of her on the lightest of breaths. "I honestly don't know what I would have done without you. Gone to pieces probably."

"Not you," he said, his voice floating. "You're not that kind."

"I am that kind. I've got emotions. Don't you think I've got emotions?"

"I know you have."

"You don't know. I've got very strong emotions. I'm very emotional, and you were wonderful tonight. You took care of everything, and I want you to know that I think you were just wonderful. I want you to know that—"

She turned suddenly on the sofa so that she was facing him and kissed him full on the mouth.

She lifted her lips away briefly and whispered, "I want you to know—" and kissed him again.

He held her with his left arm, pulling her close and kissed her hard. He put his drink on the end table and held her with both arms, kissing her harder and moving his head as if to get deeper and deeper into the kiss. She reached out and there was a faint click as she turned off the lamp at the end of the sofa. Her body convulsed in his arms and it was a few moments before he realized that she was trying to writhe out of her clothes without leaving his lap.

Her urgency accelerated the pace of his and there was more than just passion in the clash of their bodies. Her complete and wild abandon robbed it of any tenderness. Her fingernails dug into the hard flat muscles of his shoulders and held him fast to her.

It was a long while before, exhausted, they fell asleep, lax in each other's arms.

Vance awakened to find her shaking him violently, her face frightened and tight. She had on a long white terry-cloth robe that covered her to the ankles. The windows of the room were luminous with the dawn that was beginning to seep up into the eastern sky and outside the birds were beginning to whistle and chirp.

"You've got to go," she cried wildly. "You've got to get out of here. He might walk in any minute. You've got to go!"

"Wha' time is it?" he asked drowsily.

"Never mind what time it is. Just go, please!"

"Sure, sure—"

He sat up on the edge of the sofa and fumbled on the floor for his shoes. His mind was still slightly sleep-fogged. "Wes call?" he asked. "You hear from him?"

"No, no I didn't, but go, won't you, please? He'll be coming home any moment. Oh, God!"

He buttoned his shirt and stood. Shaking, she thrust and urged him toward the door, trying to get him out of the house as quickly as possible. He stopped at the door. He wanted to kiss her, but her distress was too obvious.

"I'll call you, honey," he said.

"No!" she said sharply. "He might be home. I'll—I'll call you, at the Pelican Lounge. But don't call me."

"Sure, honey."

Her eyes kept darting past him toward the road. "Oh, please *go!*" she cried. "Just go!"

He said, "Sure," again and walked to his car. He started the motor and as he backed down the driveway, he looked up toward the house. The front door was closed.

Chapter Six

It was seven A.M., a dreary hour in the Pelican Lounge, though it was never dreary there to Hully, even when he was mopping the floors and cleaning up the cigar butts and cigarette stubs. Everybody had to work. It was a natural thing, like breathing, and he could not possibly have imagined what life would be without it. With his great strength, nothing tired him and always he could look forward to that wonderful party every night when Vance was on duty and the customers came in and the juke box played and there was noise and action and laughter.

There was the usual clatter in the kitchen where Tate was peevishly making a pot of coffee, and Hully paused for a moment in his mopping to glower in that direction. Without Tate, everything *would* be perfect. If Vance owned the bar, now, that would be perfect. With Vance there would never be anything to worry about, such as getting fired, the way Tate was always saying. Tate was always talking about firing somebody because it cost too much—Vance, Cora, Hully. Always he was talking about firing somebody to cut down the overhead. Vance in particular. A smoldering rage began to accumulate in Hully when he thought about Tate firing Vance, and in a short time he could almost see and hear Tate doing it.

It would take place at night after the bar was closed. Vance would be checking the money in the cash register and Tate would come sneaking out of the kitchen, wiping his hands on his greasy apron. He wouldn't say anything to Vance. Oh, no. Tate was too yellow to come right out and say it. He would look at Vance with eyes like a rat and sneak up next to him and—and—slip him a piece of paper. That's the way he'd do, a piece of paper. Vance wouldn't know what it was all about and he would look at the piece of paper. It would be a piece of brown paper like the hamburger came wrapped in. It would be a piece of that torn off the corner. Hully ground his teeth. This was becoming more and more real as he thought about it. Tate was too cheap to buy a decent piece of paper. He'd tear it off the hamburger and there'd even be spots on it, the son-of-a-bitch.

Anyways, Vance wouldn't know what it was all about and he'd open the piece of paper and read it. "You're fired," it'd say, printed in pencil.

First off, Vance would think it was a joke because that's the way Vance was, always kidding around making people laugh, and he'd think it was a joke. Then he'd read it again and make like he thought Tate meant something else. Like, "you're hired," or something like that. A joke.

And then Tate would say in a squeaky-scared voice, "It ain't no joke."

And Vance would say, "You mean I'm fired?"

But Tate still wouldn't come right out and say so, but he'd mumble about overhead and expenses and money and things like that, and finally Vance would get the idea.

"So I'm canned!" he'd say.

And then Tate would lie and squeak that he couldn't afford it no more and he wished he could keep Vance on but he didn't have no more money, the lousy liar.

Hully was becoming excited and furious. All this was taking place right in front of him.

Vance would look at Tate and then he'd smack him right in the puss and knock him clear acrost the room and—

No. Vance wouldn't do that. Vance wasn't a guy who'd hit an old guy like Tate even if he was a son-of-a-bitch. Anyways, Vance was different. He'd laugh and say something like:

"You can't fire me, I quit."

And out he'd walk, and Tate would run to the window and watch him go away, and he'd laugh and giggle to himself because he got rid of Vance so easy. But there was one thing he'd forget. Him—Hully. Vance's friend. He'd forget all about that and stand there at the window tittering and giggling, and he, Hully, would walk up to him and say:

"Nobody gets away with anything on Vance so long's I'm around, Mr. Tate. We're friends."

And then he'd bust Tate right smack in the snoot and knock him clean through the window....

Hully's face lighted in an ecstasy of rage and his huge hands convulsed. The heavy mop handle snapped as if it had been as fragile as glass. The sound of the cracking wood brought Hully abruptly to his senses and he stared aghast at the broken handle in his hands. Now he was in for it. Tate would fire him sure for breaking the mop like that. Quickly and with sudden cunning, Hully stooped and gathered up a partial handful of dust and dirt from the floor and rubbed it on the two ends of the broken wood, disguising the freshness of the break. On second thought, he darted to the door and flung the upper half of the handle far out across the road. He darted a fearful glance at the kitchen door, but Tate had not appeared in the aperture to catch him. He leaped back to his pail of soapy water and energetically resumed mopping the floor with the broken mop. The handle was now almost two feet shorter and he had to bend over to hold it.

He did not realize the phone was ringing until Tate screeched from the john, "For crissake answer the phone, ain'cha got no ears, you dummy?"

Hully called out very cheerfully, knowing now that Tate could not possibly have seen him break the mop handle, "Just going over to pick it up, Mr. Tate. I'm taking care of it, don't worry." This was the time of morning, right after the coffee was on, that Tate always went to the can to put some gunk on his piles. Tate had bad piles and he was always running to the can to put some yellow gunk on them that he kept in a jar on the shelf over the gas stove. A couple times Hully had thought of putting snuff in the jar of gunk, but he had never quite wanted to take the chance of getting caught at it. Yet, thinking how

Tate would damn near go through the roof with a couple pinches of snuff on his piles, Hully almost laughed right out loud. Kee-rist! he'd sure like to be around to see that.

The telephone was behind the bar at the kitchen end, but Hully scooped it easily from its cradle with his tremendous reach.

"The Pelican Lounge, Sergeant Hully speaking," he said, repeating the kind of patter Vance always gave when he answered the phone. Sometimes Vance said, First Vice Bartender Vance in charge of ice cubes speaking, or, Resident Nurse Vance at your service. There wasn't nothing Vance couldn't think of to make you laugh. Hully often sat back in the storeroom laughing all night long from the things Vance said.

The phone said irritably, "What's that? What's that?"

Hully's voice was a heavy, bass rumble and was often hard to understand, and as a result he had the firm conviction that most people were hard of hearing.

He held the phone up in front of him and shouted at it, "This is the Pelican Lounge, the gin mill, just in case you're interested." Which was again the kind of thing Vance said over the phone, but funnier. Nobody could be as funny as Vance when he wanted to be funny.

The phone said angrily, "All right, all right, I can hear you. Is Wes Elwood there?"

Something congealed sickeningly in Hully's stomach. Wes Elwood. The diamond ring that was now in the cigar box with his other treasures, hidden behind the old broken-down Coca-Cola cooler in the storeroom. Hully had deliberately not thought of that diamond ring all morning, though he had ached to take it out and look at it and feel it and hold it up to the light and recapture that wild world of splendid shifting color imprisoned behind the facets of the cold stone.

His throat was thick when he asked, "Wh-who?"

"Wes Elwood. You know Wes. He always comes in. Is he there now?"

"Oh, no, no, he ain't here now. I ain't seen him. I ain't seen him today atall."

The voice swore over the phone and there was something about "stupid son-of-a-bitch" in it.

And then quickly, apologetically, "I didn't mean you. But look. When Wes comes in, will you ask him for crissake to call the office. Tell him it's important."

Relieved that it had nothing to do with the diamond ring, Hully said cheerfully, "Sure, sure, I'll tell him the minute he comes in. He usually comes in about this time."

"I know," the voice said dryly. "Tell him to call the office right away. Tell him it's about that shipment of striated plywood to panel the Roth house."

"Yeah, yeah, sure, I'll tell him."

"You got that straight now? Tell him to call the office the minute he gets in. Tell him that shipment of striated mahogany plywood for the Roth house didn't come through, and tell him old man Roth is raising hell. Will you tell him that?"

"Raising hell, yessir," said Hully, aping Vance again, remembering the kind of things Vance said over the phone. "A special hell or just general hell?"

"Oh, for the love of Jesus!" the voice said furiously, and hung up.

Hully looked contentedly at the telephone as he reached over the bar and replaced it in its cradle. That Vance, you couldn't beat him.

And Vance was his friend. That was a fact. Vance was his friend. The tears came into his eyes just thinking about it. A guy knows a lot of other guys, but one of them is his friend, and Vance was his friend. Hully's jaw dropped from the sheer wonder of it. A guy like Vance that everybody liked, his friend.

Hully had never had a friend. Nobody that had ever made the kind of fuss over him Vance did, slipped him a beer, treated him nice, didn't—Hully's heavy, narrow-browed face thickened—didn't poke fun at him. Hully's face thickened until it was almost like a fist, bunched hard in the center. They had always poked fun at him, all of them. He stared at the reflection of his clenched face in the mirror behind the bar, heavy, scowling, menacing, and in a moment of terrible clarity, he saw it exactly that way, and hated it. His big hands tightened until the knuckles were white.

"You're nothing but a goddam dumb bastard!" he said in a clotted voice, glowering at the mirror.

He heard the john door slam and he turned, and if Tate had come into the bar at that moment, Hully would have attacked him. In fact, he rested his left hand on the edge of the bar, leaned forward on the balls of his feet, extended his right arm like a wrestler, and there was an expression of grim eagerness in his heavy face. Tate. Tate the villain. Tate, the one who should be punished....

But Tate walked around the back of the passageway and entered the kitchen from the rear. Glancing up, he saw Hully standing there and said peevishly;

"Well? Well? Well? If you ain't got nothing better to do—what was the phone call? For me?"

The pendulum swung and for a moment Hully hung there dizzily at the edge of the bar, and the thing that had raged through him became servility again and he said hurriedly, "No, Mr. Tate. It was for Mr. Wes Elwood. His office wants him to call them right away. It's important, they said. Mr. Roth, it's about."

Tate always felt better after putting the ointment on his piles, but he could not resist saying ironically, "It's probably Mr. Ross, and you got the whole thing cockeyed, but the hell with it, we ain't a phone answering service. If you got the floor all mopped, you can help me stack the cartons of liquor in the storeroom."

"I'll have it mopped right away, Mr. Tate."

"And the patio?"

"Right after the floor."

"My God, what're you standing there for? You ain't even started. I'm paying you good money, so earn it, earn it!"

"Yessir, Mr. Tate, yessir. I just answered the phone, that's all. I'll get right back to it."

"All right, all right, all right. Never mind the excuses, just get to it. Finish up the floor and the patio, do the windows, then you can help me stack the cartons...." Tate's voice pottered off into a grumbling complaint about truck drivers who left cartons all over the floor and didn't stack them and what did they think he was paying good money for, and, my God, when you started figuring the overhead and the extra costs ...

Hully stopped listening and went back to his mopping. When it came to the patio, he shied away from it. He didn't want to go out there and clean up Wes Elwood's vomit. In a peculiar sort of way, he felt that if he did that, someone would discover that it was he who had stolen Wes's diamond ring. Instead of doing the patio, he got a fresh pail of hot water, into which he poured ammonia, and started cleaning the windows. He was seething inside from some unrealized fear and anger. He looked back over his shoulder as he mounted the chair to clean the window behind the fish tank. Tate was still in the kitchen, slicing onions very thinly and carefully for the hamburgers—Tate was very proud of his hamburgers—and onions had to be sliced tissue-paper thin. Hully glared down at the lazy fish swimming languidly in the tank, not a worry in the world. With a sudden, harsh gesture, he poured about a pint of the ammonia water into the tank. He watched tensely.

The fresh water came in from the bottom of the tank and flowed out through the overflow pipe at the top. The fish swam slowly, opening and closing their mouths. Hully could see the dirty streaks of the ammonia water in the tank, but the fish did not seem visibly affected by it. He glanced at the kitchen door and tipped a little more ammonia water into the tank, not much because he was afraid Tate might hear the splash and come out to inquire what it was, but enough so that the fish might be able to taste it. In that intense, needle-point of a moment, he hated the pampered fish and wanted to see them die, but he was afraid of doing anything further or more positive.

Dimly, he realized that not even Vance, his friend, would condone his killing of the fish, but he wanted to kill them. They swam, opening and closing their mouths. The ammonia water slowly disappeared through the overflow pipe, and the fish still swam with lacy fins. Frustrated, Hully turned to the windows and had to restrain himself from smashing his fist through the big plate glass pane.

Chapter Seven

Vance awakened at about eleven that morning. The venetian blinds were drawn so that the heavy morning sun would not sprawl over his bed and pin him to the mattress, and for a moment when he opened his eyes the room seemed to have that hushed, semi-gloom typical of funeral parlors, banks and sick rooms in which invalids had long lain in silent, reproachful uncomplaint. And for a few minutes he had the feeling of awakening in a strange place and not knowing where he was. Even such familiar objects as the limed oak chest of drawers across the room, the bathroom door and the tall ceramic lamp beside his bed seemed darkened and withdrawn from him like alien things in a hostile hour.

For the second consecutive day, he had a hangover caused by the mixture of beer, 'shine, rum and bourbon that he had drunk the night before. He had no headache, but his eyes had the feeling of being reluctant to open and focus and he was faintly sick to his stomach. There was also a sensation of slight apprehension, as if he had done something reprehensible the night before and was now about to be punished for it. It was the combination of all this, plus something that still lay submerged in his mind, that gave him a sense of drifting unreality.

He took a heavy breath and, bunching the pillow under his head, turned on the bed to keep the slatted light from the window out of his eyes. He tried to sleep again, but the heavy pounding of his heart and that apprehensive feeling of unease kept his eyes open and staring at the streaked surface of the hastily painted wall. The streaks and whorls gradually assumed almost recognizable shapes—a bear with its mouth open; a large, angular bird in perilous flight; something, possibly a man, falling backward from a ladder. There were unformed flowers that seemed to have burst into obscene bloom before fully ready, a long stain like the tear from a stricken giant, smoke rising from a broken oblong box—all over-laid with the bars of vertical brush marks.

But he was still sodden and flaccid with the need of more rest and sleep, neither of which were possible. After a while, he rose heavily from the bed and plodded into the bathroom. Unaccustomed to hangover, for he seldom drank very much, he had none of the usual remedies in the medicine chest over the hand basin—except for a small box of baking soda that he used to brush his teeth. He had never liked the sharp flavors of commercial toothpaste or powder which always made him feel as if he were scrubbing his mouth with candy. He poured about a quarter-inch of baking soda into the bottom of a glass which he filled with lukewarm water and drank off in a long, dogged gulp. Then he went into the kitchen and made himself a cup of strong coffee with hot water from the tap and a heaping tablespoon of what he called "that damn powdered gunk," instant coffee grains. He shambled back, after that, to the bathroom and took a hot shower followed by a cold one.

During all this time he had thought of nothing but ridding himself of the suffocating hangover. It was not until he started shaving that he remembered Maddie and all that had taken place the night before. His heart seemed to turn in his chest and clench there, like a fist, and his hand was shaking a little when he turned back to the mirror on the medicine chest door and resumed shaving.

His telephone stood on the undershelf of a lamp table beside the lounge chair at the window, but he carefully avoided even looking at it when he returned to the bedroom to dress. His physical hangover was gone, but the feeling that something irrevocable and important and possibly censurable had taken place still remained.

He took a long while dressing to keep his mind from the telephone in the living room. After a lot of fumbling around and opening and closing drawers, he finally put on a cool dark green cotton sport shirt, tan orlon slacks, straw rubber-soled sandals and no socks. He lit a cigarette and dallied in the bedroom for another ten minutes, sloppily making his bed, hanging away his clothes of the night before, putting his socks, shirt, handkerchief and underwear in the laundry hamper in the closet. When at length he went back to the living room, he walked immediately to the telephone. He stared at the curved, black handset, that sick feeling beginning to churn in his stomach again. With an abrupt, almost angry gesture, he scooped the telephone book from the shelf of the lamp table and quickly thumbed to the page on which the phone number of Wes's lumberyard was listed. He dialed the number with sharp, jabbing stabs of his forefinger. It rang for several minutes and was finally answered by the tired, harassed voice of Cassidy, Wes's yard superintendent. Vance knew him fairly well, for once a week, on Friday nights, Cassidy came to Tate's and sat at the end of the bar, drinking six or seven bottles of beer in fatigued, gloomy silence, taking no part in the bibulous and sometimes hysterical merriment that raged around him. At such times, looking at Cassidy's tragic Irish face, Vance had the fleeting feeling that he was playing host to the decline and fall of the Roman Empire amid a senseless Bacchanalian revel. Which of course was nonsense. The customers who came to Tate's were ordinary people, focused in a moment of induced relaxation.

"I'm looking for Wes, Cassidy," Vance said. "Have you seen him this morning?"

Cassidy swore wearily and obscenely and with Celtic conviction.

"No, I haven't seen him, Vance," he said finally. "I don't think anybody has seen him except the trolls."

"Have you heard from him?"

"Heard from him!" Cassidy laughed hollowly. "Vance, when he disappears like this, he goes to a place where telephones haven't been invented yet, if you know what I mean. He's in Cloud-Cuckoo Land playing footsie-footsie with the leprechauns. At times like this he becomes a shy pixie and hides in the shade of the mandrake. Only those who are born with a caul can find him."

"He couldn't be home by any chance, could he?"

"I've been calling his home every five minutes on the minute. But home! My God, home is where he'll be any place but. The last time he took off, he wound up in Key West because he wanted to play crap with the sailor boys. He was gone damn near a week and came home with a five thousand dollar diamond ring the size of a jelly glass. We lost a thousand dollars in business, and he wins a five thousand dollar ring in a crap game. Honest to God, Vance, I think the guy was born with a rabbit's foot in his mouth. We're going nuts out here at the office, and he's probably off someplace winning a yacht, matching pennies."

"Have you called the police or the hospitals?"

"Vance, I've called everybody but Walt Disney, which is probably where I'm making my mistake. I should call Disney. Wes is probably out there posing as a model for the seven dwarfs." Cassidy's voice tightened angrily. "For crissake, we're hung up on a shipment of striated mahogany plywood paneling for old man Roth, and Wes could straighten it out in two minutes. There's fifteen hundred bucks involved, plus getting the contractor sore at us, plus getting old man Roth sore at us, plus getting the shipper sore at us, plus me blowing a permanent hole in my stack. Jesus, Vance, I'd even call Jack the Ripper if I thought there was a chance I could get hold of Wes right this minute. But what am I worrying about? It's his dough, his lumberyard. I can always go on relief when the business goes kaput. But if you see him, for crissake, tie him hand and foot and bring him straight over."

"I sure will, Cassidy."

"Thanks, pal. I'll chain him to a stack of two-by-fours when I get my hands on him, though right now he's probably in Weehawken, New Jersey, winning the Forty-second Street ferry in a poker game. But how come you're looking for him, fellow sufferer? Did he borrow your car, your wife or your last pair of pajamas?"

"No, he got plotzed in Tate's last night and I meant to take his car keys away from him, but I got busy and the next time I turned around, he was gone. I just wanted to make sure nothing happened to him."

"Oh. I suppose he left his wife high and dry as usual. She sounded sore when I called her up."

"Naturally she's worried. We tried to find him last night, but as you say, he's probably in Weehawken."

"You had to run her home?" Cassidy's voice was just a shade too casual.

Vance said quickly, "You know me, Cassidy. I run the taxi service for deserted wives. Two or three times a week I have to take some louse's spouse home."

"We-ll," Cassidy said vaguely, "it sounds like nice work if you can get it."

"Don't be a jerk!"

"Sorry, lover. No offense. I've associated with low characters so long that sometimes I forget that there are some gentlemen left in the world. Anyway, if you made a pass at Wes's wife, you'd have to wear fur-lined gloves. She's a real chilled frill, a frigid Brigid."

"I'll never know," said Vance, trying to sound disgusted with the whole business. "They're all dead freight to me when I have to take them home after spending eight hours behind the bar in that rat race down at Tate's. A guy doesn't think of making a pass when his feet hurt."

"Oh, you make love with your feet? That's a new one on me."

"Go to hell, you old goat."

"I'm right there, lover. Me and a half carload of striated mahogany plywood paneling. If you'll excuse me now, I'm going out for a light lunch of fingernails."

Vance hung up and after a moment or two, called the Sanibar Police Headquarters. A different desk sergeant was on duty.

"Who's this calling?" he asked.

"Just a friend."

"What friend? We don't give out any information like that unless we know who we're talking to."

Remembering the half-joking, half-leering response he had gotten from Cassidy, Vance decided quickly to keep Maddie's name out of it.

"This is Vance, the bartender at the Pelican Bar," he said. "Elwood got drunk at our place last night and nobody's seen him since. He's one of our steady customers, and we'd just like to be sure nothing's happened to him."

"Well, as far as we know, nothing has, and if I was you, I wouldn't worry about it. Elwood pulls this stunt regular."

"Thanks."

"Okay, but the next time don't let him *get* drunk in your place. If you were any kind of barkeep, you wouldn't let a guy get in that condition."

Vance said angrily, "We do it on purpose," and hung up.

He went into the kitchen and poured himself a shot of bourbon. His hands were shaking a little, though he knew that it wasn't the pick-me-up that he needed. His hangover was entirely gone. He knew he was going to call Maddie and he knew he wasn't going to be able to keep himself from it.

Ten minutes later he called her.

Her voice was harsh over the telephone, as if she had not slept and the strain had mounted.

"Oh," she said when he identified himself, "you didn't find him by any chance, did you?"

"Not yet. I've been checking here and there, but nobody's seen him, including the police."

"At least he hasn't been in an accident, or I'd have heard. I suppose that's something to be thankful for."

"Do you want me to keep checking?"

"Go ahead, if you want to, though I don't think it'll do any good. Oh damn him anyway! I don't know why I worry myself sick over him."

Vance hesitated. "Would—you want me to come over for a little while?" he asked.

"No!" she said violently.

It was like a slap, but he quickly reminded himself that she probably was worried sick. Even if she didn't love Wes, which he knew she didn't, she'd naturally be worried. She couldn't help it. She wouldn't be human if she weren't.

"Sure, honey," he said gently. "I just thought you might want to talk to somebody, that's all."

"I don't even want to *see* anybody!"

"Sure. I'll call you if I hear anything about Wes. Somebody might have seen him someplace."

"Don't call me unless you hear something. This is a party line and I have some damn nosy neighbors."

"I know, honey—"

"And don't call me honey over the phone! Don't you have any sense? I just got finished telling you that this is party line."

"Okay. Sure. I'll keep my ears open in case I just happen to hear something."

"Go ahead if you want to," she said, suddenly and wearily indifferent. "I'm getting to the point where I don't care anymore. If he gets himself in a mess, he can get himself out of it. I won't lift a finger for him. Thank God I made him put the house in my name. At least they can't take *that* away from me if he kills or maims somebody."

Though she didn't want to talk to him, for obvious reasons, Vance was reluctant to hang up. "Why don't you lie down and try to get some rest," he said. "I'll bet you haven't been to bed at all since last night."

She said, "Please!" and hung up.

It was so abrupt that it was a moment or two before Vance realized that he was holding a dead phone in his hand. He slowly replaced it in its cradle. He wondered sickishly if she were furious because of what had happened between them the night before. He wouldn't blame her if she were. He should never have done it. She'd been drinking too much, and there was that strain she was under and—well, he should never have done it. It was as bad as making a woman drunk to get her in bed with you.

How could she possibly be in love with him, Vance thought with a growing, corrosive self-disgust. Last night was the first time he had ever really even talked to her for any length of time except the usual things you say at the bar. It had been a lousy, lousy, lousy thing to do. No wonder she was sore at him. He had picked her off when what she really needed was somebody to see her through the mess, instead of adding to it. A street-corner wolf couldn't have done a better job of kicking her when she was down.

Oh, God, he thought, *by now she's probably got the idea the whole thing was a build-up.*

It made him feel like a heel. *Call me O'Sullivan*, he thought, curling his lip.

Though he had just dressed completely, he went back to the bedroom, stripped off his clothes and put on a pair of swimming trunks, and then drove down to the beach. Again the Gulf was as calm as a plaza in a park on the Sunday afternoon and he swam for two hours, so far out at one time that the land was no more than a hazy pencil-line on the eastern horizon.

He felt tired and heavy when he walked into the Pelican Lounge to go on duty that evening. He had used the punishing crawl stroke while swimming instead of the side or breast stroke, and his arms and legs felt as if they had been stuffed with lead dust. The hours until two A.M. stretched ahead of him like a single line of discouraged footprints into a sterile desert.

Hully was sitting on a case of Seagram's in the storeroom, wearing a horrendous sport shirt of lavender and yellow and a pair of clean, unironed, though wind-smoothed, blue jeans that he washed every day and hung out to dry on a clothes line behind the tavern. His hair was finger-combed and there was a rapt expression on his face as he turned something in his huge hands, holding it occasionally to the light so that it glinted. He started when he saw Vance there and hastily stuffed the thing he had been playing with into the pocket of his jeans. He stammered a hello and looked as if he had been caught doing something shameful. Vance thought nothing of this. He knew that Hully liked to handle all sorts of brightly colored odds and ends. Hully sidled into the bar, wiping his hands down the sides of his thighs.

"You want I should stack the beer for you, Vance?" he mumbled.

He looked so much like a St. Bernard that expected to be kicked that Vance gave him a grin and said, "Sure, thanks. I don't know what I'd do without you, Hully."

Hully said fiercely, "I'd do anything for you, Vance. All you gotta do is name it, is all. Just name it."

"The beer will be all right now, thanks, pal."

Vance turned and watched the big man lumber out toward the cooler through the storeroom. *Now what brought that on*, he wondered, not knowing that Hully had been seething all afternoon with the fantasy that Tate was going to fire Vance.

He busied himself slicing limes and lemons and making juice and simple syrup while Hully devotedly stacked the bottles of beer in the small cooler under the back-bar. Vance gave him a bottle of Tropical and Hully went happily back to the storeroom to drink it, hiding it as usual under his shirt so that Tate wouldn't see it.

Cora came in at seven. She gave Vance a cold glance and no answer to his greeting and went to the back room to change into her uniform. There were no customers and she went around to the tables in the empty room, making sure that each one had a menu, a liquor list, pepper, salt, sugar, mustard and a bottle of catsup. She filled a few of the sugar bowls from the bag in the kitchen. Two men came in, but they sat at the bar and ordered whiskey with beer chasers and then sat talking quietly about a proposed fishing trip into the Gulf of Mexico. Cora wandered aimlessly around the adjoining room, but always drifting closer and closer to the service end of the bar where Vance was squeezing fruit juice for the mixed drinks. At length, she was standing there watching him and he gave her a small grin.

"Quiet tonight," he said, looking at the empty tables in the other room.

"Yeah," she said in a waspish voice, "not like last night."

"We had a nice crowd last night."

"I didn't mean that."

"What?"

"I didn't mean the crowd. I meant afterwards."

"Afterwards? I don't get it."

Cora laughed nastily. "When you took that Elwood dame home, I mean."

"Oh, for God sake!"

"Oh pardon me, I'm sure. Maybe it was just my imagination. Maybe it was Marjorie Main you took home."

Vance looked up. "Cut it out," he said angrily.

"Well, well, well, like that, eh?" Cora gave that artificial, brittle laugh again. "I'm sure I don't know what you're complaining about. Wes Elwood spends all his time in gin mills, and you can spend your time with his wife. Pretty soft, I'd say."

Vance controlled his temper. He knew that Cora was needling him now and that getting angry would just give her a little more fuel to burn him with.

"Okay," he said, going back to work. "The next time Wes gets plotzed, you can take her home."

Cora's jaw dropped for a startled moment, not expecting that response, but she tossed her head and said, "Well, well, well, I can hardly wait. But where'll you be, in the back seat with her?"

"That's right. Maybe I'll even bring a couple of other women and make a real party of it. We could park someplace and you could join us. I'll bring a light lunch."

"Don't flatter yourself. You ain't that good."

"I know, but I'm practicing to be."

"You'll never be that good, big boy, so don't kid yourself."

"I'm taking vitamins."

"Ha-ha-ha, I'm laughing. They ain't invented the stuff you could take to make you that good. The best day of your life you'll never be that good. You sure hate yourself, don't you?"

Vance pretended to consider that. He shook his head. "To tell you the truth, I don't," he said. "All things considered, I get along pretty well with myself."

"Oh, brother! Now I've heard everything."

Her face was flushed and her hands were clenched at her side. She was furious, but she didn't know what to do about it. She knew he was laughing at her and in some way or other had taken the conversation out of her hands.

"Well," she said in a clotted voice, "all I can say is you're just kidding yourself with that dame. I'll bet you didn't even get to first base with her."

"First base?" he said pretending to be puzzled. "But all I did was drive her home, not play baseball with her. It was much too dark. Anyway, football's my game."

"You kill me. A comedian, that's what you are, a real comedian."

"No, a card. I'm a card. Ask anybody and they'll tell you that I'm a card. I used to be a hot sketch, but I graduated. I took a correspondence course. Next year I'll be a comedian, but I have a little more studying to do."

"Remind me to laugh, willya?" she said, now in a deep, consuming rage.

"Okay," he said, "laugh."

She made a grating, inarticulate noise deep in her throat, beyond words for the moment.

"Well," she managed to say finally, "all I can say is, you're wasting your time with that Elwood dame. She swallowed an ice cube when she was a baby and it ain't melted since!"

Vance raised his eyes. Her mouth was shapeless and twitching and he knew that he had given her a thoroughly bad time, had rubbed her raw. Maybe it would have been better to have let her take out her spite on him and have gotten it out of her system. Instead, he had turned it back on her, and it was eating her. What she thought about Maddie and him hadn't really meant anything one way or the other, but because he had felt lousy about what had happened between him and Maddie, he had taken it out on Cora. It was a lousy thing to have done.

"Let's cut it out, honey," he said gently. "This isn't getting us any-place."

"Sure. Like last night you didn't get anyplace too."

"Let's forget the whole thing, okay?"

"What a stinker!" she said in a final effort to lash him. "You'll get yours someday, just wait. It's only a matter of time when it catches up with you, and don't worry, it always does. You'll get yours but good."

"You got customers, honey," said Vance, nodding toward the adjoin-ing room into which a party of four elderly tourists had just entered and were fussily arranging themselves at one of the tables, the two women on one side and the two men on the other, in the manner of people who had long been unadmittedly bored with one another.

Neither Vance nor Cora noticed how Hully glowered hotly after her when she walked away from the bar, her buttocks rolling with exag-gerated contempt.

The bar, as usual, started to fill up around eight o'clock, and before nine it was as noisy as a machine shop under full production, the juke box roaring as it always did. Once Vance overheard two men talking about Wes Elwood's disappearance, and he walked closer to hear what they were saying without appearing to eavesdrop. They were laugh-ing about it with good-humored pity and disdain.

"There's something wrong with the guy, that's all there's to it. You don't drink like that and go off on toots unless there's something wrong with you."

"He's not right in the head, if you ask me. It gets you after a while, drunk every night. He'll wind up in a ward, you watch."

"I don't get it. He's got everything to live for, a good business, a good-looking wife—"

"Good looks ain't everything, Walter."

"You got something there, Henry. Beauty's only skin deep, like they say. Not that I got anything against the woman—"

"Me neither. For all I know there's nothing wrong with her. But everybody knows they fight like cats and dogs."

"You can't blame her, the way he drinks. You don't drink that way and I don't drink that way and I'll bet nobody you know except him drinks that way."

"That's right. Normal people don't drink that way."

"I wonder where he disappeared to this time. The last time it was Key West, I heard."

"Well, I was talking to Joe Cruickshank and he says he heard Frank Baker saw him down in Miami this morning, orey-eyed drunk and slobbering over some woman in the park by Biscayne Boulevard."

"I didn't know he was a chaser, too. Usually drunks don't go for the women so much."

"You never can tell, you know."

"That's a fact ..."

Vance walked away from them, contemptuous. He thought for a moment of calling Maddie, but he doubted that Wes had been seen in Miami. Especially with a woman. Wes had never paid any attention to women, and he was definitely not a chaser. All Wes cared about was the bottle. Vance had seen women, good-looking ones, hang around his neck to promote a drink, and Wes had always pushed them away, even when they made an obvious play for him. When Wes was drinking, he never wanted anything but liquor. Women didn't interest him at all.

And as far as Wes being seen in Miami, Vance wanted to talk to Frank Baker before repeating that part of it to anybody. Frank Baker wasn't the sort who'd tell anybody he'd seen Wes with a woman, even if he had. Vance wanted desperately to call Maddie, just to talk to her and hear the sound of her voice, but after what he had done last night, he knew that she would have nothing but contempt for him and certainly wouldn't want to talk to him. *What a lousy thing to have done!* Vance felt sick at the thought of it, knowing that he would never have made a pass at her in her condition if he hadn't drunk so much before going to her house.

It was about eleven o'clock when Cora rushed to have all her tables completely served so that she could go out to the patio for a cigarette break. The moon was full and even the shadows of the cabbage palms seemed brilliant. She felt, rather than heard, someone behind her, and she turned quickly, because sometimes a drunk would follow her out and make a grab at her and she'd have to fight him off. She made an exasperated sound in her throat when she saw that it was only the big-shouldered bulk of Hully against the white cement block wall of the storeroom.

"It's you," she said angrily. "What's the idea of sneaking up on people, you dumb crut. Go away. You bother me. Crawl back in your dog house."

He came heavily and grabbed her by the arm. Startled, she struggled to pull away from him.

"Cut it out now," she said. "Beat it."

"I heard you in there," he said heavily.

"So what? Leggo a me, you dumb ox. Come on, leggo, dammit!"

He tightened his hand and jerked her closer. "You cut it out, you hear me?"

Cora did not know what he was talking about and she began to panic. She was struggling violently to free her arm, but his immense hand was as immovable as reinforced concrete.

"Leggo!" she cried. "Leggo or I'll scream and they'll come out and clobber you, you damn fool. Leggo!"

His left hand shot up and half circled her neck. He did not squeeze. He merely held it there against the soft fullness of her throat, but she had the feeling that if he constricted his fingers, he would crush every bone in her neck. Her eyes distended with sudden terror and she stood rigid, unable to move or even utter a sound. Her jaw wobbled and a sound like "waa-waa-waa-waa" gobbled from her.

"I heard you," he said, holding her so close that, nightmarishly, she could see the thick pores in his coarse face, the face itself an over-hanging rock that seemed about to fall and crush her. "You leave Vance alone, you hear me. I heard you going at him in there before. You lay off him."

Terror-stricken, she wanted to tell him that she would never again say another word to Vance, but the words filled her throat and choked her. Hully's face was like stone and even though his breath smelled of beer, it was the breath of doom.

Hully said menacingly, "You lay off Vance or I'll bust you. He's my friend, so you lay off him. Understand?"

Miraculously, she was able to nod her head.

"Okay," he said, "now you leave him alone."

She nodded frantically. He released her and gave her a staggering shove toward the door.

"Nobody gets away with anything with Vance so long's I'm around," he said loudly, "and I'll bust them if they try it!"

Cora fled into the tavern.

Chapter Eight

The Four Roses clock over the cash register showed midnight when the man in the tan sport shirt and dark brown slacks walked into the lounge, looked at the crowd and went straight down to the service end of the bar that was divided from the rest of it by curving chrome piping. He was a man with a flat, slab-like face and brownish-gray eyes the texture and color of putty.

Vance was busy and he patiently waited ten minutes to catch his eye and signal him with a crooked forefinger.

"Your name Vance?" he asked in a voice that matched his eyes.

"That's right—"

"I want a word with you."

"I'm sorry, friend, but this is our busy—"

The man held out his right hand, cupped, and there was a police badge in it. "Durkin," he said. "Headquarters."

Vance said, "Okay," and called to Tate who was hopping irritably around the kitchen, trying to keep up with the orders of sandwiches, hamburgers and coffee that always multiplied about this time of night. He snarled, but came out irritably when he saw Vance duck under the flap of the bar and walk toward the front door with the man in the tan sport shirt. Actually, he knew that Vance would not leave the bar at this time unless it were absolutely necessary.

Durkin walked over to a black Ford sedan and leaned against the side of it. He took out a package of cigarettes and offered Vance one. Vance put the cigarette into his mouth and Durkin lighted it with a cigarette lighter made from the brass casing of a machine gun bullet.

"We just found Wes Elwood," he remarked casually.

His tone indicated absolutely nothing, and Vance said, "He's in trouble?"

Durkin lifted one indifferent shoulder.

"Depends on how you look at it. He's dead."

Vance gasped. "He's what?"

"Dead. We all get that way sooner or later, only he got that way sooner. A couple of guys were out in the bay spearing for fish in a boat with a Coleman lantern and they saw his car in the channel off the bridge in ten feet of water. Elwood was kind of caught under the steering wheel, just sitting there. Dead. Went off the embankment just before the bridge."

"The poor guy!"

"Well, that's the way it goes. He was pretty drunk last night, wasn't he?"

For some reason, the first thought that came to Vance was how Maddie had talked about the insurance, and he said evasively, "He'd been drinking. Everybody who comes into the Lounge has a drink or two."

"But he was soused."

Vance did not want to make any positive statements and he said, "I wouldn't know."

"Nuts. He was soused." Durkin sounded as if these were dull routine questions, just something that had to be done and gotten out of the way. "Did he have any trouble with anybody here before he left?"

Vance shook his head emphatically. "He was never that kind of drunk. Why?"

"Just wondered, that's all."

"All he did here was play the piano. He didn't have any trouble with anybody."

"What time'd he leave?"

"I don't know. I didn't see him go."

"But he was soused before he went."

Durkin stated that as a fact, and Vance shrugged, flipping the ash from the end of his cigarette, looking off into the night and waiting for Durkin's next questions with the growing certainty that the detective was fully aware of almost everything that had taken place the night before. Durkin had lighted a cigarette, too, but he did not smoke it. He let it burn away between his fingers and from time to time tipped off the ash with a touch of his spatulate thumb. His whole manner was singularly incurious.

"You knew damn well he was soused," he said.

"Yes," said Vance. "But what difference does that make?"

"Why didn't you say so in the first place?"

"Would you?"

"It wouldn't make any difference to me one way or the other. If he was drunk, he was drunk. The point is that you and his missus chased over half the county looking for him last night."

Vance thought tensely, *here it comes*, but merely said, "The point of what?"

"You must of been a particular friend of his. I mean, to spend the night looking for him after work."

"I wasn't any kind of friend of his, except that he came into the bar three or four times a week. But his wife was very upset because he had been drinking and had gone off in the car like a damn fool and—"

"Oh, yes. The missus. Not a bad looking piece. Your girl-friend?"

"Hell no!"

"What're you getting sore about? It wouldn't be the first time. A guy's a lush, so the wife sleeps around. It happens all the time."

"Not with me."

Durkin tilted his head and looked at Vance with casual interest. "Something wrong with you maybe?" he asked. "From what I hear, if it ain't some guy's wife you're taking home, it's another's. You mean you just take them home?"

"Straight home," said Vance shortly.

"And that's all?"

"That's all."

"You in the war?"

"Korea."

"Oh. Got 'em shot off, was that it?"

Vance realized suddenly that Durkin was trying to make him lose his temper, for some reason, and that if he did, it would be to his disadvantage. The thought that this was a calculated routine on Durkin's part steadied Vance. Even Durkin's insults were as impersonal as the noise of an alarm clock.

He made a formless gesture with the hand in which he held his cigarette. "All I got in Korea," he said, "was a case of frostbite and a bellyache from eating too many Hershey bars one morning after the squad came back from patrol. Otherwise I'm all in one piece. Does that answer your question?"

"Yeah, but I still don't get it. You take them home, but that's all. Maybe you're a queer."

"Maybe you are. Maybe everybody is."

Durkin spun his cigarette away from him. It made a red arc in the darkness and went out in a shower of sparks when it hit the road.

"I like tough boys," he said. "The tougher they are, the better I like them. They don't bend—they break. That wasn't the first time you took Elwood's missus home, was it?"

"I've taken her a few times when he got drunk and left her stranded."

"But that was the first time you went looking for him, isn't it?"

"Yes, because he shouldn't have been driving a car, and she was ready to throw a wingding, and anyway I wasn't sleepy. I also called the hospital, the highway patrol, the sheriff, and your own headquarters. Haven't you ever done anything for anybody without expecting something in return?"

"I might have, but not lately. Where'd you go looking for Elwood?"

"The all-night joints. You know where they are, all three of them."

"Tough," murmured Durkin without looking at him. "A real tough boy. Tough as they come."

Vance said, "Nuts," and ground out his cigarette with the toe of his shoe. "Is there anything else you want to know?"

Durkin had been leaning against the car, and he pushed himself erect, rolling his shoulders a little as if he were stretching after a short nap. "Later maybe. It's all pretty cut and dried."

Unaccountably, Vance felt a sense of relief when Durkin said that. Despite the tenor of the questions about him and Maddie, it had just been routine, after all. He had a very guilty feeling about Maddie. It was impossible that Durkin could know *all* that had happened last night, but there was a stolid relentlessness about the man that was a vague threat in itself—a patient stripping away, like that of a methodical medical student dissecting a corpse with the knowledge that sooner or later every nerve and fiber would be exposed, noted and analyzed.

"Does Mrs. Elwood know?" Vance asked.

Durkin moved a noncommittal shoulder. "I told her."

Vance hesitated. "Is she all right?"

"Not exactly all broken up, if that's what you mean. She'd been hitting the bottle."

"She's had a rough time."

"Who hasn't?"

"You weren't married to the guy."

"She didn't have to stay married to him, friend. Nobody pointed a gun at her. You can get a divorce in a month down here in Florida."

"It's not always that easy."

"Easy enough. Well, I'd better be getting along. If you think of anything, give me a ring at headquarters."

He climbed stolidly into the car and Vance stood in the parking lot and watched him drive off and turn into the road to Sanibar. The red tail lights winked as the car picked up speed and passed the grove of punk trees that lined the road. Vance took a cigarette from the package in the breast pocket of his sport shirt and walked slowly back into the Lounge. For some reason, the death of Elwood made him feel hollow and dispirited. He had hardly known the man, except casually over the bar the way you know the other regular customers, but it had been a needless and senseless death, and even a little ignominious. Wes Elwood had deserved better than that.

Vance thought about calling Maddie on the phone, but decided against it. It wasn't the time. Tomorrow morning would be better. He went back to work behind the bar and Tate walked irritably into the kitchen. Hully lumbered in from the storeroom and, pretending to check the supply of bottled beer in the back-bar cooler, muttered to Vance, "That feller say something to make you mad, Vance?"

"Mad? No, nothing like that."

"You look mad."

"No. He was a cop. He told me Wes Elwood is dead."

Hully stammered, "Dead?"

"Drowned. But don't go broadcasting it."

"Don't worry about me, Vance. Anything you say goes. Drowned?"

"Yeah. Get the beer if we need it, will you?"

"Sure, Vance. Anything you say."

Hully felt as if he were walking more lightly than ever before and his hand closed happily around the diamond ring in his pocket. It was his now, all his!

Chapter Nine

Durkin had the reputation in the department of being a careful, methodical investigator who missed nothing and cleaned up a case as if he were removing dust from a small rug with a powerful vacuum cleaner. This was true enough as far as it went, but it wasn't really true. He wasn't merely methodical; he was insatiable for detail. He was like a man who omnivorously read every book he could lay hands on, regardless of the contents. It was the same with his police work. Regardless of the importance of the case, he wanted to know everything about everyone concerned in it. His memory was crammed with inconsequential data of cases that had been long settled and forgotten—but *he* had never forgotten. He gave the impression of being a lumpy, stolid man, but he could retell with great relish time and again the intimate and irrelevant facts of, say, old man Malone whose young wife had run away from him. Not with anyone, but just away, back to her parents in Nutley, New Jersey, because she had married the old man for his money and had found out that it was he who had gotten the bargain, not she. Durkin had worked on that disappearance, and when he finished, he knew everything about the woman, including her schooling, bodily functions, favorite flowers, meaningless household habits, and so on interminably. He loved such detail for its own sake, hoarding it like a miser amassing a fortune that has no real meaning for him outside its actual bulk.

Yet he was not a stupid man, and after a week he had told old man Malone that she had gone home to her mother. It was probably not a brilliant deduction, but from his endless, surfeiting questions, he knew surely where she had gone. That conclusion, however, was just the byproduct. The accumulation of the thick file of detail, that he typed very neatly on sheets of white eight-and-a-half by eleven bond paper in triplicate, was the meat of the case that satisfied his odd, omnivorous hunger.

As far as he knew, Wes Elwood had died of drowning. He had no reason to suspect anything else. The body had been taken to the Kling Brothers Funeral Home, the makeshift morgue for the city, and no post-mortem had been performed on it. Everyone knew that Elwood was a periodic drunk, and even Durkin had not been surprised when Wes had been found drowned. It had been predicted for years that some night Wes was going to get a load on and wrap his car around the nearest tree and that would be the end of it. So Elwood's death was neither unexpected nor mysterious. It had been foretold, but Durkin wanted to know everything about it, and everything about everyone concerned. Later, in another year, on a Sunday afternoon when he visited his sister and brother-in-law in Tampa, he would sit, rocking on the front porch, and retell everything in that monotonous, putty-like voice of his, until his brother-in-law yawned while his sister placidly crocheted, unlistening. Durkin visited them regularly once a month, each time bringing exactly the same gifts—candy for his sister, a box of cheap cigars for his brother-in-law, and a package of bubble gum for his nephew.

After leaving Vance, he drove directly to Dick's Bar. He was known there. The bar was outside the city limits of Sanibar, and therefore outside the jurisdiction of the Sanibar police department, a place where Durkin could drink a few glasses of beer after hours and talk to Dick. He sat at the bar and, unasked, Dick drew him a mug of beer and said, "Hi, Durk, what do you know for sure?" and as usual Durkin replied, "Everything I know is for sure," which he meant but which was always accepted as a joke.

Dick laughed and leaned against the bar. "Arrested your mother for anything yet, Durk?" he asked. This was only half a joke, for he regarded Durkin as the toughest policeman in the county. Durkin had once broken up a six-man fight in the bar with his blackjack, knocking all six unconscious and walking back to the bar to finish his mug of beer, disregarding the men who, one by one, climbed unsteadily to their feet and staggered out of the room, holding their battered heads. Also, he had once said, "Sure I'd arrest my mother if she broke the law. That's what they pay me for, ain't it?" This was also regarded as a joke, although no one was exactly sure. Jokes of this sort were usually accompanied by loud laughter, and the closest Durkin had ever come to laughter was a bunching of his mouth.

Durkin waited until the head on his beer had fully settled before he took a drink of it. He did not like a head on his beer. He glanced around the bar, taking his time. There were about twenty men in the room, four of them playing shuffleboard and another six clustered around the dart board. Two men were standing at the pinball machine, arguing drunkenly.

"Hear you had a little excitement here the night before last," Durkin said at last.

Dick cocked his head. "Excitement?"

"Carl Stover finally got himself clobbered, they tell me."

Dick laughed. "That!"

"A fight?"

"If you can call it that," Dick laughed again. "One smack and it was all over."

"It must of been quite a smack."

"It was."

"Who did it?"

"You kidding?" Dick grinned. "You know damn well who did it."

"Heard it was Vance, that bartender from the Pelican Lounge. Was it just talk?"

"It was him all right. Just one smack and Stover was out cold." Remembering, Dick became a little excited and held up his fists. "The neatest thing you ever seen. Stover swings, Vance slips inside and lets him have it. That smack didn't move more'n eight inches. I know, because I seen it. I'd of laid money Vance was in the ring, but he says no."

"Professional, eh?"

"You're not kidding, and I seen lots of fights, Durk. You know most of these comedians around here, they get in a fight and wind up for a punch like they're throwing in from left field, but this Vance, he slips that swing of Stover's and goes in tight and close and I'm telling you he didn't move his fist more'n eight inches. Stover was out before he hit the floor. That son-of-a-bitch Vance can really hit! I ast him was he in the ring, but he says no, but I'd give odds he was in the ring. I seen too many fights. I go down Miami every time there's a big fight, and I know a pro when I see one. Right?"

"If there's one thing you know, that's it," Durkin agreed, watching Dick unwinkingly. "So you think he's a pro, eh?"

"I'd give odds!" said Dick.

"Where's he from?"

Dick shrugged. "Jersey, I'd say. I'm from New York myself, and the way he talks, I'd say Jersey. Newark, maybe. He mentioned the Hudson Tubes once, and another time something about the stink on the Kearny Meadows, then something else about the Lincoln or Holland Tunnel and Bamberger's Department Store and once about Branch Brook Park. So I'd say Newark. Yeah, I'd lay money he's from Newark. I was born in Belleville, New Jersey, myself, right next door to Newark." Dick looked triumphant. "I'd give odds he's from Newark, yessir!"

Durkin mentally filed this away, and then asked, "What was it all about, anyway? A dame?"

"Yeah, but the dame was with Vance, and Stover asked for it, if you know what I mean."

"What dame was it?"

"That waitress in the Pelican, what's her name—Cora something or other. The waitress."

Having no real curiosity, only an indiscriminate thirst for information, Durkin was seldom surprised by anything. He had thought the fight might have been over Maddie Elwood, but the fact that it had been over Cora was not a surprise; it was merely a detail to be remembered.

"That guy sure gets around," he said, thinking of Maddie.

Dick looked interested. "How do you mean, gets around?"

"The waitress one night, and Wes Elwood's wife the next night. He gets around."

"Oh, you mean last night," Dick waved his hand, dismissing last night. "He wasn't with her. They was looking for Wes. The jerk was out on a binge."

"But he was with her, wasn't he?"

"Well, they was together, but he wasn't with her, if you know what

I mean."

"No, I don't get it."

"They was, well, just looking for Wes, that's all. They come in and ask if I seen Wes, but she wasn't with him. I mean, like that."

"Like what?"

"Hell, you know what I mean. She wasn't out with him."

"I heard she was his girl-friend."

Dick said warily, "I never seen them together before." He now sensed that Durkin's questions were taking a definite direction and he wanted nothing to do with that.

Durkin shrugged. "I wouldn't blame him if she was," he said. "I wouldn't mind taking a shot at that dame myself. She might be a screwball, but I'll bet she could show a man a time."

"I wouldn't know. I like a little more meat on them myself. Like that waitress. Now there's a dame—"

Durkin tried a few more questions and then realized that Dick had closed up. He knew enough not to press the matter, so he had another beer, talked about something else for a while and then left.

His next stop was Ella's Bar on the Palmetto Road south of the city. This was also in the county outside the city limits. Durkin did not like Ella's place because he could not talk to her the way he could talk to Dick. Still it was a place in which he had picked up some information from time to time just by listening to the conversation up and down the bar. Ella brought him a beer and stood there looking at him with eyes that were like wet ashes.

"I heard about Wes Elwood," she said in that harsh, ripsaw voice of hers. "Is that why you're here?"

"What'd you hear?" he asked.

"Heard he ran off the road and drowned himself in the channel by the bridge. He was drunk, they say. That a fact?"

Durkin nodded. "Who told you?" he asked, not expecting an answer.

"Bar talk," she said. "If you think he got plotzed in here, you're mistaken. I didn't even see him last night. He got drunk over at the Pelican."

"That's what I heard."

"So?"

"Just checking up, that's all," in that monotonous, plodding manner. "You have to check up. In a case like this you have to find out how drunk he was before he took the dive."

"Nuts. If he was drunk enough to drive into the channel, he was drunk enough. How drunk do you want him to be. Drunk enough to drive into something bigger, like the Gulf of Mexico, for instance. Or maybe even drunker. Drunk enough to drive into something really big, like the Pacific Ocean." Ella's derision was in the twist of her thin, long-bloodless lips.

All of this was entirely lost on Durkin.

"In a case like this," he said seriously, "you have to look at every angle. Wes Elwood was a big man in the county. He had a lot of money—"

"Sure, and a lot of cracker cousins and kin that can all put their 'X' on a ballot when it comes to vote. And it would be very nice for your bosses up in the county seat if they can make a good show on this thing for the Elwood tribe and company."

"That's right," said Durkin, who didn't know irony when he heard it. "You always have to make a show on a case like this. It looks good."

"Yeah, and instead of saying that he was just plain soused, it would look a helluva lot better if you could show that he had a what they call a temporary blackout because he drank lousy liquor in a joint like this."

"Did he?" asked Durkin interestedly.

"Ah, for crissake!" said Ella, spitting in disgust.

"He had a couple drinks of 'shine, maybe?"

"He wasn't even in here last night, I told you. You can ask anybody."

"That's right. I remember. He'd of been found here before he took the dive. Half the county was out looking for him. It's a wonder somebody didn't pick him up someplace. I just can't figure it out. He must of stuck out like a loop-de-loop, drunk driving like he was."

Ella knew that Durkin was not as dense, credulous or as naive and plodding as he sounded. She was very shrewd herself and knew a number of other things about Durkin, but not enough to trust him. There was always an element of uncertainty where he was concerned.

"What're you getting at?" she asked bluntly.

"Me? I'm just trying to get all the details."

"I know you and your details. You want to know what color drawers he had on, when he brushed his goddam teeth, how many dames he had during Lent, and what hand he uses when he gooses somebody, but you always add it up to something, so don't try to kid me. What're you getting at?"

"Was Vance, the bartender from over at the Pelican, in here looking for Elwood last night?"

"You know damn well he was or you wouldn't ask."

"Did him and Miz Elwood have a drink while they were in here?"

"*Miz* Elwood," she mimicked him, taking saturnine delight in it, "didn't come in. She was asleep in the goddam car. I seen her through the window down there." She pointed.

She was much more garrulous than usual, and Durkin made a mental note of the fact. He knew what she had in mind, of course—the bar being open illegally after the closing hour of two A.M. set by law. If it were shown that Wes had had a few drinks of 'shine in her place after two, the sheriff or his deputy, although they knew the bar stayed open all night, would have no choice but to close her up for a while and she would probably have to pay a fine. There was a very small margin of profit in a beer-and-wine joint, even with the side sale of 'shine, and a fine would hurt.

With this as a lever, Durkin said, "I'd hate to see you get in any trouble, Ella."

"I'm not going to. Wes Elwood wasn't in here last night."

"Maybe you forgot. Maybe he just had a drink or two and left, and it slipped your mind."

"Nothing slips my mind. Nothing and nobody, and specially customers."

"And Miz Elwood didn't come in for even one drink?"

"She was asleep in the car. I seen her, dammit! But what difference would it make, anyways? She ain't the one that took the dive in the channel."

"In a case like this," Durkin said patiently, "you have to get all the facts and details, and nothing can take the place of all the details."

"Okay. She had on one of them sunback dresses and she sleeps with her mouth open a little and her head was against the back of the seat and it's my guess she'd passed out—she looked it—but that's just a guess, and on top of that she thinks she's too good to come in my place though that drunk husband of hers's been in here more often than I could shake a bar rag at, and soused to the gills every time. The life she leads him from what I hear, nag, nag, nag all the time ..." She stopped abruptly, realizing that she was talking too much. "But Wes was not in here last night," she said with finality.

"It don't make much difference, I guess," said Durkin, eagerly fondling all these new details in the love-nest of his mind. He was certain now that if he could really put the screw on Ella, she could really tell him all sorts of things about people of whom he had never dreamed. But later, later, when he had more time, and could think of an angle that would open her up. The two o'clock closing law would be a good one, but he knew that he did not have that much influence with the sheriff's department. Ella paid out a certain amount each week for protection, and it would take more than just a favor for the sheriff even to think of closing her up. But an angle would come to him. She was such a fund of comprehensive information that it made him very happy to think that someday he would be able to tap it and add it to his own hoard.

In the meanwhile, there was nothing more he could get from her about Wes Elwood, Maddie or Vance. Being a man who was economical of time when there were fresh people to talk to, he drank what remained of his beer and left.

He did not get much that was new at Mush's C & C Bar on the bay west of Sanibar. He had known Mush for a long time and he knew Mush's desperate eagerness to tell you only what he thought you wanted to hear, and was therefore untrustworthy if you really wanted the true details about anything. Though almost devoid of humor, Durkin did have his moments of levity. He knew that if Mush thought that he, Durkin, wanted to hear that Vance had killed his sister on the night of January 23rd, Mush would certainly agree with him. Had Vance killed his sister? Yes, he certainly had, but what was the date? January 23rd? Yessir, that was certainly the date for a killing, a dark night, yessir. Mush would never come right out and say that Vance *had* killed his sister, but if he thought Durkin thought so, he would agree right down the line. Yessir, he wouldn't put it past Vance at all, and sooner or later everybody feels like killing somebody, and maybe Vance just felt like killing his sister on the night of January 23rd, you never could tell just by looking at a man if he had killed his sister, but he wouldn't be surprised, nossir, specially if a detective like Durkin had all the facts, yessir. This was about as far into fantasy as Durkin ever went. He knew a great many details about Mush, none of them very important except the liquor smuggling part of it, which Durkin had known for a long time, and he could pretty well predict Mush's answer to almost any given question.

In fact, that was one of Durkin's pastimes, if it could be said to be a pastime. He liked to invent conversations with people, and then try them out to see if his knowledge of detail was strong enough to keep him from being too far wrong in any situation. He knew that Dick would react in a certain way if prodded with questions about prize fighting, and Durkin liked to prod and probe just to get those reactions. He knew now that he had a lever with which to open Ella up, and he looked forward to that with relish; she would be a fund of really meaty facts; he knew contemptuously that Mush quiveringly wanted to be all things to all people, and therefore was nothing more than a tub of lard that would take any impression of your finger that you'd care to give it. A tub of lard, and worth just about as much. Less.

But Maddie Elwood and Vance. Durkin frowned. He did not have enough detail on either of them, and as far as they were concerned, you could never tell what way the cat would jump, as they say. Still, he was adding detail to detail and it would not be too long before he could prod either of them and know pretty well in advance what their answers and reactions would be.

Satisfied, he turned his car and drove back to Headquarters, arriving there at ten minutes past four in the morning. He was surprised to see a light burning in the chief's office, and the sleepy desk sergeant nodded in answer to his arched, questioning eyebrows.

"He said to see him when you come in," he told Durkin.

"Something up?"

"Seems like. You been working that Elwood mess, ain't you?"

"Yeah."

Durkin knocked on the chief's door and went in when he heard the Chief's sour and grunted command. The chief was gray and fat and heavy, though not paunchy, and his face was somewhat like Durkin's in its slablike impassivity. He waved a meaty hand at a chair and Durkin sat down, sitting somewhat forward and resting his hands on his knees. The chief was heavily studying a sheet of paper on which several lines were scrawled in messy blue ink.

"I wish they'd talk English," he complained, carefully setting the sheet of paper in the exact center of his blotter, a gesture he used when there was something on his mind. He looked at Durkin.

"You been working on this Elwood thing?" he asked.

"Ever since he was found," Durkin said. "Every minute. I been in four, five bars, had a beer in two of them."

"And you're soused," said the chief, knowing Durkin's reputation for sobriety. "But we'll skip it this time. What'd you find out?"

"Elwood was drunk and a barkeep and Miz Elwood were out looking for him till all hours of the night. Miz Elwood was asleep most of the time, maybe soused, and the barkeep, a guy named Vance from the Pelican, did most of the looking. They drew a blank and went home maybe four, five o'clock. She ain't supposed to be his girl friend, and Vance ain't got the name for being a wolf, but I could do more work on it."

"Fine," said the chief sarcastically. "Dandy. You did just exactly right. I couldn't of done better."

Uneasily, knowing something was coming, Durkin said, "In what way?"

"In every way. Any way you can think of. I couldn't of done better."

"I said I could do more work on it."

The chief's face turned a mottled red and he shouted, "Why the hell didn't you check with the undertaker, you dumb cluck? Elwood wasn't drowned. He was dead before he hit the water. He had a cracked skull and that's what killed him. He was dead before his car left the road. Doc Southall says it's a wonder he lived at all after that cracked skull, but guys have been known to walk around for days with a broken bone in their brains and nothing but a headache. But why didn't you check up, goddammit?"

Durkin looked mildly surprised. "We all thought the guy was drowned."

"Sure, all of you except the guy who'd know—Doc Southall. The guy had a fractured skull. He was slugged."

Durkin nodded. "Then he wasn't drowned. Doc Southall wasn't there when I took him into the undertaker's and there wasn't no blood because the water washed it all off, and he certainly looked drowned, down there in the channel behind the wheel of the car and all. Anybody would of said he was drowned. And here's something else on top of that ..."

The chief waved his hand, silencing him, or Durkin would have gone on and on with one monotonous detail after another. Durkin's delivery was the one thing in the world that could get under the Chief's skin like chiggers.

"Okay, okay, okay," he growled. "You thought he was drowned, but you should of checked, goddammit, and you know damn well you should of checked, so the next time, check. Remember that."

The chief's annoyance was not with Durkin, but with the fact that he now had a murder with which to cope. Ten more yards down the road, just the other side of the bridge, and it would have been in the county and the sheriff would have had to worry about it. But it hadn't been ten more yards, and it had taken place inside the city limits, and now it was going to be a pain in the ass because Elwood had always been a roaming drunk and could have gotten slugged anywhere from West Venice Avenue at the dark end, to the colored quarters in Key West. And it was a mess, because Elwood came from such a goddam mess of a family in the county that they could swing any elections if ever they could get together and agree on what they wanted to do. Now the county was going to be on his neck to clean this up, and the only detective on the force worth anything was Durkin. The chief warmed a little. Durkin. He might go over things with a whisk broom, but there was never a speck of dust left when he got finished. But the pain in the neck about that was that Durkin took forever to add one and one and get two. Durkin's method was to add things by sixteenths, or thirty-seconds or sixty-fourths, or even in millimeters, and six months later tell you the answer is two.

But by Christ, the chief warmed again, you could depend on Durkin. The answer would always be two when he got done, not two and twelve or thirteen maybes, like some of the jerks on the force. It would be two. And if the county really got impatient, he could always bring Durkin in and bore the living hell out of them. Durkin could talk forever if you let him, and those jerks from the county would just have to sit there and let Durkin go into his goddam details. The chief felt a little better, now that he had that part of it settled. If the worst came to the worst, he could turn Durkin loose on them for three or four hours. That'd fix the big-mouthed sons-a-bitches.

"Now what'd you get tonight?" he growled at Durkin.

Durkin inched a little forward on his chair, a movement that usually preceded a long accounting of facts and details. "All there was—"

The chief cut him short again. He believed him. If there were facts to have been gotten, Durkin would have gotten them. All of them, relevant and irrelevant, facts about everybody and everything. Within limits, of course, within limits. Durkin was only human. And there was the time limit, also. A killing or a simple drowning, Durkin would have all the facts.

"Fine, fine, I know I can depend on you. But let's get down to cases. This ain't a drowning no more. It's a killing. Maybe just a fight, or mugging. That's what we'll have to find out."

"No fight," said Durkin.

"Now we're getting someplace. You know that for a fact?"

"No."

"Oh, hell!"

"No fight in any of the joints. It could be a mugging. Wes Elwood wore a big diamond ring."

The chief slapped the desk and said, "The goddam ring!" and snatched up the telephone. He spoke for possibly thirty seconds and then hung up. He looked at Durkin in triumph. "It was a mugging. I just talked to the undertaker, and Wes ain't got the ring. It was taken off. He said you can see where the skin is peeled off the knuckle. It was a mugging."

Durkin considered this. "Well," he said finally, "it could of been. But on the other hand it could of been something else to make it look like a mugging. I could tell better if I knew where Wes was after he left the Pelican. I don't like the mugging angle. We got this town pretty well cleaned up."

"It has to be a mugging."

"It could be, but it don't sound like it. In a mugging, they usually just grab the wallet and run. Rings they don't like. Too hard to get rid of."

The chief put a cigar into his mouth and chewed on the end without lighting it. He seldom lit a cigar. Chewing was much more satisfying and it gave you something to put your teeth into. He respected Durkin's judgment because Durkin had cleaned up some pretty knotty ones that had come in from time to time.

"Well, what else then?" he demanded at length.

"It could of been this Vance and Miz Elwood. Her and Wes ain't been hitting it off, and Vance is a big, good-looking guy that could give her what she wanted. Rummies don't give; they just drink, and she looks like a dame that wants."

"Keep going."

"It ain't come out in the open yet between them, and maybe there ain't nothing there. She's a dame, she likes the buck, so maybe she wouldn't take no chances with Wes still around. Okay. So Wes ain't around no more, and now she can go on the town with this Vance. Now she's got the money and the time and nothing more to worry about."

The chief kept nodding heavily. "You got something to back this up?"

"A few things. Not much."

"Anything to take into court to make a case?"

"Not that much. In a couple days, maybe. I found out Vance maybe was a pug once and came from around Newark, New Jersey. I'll get a report on that. He clobbered Carl Stover with one smack the night before last, and Stover ain't easy to put down. I can see Vance for this job. Maybe him and Elwood got in an argument over the dame and he smacked Elwood maybe a little too hard. Manslaughter."

"Don't forget that diamond ring," the chief said quickly. "The diamond ring was gone."

"The ring," Durkin agreed. "That'd make it plain murder. A killing in the commission of a crime. Murder. Is that what you want?"

"I don't want anything but the facts," the chief said virtuously.

But Durkin knew that the chief would rather have a murder charge against Vance than the slighter one of manslaughter. It would be more dramatic and vote-catching. Durkin didn't really care one way or the other about it. He would accumulate his facts and present them. If they pointed to manslaughter, then it would be manslaughter; if it was murder, then Vance would have to take the big one. But no matter which it was, Durkin would never color the facts. He had too much respect for facts. Facts never lied, though you could make liars out of them, something Durkin would never consciously do.

"You want I should go into this more tomorrow?" he asked the chief.

"Well dammit, I should say so. And if you want any help, just ask for it."

"I don't need no help. Just that report on Vance from Newark, New Jersey, is all for right now."

"Put it on the wire," the chief said magnanimously. He felt easier, now that he had a logical suspect in Vance. You could always depend on Durkin.

Durkin pursed his lips, considering the details he had at his disposal.

"Vance might be kind of tough, but I think I can get to the woman if I get an angle. Women are easier."

"Work on it."

"I am working on it."

"Sure. And Durkin—"

"Yessir?"

"Get me a report on what you did tonight."

"Yessir."

Durkin left the office, plodding a little heavily. The chief hadn't had to ask Durkin to put in all the details. Durkin always put in twice as many details as necessary in his reports, even if it was only a simple hotel theft with the thief already caught. Durkin was thorough. When Durkin made up a case for you to take into court, you knew beforehand if the prisoner spit from the left side or the right side of his mouth. Nobody ever kept any secrets from Durkin.

Chapter Ten

Vance was up earlier than usual the next morning. 10:30. He usually slept until 11:00 or even noon, but the telephone went off at 10:30 and kept ringing and ringing with the dogged insistence of mechanical things that could go on forever unless stopped. Though only half awake, Vance realized that he would have to answer it or never get back to sleep again. He had slept very badly the night before, tortured by dreams of guilt, and hardly at all the night before that, and he wanted to be smothered in sleep. He reached suddenly for the phone on the second shelf of the night table beside the bed and grunted an answer.

It was Maddie and he could tell by the furriness of her voice that she had been drinking. Not that he could blame her, with Wes and all, and now the arrangements to make. The funeral and all that. A needlessly complicated business with caskets, cemetery lots, the number of cars needed for the cortège, a list of persons to be invited, the refreshments back at the house after the burial, the flowers, the notes of thanks afterward—the whole gloomy, dreary mess. "Hi, Maddie," he said, trying to get the right note in his voice, something precariously balanced between his love for her, cordiality and a timbre of proper gravity.

"I'm sorry I was foul to you on the phone yesterday, Van," she said in a voice that swayed and wavered as she must have, standing over there in that house on the Key. "I was all wound up."

"I know. Don't think about it."

"But I have to think about it. You, of all people. After all you did last night. All that endless chasing around. Which you didn't have to do."

"Don't think about it."

"But I do," she said earnestly. "I do think about it. Honestly, I think about it. You don't know how much I think about it, Van."

"Sure," he said soothingly, "sure. I know you can't help thinking about it but try not to. Just try not to think about it."

"This is going to sound awful, Van, but all I feel is a sense of relief. I'm, well, glad it's over. It's something that's been hanging over my head for years and now it seems inevitable that it's over, and in exactly the way it happened. Day in, day out, worrying about him. I suppose I'm a little numb about it. I don't feel anything very much, except that nothing seems very real, nothing. They took me over to the undertakers to identify him, but he didn't seem very real. Just sleeping maybe. Nothing seemed to have changed. I expected him to wake up. Is that normal, Van?" she asked seriously.

"Yes, very."

"You mean, it'll hit me later. Is that the idea?"

"Well, sort of," he said uneasily, not wanting to start any hysterics. "But don't let it get you down. It happens to everybody."

"But all I feel is a sense of relief. That's not normal."

"Yes it is. It's over. You don't have to worry. You know where he is now. You can sleep and not worry. It's very normal."

"Now I know why I called you up. You're so understanding. I wasn't going to call you up, but something made me. Could you come over for a while, Van?"

"If you want me to."

"I want you to. There's nobody else I want here now but you. Could you come over in a half-hour?"

"I'll be right over as soon as I dress."

"A half-hour."

"As soon as I possibly can. Sure, about a half-hour."

"I'll be looking for you."

He shaved, but left without having any more breakfast than a glass of tomato juice and a raw egg shaken up in milk with a half cup of coffee mixed into it. That would hold him. He had on a pair of slacks, a sport shirt and a pair of nylon sandals without socks. It was the quickest and easiest costume he could think of. He wanted to get to her house in a half-hour, not only because of his own desire to see her, but also and mainly because he knew she'd be watching the clock until he came. She'd made such a point about that half-hour.

The front door was partially open and he knew she'd left it that way so he would walk in without knocking. She was lying on the sofa in the living room, dressed only in a beige nightgown and holding a glass of liquor in her right hand. The hand shook ever so slightly with a small, persistent tremor. The drapes were drawn at the windows and the room was in dusk. She gave him a small smile and moved her hand to indicate that he should sit on the sofa beside her. Her body was extremely visible through the nylon gown, but he was certain that she did not realize this. She was numb from the shock, and she had not bothered to put on any clothes since getting out of bed. It made no difference, anyway, not really. That was not what he had come for. He sat down beside her and she fumblingly put her hand on his knee.

"Thanks for coming," she said. "I needed somebody here. I don't know why, but I did. I'm numb, but I wanted somebody here. Isn't that odd?"

"Not at all."

She was very restless and her hand kept moving on his knee, stroking it.

"Would you like a drink?" she asked brightly.

"No thanks. I just had breakfast."

"Would you mind making me one. The bourbon is over there on the radio. Bourbon on the rocks. I don't usually drink in the morning. I don't want you to think I lie around drinking in the morning. You understand, don't you? I know you understand. Bourbon on the rocks, up to here." She gave him her empty glass, indicating with a wavering finger that she wanted it half-full. It was a tall glass.

He went over to the radio and made the drink for her, taking the ice from a chrome thermos bucket that stood beside the bourbon bottle. There were times you had to drink, he thought, feeling miserable that she had to go through this thing. If she wanted to drink, let her. It would put her to sleep after a while, and that would be a good thing. It would smooth down some of the rough edges. Wes had given her a bad time. The most merciful thing, he thought, would be if she could have a temporary case of amnesia, just black out until the whole thing was over, but that wasn't something you could turn on or off, and liquor was the next best. He wished yearningly that there were something he could do for her, but this was one of the times when there was nothing else but to walk alone.

He took the drink back to her. She looked very drawn, he noted, especially around the eyes and mouth. Haggard. He wanted to put his arms around her, but he sat down on the edge of the sofa and put the glass in her unsteady hand.

"So understanding," she said thickly. She crooked her finger at him. "Come here—"

He bent over her because her voice was faltering and he thought she wanted to whisper something, but she clasped him with her left arm and began kissing him wildly around the mouth and chin. He had not expected anything like this and it was a few moments before he reacted at all. He crouched stiffly, immobile as she kissed him and clung to him. She held him tightly and made small moaning sounds in her throat as she tried to burrow her soft, slack lips into his unresponding mouth. But he could not return her kisses. Wes had been found dead a bare twelve hours before— He kissed her awkwardly on the cheek, but could not go beyond that. She cried out and arched away from him, and when he looked down he saw that she had spilled her cold drink, and her high breasts and the indented mound of her belly were molded by the wet fabric of her nightgown.

He jumped up and said quickly, "I'll get you a towel—"

He went into the kitchen and brought back two dish towels. She was lying limply now, her eyes slightly glazed, and he spread the towels on her, not blotting or pressing, just placing them over the wet areas of her nightgown, covering her.

"You ought to try to get some rest, honey," he told her. "You're still all wound up."

She began to cry. Fat tears welled up in her eyes and toppled down her cheeks. She stared straight up at the ceiling, breathing shallowly through her mouth.

"You're in love with that waitress," she said dully. "I could tell."

At first, he did not know what she was talking about, and then he stared at her incredulously. "With who?"

"That waitress. The one who works where you work. And she's in love with you. I could see from the way she talked to you the other night. You can't fool a woman on things like that. She's in love with you."

His impulse was to tell her that she was crazy, but he realized immediately that she was in a state of shock and also that she had been drinking too much. Her face had a dazed expression. She held her glass with both hands, raised it to her mouth and drank deeply. She took a shuddering breath as she swallowed the liquor.

"You're in love with her," she said.

"No."

"Well, she's in love with you," she said sullenly. "And if she's in love with you, she'll find a way to get at you. She's young and good-looking. And she's been with men, too. You can see that just by looking at her. She knows her way around. You can always tell that kind of woman. It's a look they get—"

"Cora's all right," he spoke quietly to soothe her. "But she doesn't mean a thing to me."

"But she's tried, I'll bet."

"We just kid around, that's all. We work in the same place, and it passes the time."

"She's on the make and don't try to tell me differently!" She finished her drink at a gulp and held out her glass. "Make me another one." It was a command and there was a sting in it.

Vance paid no attention to that. He was sure now that she was just taking out something about Wes on him. He hesitated with the bottle at the radio, and then poured her a strong drink. Her nerves were as raw as if they'd been rubbed with emery, and the sooner she passed out, the better. He went back to the sofa and she took the glass from him without a word. She scowled at the amber liquid and threw down a heavy drink of it. Her eyes were actually a little crossed now and her mouth moved formlessly. She was quite drunk. She looked up at him, still scowling.

"She's in love with you."

Vance shrugged and smiled. "But what difference does that make?"

"She'll find a way to get at you. That kind of woman, that kind, they know. They can get at you."

"Not at me."

"Ha, ha, ha. Men. They make me sick. They think they know, but a woman, that kind of woman—" Her voice trailed off and she laughed shortly. "What do you know about women anyway?"

"Not very much."

"You're damn tootin'. You don't know anything. She'll get at you, just watch and see. No scruples. What's she need scruples for? She doesn't need scruples. She's got what it takes. And she doesn't mind giving it away either, if you ask me. You can tell that just by looking at her. She's on the make."

Vance thought it best to agree with her, the way she was, and he said, "Generally speaking maybe, but not for me. I'm just the bartender."

Maddie made a harsh, derisive noise in her throat and glowered at him. "Don't give me that bartender stuff. Just a bartender! Ha, ha, ha. Since when were you just a bartender?"

"That's what they pay me for."

"Oh sure, sure. But you're not just a bartender. Bartenders—" She waved a slack, flopping hand. "Bartenders, they're fat."

"I'm on a diet."

"Oh sure, sure, you're on a diet. Bartenders go on diets all the time. Ha, ha, ha. You're not a bartender and don't try to give me that. You're a—a prizefighter, that's what you are, a prizefighter. The man said so, and he knows. I could tell he knows. All you had to do was listen to him and you could tell he knows. I used to go to the fights. Up in New York. The Golden Gloves. I liked the fights. They don't have fights like that down here. Stinking, lousy place. You ever fight in the Golden Gloves?" She stared owlishly at him.

Unconsciously, his fists tightened, but his voice was still quiet when he said, "No, I never did."

"Where did you fight? I'll bet you were good. I used to like the fights. I went all the time. The Golden Gloves I liked. They were best. Real fights. Do you think I'm a bitch?"

"Hell no!"

"Wes used to call me a bitch all the time. You bitch. Just trying to help him, that's all, the stupid, lazy cracker. Wouldn't have been anything if it weren't for me. No money, no ambition, no nothing. Put him in business. My money. Put him in business. Lumber yard. Had to keep after him. You think I'm a bitch, don't you?"

"No, I don't."

He watched her face sympathetically. Her eyes were drooping and her tongue was very thick. It would not be long now. She finished her drink and held out her glass. "Give me another one, and you don't have to be so stingy, it's my liquor."

He said, "Sure," and took her glass and put it on the floor. She didn't need another one. She was just about ready to pass out now. Her head was a lolling weight on a limp neck and her eyes were mere slits. She put out her hand gropingly and found his knee. Her fingers tightened. "We mean a lot to each other," she said loudly. "A lot." Even though he knew she was very drunk now, something leaped inside him, but all he did was pat her hand and say gently, "That's right, honey."

Her head rolled blindly toward him. "Kiss me."

He bent and kissed her on the cheek. She tried to lift her arms to hold him but they fell slackly. Her eyes opened widely for a moment and she moaned, "Oh, no!" She lay back and for a few seconds her fingers twitched, then quieted. She was asleep. He picked her up and carried her into the bedroom. He laid her on the bed and covered her with a light cotton blanket. He kissed her once again at the end of her open mouth and then walked out.

Chapter Eleven

The sun was bright and high when he walked out, and he paused, blinking, in the doorway with a vague bewilderment in his face as if he had expected it to be dark outside, the way you do when walking out of a movie house after a matinee and return to the world that is. He went down the walk, looked back at the house, and then continued to his car in the driveway. There was a sadness in him and it would not lift.

He drove aimlessly for a while and then finally turned back toward his apartment. He did not know what he wanted to do, but he thought that a long swim in the Gulf might be exactly what he needed, with the calm, clear water all around him and nothing above but the unasking calm blue of the sky. He was more tired than he knew. He was bone-tired and marrow-tired, and hidden uneasily away in the dark corner of his mind was the unanswered question about Maddie. She had said, *We mean a lot to each other*, but she had been very drunk, and when you're very drunk you say things that are severely censored later in your mind and the mind builds a callus of resentment. This was the uneasy part of it. Submerged was the knowledge that Maddie was not a woman who liked to reveal herself too much. Not that she was secretive. No. It was something else. A protective shell, possibly. Or maybe something even different than that. Considering her precarious life with Wes Elwood, she had surrounded herself with something very like the reef that sharp-edged, protecting coral builds around an atoll. There were many sharp, cutting edges around Maddie. He did not think of any of these things consciously, but he knew they were there, and it made him uneasy because vaguely he felt that it menaced his relationship with her and there was nothing that he could do about it while things were so unsettled between them. It was as if he were in a boat and trying to find a passage through the reef to a calm anchorage inside. It was an anxiety, and there was death in a coral reef, as any pilot knew.

As he drove up to his apartment, he saw a police car, with the green-and-yellow insignia on the doors, parked at the curb outside. Feeling that it was there for him in some way or other, he parked immediately behind it, just to show that he was not trying to evade them. He felt very defensive, although he told himself that he really had nothing to hide. Except Maddie. That was the rub. It had nothing to do with Wes Elwood, but it was not something that could be easily explained, if somebody wanted to make something out of it.

In the candid daylight, Durkin looked more dumpy and unhealthy than he had the night before under illusory lights of the bar. His flat face was a grayish-tan that the sun would never brown and his movements were entirely graceless.

Vance said, "Hi. What's on your mind?"

Durkin looked at the apartment house. "Let's go upstairs."

Vance shrugged and led the way into the building. Inside his apartment he said, "A drink? With ice?" Durkin's face had a lard-like shine to it.

"Orange juice, if you got it."

"I have it. Anything in it?"

"Ice."

Vance went into the kitchen and filled a tall glass with orange juice and ice and made himself the same with the addition of a jigger of Jamaica rum. When he went back into the living room, Durkin was glancing at the envelopes of three letters Vance had received through the mail the day before.

Handing him the glass of orange juice, Vance said ironically, "Find anything interesting?"

Unabashed, Durkin dropped the envelopes back on the end table by the studio couch. "Just bills, looks like. You get a lot of bills?"

Vance sat down on the studio couch, placed his glass on the end table and lit a cigarette. "The usual amount. Would you like to see the rest of them?"

Durkin appeared to think it over, but merely said, "Bills," with no interest.

"Well, what's on your mind?" Vance repeated.

Durkin remained standing, an untidy, lumpy figure. He had the air of a man whose only interest was to read the treasurer's report at a chamber of commerce meeting.

"You make pretty good money down at that bar," he said.

"I do all right."

"And you pay your bills as you go along?"

"Is this what you came to see me about? Okay. I owe the cleaner three dollars and seventy-five cents, the laundry four and a quarter, but my rent's paid to the end of the month and I've got money in the bank. If there's anything else you want to know, hell, just ask."

Irony was entirely lost on Durkin. He looked interested. "How much you got in the bank?" he asked.

"None of your goddam business."

"A couple hundred?"

"Oh, for the love of—" Vance's anger evaporated and he laughed. "Eighteen hundred and forty-five dollars," he said. "Are you thinking of asking for a loan?"

Durkin said, "Real tough, a real tough boy," but in a stolid, unimpressed voice.

"Okay, so I'm tough," Vance said angrily. "But I'm getting goddam sick of this. Either come to the point or get the hell out of here. What's on your mind?"

"Well, Wes Elwood wasn't drowned like they thought. Somebody clipped him and he's got a mashed-in head. A fractured skull, they said."

Vance stared at him, uncomprehendingly. "A fractured skull?"

"That's what they said. And somebody stole his ring."

Vance was incredulous. "And dumped him in the water?"

"Oh, he probably drove himself. They sometimes do with a fractured skull, the doc said. They go on for a while and then it hits them and it's all over. He was clipped before he went into the water. That's official."

Vance was suddenly aware that Durkin's flat eyes were fastened on him with clinical interest. He gripped his glass tightly, but his hand was very steady when he raised it to his lips.

"What was it, a mugging?" he asked.

"Could be almost anything at this stage. We'll be able to tell later, maybe."

For a fleeting moment, Vance was coldly afraid of the phlegmatic, grinding persistence of this dull man, but the feeling passed and he asked bluntly, "You think I had something to do with it?"

"Could be. This came in the mail this morning."

He handed Vance a letter. It was written on cheap note paper in a shaky hand.

> "Last night wasn't the first time Vance took that Elwood woman home, or did he take her home? Maybe Wes Elwood didn't have a accident like you think. He could of commited suicide, his wife running around with another guy."

It was unsigned.

Vance did not have to look at Durkin to know that he was being watched very closely by those putty-colored eyes. He could almost smell it. Very casually he refolded the note and held it out to the detective.

"I told you most of that last night," he said.

"Yeah. I know. Your side of it. Maybe there's two sides. Maybe there's even three sides."

Vance had never felt more wary in his life, and he knew that everything he said was being noted, tabulated and filed away in the plodding mind of the dull-looking man who stood before him.

"Three sides?"

"Yeah. Your side, the real side, and the side of the dame that wrote this." He held up the note before putting it into the breast pocket of his sport shirt.

"Dame? You know who it is?"

"Hell, yes. The waitress that works the same place you do."

"Cora?" Vance had a feeling of shock, but it was numbed.

"Yeah, her. I thought it sounded like a dame. Jealous, you know? So I checked a couple places. The super market she has a charge account in, she has to sign a slip. It was her, all right. I had an idea it was her right from the beginning. She was the dame you clipped Carl Stover on account of. I got all that. Maybe she thought she was in or something. I don't know. Anyway, she got all hot and bothered when you went out with this Elwood dame, so she wrote the note. There was nothing to figuring that one out. You can usually figure it out if you stop to think. That part of it's easy."

Vance had a sense of almost complete unreality, with Durkin's dull, teacherish voice droning on and on, making point after point in a logical, monotonous manner, in direct contrast to the terrible information he was conveying—Wes Elwood's violent death, Cora's anonymous note and the implications.

"So she wrote the note," he said. "So what? It doesn't mean a thing."

"Maybe not, but it's something to keep in mind. Here's something else."

He took his wallet from his hip pocket and removed a folded sheet of onionskin paper from it. He opened it and read it carefully, as if to refresh his mind, before handing it to Vance. Vance read only the dateline, Newark, N. J., Police.... He felt as if he was reeling, but automatically his eyes scanned the typewritten page. It was a report on him from Newark. It stated that Vance had been in the ring as a promising light-heavyweight. The man who had written the report had liked Vance because it described him as a good boy and a clean fighter who could use both hands and was almost as strong with the left as with the right. It said that he'd had the bad luck to have been under-matched one night and had almost killed his opponent in the first round in a series of lefts and rights to the head. The referee stopped the fight and the opponent spent three weeks in the hospital but finally recovered. Vance had then disappeared from Jersey boxing circles.

"If he's fighting again, keep your eye on him because he's a damn good kid," the report said. "Hope he's not in any trouble. He never was in any trouble up here."

The rest of the report was routine. It gave his place of birth as Union City, N. J.; he had moved to Tenafly with his parents at the age of twelve, graduated from the Tenafly Elementary School there and shortly thereafter moved to Kearny, N. J. Graduated from Kearny High School and attended Rutgers University, taking a course in accounting and business administration, paying his tuition from the money he made in the fight ring. Unmarried. No known police record.... It was signed by Police Captain J. J. Doyle.

Holding the thin sheet of paper in his hands as if it were a leaden slab, Vance said automatically, "The captain always bet on me. He was a fight fan. He used to come around to the gym all the time when I was training. But it wasn't just me. He was always in the gym. He was nuts about the ring. He couldn't stand a crooked fight, and he could always spot them."

He was just talking. It was just something his voice said. It had no meaning. It was a mechanical response. His mind was locked, like a fist.

Durkin watched him, noting all this. He was interested because, aside from the police angle, you could read everything in Vance's face—shock, horror, guilt, fear, anger, and also a clenching toughness. Durkin was a little uneasy about that toughness. Despite what he had said, he did not like genuine toughness, that hard core of fibre. Surface toughness, hard-talk and bravado, he did not mind, but he did not like the kind of toughness he saw in Vance. If Vance were made of wood, he would be of a toughness that would blunt a knife or an ax. Durkin did not like that kind of toughness at all. He had met it before, and it baffled him. It was something that would not break down, even in the face of facts, and Durkin believed in facts. Facts were the keystone of everything. They held everything up. And they were also the clear, hard burning flame that destroyed all that was false. Yet, this was the kind of toughness that facts could not touch, and Durkin felt resentful.

"You must have quite a wallop," he said.

Vance looked at the paper in his hand and said vaguely, "He had a reputation. He had never been knocked out. They called him The Iron Man. I tried to get him in the first round. He was just a dumb kid they were trying to push too hard. He had a neck like a tree trunk and a jaw that ran straight across his face, no chin. The ones with a long chin are easy to tag. I thought I'd have trouble with him, and I wanted to get it over, so I went in hard in the first round. He was hard. I tagged him with a straight right, and he didn't even blink. I must have hit him twelve or fifteen times on the button before he went down. He didn't even know how to roll with a punch. He just took it, but you can't keep on taking it. He didn't know any more about protecting himself than a bowling alley. All you had to do was roll the ball down the middle."

"Quite a wallop," Durkin repeated.

Vance moved his hands formlessly. "Yeah."

Durkin watched. "Carl Stover," he said. "Just one smack."

Vance kept talking as if hypnotized, as Durkin knew he would, his hands moving in vague, explanatory gestures.

"I shouldn't have hit him. He was wide open. You could have had a parade inside one of his swings. I let him swing, that's all. It was like walking through a gate. It swings open, and you walk in. I walked in and tagged him. I didn't want to hurt him. I just wanted to put him out." Vance shook his head and he looked up. His eyes came to life. His face, which had been slack, became taut and his mouth hardened. "And nuts to you!" he said harshly.

Durkin knew that he had missed his chance, but he was not altogether disappointed. He had learned a number of things about Vance, and he would remember them. It was not the conclusion of a case that mattered; it was what you found out while it was going on. In fact, the ending was, most times, an anti-climax. Yet, he knew that he was going to have trouble with Vance, and he did not like that. He liked the slow accumulation of facts, and then later to present them in an overwhelming fashion. But you had to have somebody against you who believed in facts, too, and for the first time in his life he had the feeling that he had met somebody who didn't believe in facts. As evidence, as something indisputable. And then there was nothing to do about it except to accumulate more facts until the sheer weight of them was too much to bear. This did not go through Durkin's mind in an orderly fashion, but it went through all the same and came out with the realization that he would have to shift his attack if he were going to get anything from Vance.

"Well," he said in a reasonable tone of voice, "I have to consider all angles in a case like this and you just happen to be one of the angles. You got to admit that."

"Admit what?"

"That you're an angle, so why get sore about it? I'm a cop and I got to ask questions. Right?"

"You mean, did I smack Wes Elwood?" Vance asked bluntly.

"I didn't say that."

"Cut it out, for crissake. You've said it a dozen different ways."

Durkin nodded. "Well, let's put it this way. A bartender's in a rough spot. A customer gets tough in a bar and there's nobody but the bartender to take care of him before he hurts somebody. There's no time to call the cops usually, so the bartender's got to do it himself. A bartender that can't keep peace in his bar might just as well start looking for some other line of work. Right?"

"I wouldn't know. I never worked in a place where the bartender had to be the bouncer, too."

"It happens in the best places, and a drunk don't care where he is when he feels like making trouble. I been on the force a long time and I've seen all kinds. I know just what a bartender is up against."

"Yeah, we sure have it tough. That's why we're all nervous wrecks."

Durkin was impervious to sarcasm and he continued calmly. "Let's say a drunk takes a swing at the bartender and the bartender has to swing back, just to quiet him down. Let's say in this case the drunk fell down and fractured his skull, but it don't show right away. Fracture cases sometimes don't. So the drunk gets up and drives away in his car. He goes a little ways, then it hits him and he's dead. Okay. So where's it leave the bartender? A killer? Self-defense? What would you say?"

"Where was all this supposed to take place? Anybody who was in the bar that night can tell you that Wes Elwood didn't make any trouble for me or anybody else."

Durkin ignored that. "Me, I'd call it self-defense. Like I said, a bartender can't call the cops every time a drunk gets out of line. He's got to keep his bar in order himself, or people won't come in."

Vance said flatly, "I didn't lay a finger on Wes Elwood."

"I'm not asking you, I'm telling you. I'm putting it to you this way, if you smacked him and he was drunk and making trouble, you ain't got a thing to worry about. Covering up is what makes it look bad, know what I mean?"

"Damn it, I didn't touch him, I told you!"

"But if you did, it would be better—"

"I didn't. Is there anything else on your mind? I want to go down to the beach and take a swim."

Durkin shrugged and carefully placed his half-finished glass of orange juice on the small table at the end of the studio couch.

"Well," he said, "it's going to be just too bad for you if I find out different. And maybe too bad for Elwood's wife, too, if she's in it with you."

He turned and walked out of the apartment. Vance pressed his lips together and then after a few minutes he picked up the phone and dialed Maddie's number. This was something she'd have to be told immediately. It was not until the phone rang a dozen times that he remembered that she was out cold and probably would not awaken for several hours. He replaced the handset in its cradle and swore. He'd just have to keep trying to get her by phone. He couldn't take the chance of driving out to see her. For her sake.

Durkin was standing in the hall with his ear pressed against the thin panel of Vance's door. He heard the whirring sound as Vance spun the dial of the phone, and he nodded to himself. He knew Vance was calling Maddie. He knew that very surely and he could have predicted it before he left the apartment. Whether or not there was something between the two of them, Vance was the kind who'd call her and tell her the score. He wouldn't want her to have to take it cold when the police walked in. He'd warn her in advance. To protect her, or something. Durkin had that much figured, but he also knew that it didn't mean very much until he heard what Vance said to her and how he said it. That would be the tipoff.

He waited and a frown gathered between his eyes. Then he grimaced when he heard Vance replace the handset in its rack and swear. Durkin straightened up and walked down the hall toward the stairs. He was disappointed but he didn't swear. He knew that sooner or later he'd get the break for which he was looking.

Chapter Twelve

Durkin went to his car and sat behind the wheel for a few minutes before deciding to drive out to the Elwood house on the Key. There was the chance that the woman had been on the beach and hadn't heard the phone, and he wanted to talk to her before Vance could warn her. He would have preferred to have heard what Vance would say to her, but this was the second best choice. Give it to her cold and watch her reaction.

He was at Maddie's house within fifteen minutes, driving the car wide open almost all the way. The front door was open about six inches. He pressed the brass button on the frame and heard the chimes ring mellowly inside the house. He rang them several times within the next five minutes and then walked around the house and scanned the stretch of white beach, expecting to see her lying there on a beach towel in the sun. The beach was empty. He walked slowly back to the house. He rang the chimes again and called:

"Mrs. Elwood—"

He pushed the door open and walked into the house. He saw the tall glass with part of a drink still in the bottom of it on the cocktail table in front of the sofa, and then his glance picked up the beaded thermos ice bucket and nearly empty bottle of bourbon on the radio. He walked over to the cocktail table and picked up the glass. It was still a little cold from the ice cubes that had melted in it. He nodded. He should have thought of that. She'd been hitting the bottle. Probably had been at it steady. She was a drinker.

He prowled through the house and found her asleep on the bed where Vance had put her. She was lying on her back, still covered with the light cotton blanket. Her mouth was open and she was breathing with shallow, panting breaths. She was dead drunk, all right. Durkin crossed to the bed, noting the fine network of wrinkles at the ends of her eyes, the faint lines from her nose to her mouth.

Crowding forty, he thought. But still a good-looking woman, good-looking enough for a young guy like Vance to make a play for her. And maybe a nymph, too. A woman that age, especially with a lush for a husband like Wes Elwood, they go crazy for sex sometimes, like it was the last chance and they didn't want to miss out on anything, and sex was something you didn't get from a lush. A good-looking big guy like Vance, he'd be just about right to make a play for. And being a drinker the way she was, just thinking about it would get her all steamed up.

He bent over her and smelled the sour fumes of undigested whiskey. He shook her shoulder and said loudly, "Mrs. Elwood. Hey, Mrs. Elwood—" He did not expect any response because he could see that she was really under, but he had to make sure. She merely rolled limply under his hand and her eyelids did not even flicker. She was really out cold and she'd probably stay that way for a good five, six hours.

Durkin was half way to the door when the phone beside the bed rang shrilly. He turned and looked at it thoughtfully while it rang another dozen times. He was not tempted to pick it up because he was almost certain that it was Vance calling again. When the phone stopped ringing, Durkin went over to it and lifted it from its cradle. He laid the handset on the floor. That took care of that. Now nobody could call her, and he was sure that Vance wouldn't take the chance of driving out to see her. Now Durkin felt more satisfied. Things were beginning to go his way just a little bit.

As he drove back toward the mainland, he passed the deputy sheriff's cruiser patrolling the Key road. He waved it down, stopped at the side of the road and walked back to it. The deputy leaned out the window and said, "Hi, Durk, what's up?"

Durkin said, "Hi, Al," and tilted his chin at the road behind them. "I just come from the Elwood house. Mrs. Elwood, she's out cold. Been drinking. She's there all alone and that's not so good. It's pretty lonely out here. This is your beat, so I thought I'd tell you. Do you think if maybe I gave you a hand you could take her over to your place so's your wife could keep an eye on her?"

"She's that soused?"

"You could shoot off a gun."

The deputy pursed his lips and looked back through the rear window of the car. "To tell you the truth," he said, "I don't want any drunks laying around my house on account of the kids. Know what I mean?"

"Maybe your wife could come over and stay with her. Or somebody."

"Yeah. That'd be better. Too bad about Wes, wasn't it? I felt sorry for the guy. The wife's taking it pretty hard, eh? Can't blame her, I suppose, but you'd think she'd lay off the liquor at a time like this. I mean, knowing what it did to Wes and all. But it's none of my business."

"Yeah. You'll bring your wife over right away?"

"I'll pick her right up."

"Good. Tell her Mrs. Elwood's in a pretty bad way and I don't think it would be a good idea if any outsiders came in and bothered her till she kind of snaps out of it. You know how it is."

"Yeah. People can be a pain in the neck. I'll tell Janie to keep the rubbernecks out."

"Fine. See you, Al."

Durkin felt even more satisfied now as he drove toward the Pelican Lounge. This sewed the Elwood dame up till he could get to her. Al's wife had a mind of her own and nobody, including Vance, would get by her at the door.

Tate and Hully were alone in the bar when Durkin walked in. Hully was working in the storeroom, restacking the cases of liquor and Tate was reading a newspaper at the end of the bar near the kitchen from where he could keep an eye on the big pot of chili cooking on the stove. The story about Wes Elwood was on the front page of the paper with a one-column picture of Wes. Tate's thin mouth was drawn up into a sour pucker. He greeted Durkin with a short, suspicious nod. Durkin took a stool at the bar and ordered a beer. He glanced casually at the paper. He had already seen the story. Wes's fractured skull was mentioned in it, but only as part of the accident. The police had given no other statements to the press.

But Durkin was pretending casual interest in the story when Tate brought him the beer.

"That's a shame about Wes Elwood," he said. "Drinking like that."

"He didn't get it here," Tate snapped. "He was drunk when he walked in. I saw him myself."

"I wasn't thinking about that. I was thinking about his fractured skull."

Tate's eyes sharpened. "What do you mean? That happened in the accident, didn't it?"

"Well, not exactly. The way it looks, he fell down and cracked his head on a rock or something before the accident. That's what killed him."

"I thought he was drowned."

"That's what we all thought, but it was the crack on the head that did it. That's what the doc says, anyway. Not that it makes much difference, a guy falls down and cracks his head or he drowns himself."

There was no mention of the theft of Wes's diamond ring in the story. That had been kept quiet for the time being. Durkin wanted it that way. People like Tate would be more likely to talk if there was no robbery involved. The part about the ring could come out later.

Tate said sharply, "Well, if he fell down, he didn't fall down in here. 1 saw him walk out under his own power."

"Drunk?"

"I just got finished telling you he was drunk when he came in, didn't I?"

"Yeah, that's right. Anybody help him out to his car? I mean, a guy that drunk, sometimes the bartender gives him a hand or something."

"He walked out by himself. He didn't need any help from the bartender."

"It must have been some other bar. I mean, the bartender had to give him a hand."

"It must have been because it wasn't here. Vance didn't leave the bar all night. We were busy. Anyway, Wes wasn't that drunk when he walked out. If he was that drunk, Vance wouldn't have served him," Tate added quickly. "We don't serve drunks. That's a rule of the house."

Durkin knew that Tate was lying, but he let it pass. Tate would naturally not want any part of Wes Elwood's death connected with the Pelican Lounge, and he'd lie by the clock to give the bar a clean bill.

Durkin glanced toward the storeroom where Hully was working. "Was he here that night?" he asked.

Tate hesitated but, knowing that it was something that could be too easily checked, grudgingly admitted that Hully had been in the bar all that night.

"But you won't get anything from him," he said. "He's too dumb to see anything that goes on. You'd just be wasting your time."

"I better talk to him anyway. Maybe Wes fell getting into the car."

"You're just wasting your time with that dumb ox," Tate said uneasily. "He's so dumb I don't know what he's talking about half the time and I don't think he does either."

Durkin said vaguely, "Well—" and walked back to the storeroom.

Hully had been watching him covertly, he knew, but he was unprepared for the glowering scowl that greeted him.

"You're the cop," Hully said heavily.

Durkin knew that he would have to be careful, so he said mildly, "Sure, that's right. Why?"

"You're the cop that made Vance mad last night."

"Made Vance mad? I didn't make him mad. He wasn't mad when he was talking to me."

"He looked mad."

"He must have been mad about something else then. Vance and me are the best of friends. Did he tell you I made him mad?"

Hully's face cleared. "No, that's right. He said you didn't make him mad. I just thought you did, is all. He said you didn't. Vance—he's a friend of mine."

"He's a friend of mine, too. I wouldn't do anything to make him mad."

Hully swelled his chest. "I'd bust anybody that tries anything with Vance."

"Sure. That's what friends are for. Vance is a nice guy. Everybody likes Vance."

Hully grinned happily. "He's a swell guy."

"You're not kidding. That's what everybody says, the way he helped look for Wes Elwood that night."

Hully did not know that Vance and Maddie had searched the county for Wes that night and thought Durkin was speaking of how Vance had searched the parking lot behind the Pelican.

"Yeah, we looked all over for him," he said.

"You were along?"

"I was right here all the time. Me and Vance, we went out back and looked all over, but he had took his car away by that time."

"Oh, here," Durkin glanced toward the door to the patio. "You mean out there."

"Yeah, right back there. We looked all over, both of us. Wes, he was soused."

"So they tell me. Mind showing me where you looked? My name's Durkin, by the way. What's yours?"

"Mostly they call me Hully."

"Glad to meet you, Hully. Always glad to meet a friend of Vance's."

Durkin held out his hand and Hully grasped it, looking pleased. "We looked out back," he said. "I'll show you." He still had not cleaned the patio, but he had forgotten about that. Durkin's quick eyes immediately noticed the large mess on the patio floor where Wes had been sick that night.

"Was Wes out here?" he asked.

"Yeah, he—" and then Hully saw it and his jaw sagged. Durkin walked over and looked at the spot. "He was sick, eh?"

"No, that—that happened last night," Hully stammered. "I clean up out here every day. Mr. Tate, he makes me clean up every day. That's something I got to do."

Durkin saw the dried brown smear of blood on the edge of the concrete table, but by this time he knew that he would learn nothing if he attempted to question Hully about it, especially if Vance were concerned. He pretended no further interest in it.

"The parking lot's right behind here, eh?" he said.

Hully nodded quickly. "That's right. Vance went right out to the parking lot. To see the car. If Wes left in the car."

"Did you go with him or were you in the storeroom?"

"I came out with him but I didn't go in the parking lot. I mean, I was right about here and Vance was out in the parking lot but Wes wasn't here no more. His car was gone."

Durkin felt an unaccustomed excitement. There were a lot of threads still to tie and a lot of facts still to gather, but he was as sure as he could be that Wes Elwood had fractured his skull on the edge of that heavy concrete table on the patio.

"Show me where Vance went in the parking lot, would you, Hully?" he asked casually.

"Right over there, out back."

Durkin took out his handkerchief and moistened a corner of it in his mouth. He leaned against the table, the handkerchief still in his hand.

"Just about where was Wes Elwood's car?" he asked. He casually put the wet portion of the handkerchief over a part of the brown smear on the edge of the table and rubbed it with his forefinger while Hully stared, puzzled, out into the parking lot. Hully shook his head.

"Out there someplace. It was dark."

Durkin said, "Oh yeah, that's right," and put the handkerchief back into his pocket after covertly making certain that he had transferred some of the stain from the table to the fabric. This was something he had to do without Hully becoming aware of it. There was danger in Hully. Durkin was not an imaginative man, but he knew that it would take no more than a suspicion in Hully's mind to make him really dangerous to the point at which even a gun would have small meaning. Vance was the biggest thing in Hully's meager life, and Hully would never permit Vance even to be threatened.

The smear on the edge of the table *might* be a threat against Vance, but Hully could not be allowed to think so. If it were blood, there would be enough on the handkerchief to establish that fact, and that would be enough for Durkin.

To lull any suspicions that Hully might have, Durkin asked, "About how long did Vance look for Wes, Hully?"

Hully ran his tremendous hand up and down the side of his massive jaw. "I dunno, but he looked all around for the car. It was gone. It wasn't there. He looked."

"I'm sure he did. A guy like Vance'd do everything he could to help."

"You're not kidding," Hully said eagerly. "That's just the way he is. He's a swell guy. And you know what else he done? He drove Wes's wife home cause she was stuck. Wes had the car."

"I'll bet *she* didn't mind," said Durkin, winking significantly. "A good-looking guy like Vance."

Hully laughed. "The babes all go for Vance, but he gives them the brush-off."

"This Elwood dame, too? Does she go for him?"

"They all go for him," Hully boasted. "He can have any dame he wants."

"That Elwood dame is pretty hot stuff, they tell me."

"Aaaaah, Vance'd give her the brush-off the same as the rest of them."

"You can't tell about things like that. It wasn't the first time he took her home."

"Vance don't have to make a play for none of them. They fall in his lap."

"Yeah, but there's something about that Elwood dame—" He stopped because he saw a scowl beginning to gather in Hully's heavy face. He winked again and waved a hand. "What I mean, I wouldn't mind having a shot at that babe myself."

"Maybe you might, but Vance, he don't play around."

Durkin knew it was time to go before he aroused Hully's hostility. Hully might come in handy later.

"There's nobody like Vance," he said. "He's one of a kind."

Hully's scowl melted.

Durkin went to the phone booth in the bar and called the Elwood house, but it wasn't until he heard the buzzing busy signal that he remembered that he had deliberately left the phone off the hook. He made a small sound of exasperation in his throat. The precaution was unnecessary now that the deputy's wife was staying with Maddie. He should have gone back and replaced the phone the moment he knew that someone was going to stay with the woman. He shook his head. It was not very often that he was guilty of an oversight like that.

Leaving the bar, he drove straight to the Sanibar Memorial Hospital. He went into the laboratory and gave his stained handkerchief to the technician, who had worked with the police department before.

"Can you tell me if this is blood and what type it is?" Durkin asked.

The technician looked at the stained cloth. "Couldn't you do better than this? There's not much to go on."

"Can you do it?"

"I guess so. Whose is it?"

"Maybe Wes Elwood's. Is he on file here?"

"He's a donor."

"How soon can I have that?"

"Would it be all right if I gave it to you for your birthday?" the technician asked wearily. "An hour."

An hour later Durkin was told that it was blood and that it matched Wes Elwood's type.

"Does that wrap it up for you?" the technician asked.

"It's a piece of the string," Durkin said.

Chapter Thirteen

Cora walked into the Pelican Lounge at quarter past six that evening instead of her usual seven o'clock. Her eyes were suffused and her face was puffy, as if she had been crying. Vance was juicing limes at the service end of the bar, and she hesitated before she walked over to him.

"Can I talk to you for a minute, Van?" she asked in a sick voice.

He looked up. "Sure. What's the matter, honey? Don't you feel well?"

"I feel lousy."

"Take the night off, then. I can take care of the tables."

"It's not that kind of lousy. Did you see the afternoon newspapers?"

"Just the morning paper. Why?"

"They don't have it. Wes Elwood, I mean. They think somebody killed him and stole his ring."

"I know. A detective named Durkin told me."

"They're after you?" Cora asked anxiously.

"He just asked a lot of questions, that's all." He looked at her more closely. "But what is all this?"

She began to cry. Not sobbingly, but with sick, helpless tears that swelled in her eyes and trickled down her cheeks. She did not seem aware of them.

"I think I got you in trouble maybe," she whispered.

"You got me in ... oh." He suddenly remembered the anonymous note she had sent to the police. "That."

"You know about it?"

"The note? Yes. Durkin showed it to me."

"Oh, Van!" Her mouth was sick with shame and despair. "I don't know what got into me, honest to God I don't. I never done a thing like that before. I been a lot of things, but I never been a rat like that. I don't know what got into me!"

I suppose I should be sore because it was a lousy trick, he thought, but all he could feel toward her was pity, and he reached across the bar and lightly knuckled her trembling chin. He grinned at her.

"Forget it," he said. "That note didn't mean a thing. I'd told Durkin all about that the night before."

"I don't know what got into me, Van! Honest to God, I don't know what got into me. Even when I was doing it I didn't want to do it, but something kept making me do it, even when I put it in the mailbox I didn't want to do it. I knew in my heart it was a stinky thing, and I didn't want to do it, but I just kept on doing it. I couldn't stop!"

Her face was clenched in the despair and shame she felt, and her hands were beginning to shake as if palsied. She was very close to hysterics. Vance quickly poured a drink of bourbon and set it on the bar in front of her.

"Drink it up," he said, "it's on the house."

"I don't need that," she said miserably. "What I need is a good poke in the snoot."

"Forget it."

"I can't forget it. I'll never forget it."

"Sure you will, and you can start as of now."

"I'll never, never, never—"

He saw that she was very close to breaking down completely, and he picked up the glass of bourbon and held it out to her.

"Drink it down," he said. "That's an order."

Shaking, she took the glass, spilling a little, and drank the bourbon. She looked straight at him and wailed, "I want to die, Van, I want to die!"

Vance turned toward the kitchen and called, "Take over for a couple minutes, Tate. I'll be right back." He ducked under the flap of the bar and, taking Cora's arm, led her toward the exit to the patio. "Come on, honey, we'll get it out of your system once and for all."

Hully, monolithic in a violently patterned red and green sport shirt and bleached jeans, was sitting on a case of Seagram's in the storeroom, sucking at a wad of Copenhagen snuff stuffed behind his upper lip. He looked eagerly at Vance and, though he moved only a hand in eager greeting, he gave the impression of wriggling like a huge, affectionate dog.

"Anything I can do, Vance?" he asked quickly.

"Keep an eye on the bar and see that nobody steals it."

Hully looked at Cora and then spoke as if she were not really there. He tilted his massive chin at her. "She ain't trying to give you no trouble, is she, Vance?"

"Nobody gives me trouble, Hully. Relax."

"Sure, Vance. Anything you say. But if anybody gives you trouble, let me know and I'll bust them for you."

"Relax."

Cora shivered and pressed close to Vance as they walked out to the patio. "He scares me," she whispered.

"Hully?" Vance looked at her in surprise. "Hully's nothing to be afraid of. He's just a big good-natured guy, that's all."

"You don't know," she muttered.

Vance closed the storeroom door and led her to one of the concrete benches. The patio floor had been scrubbed and there was a white streak on the concrete table where Hully had washed off the bloodstain.

Vance sat on the bench beside Cora. "I don't know what?" he asked.

"He almost broke my arm last night because he thought I was making trouble for you or something."

"You're imagining things. Hully wouldn't hurt a fly."

"He grabbed me and said he'd bust me if I made trouble for you. You don't know how strong he is."

"I know, but he won't hurt you."

"I wonder what he'd do if he knew I wrote that thing to the police!"

"Cut it out, I told you!" He gripped her knee, then patted it. "You didn't do anything. I told them all about that long before they got the note."

"I wanted to hurt you."

"You didn't, so forget it."

She snatched up his hand and held it to her mouth, kissing it wildly, clenching tighter when he tried to pull away. "I'm nuts about you, Van," she sobbed. "That's why I done it. I'm nuts about you and I was crazy-jealous over that Elwood dame. I didn't really want to hurt you. I just wanted to bust it up between you, that's all, honest to God."

"There's nothing to bust up," he said uneasily.

"I was crazy-jealous. I'm nuts about you. I'm like Hully. I want to do everything I can for you. I'll go to the police. I'll tell them I lied. I'll tell them I was just jealous."

"I said forget it. The note didn't mean a thing." He eased his hand away from her mouth.

She was crying dully and with a kind of hopelessness, her own hands sagging in her lap. "I ain't no better than I should be," she said, staring across the patio with clouded eyes that seemed to be looking back into her past. "I done a lot of things I should be ashamed of, but I ain't, except for that note. I went to bed with guys, but I ain't ashamed of that. It was okay, and I never let nobody's husband make a pass at me. That's one thing I drew the line at. I didn't have nothing to do with married men. It's different with single guys. They need it once in a while, but married men, I wouldn't have nothing to do with them. You know what I mean?" She looked pleadingly into his face.

Vance took a cigarette from the package in the breast pocket of his sport shirt and lit it. He leaned forward, resting his hard forearms across his knees so he would not have to look into her stricken face.

"You don't have to tell me about any of that," he said woodenly, thinking of how he had been with Maddie on the very eve of Wes Elwood's death, taking her, not in love, but just in the blind animal surge, shaming both of them. "We all do things—"

"You're not sore at me?"

"Who am I to be sore at anybody?"

"I mean, on account of the note."

"I said, forget the note."

Her hands moved in her lap, twisting together, and she looked down at them. "I'm like my mother, I guess. My old man used to come home drunk once in a while and bust things around the house. Once he started busting the dishes and she called the cops. They took him down to the station. Ten minutes later she was down there after him, begging them to let him go, but he was cockeyed and they kept him there overnight. She cried all night. I know because I heard her and she was down at the station the first thing in the morning. The cops were pretty nice about it and he didn't have to pay no fine or nothing. The sergeant just gave him hell. But what I mean is, all that night my mother wanted to die on account of what she done to him, getting him arrested. She didn't mean it. It was just something that come over her, like me and that note."

"Forget the note."

"All right, so long's you say so."

"I say so."

"I'm nuts about you, Van. Wait a minute. I'm not throwing it at you. I know you're not nuts about me, but that's all right. I don't mean I don't care. I do. What I mean is, I ain't going to throw no more wingdings. I ain't going to do nothing against you, honest."

He said, "Well—" and stood up, flipping his cigarette off into the darkness. "If you don't feel like working, I can take care of things tonight."

"Oh, I'll be in." She touched her puffy cheeks with slightly trembling fingers. "I'll bet I'm a mess. I better put some cold water on my face before I come in. I don't want everybody to know I been crying my eyes out."

"I'll see you, honey," he said, and walked toward the door.

Hully was still sitting on the case of Seagram's, and he grinned quickly when Vance walked in. "Anything you want me to do, Vance?" he asked.

Vance stopped and looked down at him. "Yes," he said, "leave Cora alone."

"Sure, Vance, but—"

"And no buts. She said you almost broke her arm last night when you grabbed her."

"I didn't break her arm. She was making trouble for you and I told her off, that's all."

"Now listen to me," Vance said sharply, "lay off that kind of stuff. You're not going to bust anybody, you understand? I can take care of things myself. If I need any help I'll let you know. But in the meanwhile, keep your hands to yourself."

"I didn't mean nothing—"

"All right, but just remember what I said."

Hully sat stunned as Vance turned away, and then his heart lurched greasily, like live suet. Knowing that Cora was still out on the patio, his head swung heavily toward the door and his tremendous hands knotted on his thighs. The bitch! She had poisoned Vance against him. A murderous fury filled his chest and he half-rose to his feet, starting toward the door, but remembering Vance's sharp warning, he sat back on the case of Seagram's, grinding his fingers impotently into the palms of his hands. She had done this to him. She had poisoned Vance, and she was against Vance. All she wanted to do was make trouble. She was no good. Vance didn't know it, but she was no good. All she wanted was what she could get, and if she couldn't get it, she'd make trouble, like with Vance. She was against Vance, and Vance didn't know it. What he should do was go right out there and bust her, but Vance had said no. Hully felt as if he were being torn apart. She was against Vance and there was nothing he could do about it. His eyes narrowed and his jaw hardened. His face became a mask of savage cunning and his hands bunched, white-knuckled.

Maybe there was nothing he could do about it right now, but there could be another time. Tonight would be bad because of what Vance had said, but maybe tomorrow or the day after. It wouldn't take much, just one hand around her neck. He'd bust her! His glance moved and stopped on the goldfish tank in which the fish were languidly silhouetted with the cool green lights behind them. His glance moved again and stopped on the broom that leaned against the wall of the storeroom. He could go in and sweep the floor in there and hit the tank with the end of the broom and bust it and the fish would be all over the floor, flopping and dying and he could step on them and ...

Vance walked back to the bar. His teeth were clenched and he hit the side of his right thigh with his fist. He felt as if he had kicked a trusting dog, but hell, he couldn't let Hully go around hurting people. He looked back, grinned and waved his hand, but Hully did not see him. He ducked under the flap of the bar and went back to juicing limes for the night trade. He'd make it up to Hully later. You didn't go around kicking people just because— Because what? He paused with his slicing knife half through a small key-lime. Because what? Why had he given Hully a beating like that, knowing how the guy felt. What had been the point? Hully hadn't really hurt the girl, he was sure. Just scared her. Just grabbed her, that was all. But that was bad enough, he thought. He didn't need any self-appointed bodyguards. All the same, he shouldn't have booted Hully like that. He'd make it up to him later. Give him an extra beer or something. He sliced through the small lime.

Hully was hunched on the case of Seagram's like a huge crouching bear when Cora came in from the patio. He glowered at her for a moment, and then looked away. Instead of passing him without a word, as she usually did, she hesitated, then sat down beside him on another case.

"You're mad at me," she said.

He grunted, but did not look at her.

She sat beside him, but did not touch him. "Vance say something to you? That why you're sore?"

This time he did not even grunt. He stared stolidly at the opposite wall of the storeroom, his hands knotted on his knees. Cora nervously rimmed her lips with her tongue.

"I didn't mean to snitch on you," she said.

He turned his head slowly toward her. "Go to hell," he said heavily.

She realized that she was close to something very dangerous and her heart beat wildly, but she went on. "You hurt me, that's the only reason I said anything. My arm's all black and blue. I wouldn't of snitched."

He snarled wordlessly at her.

She wet her lips again. "I'm for him, Hully. I'm not against him. I'm for him. You got to listen to me. I'm for him."

He said, "Aaaagh!" and looked away from her.

Shakily, she touched her fingertips to his iron forearm. "Honest to God, Hully, I'm nuts about the guy!" She began to cry again.

He heard her sobbing and it made him uneasy. That, and what she had said and what Vance had said. It confused him. He didn't know what to think now. Vance wasn't like he used to be.

"You tried to make trouble," he muttered thickly.

"I'm nuts about him, Hully. I can't think of anything but him. I go to bed at night and close my eyes, and all I see is him. I think about him all the time."

Hully's hands loosened a little on his thighs. He didn't know what to think. "He ain't like he used to be," he mumbled. "Somebody's making trouble."

"It ain't me, Hully, honest."

"It's somebody."

"It's that Elwood dame, that's who it is."

"I'll bust her!" Hully said fiercely.

"No!"

"I'll bust her, I said. Nobody makes trouble for Vance when I'm around."

"No, no, listen, Hully, leave her alone. Vance wouldn't like it if you busted her. Leave her alone. He'll find out by himself. She ain't no good, but she can't hurt him."

"Then it's that other guy, the cop."

"Leave him alone too!" Cora cried anxiously, frightened at the tempest she had started in the huge man beside her. "Vance can take care of himself. You know Vance. They can't do nothing to him. Vance is smarter'n me and you put together."

There was not much fury left in Hully, and he nodded, warming. "He's smart, all right. They don't come smarter'n Vance. You can't put nothing over on Vance."

"I'm nuts about him, Hully."

"You're on his side?"

"Yes, I'm on his side!"

"Then we'll both see that nobody makes trouble for him, okay?"

"Okay!" cried Cora gladly.

Sitting side by side, they looked into the bar where Vance was standing at the house phone at the end of the bar. His back was toward them. The phone had rung but a moment before, but they had not heard it.

Vance was talking to Maddie.

"I'm down at that stupid boat-and-bait place by the bridge to the Key," she said peevishly. "Did you bring that woman into my house?"

"Woman?"

"I woke up a little while ago and there she was, dirty dress and all, trying to tell me what to do. But I fixed her. I locked her in the bathroom. Who is she?"

The first thought that came to Vance was *policewoman*, but he said, "I wouldn't know, honey. I didn't bring her."

"Domineering bitch! Tried to keep me in bed. I fixed her. Locked her in the bathroom. What was she doing in my house, anyway? Who brought her?"

"I wouldn't know, honey." Then, very casually he asked, "Did she say why she was there, or anything?"

Maddie laughed harshly, and Vance knew that she had been drinking again.

"Sure she said. She said for me to stay in bed and she'd take care of everything. Who did she think she was, my mother? I can take care of everything myself. I don't like strangers telling me what to do in my own house. Where'd she come from, anyway?"

"Is that all she said?"

"My God, no. I couldn't shut her up. How do you feel, dearie? Can I get you something, dearie. Sure, I said, get me a bourbon and soda, and damn it if she didn't pat me on the head and coo that she was sure a bowl of soup would be much better for me. Soup, my God! As far as I'm concerned, they can take all the soup in the world and pour it back into the crankcase. Soup. Are you sure you didn't plant her there?"

"Honestly I didn't."

"The hell with her. I locked her in the bathroom. Patted me on the head and said she wouldn't let anybody bother me. She bothered me, that's who bothered me. The hell with her."

Vance realized by this time, thinking back, that it could only have been Durkin who could have brought the woman into Maddie's house for the purpose of isolating her for questioning. It was very clear.

Maddie said crossly, "Well, when can you pick me up? I'm sick of sitting around in this smelly hole."

Vance glanced quickly around the empty bar and hunched over the phone. "I don't think I should right now, honey," he said.

"*What!*"

"Wait a minute. You know that detective—Durkin?"

"What about him?"

"He was in to see me this morning ..."

Swiftly Vance told her the gist of what Durkin had said, including the threat against her.

"He didn't say anything definitely, honey," he said. "That's just about all there was to it, but there it is, and I don't think it would be such a good idea if I came over and picked you up right now."

There was a long silence on the phone and then Maddie said slowly, "He said it would be just too bad for me, is that what he said?"

"Not exactly—"

"What do you mean, not exactly! He either said it or he didn't say it!" She sounded very sharp and very sober now.

Vance made a conciliatory gesture with one hand. "He said—"

"He said, he said! Just what did he say?"

Her voice rasped, and it came to Vance like a blow that she was thinking only of herself. His shoulders hardened.

"He said," he said very distinctly, "that if we had anything to do with Wes's ... death, it would be just too bad for us. That's exactly what he said."

He did not try to soften it for her.

When she spoke again, her voice was very cold. "You're perfectly right. We mustn't be seen together. Don't even call me again."

"I won't."

He heard her suck in her breath.

"Do you know something?" she said harshly.

"What?"

"You're a son-of-a-bitch!"

"Probably."

"You got what you wanted, and now you're leaving me to pay for the room. You're a real bastard, and I mean that."

"Right."

"Damn right, it's right. Bartender. My God! I must have been out of my mind. But when you get mixed up with cheap people you have to expect—"

Vance hung up. He replaced the handset quietly on its hook and turned back to the bar. He looked down at the slicing knife and the bowl of limes, glanced back at the telephone, then picked up a handful of halved limes and started juicing them. He should feel something, he thought, but there was nothing. He felt neither sorry nor glad, but also he could not entirely believe that it had happened.

Hully and Cora watched him from the storeroom. To them, he looked like a man who had been struck heavily on the head, not enough to knock him unconscious, but enough to leave him dazed.

"Who was that?" Hully asked heavily.

Cora looked at him. "On the phone?"

"Yeah."

"How would I know?"

"Yeah. The dame, you think?"

"How do I know? Hully. Listen! Don't go off halfcocked. Don't go busting anybody. You don't know who it was. Don't go busting anybody."

"I ain't going to bust nobody, but it sure knocked him for a loop, didn't it. Just take a look at him. He don't even know where he is. That cop you think, maybe?"

"Hully, for God sake!"

"Okay, okay," his fists clenched and unclenched. "It was somebody making trouble for him though. You can see that. You just take a look at him and you can see that. He don't even know he's alive. I'll betcha it was the cop or the dame, that Elwood dame like you said."

Cora cried desperately, "But we don't know, Hully. Don't do anything, please for God sake, don't do anything!"

"I ain't going to do nothing—yet."

"Listen, Hully," she clung to his arm now, trying to drag his lowering attention from Vance, "listen to me, Hully. Let me find out who it was before you do anything. We're both Vance's … friends, ain't we? We're his friends. We're the ones that want to help him, me and you. Let me find out."

"Okay," he said, "you find out and leave the rest to me."

"All right. I'll find out. I promise you. I'll find out. But promise me you won't do anything till I find out. Promise me that, Hully. Promise me that much."

"I said okay, didn't I? Just don't take too long, that's all. Sometimes—" he was struggling with a thought, straining. "Sometimes you gotta do something for a guy even if he don't like it. You just gotta."

Cora opened her mouth. There was something she had wanted to say, but she couldn't. Something very much like terror was beginning to build up within her, burying everything else.

Chapter Fourteen

Durkin passed Maddie Elwood on the beach road when she was striding away from her home, clad in a pair of navy blue slacks that trimly accented the thrust of her hips and the slim length of her legs, a striped Basque T-shirt that made the lift of her high breasts more prominent, and a pair of thonged-leather sandals.

He was on his way to her house when his headlights picked her up. He could tell from the way she was walking that she was angry, and he also knew that the nearest place at which she could get a drink was the boat-and-bait house at the eastern end of the Key bridge. From the way she was walking, he had the feeling that she was escaping from her house and the deputy's wife, and that she was furious about it. She would go to the boat-and-bait house, he decided, and from there she would call Vance. There was a telephone there, he knew. That would be the pattern. He was satisfied now that he knew enough about both Maddie and Vance to predict that much. She would call Vance, and Vance would warn her and tell her that it would be better if they were not seen together. She would be even more furious after that.

And that, he thought, would be the time to pick her up and offer her a ride back to her house.

He drove on for another mile or so, turned his car and drove back to the boat-and-bait house at the eastern side of the rickety planked Key bridge. He was sitting inconspicuously at the dark end of the plywood bar with a bottle of beer in front of him when she walked in. She paid no attention to him or anyone else in the room. She walked to the bar and rapped imperiously on it with her knuckles and demanded a bottle of beer. She drank it straight from the bottle and looked around the room until she spotted the telephone booth in the far corner. She kept eying the booth but did not go to it until she had drunk a second bottle of beer. Clinically, Durkin noted the flutter of her fingers. *Hangover*, he thought, *and on her way to another bender. She's really hitting it up.* The thought gave him a good deal of satisfaction. This time he did not intend to let her pass out before he could get to her, but the hangover would soften her up and if she had a few drinks it would soften her up even more and he could put the boots to her.

He watched her go to the phone booth and make the call he had expected. She was furious when she came back to the bar and demanded another bottle of beer. Furious and a little frightened, he noted. The tremor in her hands was very noticeable and her eyes looked wider. She fumbled in the pockets of her slacks for money to pay for the three bottles of beer, and then she said loudly to the bartender:

"You'll have to charge it. I don't have any money with me."

The bartender smiled. "That's all right, Mrs. Elwood. We trust you."

"Why shouldn't you trust me?" she said truculently. "You don't think I'd cheat you out of seventy-five cents, do you?"

"Not at all, Mrs. Elwood."

"Seventy-five cents. My God. Give me another bottle and make it an even dollar. Send me the bill."

"Any time at all, Mrs. Elwood," the bartender uncapped another bottle of beer and set it on the bar in front of her. "Don't worry about it."

"Worry about a dollar?" she laughed jeeringly. "I'll worry myself sick. I'll go into a decline."

The bartender said, "Sure," and walked away from her.

She was weaving a little as she stood and drank the beer from the bottle. She looked around the room, which was crudely decorated with old fishing nets and dusty, mounted tarpon. She said, "Oh my God," and finished her beer and walked out.

The bartender looked at Durkin and shook his head. "They're a pain in the neck when they get that way," he said. "All they want to do is start something. They're worse than the men."

"They always are."

Durkin gave her a fifteen minute start and then went out to his car. His headlights picked her up on the beach road, halfway back to her house. He stopped and leaned out the window.

"Can I give you a lift, Mrs. Elwood?" he called.

She walked over to the car and peered in at him. She was unsteady but not really drunk yet.

"Oh, it's you," she said. "I was expecting you'd turn up sooner or later." She slid into the front seat beside him. "Well, let's go back to the house and get it over."

Durkin drove slowly. He knew she'd start drinking again the moment they arrived at her house, and he wanted to get it across to her before she became really drunk. He was sure that he could break her down. Vance was tough, but she was the weak one. She was the one he would be able to get to.

"I suppose they told you about poor Wes, Mrs. Elwood," he said.

She nodded curtly. "I heard."

"Too bad. I mean, he shouldn't of gone around flashing a ring worth that much money. Five thousand, wasn't it? A thing like that, you're practically asking for trouble, specially these days. Not that the guy that robbed him could get that much. He'll be lucky if he gets five hundred out of it, but wearing a ring like that, it was an awful temptation."

Maddie said bitterly, "You couldn't tell Wes a thing. I told him time and again, but would he listen? No. He never listened to a thing I told him. A ring. My God! He needed a ring like I need a third leg. A ring. Insurance, that's what we needed, not a ring!"

"Didn't Wes have no insurance, Mrs. Elwood?"

"Insurance? Sure he had insurance. Two thousand dollars, that's what he had!"

They were at the house now and Durkin parked in the driveway. Maddie got out and slammed the door. "I suppose you're coming in," she said.

"Well, there are a few things I have to ask you," Durkin said, trying to give the appearance of apologizing. "I don't like to bother you at a time like this, but I have a job to do. You know how it is."

"Bother me! Everybody bothers me, so why should you be different. Come on in. I don't suppose I could stop you anyway."

She turned her back and walked into the house. He followed her, smiling a little to himself. She mixed herself a stiff drink of bourbon and sat belligerently on the edge of the sofa.

"Well, what do you want this time?" she demanded.

He looked vaguely around the room and sat in the lounge chair at the window so that the light would be behind him. Looking into the glare of the lamp behind him, she would see only his silhouette.

"There are just a few things, Mrs. Elwood," he said, scratching his head. "Let's see if I can think of them now. I should of written them down, I guess. Oh, yes, the ring. Everybody knew about it, didn't they?"

"My God! He wore it like a license plate."

"That's what I heard. I never did go much for rings and things like that myself. He had insurance, you said?"

"Not on the ring," she said angrily. "Just life insurance. Two thousand dollars."

"Well, it's a lucky thing you don't have to depend on that then. The insurance people sometimes hold up payments in cases like this. I mean, till it's settled."

Maddie froze with her glass half-raised to her mouth. "What do you mean, till it's settled?" she asked sharply. "Until what's settled?"

"Well, the cause of death, and all that. Their investigators have to look into it."

"Into what?"

"How he died and all the rest of it. It ain't as though it was pneumonia or something."

"You mean I'm not going to get the money? Why not? I kept the policy paid up. Why shouldn't they give me the money? It's coming to me. Why shouldn't I get it?"

"Oh, you'll get it, Mrs. Elwood, but it might take a little time. Till this is settled, I mean. They always look into things like this. Who killed Wes, and all that."

"Do you mean to tell me that they won't give me the money until they find out who killed Wes?" Her voice was becoming strident, and, angrily, she set her glass down on the cocktail table in front of her. "Suppose they never find out. Does that mean I'll never get the money?"

"No-o, but they can hold it up quite awhile."

"Insurance!" she said shrilly. "I've heard of things like that. You pay and pay and pay, and when the time comes, they don't want to pay you. That's what Wes always said. Getting money out of an insurance company is like getting blood from a stone. How long can they hold it up?"

Durkin kept his smile hidden behind his lips. Now he knew that he was on the right track. Now he knew where she lived. Now he could really get at her.

"Well," he said, "sometimes the insurance companies take the word of the local police, and in that case it ain't held up too long."

"Take the word of the local police for what?" she yelled at him, beating against her thighs with her fists, leaning forward. "What's there to take your word for?"

"Well—that you didn't have nothing to do with it."

"Of course I didn't have anything to do with it. My God. Any fool would know that."

"They have to be careful, Mrs. Elwood. That's the only thing. You'd be surprised at the people that try to gyp the insurance companies, and they got to be careful. They always look into things. But you don't have anything to worry about. You'll get expenses. You'll be okay till this is settled."

"Expenses!" She sat up very straight, quivering with fury. "Expenses! Exactly what do you mean by that? Expenses! I'll get more than expenses. I've got an income and a pretty damn good one. Wes might have been a damn fool in some ways, but he had a good business head. I'll get more than expenses."

Durkin said with every appearance of regret, "Sure you will, Mrs. Elwood. Everybody knows Wes left you pretty well off, but in cases like this the county attorney usually freezes the estate till things get cleared up. Not that you're under suspicion or anything like that," he added apologetically. "It's just routine. But there's nothing to worry about. The widow always gets expenses."

Maddie stared at him incredulously. "You mean the county attorney can tell me what I can or cannot do with my own property?"

"Not exactly, Mrs. Elwood. But you couldn't touch anything till the will is probated, and he can hold that up."

"How long will that be?" she demanded.

Durkin shrugged. He had her now, he knew. Money, that was the touchstone. Everybody had a weakness you could get to them through, and hers was the money. As soon as he got out of here, he thought quickly, he'd have to give the county attorney a ring and tip him off to lay it on thick when Maddie called, and she would surely call to find out where she stood. Durkin knew that positively. She would call because she would want the money Wes had left to her in his will. The county attorney was okay. He'd work right along with the set-up.

"It's hard to say, Mrs. Elwood," he droned, pretending to be just as much in the dark as she was. "Sometimes these things drag on for quite a while."

"You mean I can't touch any of the money?"

"Not if he ties it up, and he usually ties it up till it's all over. But he'll see to it that you get living expenses. You don't have nothing to worry about."

"My God!" Furiously she swept out with her arm and sent her glass clattering across the floor, knocking it from the cocktail table in a shower of bourbon and ice cubes. "It's *my* money. He can't do that. He can't tell me what to do with my money. It's mine. What's he got to do with it? It's mine. Mine! He can't keep it away from me. He can't force me to live on nickels and dimes until he gets good and ready to let me have the rest of it. I'll see a lawyer!"

Durkin nodded. "I would, if I was you, Mrs. Elwood," he said earnestly, the family friend and advisor. "If you're really strapped for dough, you should get a lawyer. I know how these things go. The county attorney can be a son-of-a-bitch—excuse me, he can be pretty tough and tie things up—and I mean tie things up—till the will is probated. There's an estate up in Tallahassee, for instance, that's been tied up for five years. Nobody can touch a cent of it. That's the way it goes sometimes."

Maddie sat speechless. She reached for her glass but it wasn't there. "Excuse me," she said. She rose and walked out into the kitchen for another glass. She built herself another drink and returned to the sofa. She put the glass down on the cocktail table before her and looked at Durkin.

"It's really up to you then, isn't it?" she said.

"It's not up to me at all, Mrs. Elwood," he protested. "I don't have nothing to say about it. I don't do nothing but turn in my report and that's all. I don't have nothing to do with tying up your money."

"But your report is very important." Her fingers, beginning to become knuckly, were drumming on her knee.

"That part of it's up to the county attorney. I don't have nothing to do with that. I just turn in my report." And then slyly he added, "Not that you're under suspicion or anything like that, but it's just, well, too bad you're tied up with that bartender, what's his name, Vance."

"I'm not tied up with him in any shape or form!" she said loudly. "I hardly know the man."

"Well—you know what I mean. You and him, you went out looking for Wes that night, and things like that have to be taken into consideration."

"I don't have anything to do with Vance!"

"I didn't say you did, Mrs. Elwood. It's just the looks of the thing, that's all. I'm thinking about the insurance company and the county attorney," he added quickly.

"Is he under suspicion? The bartender?"

Durkin made an elaborate thing of hesitating, as if there were something he could divulge, but because of his position in the police department could not, as much as he regretted it.

"Well," he said, purposely vague, "let's put it this way. This bartender, Vance, nobody around here knows much about him, and we're kind of looking into things. You know what I mean?"

"I know exactly what you mean," she snapped. "I don't know anything about him either. Whatever made you think I did?"

"I don't, Mrs. Elwood. If I thought you knew something about him, I'd of asked you. But," he made an apologetic motion with his hands, "it's things like that ... I mean, we have to look at all the angles. The county attorney, that is. And the insurance company. I'd get a lawyer, if I was you, Mrs. Elwood. Things like this can drag on forever, and a woman like you, I mean, all that money and all, don't want to live on coffee and doughnuts."

"I don't intend to!"

"I don't blame you." He stood, contriving to look as stupid and fumbling as possible. "That's about it, Mrs. Elwood. I'd like to help you if I could. If there's anything you want me for, you can get in touch with me at Headquarters. The name's Durkin."

She was staring fixedly at her glass on the cocktail table when he walked out.

Chapter Fifteen

Durkin drove rapidly to the boat-and-bait house and called the chief of police at his home.

"Set up a meeting with the county prosecutor right away," he said. "And tell him if Mrs. Elwood calls not to answer any of her questions. Tell him it's important to talk to me first."

"You got a break on the Elwood case?"

"Just about. I'll meet you at the prosecutor's office in about an hour if you can set it up for me. Tell him it's important."

"He'll be there," said the chief. "He'll be there if I have to point a gun at him. I'll call him right away."

Durkin had one stop he wanted to make before meeting the prosecutor. He wanted to search Vance's apartment for Wes Elwood's ring. It was an hour and a quarter before he drove up to the prosecutor's office, a little annoyed because he had not found the ring. He was certain Vance had it and, knowing that Vance would be on duty at the bar until two o'clock, he made up his mind to go through the apartment again more carefully.

The prosecutor was a young stocky man named Van Meter and he greeted Durkin with an aggressive handshake.

"The chief tells me you have the Elwood case pretty well wrapped up," he said. "Wonderful, wonderful. I don't like these things to drag out."

"I only said I think I'm going to get a break on it," Durkin corrected him.

The chief was sitting on the bench at the side of the room, smoking a cigar. "The same thing, the same thing," he said peevishly. "Durkin's the kind of guy, Van, who won't say black is black until he's had it tested by a half dozen laboratories. If he says he's getting a break on the case, you can depend on it that it's just about ready to bust wide open."

The prosecutor said, "Good, good," but with visibly less enthusiasm. He sat down behind his desk. "Just what is this break, Durkin?"

Durkin took the chair at the side of the desk. "Can you tie up the Elwood estate?" he asked. "I mean, can you fix it so the dame can't draw a nickel from it outside of just expenses?"

"If you can give me a good reason. I'd have a half dozen lawyers on my neck if I tried any tricks. What's your reason, and it's got to be a good one. Is she implicated in the killing?"

Durkin considered this carefully. "No, I don't think so."

The chief said, "Oh, for God sake," and clamped his teeth down on his cigar, looking irritably at Durkin. He had never, he reminded himself, liked this stuffy, careful man. He was a good detective and all that, but he took forever to get things done and fiddled around with things like the name and complexion of somebody's mother-in-law, whether it had anything to do with the case or not.

"For God sake," he repeated, "if you got a break, tell us. Without trying to write a book about it."

"I think we can get a break if we tie up the estate."

The prosecutor looked at the chief with exasperation. "This isn't getting us anyplace. We're just going round and round. I don't mind working with you boys, but you've got to give me something to go on."

"What's this break you're talking about, Durkin?" the chief demanded.

But Durkin was not ready yet. He had to present things in an orderly fashion. He had his facts marshaled, and they had to be given in logical sequence.

"Well," he said, unmoved by their annoyance at him, "in the first place I think Vance—that's the bartender down at the Pelican Lounge—has been laying this Elwood dame on and off for quite a while now."

The prosecutor and the chief exchanged glances and Van Meter asked, "You're sure of that?"

"Not positive, no. But pretty sure. That's part of the break we're going to get if we can tie up the Elwood estate."

Van Meter rolled his eyes upward toward the ceiling. "Round and round," he said. "So you have no evidence that Mrs. Elwood and this Vance have been doing it on the side. You have to have evidence, damn it!"

"That part of it ain't so important."

The chief said, "Oh, Jesus! I should have brought a pillow. We're in for the duration. Make yourself comfortable, Van. This can go on for quite a while. In a few minutes he'll start giving us the family history back to the year one." He glared at Durkin, "If you got something to say, why can't you come right out and say it, like everybody else? I don't give a damn about this dame's sex life if it doesn't have anything to do with the case. Now does it or doesn't it?"

"In a way," Durkin told him.

"But you say she didn't have anything to do with the killing, so why the build-up? Do you have any idea who did have something to do with it."

"Vance," Durkin said.

The prosecutor said sharply, "You're sure of that."

"Yes."

"Evidence?"

"Yes."

He told them about the blood on the edge of the concrete table and that he had been told by both Tate and Hully that Wes Elwood had left the bar by way of the patio and that Vance had left the bar to look for him.

Van Meter's fingers thrummed the desk blotter before him. "You mean he followed Elwood out?"

"Well, one story I had was that it was quite a while later, but that don't have to be a fact. He could of gone out right after him. That's one of the things I think we'll get a break on."

"All right. So you think Vance followed Elwood out and stole his ring—"

Durkin held up his hand. "I didn't say that. I don't think the ring's got much to do with it. I don't think Vance would go after Elwood just for that. I think the ring was just a kind of sideline, and it could even be just something to make it look like a mugging. That ring business was just kind of thrown in."

"What was the motive then?"

"The dame, and Wes Elwood was pretty well off, too. It's like this. Vance was laying the dame, so he thought he had an in, but she's married and he can't get at the money till he knocks the husband off. Wes was a souse, see, so Vance has a nice set-up. Rummies are always getting themselves in trouble, and nobody's surprised when they get themselves knocked off. A fight, an accident, even a mugging. Elwood was a perfect set-up."

Van Meter frowned. "It sounds good, but there are still too damn many ifs. It's all guesswork. You don't even have any evidence that Vance and this Elwood woman were having an affair."

"We'll get that part of it," Durkin said with assurance. "All we have to do is tie up the estate for a little while."

The chief groaned and Van Meter's face assumed an expression of weary patience. "I suppose you'll get around to it after a while," he said. "Keep on going. We've got all night, and maybe all day tomorrow, too."

"It won't take that long," said Durkin, looking a little surprised. "I'm coming to that right away, but there are a couple things I have to tell you first."

"Just a couple," growled the chief, "just a few biographies of some-body's cousins and uncles, and who had what for dinner the night be-fore Lincoln was shot—"

"Hold it for a minute," the prosecutor interrupted. "I think I'm be-ginning to see what he's driving at. Keep going, Durkin."

Durkin looked at Van Meter with approval. He liked people who could appreciate facts and listen when they were presented in the right order.

"Well," he said, in that stuffy, didactic voice of his, "I don't think Vance had the inside track he thought he had with the Elwood dame. I don't think she gave two hoots for him. He was just something on the side, her not getting enough attention from Wes on account of him being a rummy."

"So you think she'll give him the boot when the time comes," Van Me-ter said.

"If she thinks it's on account of him she can't get at Elwood's money. If she thinks the money's going to be tied up, she'll go nuts. She wants to get her hands on it. So you tie up the estate and she'll blow her stack. She'll give Vance the boot so fast he won't know what happened to him. I already gave her the business about an estate up in Tampa being tied up for five years, and she almost flipped her lid. I'll bet right now she's got her lawyer on the phone and raising holy hell. She'll go nuts if she thinks she can't get at Elwood's money."

Van Meter nodded and looked at the chief. "I think your boy's got something," he said. "I really think he's got it. Play the woman against Vance. It won't be the first time a woman threw a man to the wolves." He looked back at Durkin. "And you really think she'll do it?"

"Oh, sure. And here's the way you can tie her up with Vance. Him and her went all over the county that night looking for Wes. Out all night together, practically. He didn't get back to his apartment till morning. I found that out from the janitor. But it all depends on if you can tie up the estate."

"Man," grinned Van Meter, "I'll tie that estate up so tight that she'll have just as much chance of getting at it as she would of getting samples from Fort Knox!"

Chapter Sixteen

Maddie was in a towering fury when Durkin left. She strode to the radio and poured herself a stiff drink of bourbon. The phone rang and she ran to the bedroom to answer it. It was Vance.

He said, "Listen, honey—"

She yelled, "Damn you!" and slammed the handset down into its cradle. She stood there cursing him. She felt as if someone had jammed a fist into the back of her head. Then she remembered what Durkin had said. "The lawyer!" she said aloud. "The lawyer the lawyer the lawyer!" Stancik, that was Wes's lawyer for the lumberyard. Stancik. She snatched up the telephone book, ripping the pages as she thumbed frantically through it to find his number. Twice she dialed the wrong number, and when she finally did reach him, she could hear the sound of music and laughter behind his voice.

"Stancik?" she said sharply. "I want to see you right away. Right now!"

"I'm sorry, Mrs. Elwood, but this is my wife's birthday and—"

"I don't care whose birthday it is. I want to see you right now, right this minute. It's important. It's damned important."

"So important that it can't wait until morning, Mrs. Elwood?" the lawyer asked stiffly.

"It can't wait!" she screamed at him. "It can't wait till morning. It can't wait another minute, so get yourself over here or I'll get another lawyer. Wes has been paying you plenty every year, so get over here and earn your money for once."

"Could you tell me over the phone—"

"I'll tell you when you get here!"

Again she slammed the receiver back into the cradle. Pounding her right fist into the palm of her left hand, she strode back into the living room and went straight to the bottle on the radio and poured herself another drink. Her mind was in a frantic, furious turmoil. She cursed Durkin, she cursed Wes, she cursed Stancik and she cursed Vance. She hurled her glass across the room and took another drink straight from the bottle. She prowled around the room, knocking over lamps and end-tables with furious sweeps of her arm when she passed them.

Stancik came about a half hour later. He was dressed in a white dinner jacket, a dark red cummerbund and black formal trousers and was obviously annoyed that he'd had to leave his wife's birthday party. But that feeling fled when he saw Maddie. She was standing in a corner of the living room with smashed lamps and broken end-tables all around her. Her hair was in wild disorder, her eyes blazed and she bared her teeth at him. He was shocked at what he saw. She looked like a cornered animal.

"Good God, Mrs. Elwood!" he gasped. "What happened? Did somebody attack you?"

"You took your own damn time about getting here," she cried shrilly. "I told you to come right over!"

"I came over immediately, Mrs. Elwood," he soothed her. "Now if you'll tell me—"

"The county attorney's going to tie up Wes's estate so I can't touch it. Can he do that?"

Stancik was momentarily confused by the abruptness of this, partially because it did not seem to have any connection with the condition of the living room.

"Well, I don't know—" he stammered.

"Why don't you know, damn it? You're supposed to know. You're a lawyer, aren't you? Can he do it or can't he?"

Stancik was about to answer angrily, but he saw that she was on the verge of hysterics and he spoke quietly, "I can't say, offhand. Were you given any reason?"

"They said, until Wes's death was cleared up."

"Well, the prosecutor has the right to freeze an estate," Stancik said cautiously. "That is, if he has any suspicion that, well, you might be directly or indirectly concerned in the death. He has that right."

"But I'm *not!*" she screeched. "I didn't even know about it till they told me!"

"They must have some reason. But let's sit down and talk this over calmly. We're not going to get anywhere losing our tempers and shouting at each other. You'll have to tell me the facts before I can give you an opinion, or even do anything."

"All right, we'll sit down." She kicked a fragment of broken lamp out of her way as she strode to the sofa, but she was much calmer when she sat down. She ran her fingers through her disheveled hair, making a very obvious effort to control herself.

"Now exactly what is the situation?" Stancik asked.

She told him what Durkin had said, adding the fact that she and Vance had made every effort to find Wes that night. She omitted entirely, however, the fact that she had made Vance go to bed with her.

Stancik thought, *She's lying; she was having an affair with that man. Good God, they'll crucify her!* All that was very obvious in her manner and bitterness toward Vance.

Aloud, Stancik said, "The best I can do at the moment is find out if Van Meter *is* going to freeze the estate. After all, you've had no official word as yet. This policeman's word doesn't mean very much. Where's your telephone? I'll call Van Meter at his home."

"It's in the bedroom," she said sullenly.

He walked into the bedroom. She was in a very bad position, he thought, very bad, getting mixed up with a bartender. A bartender, of all people. He had always had his suspicions about her. Her sharp tongue had made poor Wes's life hell. That was why Wes drank. To find some peace. God only knew what other shabby affairs she'd had behind Wes's back. If she were in any real trouble, it would be bound to come out.

He called Van Meter's home and was told that the prosecutor was out and that no one knew when he would return. Stancik went back into the living room. Maddie had a fresh drink in her hand.

"He's out," he told her. "I'll keep trying to get hold of him. I'll call you if I find out anything."

"Call me!" Her eyes blazed. "You'll stay right here until—"

"It's my wife's birthday, Mrs. Elwood," he said firmly, "and I'm going back to the party. Furthermore, there's no point in my staying here. I can call Van Meter just as easily from my own home. I'll let you know when I learn something."

"Oh, go to hell," Maddie said nastily.

"I'll call you," said Stancik curtly, and walked out.

Maddie continued to drink but it was not until after midnight that she passed out on the sofa. She was awakened at eight-thirty the next morning by the ringing of the telephone. She had a savage hangover, but her senses came sharply to focus when she heard Stancik's voice on the phone.

"I couldn't get Van Meter last night," he told her. "I just got hold of him at his home."

"Well?" She gripped the handset.

"He has frozen the estate. You'll get an allowance but—"

"Oh, damn it! Damn it to hell!"

"Please control yourself, Mrs. Elwood," Stancik said coldly. "Wait until I finish. He told me he took the action chiefly because of your association with this bartender. He said that it was a purely routine action."

"Can't you get a court order, or something?"

"I'm afraid not. He's entirely within his rights."

"Isn't there anything I can do?"

"Well—I'd suggest you go down and have a talk with him. You'd have to do that anyway to make provision for your allowance. He's a very reasonable fellow, and I don't think you'll have any trouble with him. I'll go along with you, if you wish."

"You!" she said contemptuously. "What good would you be? You haven't been any more help than a flat tire."

"That's up to you, of course."

"You're damn right it's up to me. It's been up to me all along. You were nothing but a waste of time."

She hung up. She tore at her fingernail with her teeth and then sat up straight and folded her hands in her lap. She felt suddenly very calm. She called the prosecutor's office.

Durkin was waiting there and Van Meter covered the mouthpiece of the phone with his hand and winked at him. "It's her," he said. And then into the phone, "Of course I'll be glad to see you, Mrs. Elwood. I'm awfully sorry to have to cause you this inconvenience, but it's only something we do as a matter of routine in cases like this. A half hour? Fine, fine. I'll be waiting for you."

He hung up and looked at Durkin. "I think it'll go better if you're in the other office when she comes. You'll be able to hear everything through the door."

"How'd she sound?"

"Just about the way you said. Ready to blow her stack. You should have been a psychologist."

"What for?" asked Durkin in surprise.

"The way you called your shots on that woman."

Durkin's estimation of Van Meter dropped a little. Durkin's ego was not one that fed on praise. He was merely surprised that the prosecutor could not see something that was very obvious to him, and what did a psychologist have to do with it? Those long-hairs didn't know which way was up and all you ever got from them was double talk.

"I didn't call any shots," he said. "It's just the old story. You put the pressure on them and they start giving at the seams."

"And you think she'll turn this Vance in?"

"She's bound to. We got hold of her where it hurts and she wants to get off the hook. Mind if I say something?"

"Go right ahead."

"When she comes in, make like you're on her side. Make like it's all this Vance's fault. Make like she's getting a dirty deal but your hands are tied and there's nothing you can do about it. But don't let her think that she'll get her hands on that money till at least 1960. I mean, that's the way I'd do it."

"I'll keep it in mind."

Durkin nodded and walked into the other office. He placed a chair beside the door so that he would be comfortable while he was listening. He glanced at his wrist watch. A half-hour? Twenty minutes would be more like it. She'd be early.

She was. He bent over and put his ear against the door when he heard her say shrilly, "Mr. Van Meter? I'm Mrs. Elwood." He nodded to himself with satisfaction. All wound up like a fiddle string. One more turn of the peg and she'd bust. He did not have to see her to know how she looked—white, strained face, mouth a little rubbery, eyes anxious, and a hangover raging inside her and clawing at her nerves. Van Meter wouldn't have to do a thing except say something about Vance from time to time. She'd do it all herself. She was ripe.

"What is all this about freezing my money, Mr. Van Meter?" she demanded imperiously.

Durkin listened to Van Meter's murmured answers, pleased with the way the prosecutor kept turning the explanations toward Vance.

Durkin pressed his ear more tightly to the door when Maddie said sharply, "But I have nothing to do with that man, nothing whatever!"

"I didn't mean it that way, Mrs. Elwood. But we have certain information regarding him and, well, he's a dubious character, to say the least. Prizefighter, bartender, known to have a very hot temper. You understand, of course, that there are certain precautions that have to be taken in cases of an unexplained death, such as your husband's. Until the mystery is cleared up, I mean."

"What has that got to do with me?" The shrillness in her voice was more pronounced. "Do you mean that I'll have to live on an allowance indefinitely? Until you get good and ready to let me have my money?"

"I hope it won't be too long, Mrs. Elwood. The moment we clear this thing up—"

"You may never clear it up, damn it! Don't give me that. Half the cases the police get are never cleared up!"

"Let me ask you something, Mrs. Elwood. When your husband left the bar that night, did the bartender go out after him immediately?"

She hesitated and Durkin could almost see her wetting her lips before taking the plunge. "Yes," she said finally, "he went right out after him."

"Was there any particular reason for his doing that, Mrs. Elwood?"

"Wes was—drunk."

"Oh? And did the bartender usually follow drunks out of the bar."

"Sometimes."

"How long was he gone?"

"I don't know. Perhaps fifteen minutes."

"How did he seem when he came back?"

"Annoyed. Angry."

"Did he say why?"

"He said he couldn't find Wes."

Her voice had changed. The shrillness had gone out of it, and some of the strain, and she was answering Van Meter as quickly as he asked the questions. She's made up her mind, Durkin thought, she's going to nail him to the cross.

"Now let me ask you something else, Mrs. Elwood. Did this Vance offer to help you look for your husband that night?"

"He suggested it."

"Wasn't that a rather unusual thing for him to do? He had never done that before, had he? I know he had taken you home on other occasions when your husband had drunk too much, but he had never offered to search for your husband before, had he?"

"Never."

"Didn't it strike you as being unusual, then?"

Maddie hesitated again. "I didn't think. I was worried about Wes."

"Of course. Quite naturally. Now, after looking in several places for your husband, this Vance took you to your home, did he not?"

"Yes."

"At what time was this?"

"I really don't know. I was exhausted."

"Did he go inside with you?"

The strain began to show in Maddie's voice again. "He said he'd like to have a nightcap. Or one for the road. Something like that."

"Ah, yes. So he went into the house with you. Now tell me, Mrs. Elwood, exactly what were his actions after he went into the house with you?"

"He made a pass at me," she said viciously.

"And did you—"

"I certainly did not!"

"Did he force his attentions on you?"

"He tried."

"But you resisted?"

"I told him to leave."

"And did he?"

"Yes, but—only after I locked myself in my bedroom."

Durkin did not believe that, but it was all right. The main thing was to show that Vance had made a play for her.

Van Meter wrapped that up. "And has this bartender made any advances to you since?"

"He came to my house yesterday morning."

"Did—anything happen?"

"I was sick."

Drunk, thought Durkin. But that didn't make any difference either. She was really putting the screws to Vance, and when the time came, Vance would put the screws to her. They'd be falling all over themselves accusing each other.

Maddie was saying angrily, "And he's been calling me up every other minute since then. I hung up on him last night."

"In other words," Van Meter said, "he was making a very serious play for you. Did he ever mention marriage?"

"I laughed at him!"

"Perhaps I should have told you this before, Mrs. Elwood," Van Meter said blandly, "but my secretary has been taking notes of this conversation. Over the intercom. Merely for my own records. This would have no legal standing. But would you be willing to sign a statement. It would help us to clear up this matter more quickly."

"And release the estate?" Maddie asked sharply.

"Of course."

"I'll sign."

Durkin jumped up from his chair and broke for the phone on the desk across the room. He dialed police headquarters and asked for the chief.

"Have the boys pick up Vance," he whispered. "She just nailed him to the cross!"

Chapter Seventeen

Hully, anxiously clad in a clean green and yellow sport shirt and a fresh pair of jeans, knocked at the door of Vance's apartment and waited worriedly for an answer. He had dressed up especially for this visit and had even wet his hair and flattened it back on his head with the palm of his hand. He had wanted to look his best.

Vance answered the door almost immediately. He had on a pair of swimming trunks and had a towel thrown over his right shoulder.

"For God sake," he said, "what're you doing here? I thought you were working."

"I kind of took time out," Hully mumbled.

"You've got it coming, God knows, working seven days a week down there. But what's on your mind?"

Hully avoided Vance's eyes. "You sore at me, Vance?" he blurted.

"Sore at you—" Vance remembered how he had spoken to Hully the night before. "No, I'm not sore at you, you big lug. Only you shouldn't have grabbed Cora like that. You could have hurt her, that's all. Is that why you came over?"

"I didn't want you sore at me, Vance. You're my friend, and I didn't want you sore at me. I didn't mean nothing."

"Come on in, jerk," Vance said affectionately. "Want a cup of coffee?"

"You ain't sore at me?"

"No, I'm not sore at you. Come on in and have a cup of coffee with me. I'm going down to the beach for a swim. You can come along, if you want."

"You mean it, Vance. You ain't sore at me?"

"No, I'm not sore."

"You're the only friend I got, Vance."

God help you, Vance thought, but he grinned and knuckled Hully's massive chin. "Cut it out or there won't be a dry eye in the house," he said. "Let's have a cup of coffee and then go down to the beach."

"I was afraid you was sore at me," Hully said happily, "I brung you something."

He handed Vance a long, flat box. There was a cheap rayon tie in it, pink and black, and lettered across it was *Souvenir of Sanibar, Florida*, over a stylized pink flamingo.

"Well, how about that!" Vance said, holding it up, "I was going to get myself one of these the other day but it slipped my mind. Thanks, kid."

Hully beamed. "I knew you'd like it, Vance. It's got all them pretty colors in it."

"I'm nuts about it."

Hully refused to sit down in the apartment while he was drinking his cup of coffee. He was so happy that he could not even stand still, and every time Vance glanced at him, a grin leaped to his lips and he said, "Anything I can do, Vance. Anything you want me to get you?"

My God, thought Vance, how long had this been going on? It made him uncomfortable because he had always treated Hully with half-humorous tolerance and nothing more. Now, all of a sudden, this! The poor bastard.

"Let's get down to the beach," he said.

As they drove toward the secluded spot south of the municipal beach where Vance liked to swim, Hully said happily, "Jeez, Vance, wouldn't it be swell if you bought the bar from old man Tate and you was the boss and I worked for you and we got rid of that old son-of-a-bitch. Wouldn't that be swell?"

It was an extremely remote possibility, but Vance said, "It sure would, Hully."

"It'd be swell working just for you, Vance. When you buy the bar, I'll work for you, even for nothing. That Tate, he's a son-of-a-bitch, ain't he?"

"He doesn't bother me, Hully. Forget him."

"I mean, talking about firing you all the time."

"He's not going to fire anybody. He's just a lot of talk."

"All the same," Hully said earnestly, "if he tries anything with you, Vance, I'll bust him."

"Damn it, Hully, get those ideas out of your head. You're not going to bust anybody. Remember that."

"Sure, Vance," Hully said meekly. "Anything you say."

Vance turned off the narrow, sandy road into a break between the cabbage palms and palmetto. They walked down to the wide, white beach.

"I'll watch," said Hully.

"You will like hell. I don't want anybody watching while I flap around out there like a flounder. Take a walk up the beach and—well, get me some shells. Big ones. The bigger the better. I need them for ashtrays."

"Why didn't you say so before, Vance? I could of got a whole bushel of them down the fish house."

"I like the ones you get on the beach better. They don't stink so much.

You get me some shells while I take a swim."

Hully beamed. "Sure, Vance. I'll get you all the shells you want. I'll get you big ones."

Vance grinned as he watched the big man lumber up the beach toward the lone gray and yellow-trimmed beach house that stood about two hundred yards south. The windows were boarded up, and it had not been in use for the past two months. It belonged to one of the local rich who was on one of his periodic Caribbean cruises. It was as large as a good-sized bungalow, and was actually a guest house, for it had a kitchen, a living room with a fieldstone fireplace and three bedrooms. Hully bent over from time to time, picked up a shell, weighed it in his hand and invariably tossed it aside. Vance wanted big ones and Hully was going to get the biggest there was. Vance thought, *the big lummox,* and felt a warm affection toward him. He had never suspected the dog-like devotion Hully felt toward him.

Vance left his towel hanging on the handle of the car door, sprinted down the beach and made a leaping shallow dive into the cool, pellucid water. He swam energetically for about a half-hour, thinking of Maddie in a detached manner as if she were an almost total stranger to him, or someone whom he could regard objectively. He still loved her, he was sure, but temporarily she had turned into another person, probably from shock and fright over the pending police investigation. He felt a deep sympathy toward her, but he knew that, as much as he loved her, the only way he could help her through this troubled period was to stay away from her entirely and perhaps not even call her on the telephone. But he'd try just one more telephone call, he decided. Just one more that afternoon, and if she still reacted violently, he would leave her alone. It would be hard to do because he yearned to see and talk to her all the time, but it would be the best way. There was enough on her mind without his complicating things further for her.

He swam back to shore and ran up to the car for his towel. He slowed down as he saw the police car standing behind his, blocking his egress, and Durkin standing there with a gun in his hand. This was unlike the phlegmatic detective, for he had never before made a dramatic scene of any of his arrests. He appeared a little excited and nervous, and he watched Vance warily—a little more warily than Vance watched him.

Vance stopped about six feet away, for Durkin had lifted the gun slightly in an unspoken warning.

"Now what?" Vance asked.

"I thought you'd be down here," Durkin said in an unusually high voice. "I knew this was where you always swim. I made it my business to find out."

"So what? Is it against the law?"

"It's against the law to murder Wes Elwood. I'm taking you in, Vance, so don't make any trouble, I'm warning you."

Vance felt no real surprise and he said disgustedly, "You're out of your mind. You'll never make it stick. You're going off half-cocked."

"Half-cocked, eh?" Durkin looked at him, exulting. "Well for your information, your girl-friend went down to the prosecutor this morning and spilled her guts in our lap. She tied you up like a Thanksgiving turkey. She sank you like a stone, so come along and don't make any trouble. It won't do you any good."

Durkin's unaccustomed nervousness increased. Vance looked bigger and more hard-muscled in just swimming trunks than he did when dressed, and there was a look of lean danger in his suddenly sharpening face. He should have brought another man, Durkin knew.

"She didn't have anything to spill!" Vance said sharply.

"Maybe you didn't think she did, but she spilled plenty. Enough to tie you up tight. That you tried to rape her, for one thing."

"You're a goddam liar!"

"Am I? It's down in black and white and she signed it. She was lying like hell and the prosecutor knew it. You been laying her all along, and I think we'll be able to break her down on that point. But we wanted it down in black and white, so we could nail her later. Oh, we'll get her, too, don't worry about that."

Vance felt as if something were raging inside him and he said furiously, "You're nuts! You're absolutely nuts!"

Durkin's laugh was high-pitched and he was beginning to get carried away a little with his own triumph. "Don't even think so, big boy. We got the pair of you, and I wouldn't be surprised if the prosecutor indicts her with you. All it needs is a little more leg work, and we'll tie up the both of you. We got the motive right in our hands, killing her husband."

Vance made an involuntary movement of fury, his hands jerking up and balling into hard fists. Durkin leaped back, tripping in the thick sand, and his gun exploded, the bullet slamming into the hood of Vance's car. He yelled, pointed the gun at Vance and pulled the trigger again, but he did not know how fast Vance, a trained boxer, could move. Vance ducked and as the second bullet whined over his ear, he took three lithe, crouching strides and hit Durkin heavily on the point of the jaw. He hit him three more times in the same place as the detective sagged, unconscious, to the sand.

Vance knew instantly that this had been a mistake, although Durkin had tried to shoot him. The arrest was a damn fool idea and he should have submitted quietly, but he had blown off at Durkin's trying to drag Maddie into it. He picked the detective up and propped him against the car. As he turned to go to the Gulf to wet his towel to revive the man, Hully came lumbering up, panting, his eyes the size of ashtrays.

He looked at Durkin and stammered, "What—what—" He saw the gun lying on the sand. "He wanted to shoot you, Vance?"

"It was a mistake. Don't worry about it. Here, wet this towel and bring it back to me. I want to snap him out of it."

"Why'd he try to shoot you, Vance? Why'd he want to do that, huh?" And then, as it burst on him, "He wanted to arrest you!"

"Don't worry about it, will you? Just wet the towel and bring it back."

Hully's tremendous hands began to work ominously. "That's why he was asking all them questions about Wes Elwood, on account of he wanted to arrest you."

"Okay, so he wanted to arrest me," Vance said impatiently. "But he's off his trolley, so forget it. Now wet the towel, will you, or I'll do it myself."

"You gonna *let* him arrest you!" Hully said incredulously.

"Yes I'm going to let him arrest me, if only to show him up for a damn fool."

"But you can't do that, Vance!" Hully cried excitedly. "They'll get you down the police station and get you to say a lot of things you don't mean and give you the third degree and stuff like that and you'll be in jail before it's all over. You can't let him—"

Vance said impatiently, "Oh, for God sake," and started toward the water with the towel.

Hully yelled, "You can't do it, Vance!" hesitated, and hit him on the side of the neck with his forearm. Vance went down as if clubbed.

Hully moved more swiftly than he had ever moved in his life. He scooped Vance up and ran to the car with him, putting him on the floor of the back seat, with some vague notion of concealing him there. Then he leaped into the front seat and tried to start the car, but Durkin's first wild bullet, which had punctured the hood of the car, had destroyed the carburetor. He swore impotently and looked at Durkin's car, realizing, however, that he could not be seen driving an official car with the police insignia emblazoned on both doors. He would be picked up by the first police cruiser he met. He looked wildly around, not knowing what to do. He spied the boarded-up beach house and uttered a triumphant exclamation. Folding Vance over his big shoulder, he trotted down the beach toward it. There was a padlock on the door, but Hully pulled it off with one wrench of his thick hand, ripping the hasps from the brittle wood. He hastily took Vance inside. He glanced quickly around and then trotted into the first bedroom he saw and dropped Vance on the bed. He knew this wasn't the end of it, however. He would not be able to keep Vance there. Vance would want to get himself arrested and that was bad because they'd put him in jail. Vance was beginning to stir limply and so Hully, muttering apologetically, "I don't want to do this, Vance, honest," hit him again on the side of the neck. Vance dropped back, motionless. Hully ran frantically into the large living room. His mind was beginning to scatter and he did not know what to do. Then he spied a small sailboat-anchor with a coil of white nylon line in the corner near the door to the beachfront porch. He uttered another small cry of triumph and pounced upon it. In five minutes, he had Vance trussed securely to the four posts of the bed by wrists and ankles. He bent over and shakily patted Vance's still shoulder.

"Don't worry, Vance," he said reassuringly. "I'll take care of everything, honest. I'll take care of it. I'll be back."

He ran out of the house and with unexpected cunning, replaced the padlock and hasps, smoothing the splintered wood so that a casual glance would not show that it had been broken. Then he went back toward Vance's car. There was only one thought in his mind. Durkin had to be silenced. That was his idea of taking care of things. Of course, that was only the first step. There would be other things to take care of, though he did not know what they might be. They'd turn up, though, and he'd take care of them, one by one. However, the first thing to take care of was Durkin.

He burst through the underbrush of palmetto and stopped, aghast. The police car was gone, and so was Durkin. Hully swore savagely and ran down the road to see if he could spot the car, but there was nothing in sight. He raised his huge fists and shook them impotently, his face convulsing in anger against Durkin for escaping a just punishment.

He gradually calmed down. It didn't make much difference anyway. Vance was safe where he was and he'd keep him there till it blew over. Hully knew that Vance had not killed Wes Elwood. He knew that it was his own blow the night he had stolen Wes's ring, but it did not occur to him to give himself up to the police. All he could think of was that Vance was innocent and that the police would realize that sooner or later and everything would be all right. Hully believed inflexibly that everything would always turn out all right for Vance because Vance was a swell guy, but sometimes you had to stop him from doing things that were wrong, like now. He felt much better as he started the long walk up the beach road toward the Pelican Lounge.

Chapter Eighteen

It was shortly after noon that Cora came running into the Lounge, so upset that the newspaper in her hand shook. She spied Hully working placidly in the storeroom and, ignoring the curious stares of the three men drinking beer at the bar, ran nervously in to him.

"Come out to the patio for a minute, Hully," she whispered in a voice that was barely audible.

He nodded and followed her amiably. She was Vance's friend, too. Outside, she grasped his arm and whispered urgently, "We got to find Vance, Hully. They're after him, even the state police. Look."

Trembling, she opened the newspaper. There was a five column banner headline across the tabloid:

Murder Suspect Escapes

There was also a two column picture of Maddie, dressed in black and sitting on the sofa in her home, weeping. The cut line was, "Widow Mourns Murdered Husband." There was also a side bar story that was headlined:

Widow Charges
Attempted Rape

Hully was less interested in the reading matter than in the picture of Maddie. He put his finger on it.

"That's the Elwood dame," he said.

"She's the one that got Vance in all the trouble!" Cora said wildly. "Her and her lies, saying Vance done it."

Hully's face became very still and he said, "Her!"

"Yes, but we got to find Vance. We can't let them get him. Not till we can prove she lied. I don't know how we'll do it, but we will. You and me, Hully, it's up to us. But we got to find Vance first!"

Hully grinned. For once he had everything under control. "Don't worry about Vance," he said.

"What do you mean?"

Hully hesitated and then remembered that she was Vance's friend, too, and they were both going to help Vance. "He's okay," he said.

Cora seized his arm and shook it. "Tell me, tell me!"

He winked at her and bent over and whispered in her ear, "I got him stashed away."

Cora looked as if she would collapse from sheer relief. "Thank God," she breathed. "I was afraid he'd get some damn fool idea about giving himself up or something. You know how he is, not scared of nothing."

"Yeah, but he wanted to get himself arrested. The cop tried to shoot him. Twict. I was right there."

Cora stared incredulously at him and began to shake badly and, for a few moments she was wholly inarticulate though her lips moved and tried to form words.

"Give—give himself up?"

"Yeah, but I fixed that. He ain't gonna give himself up, like you say."

"You talked him out of it?" Then wildly, "I don't believe it. You couldn't, if he wanted to give himself up."

"I tried to talk him out of, but he wouldn't listen. He wanted to get arrested. I tied him to the bed."

"The bed? What bed?"

"The bed out there on the beach. That house down there. They won't find him. It's all boarded up and I put the lock back. I tied him up. He can't get away. I—" he looked defensive, "I had to hit him, too."

"But—but you're sure he can't get away?"

"I tied him myself. Sure I'm sure."

"Thank God—Hully, I can't—oh thank God—where is this house?"

"The beach, the gray-and-yellow one all the way down the end, know what I mean. I pulled the lock off but I put it back."

"Oh, thank God, Hully! You're sure he's all right?"

"Sure. It's kind of hot in there on account of it's boarded up, but he's okay."

"I'll go right down. I know the place. It's the Roebuck house. He's away. I know where it is. I'll take an electric fan. And something to eat for him. And some water." She was beginning to sound as if she were babbling in her eagerness. "We'll take care of him, Hully, you and me. We'll take care of him."

"Yeah," Hully's face darkened, "and I'll take care of the cop, too!"

Cora cried, "No, Hully, no! That'd only make it worse for Vance. Anyway," she pleaded, "there's always another cop to take his place. Don't lay a finger on him. Leave him alone!"

"You think so?"

"I *know* so. You can't go around doing things to cops. You'll just make it worse for Vance."

"Well—if you say so."

His eye fell on the newspaper picture of Maddie, but with another flash of cunning, he said nothing about it. "Okay," he said, "I was going to bust the guy, but I'll leave him alone if you say so."

"Promise, please!"

"Sure I promise. I wouldn't do nothing against Vance."

"I know you wouldn't, Hully. But I got to go now. I got to see how Vance is ..."

She ran off the patio and across the parking lot to her car. It was about three-quarters of an hour before she walked into the beach house, carrying a small electric fan, a gallon thermos jug of cold water and a large paper bag of easily prepared groceries.

Vance glared at her from the bed. His wrists and ankles were raw from his struggles to burst loose from the nylon line and he was drenched with perspiration. The heat was terrific in the boarded-up house.

"Did Hully do this?" he demanded furiously. "Get me out of this!"

Cora tried to speak soothingly, but her voice shook. "No, Van, you can't. They're after you, even the state police, and—"

"All the more reason, damn it. Get me out of this!"

"No, Van, that'd be the worse. She lied about you and they believe her. You'd give yourself up and they'd put you in jail." Her tongue refused to say that they might even execute him for the killing of Wes Elwood. She did not want to think about that.

Then with a forced cheerfulness, she said, "Look, I brought you an electric fan. Lucky I could turn on the electricity at the meter outside, wasn't it. All you do is pull down the handle and it goes on. I'll set it up right here."

He swore furiously and struggled against the ropes that bound him, but she ignored that and set up the fan on a small table beside the bed.

"And I brought you some water and something to eat. I got soup and cold cuts and potato salad and cottage cheese and milk and powdered coffee and there's an electric icebox in the kitchen and it'll all keep.

I'll come three times a day and—"

"Just take these goddam ropes off me!" he raged.

"— make something to eat for you," she continued with false calm, trying to soothe him. "They'll find out she's lying and then everything will be all right."

He quieted himself with effort.

"Look, Cora," he said, "I know you and Hully mean well and all that, but this is the worst thing I can do. I have to give myself up so I can prove I didn't have anything to do with Wes Elwood's killing. Can't you see that? I can't prove anything as long as I'm tied up here, and it'll just look as if I'm in hiding, and that's the worst thing that can happen. So untie me and let me handle it myself."

"We'll talk about that later," she chattered, adjusting the fan so that it would blow upon him. "I think you ought to have something to eat first. It'll make all the difference. My goodness, a man has to eat. Can I give you a glass of water. I got it nice and cold. Look, I got one of them thermos jugs, just so's to keep it nice and cold."

"For the love of Christ, listen to me, will you! Every minute I stay here, the more trouble I'm going to be in. Can't you get that through your head? As far as the police know, I'm running away, damn it. That's practically a confession of guilt, for God sake, and when they do get me, they'll bring it up at the trial. Can't you see how that's going to look in front of a jury?"

"We'll talk about that later. I'm going to make you something to eat. How's about some cottage cheese and sour cream and a nice cup of coffee and a sandwich. I got ham and Swiss cheese, or you can have a hamburger. I got hamburger and a Spanish onion."

"Damn it, listen to me, will you!"

"Eat first," she said with a show of firmness.

She took the bag of groceries out to the kitchen, pretending to pay no attention to his furious swearing. Her hands were trembling badly again, and she tried to put Vance's arguments out of her mind. They had sounded very logical, but she did not want to think about it. She had a strong, formless dread of his being arrested. When you were arrested, you were in trouble and they put you in jail, and in a case like this, maybe even kept you in jail. They were after Vance and she knew that it was very serious. She could not think beyond that, except that she was determined to keep him away from the police.

She prepared a cup of coffee, a bowl of cottage cheese and sour cream and a ham-and-Swiss sandwich and carried it into the bedroom on a tray that she had found atop the refrigerator. She wished Vance wouldn't look so mad, but he'd feel better after he ate. Food always made the difference, and maybe he'd think it over and know they were only doing it for his own good. She smiled tremulously at him and set the tray down on the edge of the bed.

"Eat first, then we'll talk. I'll unloosen your hand so's you can eat."

He veiled the gleam in his eyes. "Yeah, you better do that, I don't want to be fed like a baby."

She untied the line at the bedpost to which his right wrist was bound, and as she did, he gave his arm a sudden jerk but, expecting this, she had kept the line wound around the post and had held it firmly in her hand so that it did not give an inch when he pulled at it. She pretended not to notice. It would just start him off again if she said anything. She let out the line just far enough for him to get his hand to his mouth, but not far enough so that he could get at the knots with his teeth. Then she retied it expertly and strongly, tucking the end of the line behind the bed so that he could not get at that either.

"There!" she said. "You'll be more comfortable too. Now eat the nice lunch I made you and we'll talk." He swore and shoved the tray off the bed.

"Oh, Vance!" she cried in dismay, looking at the spilled coffee, the upside down bowl of cottage cheese and the scattered sandwich. "You got to eat. You can't go without eating."

"I don't want any of the goddam crap. I just want to get out of here, you fool!"

She knelt and hurriedly began gathering up the spilled food. "I can't let you go, Van," she said in a smothered voice. "So please don't ask me. Honest to God, we're doing it for the best. You don't know all that's going on."

"I know damn well what's going on."

"No you don't. Here, I'll show you." She jumped up and ran to the lounge chair in which she had laid the newspaper and her purse. She brought the newspaper back to the bed and held it up so that he could see it.

"It says here that local, county and state cops got road blocks up for fifty miles all round," she said hurriedly. "Every cop in the state's looking for you. The chief of police says, right here, see, he says a fly couldn't get through the net they got up. And this other cop, the one you smacked, he says he's sure you're hiding out in Sanibar. He says it's only a matter of hours before they catch up with you, he says. He says, the police chief that is, he says they got enough on you to convict you twice over. And the—the prosecutor, he calls it a perfect case against you."

"And that's exactly the reason you've got to let me go, Cora," said Vance with forced calm. "Can't you see you're just helping them build up the case against me? When you hide out, you practically admit you're guilty. I have to prove I didn't have anything to do with it, and I can't do it while I'm tied up here. Cut me loose. I can handle it. I can take care of myself."

She hesitated shakily, almost convinced, but she shook her head and cried, "Please don't ask me, Van. Please don't keep asking me! I can't let them put you in jail!"

"Jesus-Christ-goddam-it-all-to-hell!"

"Look here," she said, pointing to Maddie's picture in the paper. "She says you tried to rape her."

"They made her say it."

"No, no! She went down to that prosecutor of her own free will, it says, and she signed a—a statement. It says so right here. And she says you went out right after Wes that night, and she says you have a bad temper and she's afraid of you. That's what she says."

"I don't believe it."

"But it says so right here," she pleaded. "They wouldn't put it in the paper if she didn't say it. And the prosecutor, he says he's going to charge you with attempted rape, too. They believe everything she says, Van, and they won't believe you. In a case like this, they always believe the woman. Time and again you read in the paper how some guy gets hooked because a dame claims he made her pregnant, and half the time, you know as well as me, he didn't have nothing to do with it. They always take the woman's word for it."

"They forced her," Vance said harshly. "They got at her when she was hysterical. They made her say things she didn't mean."

Cora said flatly, "Don't kid yourself. That dame never says nothing she don't mean. She looks out for number one. It might even of been her that killed Wes and she's just putting the blame on you."

Vance looked at her with hard eyes. "Get out!"

Her mouth worked as if she were going to cry and then suddenly she bent over the bed and kissed him on the mouth. "I'm nuts about you, Van," she whispered. "Honest to God, I'm nuts about you, and all I want to do is see that you don't get in no trouble. *I'm nuts about you, Van!*"

His mouth was rigid beneath her warm, tremulous lips, and he stared stonily at the ceiling. She kissed him again and then stood up and said shakily, "I just want you to know I'm nuts about you. Here, put the water jug and a glass on the bed where you can reach it. I'll come back tonight and make you something to eat. You got to eat."

He did not answer and she walked out, picking up her purse from the chair as she went.

She was stopped by a red light at the Sanibar end of the beach road, and Durkin drew up beside her in a police car. He waved her over to the side of the street. Her heart thumping heavily, she obeyed. He slid out of the police car and walked to her window. His face was a little swollen around the chin where Vance had hit him. There was a tight, grim expression in his eyes that had not been there before.

"I don't suppose it's any good asking you if you know where Vance is hiding out," he said abruptly.

She shook her head, frightened, not trusting herself to talk.

"You know where he is though," Durkin said in the same hard, abrupt voice.

Again she shook her head, wet her lips and whispered, "I ain't heard from him."

He looked searchingly at her. He did not think it very possible that Vance would get in touch with Cora if he were hiding out in Sanibar, especially after she had written that anonymous note. Still, there was always the outside chance.

"There might be a reward," he said. "You could cash in on that. You don't owe the guy a thing after the way he two-timed you with that Elwood dame. I'll see that you get every cent of it. Keep it in mind."

"I'll do that."

"The name's Durkin. You can get in touch with me through the desk sergeant at headquarters. Just leave word that you want to see me. You won't have to say another thing. Just tell him you want to see me."

"If I hear from him," said Cora, wishing desperately that he would go away. She was terrified of him.

He nodded crisply and walked back to the police car. She drove jerkily away, her heart beating so thickly that it made her a little sick to her stomach. There was something about Durkin that told her that he would never let up. He made her and Hully seem like a pair of kids fumbling around in the dark.

Chapter Nineteen

Hully quickly finished his work at the Lounge and told Tate that he had to go downtown to get a new pair of blue jeans. Tate was startled at the take-it-or-leave-it note in Hully's voice, so instead of saying shrilly that Hully could not leave until the storeroom had been straightened up, he grumbled peevishly, "All right, all right, all right, but don't take all day about it. We got a bar to run here and we're short-handed."

With what he thought was great cunning, Hully said earnestly, "Oh, I won't be long, Mr. Tate, but I got to get me a new pair of blue jeans. The ones I got on're beginning to give out in the seat. I got to go down the Army-Navy store and get another pair or go bare-ass."

"I said all right, didn't I. Get back as fast as you can."

Concealing a narrow grin, Hully walked out of the Lounge. He walked about a hundred yards down the road toward the city, then doubled back through the grove of Australian pine toward the Elwood house on the Key. Despite his tremendous bulk, Hully could move very quickly and silently. It took him less than three-quarters of an hour to reach Maddie's house. He concealed himself in the screen of thickly-leafed sea grape shrub at the south boundary of the Elwood property, lying flat to the ground and surveying the open space beyond the shrubs. He nodded once with satisfaction when he saw the uniformed policeman leaning against the coconut palm beside the house, smoking a cigarette. He had expected that there would be a cop there. Something had told him that they'd put a cop on guard. The palm tree was fairly close to the sea grape and mangrove underbrush, and he had no difficulty in getting close to the policeman without revealing himself. His last few swift strides were muffled in the soft sand. He hit the unsuspecting guard heavily on the side of the neck with his forearm and smiled grimly when the man dropped. Now the hard part was over. If the cop had been in the house, he might have had some trouble, but it was all right now.

He slipped around the house and entered it through the kitchen door on the north side. He was wearing a pair of old, tattered rubber-soled canvas shoes, and his footsteps made no noise on the terrazzo floor. It was unnecessary for him to tiptoe, but he felt that he had to. It made him feel as if he were concealing himself just a little more, and he moved close to the walls. He knew what he was going to do—that had all been decided in his mind—and he felt a great calm. He opened the swinging door to the living room and peered through the crack. He smiled grimly again when he saw Maddie lying on the sofa, apparently asleep. He noted the bottle and partially-filled glass on the cocktail table, and he knew that she had been drinking and had passed out. Everything was in very sharp focus. There was a brilliant clarity in his mind as if he were looking upon a scene that was strongly lighted. He tiptoed across the room and looked down at the sleeping Maddie, exulting. This was going to be much easier than he had ever imagined, and there was a bubbling excitement in him. He wanted to laugh and his lips twitched with the feel of it. Purposely he waited and stood there looking down at the sleeping woman so that he could enjoy this feeling the more. It was a tremendous thing. It filled him and he felt twice as big as he had ever felt before. The sensations were indescribable, and for a moment he felt a little giddy as they bubbled through him. It was with an effort that he kept from laughing aloud. He had never felt like this before, and it was wonderful.

It was almost with reluctance that he knelt down beside the sofa and took her chin in one hand and placed the palm of his other hand at the back of her head. The bubbling sensations were racing through him now and almost gently he rolled her head between his two huge hands. He wanted to keep this up indefinitely, but something told him to do it now and get it over. Smiling, he hunched his shoulders and gave her head a sudden, hard twist, laughing as he heard the bone snap.

He stood up, rubbing his hands down the sides of his thighs, and looked at the dead woman.

"That'll learn you," he whispered. "I don't let nobody get away with nothing with Vance. Now you know."

He laughed again and ran swiftly to the kitchen door. When he went outside, he saw the policeman sitting dizzily against the coconut palm, but it was no trouble to run unobserved through the thick screen of sea grape and mangrove.

He was in a tremendous state of excitement all day and he hardly knew what was going on around him in the Lounge. He worked in the storeroom, but later he could hardly remember that either. He kept thinking of how easy it had been and surges of pleasurable excitement ran through him.

There was a curious, capacity crowd in the Lounge that night, and Tate tended bar himself. Hully did not know that the late edition of the paper carried a report of Maddie's killing, and Cora had come in too early to have seen the late paper. Hully kept trying to catch her eye and wink at her to reassure her that everything was all right for Vance, but she hardly glanced into the storeroom.

She was pale under her make-up and seemed under a terrific strain. The night passed easily for Hully and he spent most of his time in the storeroom, playing with Wes Elwood's diamond ring, cupping it in his hand and letting the light flame into the living facets of the stone. He had gotten over his fear of the ring and the feeling of guilt about it. When he was not looking at it, he held it tightly in his hand, enjoying the solid feel of it. It was his and it was the most beautiful thing he had ever had and nobody could take it away from him now. He sat entranced. He felt as if he could fly.

He went to work the next morning at seven o'clock. The sensation of exhilaration was a little abated, but it was still in him and every now and again he paused with his mopping and laughed to himself.

Tate was working morosely in the kitchen. He was in a very bad humor, and Hully called happily to him, "Don't worry, Mr. Tate, everything'll be all right when Vance gets back."

Tate slammed down a pot. "He ain't coming back!" he snapped.

It was as if he had struck Hully in the face. "Sure he's coming back," Hully stammered. "He'll be back in a week or so."

"Not here he ain't. Not after what he done," Tate came out of the kitchen, untying his apron. "He's finished. You couldn't give him to me for nothing. Anyway, the cops'll take care of him for good. I'm going to the well for some water. If anybody comes in, tell him to wait a minute and don't try to draw him any beer. I'll take care of it when I get back."

He walked out and Hully watched him, stunned. Vance not coming back! And all on account of old man Tate. Hully shook with a sudden fury and, convulsively, the remaining short handle of the mop snapped in his hands. He looked wildly around the room. He wanted to smash something and then he spied the goldfish bowl and the fish swimming placidly in it. He made a sudden move toward it but checked himself. He wouldn't bust it. No. He took a table by the edge and swung it over beside the tank. He jumped up on the table and, standing there, urinated into the water, laughing as the small fish swam frantically. He was still standing there when Tate walked in, carrying a five gallon jug of water from the well across the road.

Tate's jaw dropped when he saw what Hully was doing, and then his face turned a fiery red.

"You're fired!" he shrieked. "Get out of here. You're fired!"

Hully had a moment of absolute panic, and then with a roar he leaped from the table, smashing Tate to the floor. Smiling, he crouched over the unconscious man and slowly reached with both hands for Tate's chin and the back of his head....

Chapter Twenty

It was just about seven o'clock, too, that Cora walked into the beach house, fearful of the reception she knew that she was going to get from Vance. She had spent a sleepless night, dreading this moment. His bloodshot eyes did not waver a fraction toward her when she walked into the room where he was trussed on the bed. His lean face was drenched with fatigue and his eyes stared heavily at the ceiling. His wrists and ankles were now bloody from his fruitless struggles against the hard, narrow nylon lines that bound him. He lay locked in cold fury.

She had left the newspaper in the car. It contained the story of Maddie Elwood's death, and Cora's only reaction to it was a feeling of fervent relief that Vance had been tied up in the beach house. She had been fearful that he might have escaped, but he was still there and, naively, she believed that he could not possibly be linked with the killing of Maddie. Maybe now, she thought irrationally, the police would start looking for somebody else who killed Wes Elwood. In her eyes, the death of Maddie was proof that Vance had not had anything to do with the killing of Wes.

The dinner of coffee, cold cuts and bread, that she had made him the night before, lay scattered on the floor with the over-turned tray, and, saying nothing, she knelt and gathered up the debris. When she finished, she carried it out into the kitchen and put it into the small garbage container under the sink. She went back to the door.

"If I make you breakfast, will you eat it?" she asked timidly.

He did not answer or even look at her. She stood there, undecided, and then said, "I'll make something for you. You got to eat. And—" she thought of the story in the newspaper, "don't worry. Everything's going to be all right."

She prepared a tray of sandwiches and took it in to him. She opened the water jug and looked into it. It was almost empty. At least he had been drinking water. That made her feel better. She refilled the jug in the kitchen and put ice cubes into the water. She placed it on the bed within reach of his hand.

"Try to eat something," she urged. "You can't go without eating."

His only answer was a hard tightening of his jaw muscles. His rejection of her was so complete that tears came to her eyes.

"Don't be mad with me, Van," she begged. "We're only doing this for your own good, me and Hully. I'm nuts about you, honest to God, Van, and I don't want nothing to happen to you!" Anxiously, she watched his face, hoping that he would relent, but his lean face was coldly closed against her. For a moment, she wanted to blurt that Maddie was dead, but she had a feeling that it would be the worst thing she could do. That was something he was going to have to find out by himself. She didn't want it to come from her.

Forcing a small note of cheerfulness, she said, "Try to eat, Van, I'll be back around lunch time and fix you something else."

She went back to her car and cried for a while. Then she dried her eyes and reread the story of Maddie's killing in the newspaper. She had not read it closely before. She had merely glanced hurriedly through the paper to see what they were saying about Vance. There was a story about the police in five neighboring states being alerted, but that did not upset her. She knew where Vance was, and the police wouldn't be able to get at him there. There was more about Vance in the story of Maddie's murder, something she had missed on her first skimming through. Near the end, the police chief was quoted as saying, "We don't know who killed Mrs. Elwood, but my men have orders to bring Vance in dead or alive. But there is a chance that he had nothing to do with the killing of the woman."

She fastened on that one sentence and repeated it happily to herself over and over again. "There is a chance that he had nothing to do with the killing of the woman." She *knew* Vance had nothing to do with it, and now the police were beginning to realize it, too. "There is a chance that he had nothing to do with the killing of the woman." Maybe they already had somebody else in mind. The police were smart. It wasn't often they let you get away with something. Just look at the way they could track down a murderer with practically nothing for a clue, maybe just a footprint, or a cigar butt, or something. Why, they were probably working on that angle right this minute. That Elwood dame was a bitch. Everybody knew how she nagged poor Wes, and he wasn't the only one that had ever gotten the rough side of her tongue. She had enemies all over town. Look at the way she had chewed out Hoke Moylan, the septic tank man, just because he was a half-day late that time. Called him things Hoke said he wouldn't repeat in front of a lady. Hoke was really burned that time. And there were others she had given a bad time. Why, if you started adding them up on your fingers, almost anybody could have killed—

Something cold and horrifying slid into her mind like a knife. She remembered Hully saying ominously of Durkin, "I'll take care of that cop, too." And another time he had said of Maddie, when he thought she was a threat to Vance, "I'll bust her!" There was no doubt in her mind that Hully had meant it both times. That was Hully's idea of helping Vance. And suddenly it was chillingly clear to her that Hully had carried out his threat and had killed Maddie because of what she had told the police. Hully. She could close her eyes and hear him saying in that rumbling, menacing voice of his, "I'll bust her." And that's just what he had done. He had busted her.

She reached for the key in the ignition lock to start the car. There was only one thought in her mind, to talk to Hully. She knew that if she talked to him, she'd know right away if he had killed Maddie. Oh, she wouldn't come right out with it or anything like that, she thought, planning it in her mind, but she could lead up to it one way or another. She could say, "Well, the one that knocked off that Elwood dame sure did Vance a favor." She was sure that if she put it that way, Hully would give himself away. She had no feeling of loyalty toward Hully whatever. All she wanted to do was to get Vance out of trouble, even if it meant turning Hully over to the police.

As she drove past the intersection of the beach road and the street into the business section of Sanibar, she saw Durkin sitting there again in the police car. He looked hard at her, but did not wave her down this time, for which she was grateful. She did not want to waste time with Durkin. Later she'd talk to him, but she wanted to talk to Hully first. She wanted to find out for sure, and she could. Hully was so dumb, he'd give himself away the first time he opened his mouth, especially if it had something to do with Vance. If she put it the right way, Hully would boast how he had helped Vance out of the jam. She'd pretend Hully had done something wonderful, just to get him talking. She knew how to handle Hully all right. All she'd have to do was say Vance, and she'd be able to do anything she wanted with Hully. This was not betrayal. This was just getting Vance out of trouble.

She parked her car behind the Pelican Lounge and walked into the bar through the patio door. She stopped and, for a moment, felt as if she would faint. Tate was lying on the floor with his head twisted back and to the side at a gruesome, unmistakable angle and there was no doubt that he was dead. Hully stood astride the body, breathing heavily. Cora smothered a scream and Hully turned his head slowly and looked at her.

"He wasn't going to let Vance come back," he said thickly, "and he just canned me."

Cora knew that she was in deadly danger, for Hully's eyes still glittered from the excitement of killing, and he would kill again while the excitement was in him. Cora fought down the shriek that rang through her. She had to. She had to appear calm. She had to appear as if she approved of what Hully had done.

"We—we couldn't let him do that to Vance, Hully," she quavered.

Hully turned from her and looked down at the body. "I should of busted him a long time ago. He was always trying to fire Vance and get rid of him."

"We can't let anybody get away with anything as far as Vance is concerned," Cora said desperately.

Hully laughed. "Don't worry about that. Is Vance okay? You taking care of him out there?"

"I—I just made breakfast for him. And gave him more ice water."

"You're a good kid. Vance don't have nothing to worry about with us around, right, kid?"

"That's right, Hully. We'll—we'll take care of him, me and you. We won't let nobody get away with nothing. I see in the papers that Elwood dame got hers, too." She clasped her hands together at her waist to conceal their trembling, but her throat filled sickeningly as she waited for his answer. This was the climax and it would go one way or the other. She wanted to scream.

Hully laughed again and winked at her. "I busted her good, kid. She won't make no more trouble for nobody, the way she told them lies about Vance. Okay, kid?"

"You—you did just right, Hully," Cora stammered. "She had it coming."

Cora had gone as far as she had planned, and now she did not know what to do. She was afraid to try to leave for fear that Hully would stop her, and if he stopped her, he'd stop her for good. His eyes still had that queer glitter in them. He looked at the front door.

"We better lock that in case somebody comes in," he said, crossing to the door. He regarded Cora happily. "You're really Vance's friend, kid. Right?"

"We're both his friend."

"You're damn right. You're okay, you know that? The way you're taking care of Vance, you're okay. And you're okay with me, too."

"And you're okay with me," she said, wondering desperately how she could get away from him.

He tilted his huge head to one side and regarded her with great affection. "I got something for you," he said, "on account of you're Vance's friend, like me."

For a wild moment when he walked toward her, she thought he was going to attack her, that strange glitter in his eyes, but she stood frozen, unable to move. But he merely winked happily at her and went into the storeroom. She heard him fumbling with something that sounded like a box, but she did not dare turn her head to look. He came back and she started violently when he took her hand and pressed something into her palm.

"On account of how good you're taking care of Vance," he said.

She gasped when she saw what he had given her. It was Wes Elwood's ring. She had seen it many times and recognized it immediately. She had never thought of Hully as Wes's killer, and she was more shocked by that than by the other two killings. Hully took her by the arm.

"Let's go and tell Vance everything's okay," he said excitedly. "Let's go and tell him he don't have nothing to worry about no more."

"Yes, let's go right away!" she cried. "Right now. Let's go right out and tell him."

"But I want to be the one to tell him," Hully said jubilantly. "I was the one that done it for him."

Cora's legs felt so weak that she was hardly able to walk out to the car with him, and she prayed desperately that his mood would hold until they were able to untie Vance. After that, Vance would be able to handle Hully—

Chapter Twenty-one

Vance heard the beach house door open, but he did not turn his head, thinking that Cora had returned. He jerked when he heard Durkin's voice say, "What the hell—"

Vance raised his head from the pillow. "Get me out of this," he demanded.

"Don't worry about that," Durkin said grimly.

His jaw was swollen and discolored. He was holding a gun and he reached into his pocket with his left hand and took out a small, bone-handled pen knife.

"I thought maybe you were down here someplace," he said. "Two days running I saw that waitress girl-friend of yours coming from the beach road, and I knew you couldn't of gone far on foot, your car being busted. I thought I'd take a look, and there were her tire marks in the driveway outside and the lock broken on the door."

"Just untie me, will you?" Vance said angrily. "This wasn't my idea, and I'm not hiding out."

"Oh sure, sure," said Durkin, mockingly. "You're just spending your vacation here. You're not kidding anybody, killer. This tie-up gag wouldn't fool a Boy Scout."

He went to the bed and cut the lines that held Vance's legs, all the while pointing his gun at Vance's belly. "Don't try anything the second time," he warned. "I don't miss twice."

"Just cut me loose," Vance said wearily. "All I want to do is get out of here."

"You're getting out of here all right. Out of here and down to headquarters."

He pressed the muzzle of his gun deep into Vance's belly when he cut the other two lines, then leaped back quickly. "Now let's go," he said, "and keep it in mind that nobody cares how many pieces I bring you in. Stay about six feet away and follow me out to the car. Dead or alive, the chief said, and that's the way I'll take you in."

He backed slowly toward the door. Vance started to say, "I'm not making any trouble—" when he saw Hully loom up silently behind the detective. Before he could cry a warning, Hully's forearm came down and struck Durkin a glancing blow on the side of the head. Durkin sagged against the door frame and the gun dropped from his hand. Hully kicked the gun into the sand and seized Durkin by the neck, laughing with a bubbling kind of excitement. There was a scream and Cora appeared from behind Hully and frantically grabbed his arm. Her weight was just enough to stagger the big man, and it gave Vance the time to leap forward and hit Hully on the side of the jaw. Hully dropped the detective and lurched against one of the porch posts. Durkin was not entirely unconscious, but he seemed incapable of movement as he lay on the floor, staring up at Hully with slightly glazed eyes.

"Don't touch him again!" Vance said sharply to Hully. Hully touched the side of his face and said pleadingly, "But I couldn't let him—"

"Never mind what you couldn't let him. I'll take care of myself from now on."

Cora stepped back three paces from Hully. "He just killed Tate," she told Vance in a horror-stricken voice. "He's crazy."

Vance said, "*What!*"

"He just killed Tate. Broke his neck. And he killed that Elwood woman the same way. He told me."

Vance looked incredulously from her to Hully. "*He what?*"

"She told lies about you, Vance," Hully was still pleading. "I don't let nobody get away with nothing with you, Vance, you know that. And Tate wasn't going to let you come back and he fired me. I should of busted him a long time ago."

Vance whispered, "Dear God!"

"And look what he just gave me." Cora held out a shaking hand with Wes Elwood's diamond ring in the palm of it. "He killed Wes Elwood, too!"

"I didn't mean to, Vance!" Hully blurted defensively. "I just kind of pushed him and he hit the table with his head. I didn't mean nothing. Honest to God, Vance, I didn't mean to hurt him."

Vance stood very still. "But you can't go around killing people, Hully," he said quietly. "You know you're not supposed to do that."

"I wasn't letting nobody get away with nothing with you!" Hully said loudly.

"But Wes wasn't trying to get away with anything. Why did you go after Wes?"

"I just wanted to look at his ring, is all. I didn't mean nothing."

"And he tried to stop you?"

"He took a swing at me and I just kind of pushed him away. I didn't have nothing against him. I didn't even think I hurt him. I just kind of gave him a little push. Not like the other two. They was against you."

Vance took a deep breath. "You'll have to tell this to the police, Hully."

"No! I ain't telling nothing to no police. They don't listen. All they want to do is stick you in jail."

"You'll have to, Hully."

"I only done it for you, Vance, honest to God, I only done it for you."

"But it's against the law, Hully. You can't go around—busting people." Vance felt abysmally sorry for the big man, but Hully had turned into a killer and he had to be stopped before there were more killings. "I know what's best, Hully. Do what I say. Go to the police."

Hully turned furiously on Cora. "You turned him against me!" he yelled.

He leaped at her, but Vance sprang at almost the same moment and hit him heavily on the side of the face. Hully twisted from the force of the blow and fell off the porch into the sand.

Vance said sharply to Cora, "Lock yourself in the house!" He walked to the edge of the porch and said quietly, "I'm not against you, Hully. Cora didn't turn me against you." He felt like a Judas, but it was the only thing he could do. "Do what I say, Hully."

Hully rose slowly to his feet and, rubbing his huge hands up and down his thighs, glowered past Vance at the doorway through which Cora had run.

"I'll bust her," he said in a clotted voice. "She turned you against me."

"She didn't, Hully."

"Don't try and stop me, Vance, or I'll bust you, too. You're against me. We ain't friends no more. She turned you against me." He started up the four steps to the porch. "Get out of my way, Vance. I'm warning you."

Vance swung a hard, straight right and caught Hully flush on the point of the chin. Hully shook his head and, with a bellow, charged, holding his arms spread like a wrestler. Vance hit him twice again in the face and dodged to the side of those thick, grasping arms. Hully turned.

"We ain't friends no more after that," he snarled and charged again. Vance pumped a whole series of hard rights and lefts into Hully's unprotected jaw and again slipped away from the thick, reaching hands. Hully turned and plodded at him. The porch was about fifteen feet wide and Vance dodged to keep himself in the middle of the floor so that he would not be pinned against either the wall or the railing. As Hully came in, he hit him as hard as he could on the side of the jaw near the hinge. Four times he struck, using both hands. Hully laughed with an odd, lilting excitement in his voice and cried out with triumph as his fingers hooked into the open neck of Vance's sport shirt. He yanked to pull Vance into his grasp, but the thin fabric tore away, leaving Vance naked to the waist. But the pull was just strong enough to jerk Vance off balance for an instant, his left arm flailing. Hully cried "Aaaargh!" in jubilation and grabbed his wrist in iron fingers. His grin glittered and, enjoying it, he started to pull Vance slowly toward him.

"Now!" he said.

He threw back his head and laughed uproariously just as Vance's desperate right fist hooked for his chin. Vance missed the chin but his hard knuckles struck Hully full in the throat. Hully's eyes started and, choking, he dropped Vance's wrist and grasped his throat with both hands. He staggered against the side of the beach house, lurched back, stumbled across the porch and fell into the sand. He staggered to his feet and ran heavily away from the house, still holding his crushed throat with both hands. Vance leaned weakly against the side of the house, listening to the diminishing sound as Hully crashed southward through the dry palmetto.

"He won't get far," said a voice.

Vance looked around. Durkin was standing at the head of the steps.

"Who does?" said Vance in a sodden voice.

"He's got about a half-mile to go," said Durkin, "then it's all mangrove swamp. He can't get far in that stuff. He'll be a sitting duck." He went down the steps. "I better call headquarters." He stopped and, turning, looked up at Vance. "You're a lucky son-of-a-bitch. I'd of nailed you sure. The facts were all against you."

Vance ignored him and looked down at the floor, panting.

Durkin went on in an uncertain, complaining voice, "The facts were all against you. I had it all lined up. You didn't have a chance. I had all the facts. You were all sewed up, all the facts I needed, and you couldn't go against the facts—"

Vance still did not answer and Durkin turned away and plodded through the thick sand toward his car, a kind of bewildered defeat in his sagging shoulders.

Cora came out of the house and stood in the doorway looking timidly at Vance.

"You're sore at me?" she said hesitantly.

He shook his head.

"All I wanted to do was help," she fumbled. "Just keep you out of trouble, is all. You're everything I got, even if you don't want me. Just don't be sore at me."

He gave his head a vague shake. "I'm not sore. I'm not anything."

"Would—would you like a hot cup of coffee maybe?"

"I could use something, I guess."

He was unresisting when she took his arm. They went into the house together.

THE END

Lorenz Heller Bibliography
(1910-1965)

As Frederick Lorenz

Novels:
A Rage at Sea (Lion, 1953)
Night Never Ends (Lion, 1954)
The Savage Chase (Lion, 1954)
A Party Every Night (Lion, 1956)
Ruby (Lion, 1956)
Hot (Lion, 1956)
Dungaree Sin (Chariot, 1960)

Stories:
Backbite (*Justice*, Jan 1956)
Big Catch (*Justice*, July 1955)
Living Bait (*Justice*, May 1955)

As Laura Hale

Novels:
Wild is the Woman (Rainbow, 1951)
Lovers Don't Sleep (Falcon, 1951)
Kiss of Fire (Rainbow, 1952; reprinted in Australia as
   Kiss Of Death, Phantom, 1953)
Woman Hunter (Falcon, 1952; reprinted in Australia,
   Phantom, 1953)
Desperate Blonde (Beacon Australia, 1960)
Lessons in Lust (Beacon, 1961; re-write of *Woman Hunter*)
Sensual Woman (Beacon, 1961; re-write of *Lovers Don't Sleep*)
The Zipper Girls (Beacon, 1962; re-write of *Wild is the Woman*)
The Marriage Bed (Beacon, 1962; re-write of *Desperate Blonde*)

As Larry Heller

Novels:
I Get What I Want (Popular, 1956)
Body of the Crime (Pyramid, 1962)

Story:
Blood Is Thicker (*Guilty Detective Story Magazine*, Mar 1957)

As Larry Holden

Novels:
Hide-Out (Eton, 1953)
Dead Wrong (Pyramid, 1957)
Crime Cop (Pyramid, 1959)

Stories (alphabetical listing):
...And Death Makes Ten (*Detective Tales*, June 1947)
Another Man's Poison (*Shadow Mystery*, Apr/May 1948)
Any Corpse in a Storm (*Dime Mystery Magazine*, Aug 1949)
Anybody Lose a Corpse? (*Mammoth Detective*, Aug 1946)
The Big Haunt (*10-Story Detective Magazine*, Oct 1948)
Blackmail Means Homicide (*15 Story Detective*, Feb 1950)
Bloody Night! (*Dime Mystery Magazine*, Oct 1949)
Bodyguard (*Thrilling Detective*, June 1951)
Bullets for Beethoven [Dinny Keogh] (*Mammoth Mystery*,
   June 1946)
Coffin Key (*Detective Tales*, Oct 1951)
A Corpse at Large (*Ten Detective Aces*, July 1949)
Corpse in Waiting (*New Detective Magazine*, Nov 1950)
A Corpse to His Credit (*Dime Detective Magazine*, May 1947)
Criminal at Large (*Suspense Magazine*, Summer 1951)
The Crimson Path (*Detective Tales*, Sept 1947)
Cry Murder (*New Detective Magazine*, Oct 1952)
The Crying Corpse (*Ten Detective Aces*, Sept 1948)
Death Brings Down the House (*10-Story Detective Magazine*,
   Apr 1948)
Death Carries the Mail (*F.B.I. Detective Stories*, Aug 1950)
Death for Two! (*Detective Tales*, Dec 1952)
Death in Dirty Linen (*Shadow Mystery*, June/July 1947)
Death in Six Reels (*Doc Savage*, July/Aug 1948)
Death in Thin Ice (*Shadow Mystery*, Feb/Mar 1948)
Death Is Where You Find It (*Suspect Detective Stories*, Nov 1955)
Die, Baby, Die! (*Detective Tales*, June 1948)
Don't Crowd My Shroud (*10-Story Detective Magazine*, Dec 1948)
Don't Ever Forget (*Detective Story Magazine*, Mar 1953)
Don't Wait Up for Me (*Triple Detective*, Fall 1955)

The Eighteen Screaming Corpses (*Detective Tales*, Jan 1948)
The Expendable Ex (*Dime Detective Magazine*, June 1952)
Face in the Window (*Detective Tales*, June 1951)
Fall Guy (*Detective Tales*, Aug 1953)
Forger's Fate (*Dime Detective Magazine*, Apr 1951)
The High Cost of Chivalry (*Dime Detective Magazine*, Dec 1951)
Home for Christmas (*Thrilling Detective*, Dec 1947)
House of Hate (*10-Story Detective Magazine*, Apr 1949)
Humpty-Dumpty Homicide (*Detective Tales*, June 1949)
If the Body Fits— (*Dime Mystery Magazine*, Dec 1947)
If the Frame Fits— (*Detective Tales*, Dec 1951)
I'll Be Home for Murder! (*Detective Tales*, Apr 1948)
I'll See You Dead! (*Detective Tales*, May 1947)
In Her Mother's Best Bier! (*Detective Tales*, Dec 1948)
Keeping Honest (*Doc Savage*, Winter 1949)
Kickback for a Corpse (*All-Story Detective*, Apr 1949)
Killer's Kiss (*Detective Tales*, Aug 1949)
Lady in Red (*Detective Tales*, Oct 1948)
Lady-Killer (*Dime Detective Magazine*, Dec 1952)
Lethal Boy Blue (*Detective Tales*, May 1949)
Love Me, Love My Corpse! (*Detective Tales*, Aug 1948)
Make Mine Mayhem (*New Detective Magazine*, Jan 1949)
Man with a Rep (*Detective Tales*, Dec 1949)
Mayhem at Eight (*New Detective Magazine*, May 1950)
Mayhem's Mechanic (*Detective Tales*, Sept 1946)
Morgue Bait (*New Detective Magazine*, Dec 1951)
Murder and the Mermaid (*Dime Detective Magazine*, Oct 1952)
Murder Never Gets Too Old (*Private Detective*, Jan 1950)
Never Dead Enough (*New Detective Magazine*, Sept 1947)
Never Turn Your Back (*Mike Shayne Mystery Magazine*, July 1959)
Nightmare (*Detective Tales*, Oct 1952)
No Dead End (*Triple Detective*, Spring 1955)
On a Dead Man's Chest (*Thrilling Detective*, Apr 1953)
One Dark Night [Dinny Keogh] (*Mammoth Mystery*, Dec 1946)
One for the Hangman (*Suspect Detective Stories*, Feb 1956)
Operation—Murder (*F.B.I. Detective Stories*, Aug 1949)
Orphans Are Made (*Mobsters*, Feb 1953)
Out of the Frying Pan... (*15 Mystery Stories*, Oct 1950)
Port of the Dead (*New Detective Magazine*, July 1947)
Prelude to a Wake (*Dime Detective Magazine*, Feb 1952)
Red Nightmare (*Dime Mystery Magazine*, July 1947)

Sailor, Beware! (*Detective Story Magazine*, May 1953)
Save Me a Kill (*New Detective Magazine*, June 1953)
Self-Made Corpse (*Detective Tales*, Apr 1949)
She Cries Murder! (*New Detective Magazine*, June 1952)
Sing a Song of Murder (*Dime Detective Magazine*, Aug 1952)
Snow in August [Dinny Keogh] (*Mammoth Mystery*, Aug 1946)
The Spice of Death (*Private Detective*, Dec 1950)
Start with a Corpse [Dinny Keogh] (*Mammoth Mystery*, Jan 1946)
There's Death in the Heir [Dinny Keogh] (*Mammoth Mystery*,
    Aug 1947)
They Played Too Rough [Dinny Keogh] (*Mammoth Mystery*,
    Mar 1946)
This Shroud Reserved (*New Detective Magazine*, Oct 1951)
Those Slaughter-House Blues (*Mammoth Detective*, Feb 1947)
A Time for Dying (*Dime Detective Magazine*, Aug 1951)
Too Many Crosses [Dinny Keogh] (*Mammoth Mystery*, Feb 1947)
Tragedy in Waiting (*Invincible Detective Magazine*, Mar 1951)
The Trouble with Redheads (*Mike Shayne Mystery Magazine*,
    Apr 1959)
Two-Headed Killer (*15 Mystery Stories*, Feb 1950)
Undressed to Kill (*New Detective Magazine*, Sept 1949)
Vicious Circle (*Detective Tales*, Nov 1949)
The Voice That Kills (*15 Mystery Stories*, Aug 1950)
Wake of the Ermine Chick (*15 Story Detective*, Dec 1950)
When Cops Fall Out (*Detective Tales*, June 1953)
With Hostile Intent (*Fifteen Detective Stories*, Dec 1954)
With Love and Bullets! (*Detective Tales*, Feb 1953)
Written in Blood (*Ten Detective Aces*, May 1948)
You Can't Live Forever (*New Detective Magazine*, Aug 1952)
You Die Alone (*Fifteen Detective Stories*, Oct 1953)
You'll Die Laughing (*Detective Tales*, Oct 1950)
You're Killing Me (*Detective Story Magazine*, Sept 1953)

Dinny Keogh series:
Start with a Corpse (1946)
They Played Too Rough (1946)
Bullets for Beethoven (1946)
Snow in August (1946)
One Dark Night (1946)
Too Many Crosses (1947)
There's Death in the Heir (1947)

As Lorenz Heller

Novel:
Murder in Make-Up (Messner, 1937)

Stories:
Blood Money (*Suspect Detective Stories*, Nov 1955)
A Tasty Dish (*Suspect Detective Stories*, Feb 1956)
Twilight (*Short Stories*, Nov 1956)
The Hero (*Mystery Tales*, Dec 1958)
The Last Hunt (*Adventure*, June 1959)

As Burt Sims

Television Scripts:
1953: "Death Does a Rumba" (Season 2, Episode 12, *Boston Blakie*)
1953: "Island of Stone" (Season 2, Episode 1, *Chevron Theater*)
1954: "Tailor-Made Trouble" (Season 1, Episode 11, *Waterfront*)
1956 - 1959: Seven episodes of *Sky King*
1958: "Beautiful, Blue and Deadly" (Season 1, Episode 14,
  Mike Hammer)
1958: "Texas Fliers" (Season 1, Episode 18, *Flight*)

A TRIO OF LIONS

From the early 1950s—the golden age of the paperback!
Three noir crime novels in each volume!

Lion Books began in 1949 as Red Circle Books, part of the
Martin Goodman publishing empire that also included such
magazines as *For Men Only, Stag* and *Movie World*, as well
as various pulps and the early version of Marvel Comics. Lion
Books only lasted for nine years, but during that time at least a
third of their books were noir reprints and originals, and featured
authors like Jim Thompson, David Goodis, Robert Bloch, Richard
Matheson and Day Keene.

Kermit Jaediker: Hero's Lust
Shel Walker: The Man I Killed
Clayre & Michel Lipman: House of Evil
978-1-944520-02-1 $19.95
"A real ten-knuckle page-turner."—Kristofer Upjohn, *Noir Journal.*
"Reading these books are like watching late night film noir on late
night TV with the lights out."—Rick Ollerman.
Introductions by Gary Lovisi and Dan Roberts.

Kermit Jaedeker: Tall, Dark & Dead
Frederick Lorenz: The Savage Chase
D. L. Champion: Run the Wild River
978-1-944520-75-5 $19.95
"As hard-boiled as they come."—Paul Burke, *NB*.
"…really races along."—James Reasoner.
"…unequivocally recommended."—*Paperback Parade*.
Includes an interview with editor Arnold Hano.

"Lots of tough-guy, wisecracking fun… reads like a
65-70 minute RKO private-eye movie."—*GoodReads*

Stark House Press

1315 H Street, Eureka, CA 95501, 707-498-3135, www.StarkHousePress.com
Retail customers: freight-free, payment accepted by check or paypal via website.
Wholesale: 40%, freight-free on 10 mixed copies or more, returns accepted.
All books available direct from Publisher, Ingram or Baker & Taylor Books.

www.ingramcontent.com/pod-product-compliance
Lightning Source LLC
Chambersburg PA
CBHW071737190726
48292CB00003B/782

A RAGE AT SEA

Frank Dixon has just lost his ship in a crap game, and is about to lose his woman as well, when Addams offers him a job captaining the *Almacor*. All he has to do is take the owner and his drunken guests around the Caribbean. Trouble is, Dixon hates Addams—doesn't trust him, knows that Addams will sabotage him if he can. But Dixon only has this one chance to climb out of the bottle, one shot at redemption, and agrees to helm the yacht. Thank goodness he has young Wirt aboard. There's one seaman he can trust. It's not long before the drinking starts, the owner takes a swing at Wirt, and all hell breaks loose. Dixon knows that Addams is only waiting for his opportunity to stab him in the back, and this could be it.

A PARTY EVERY NIGHT

Vance is the perfect bartender—tall, good-looking, funny, he charms them all. Particularly the waitress, Cora. But Vance only has eyes for Maddie. Unfortunately, Maddie is married to the town lush, Wes Elwood. Almost every night, you will find Maddie and Wes at Vance's bar, belting down the Scotches and hating one another with a white heat. Tonight is different. Tonight Wes disappears in his car, and no one can find him. After closing, Vance takes Maddie out to all the after-hours bars looking for him, but all they get is one run-around after another, and no Wes. Then Wes is found drowned. And that's when Durkin steps in, a cop who collects facts like some people collect stamps. Durkin has his own idea of what happened to Wes, and as far as he's concerned, all those facts lead him back to Vance.